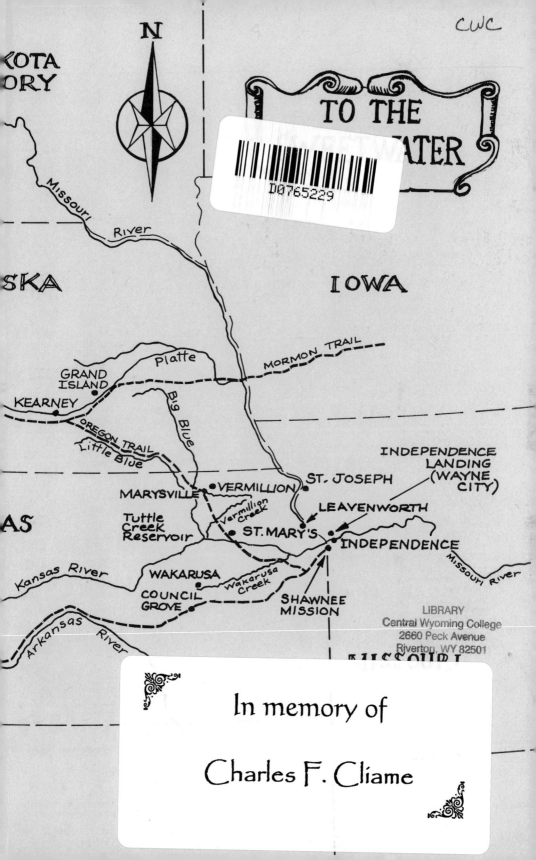

cwc

N

TO THE ...ATER

D0765229

...KOTA
...ORY

Missouri River

...SKA

IOWA

MORMON TRAIL

Platte

GRAND
ISLAND

KEARNEY

OREGON TRAIL

Little Blue

Big Blue

INDEPENDENCE
LANDING
(WAYNE
CITY)

MARYSVILLE

VERMILLION

ST. JOSEPH

Tuttle
Creek
Reservoir

Vermillion Creek

LEAVENWORTH

...AS

ST. MARY'S

INDEPENDENCE

Kansas River

WAKARUSA

Wakarusa Creek

Missouri River

Arkansas River

COUNCIL
GROVE

SHAWNEE
MISSION

...SOURI

The Sweet-water

by Jean Rikhoff

The Sweet-water

JEAN RIKHOFF

THE DIAL PRESS
NEW YORK
1976

Excerpts from Gold in the Black Hills, *by Watson
Parker: Copyright 1966 by the University of
Oklahoma Press. Used by permission.*
Excerpt from The Great Plains, *by Walter Prescott
Webb:* © *Copyright, 1959, 1931, by Walter Prescott
Webb. Used by permission of the publisher, Ginn and
Company (Xerox Corporation).*

*Library of Congress Cataloging in Publication Data
Rikhoff, Jean.
  The sweetwater.
  I. Title.
PZ4.R573Sw [PS3568.I377]   813'.5'4   76–10745
ISBN 0–8037–8436–8*

This book is for Bruce MacDonald

ACKNOWLEDGMENTS

Part of the research for this novel was done in 1973 on a summer fellowship from the University Awards Committee of the State University of New York out West retracing the Oregon Trail.

On the Indian material grateful appreciation is extended to the following: Robert Lowie's *Indians of the Plains*, Mari Sandoz's *Crazy Horse*, Thomas Mails's *The Mystic Warriors of the Plains*, *Legends of the Mighty Sioux* (compiled by the Workers of the South Dakota Writers' Project, Work Projects Administration), and Dee Brown's *Bury My Heart at Wounded Knee*.

A note of thanks to Joyce Shuman for helping to type parts of this manuscript, to my son Jeff for accompanying me over the old Oregon Trail, and to my daughter Allison who had the painful task of collating this work.

Contents

1876

There has been no other phenomenon like this in American history, and it is doubtful if world history offers a parallel case. It is significant that the immigrants went all this distance [two thousand miles of unoccupied country] to a wooded and well-watered environment similar in practically all respects to that which they had known in the East; in fact, they passed over the fertile Prairie Plains of the Middle West, where, as time has proved, the agricultural opportunities were far better than they were on the Pacific coast. They were bound for the land where the simple plow, the scythe, the ox, and the horse could be used according to the tradition that had been worked out in two centuries of pioneering in a wooded country. It has been estimated that each mile of the two-thousand-mile journey cost seventeen lives—a total of thirty-four thousand lives.

. . . They were in reality seeking the familiar and shunning the necessity of working out new ways in the Plains. The heroism lay in getting to Oregon and not in living there. The deserts, the waterless drives, the sand storms, the treacherous quicksands of the rivers, the prairie fires, the hostile Indians, the stampeding buffalo found on the Plains—all were a part of that great obstacle.

Walter Webb, The Great Plains

One

Independence
Landing

I

There's jest a limit to everythin', John
Buttes told himself as he reined in and looked
down on the sprawling shacks ahead. Ever since he'd left
home in the Adirondacks over a thousand miles back he'd
been saying to himself, *When I git to the Missouri, thin's are
gonna be better. Once I git to Independence I'm gonna be free. I'm
gonna git rid of that crazy Mason Raymond and git off on my own.
I'm gonna be free.*

The shacks vaguely outlined against the sky perhaps a half
mile ahead meant the Missouri and the Missouri meant freedom.

A sarcastic voice inside said, You wanna bet? What makes
you think you're gonna be able to git rid of him now?

Because I can't take no more, John told that inner side of
himself that was always plaguing him one way or another. No
way under the sun to get it to shut up, and it was always so
goddam right. Nuthin' worse in the world than a voice that
was never wrong.

He scanned the empty skyscape. The land ran like a thin
blade of gray against the blue sky. The sky overhead seemed
a bowl of blue filled with whirling blackbirds. Where in the

] *3* [

name of Judas had that dumb dodo disappeared to? And how was it possible he could evaporate the way he had? There wasn't any place to hide—just the long endless flatness and the empty blue bowl and the blackbirds whirling about.

Hidin' in some hole prayin' agin, John thought. The mystery of Mason Raymond's praying filled his mind. All the way cross-country Mason Raymond had been burrowing down in some out-of-sight place and sending his messages out into space. He believed that he could close his eyes and telegraph thoughts directly to the divine. He wanted to be forgiven killing a man, but to John's way of thinking Mason Raymond'd been doing penance for so long now that if he hadn't been forgiven, he never was going to get a pardon. Some things maybe you never get a dispensation for; they just go on and on.

I'm jest plain wore out, John thought. It had been hard enough lugging himself out to the start of nowhere, but to be caretaker to a crazy cousin in the bargain was asking the impossible. *In my view,* he reminded himself. You had to try to be fair.

You could try a little harder, the voice crouched down hiding inside said. Everyone can always try a *little* harder.

That goddam voice and that goddam Mason Raymond. It's them wore me out.

All the way out Mason Raymond had been losing them, getting mixed up on compass points, befuddled by the simplest maps, taking wrong forks in the road, until at last John had come to the conclusion Mason Raymond must have been born with an infallible sense of going wrong. A born loser.

John took off his sweat-stained hat and beat it against his thigh. Dust blew up around him like some windfall from the stars. The stars fascinated Mason Raymond. He was always talking about how they shot out silent rays of precious things that went into the ground. They made gold. They sent diamonds into the earth. They made mysterious minerals that caused plants to grow tall. If they wanted, Mason Raymond said, they could implant strange and secret knowledge inside a man's head. Or they could lean down and cook a man's brains.

] *4* [

According to Mason Raymond's view it was the stars and planets shining down with their powerful rays that had made the earth nuggetted with gold up north in the Hills where John wanted to go, where the Indians and Army were trying to keep him out. Well, he, John Buttes, didn't care how the gold had got in the Hills; he was just happy it was there. And he was on his way to get hold of some. Get rich. The rich had power. They could make people do what they wanted. They could live the way they wanted instead of being told. The rich weren't driven like oxen the way men were on the farms back home; they could pick and choose the time they got up and when they felt like going to bed. They weren't driven by debts at the bank and an earth that gave up more stones than crops.

Mason Raymond had money, of course. He didn't have to go looking for gold. Why the hell then did he want to come along—because he was peculiar, that was why, touched in the head. John couldn't think of another person in the whole wide world that had such strange notions as Mason Raymond. Mason Raymond, for instance, had insisted on Independence, even though it was out of the way because he said in the year of the country's centennial everyone should be able to make some sacrifices for symbols; he himself was willing to pay for the pleasure of the name itself (Mason Raymond had a goddam thing about names; he and his names had been the start of the whole thing) and so they had swept from Albany south to go back up north, just exactly the crazy turned-around way Mason Raymond would do things. Well, he's paying for it, John thought. The rich can afford symbols—*symbols*, another Mason Raymond notion. He saw signs in everything.

Where the hell *was* he?

Mason Raymond might not have any skills to survive—he was weak and worthless in every way John could count up: He had no sense of direction and got himself lost if he was turned loose on his own for even a minute; he couldn't and wouldn't shoot (even counting he'd once killed a man); he couldn't lay a trap and he was squeamish about food; but worst of all, the absolute worst of anything as far as John Buttes was concerned, was that Mason Raymond was a hanger-on, someone who attached himself and stuck like a burr and there was no way to pry him loose and get rid of him—and all because he was "family," a first cousin, and had high moral principles and whatever else it was with people like him that, though they were weak as brackwater and wishy-washy as bark tea, had learned the knack of using the strong to get their own way.

Well, he had done his best—had got Mason Raymond to sit a horse so he didn't slide first this way and then that, had got him to pray off by himself behind a rock or a tree or some brush so that John didn't have to try to explain his carryings-on to other people, had got him to stop giving his money and clothes and equipment away to tramps and beggars and no-good ne'er-do-wells. The only thing he hadn't been able to do was convince Mason Raymond that his wanting to go out West and "do something" for the Indians was a lot of nutty nonsense which would—

Would what?

John didn't know—jest get him in trouble, was the way John thought of it. But he's always in trouble, John thought now. What difference does it really make, speaking in a geographical sense, where he's making a fuck-up of things?

He wiped his face again with his hat. He was tired and hot and thirsty—bone tired—but there was nothing to do but start scouring the landscape for Mason Raymond, who was probably crouched down somewhere (for the hundred thousandth time) asking for forgiveness.

Yet a perverse kind of admiration pervaded John for the whole episode over which Mason Raymond mourned so much and which seemed to John (and most people back home at Buttes Landing) the only really admirable thing Mason Raymond had ever done in his life. To kill a man meant you weren't average or ordinary, and if there was anything John Buttes despised it was the average and ordinary.

I don't understand how he ever done it, John Buttes thought. He had had that question to ponder for seven years, and there was still no answer. He come runnin' out of the woods, John thought, like he was never goin' to stop, run right past us, run three, maybe four miles already from where Hart and that bear and that dog was strung out, run right past us like he never even seen us, and I took after him, couldn't catch him no way he was goin' so fast. I can see him plain as if it was happenin' right now: runnin' like God Hisself had dropped down out of the skies and was gonna grab hold of him if he didn't outrun Him.

Shoutin' didn't do no good. Hollered my head off and he didn't even hear the whisper of a word. He was deaf, dumb and blind runnin' to the end of the earth and then he was jest goin' to jump off.

Runnin' and runnin' and I was never goin' to catch him: then the scream. Inside his head, here near the Missouri, John heard the grinding cry of a man's spirit being wrenched right out of him. Mason Raymond had stopped still and shrieked and then he had dropped to earth, as if dead, and John had run up to him and crouched down looking into the bubbled face of a man in the midst of a fit.

He ain't never been right since, John thought.

He could still picture Mason Raymond thrashing about in the pine needles and small crusty cones of the mountainous Adirondacks, Mason Raymond's eyes turned back until they were white, foam and froth on his mouth, Mason Raymond's tongue a tangle against his teeth.

He been touched ever since he had that fit, John thought.

The empty dead landscape ahead was almost the opposite of the pine mountains and rushing rivers back home, and it was a fact, another of those queer reversals of living that made no sense when you examined them but which existed nevertheless *as* facts, that it was from Mason Raymond that John had first listened to the poetry of the desert names; it was Mason Raymond who had had the original longing to leave the Landing, the Adirondacks, and strike out all alone to the far country to make a place for himself—that is, before the "accident."

"You ever think about names?" he asked John.

"Names?"

"You know, how some names seem to mean so much more than others, how the names of some places just seem to call out to you?"

Of course John never wasted time on such crazy thoughts. Who would? But Mason Raymond was serious, leaning forward in sweaty earnest adolescent confidence. "All those

] 7 [

names out West—even the way they talk about the land out there, gulches and prairies and canyons, they're like a whole 'nother world—and there are names of places—the Rockies and the Tetons, Colter's Hell and Tombstone, Grand Canyon and Yellowstone—that make you just want to go and see them. But you know the name that I think about the most, the one that comes to call just to me?" He wanted for John to ask, and John shrugged his shoulders, what did he care if Mason Raymond had some special name he liked? "There's one place I'm going to go some day and that's The Sweetwater, The Sweetwater at South Pass where the mountains finally rise out of the Plains and the people know the air's cool and the water's good again and a whole new world begins."

He was probably crazy even back then, John thought, before he even went into that fit. Whoever heard of anyone in his right senses talking like that? I should of knowed then there was something not right with him; nobody normal would talk like that. But, hell, at twelve why was I supposed to see what grown-ups theirselfs couldn't lay a hand on?

But back then, six, seven years before, John had just thought Mason Raymond was romanticizing, part of the kind of silliness that came from too much schooling ("buried in his books," John's mother said), but now—the desolate land actually before him—John had sense enough to see that back then at the Landing Mason Raymond had known he would never be anything but "that rich Raymond boy" (and "spoiled" was of course implied), and he had wanted to go someplace where he could just be himself. Why The Sweetwater? Who knew *then*? But now there were so many reasons, John couldn't lay his hands on one single focal point, unless perhaps it might be the everlasting "atoning" Mason Raymond was always talking about and which, at this moment, he was probably engaged in, down on his knees under the Kansas sun asking God to forgive him because once in his life he'd had the guts to take up a gun and do what had to be done. It was no crime to kill a dying man in mortal misery—that is, not to anyone but Mason Raymond. Any hunter would have done what Mason Raymond had done, but of course (again) the whole point was that Mason Raymond wasn't a hunter; he'd refused to carry a gun,

] *8* [

even during that crazy coon bet John's father had made back at the Landing with Frank Lite.

"How'd you like to run a couple of boys on a hunt, Frank, first one that trees and brings in a coon wins the bet?" John's father had had that hard, no-nonsense look on his face. Treeing to everyone meant getting a coon up in the branches and shooting him down. To everyone but Mason Raymond. He'd brought his coon in *alive* in a bag. Lite was so mad he went and shot Mason Raymond's dog; John shook his head in wonderment, remembering.

Lite was an evil man. Everyone knew it. But he had power because people were afraid of him. To get respect in this world people had to be afraid of you. Money makes people afraid of you sure enough, John thought.

Still, Mason Raymond had money and nobody was afraid of him. Mason Raymond got him all mixed up. I wish I'd never laid eyes on him, he thought in disgust. He's done nuthin' but git me turned around ever since I got mixed up with him. People like him shouldn't *exist*; they jest confuse everything.

I'm here and I got him on my hands and he's gone and disappeared on me again, and I'm wasting time again because of him when I could be getting on.

Ahead of him lay Independence, Missouri, three miles from the river, and past Independence, the Great Plains; he was near the 95th meridian, which divided the United States in this year of the centennial into two distinct halves—the crowded, settled, civilized East and the lonely, wild, unpredictable West, and all that was holding him up was his crazy cousin. "You know it won't be like it is here at the Landing, out there in the West. That's a long way away, a lot longer than distance. People feel different out there," his father had said, wanting to discourage his going. People never seemed to want you to do what you wanted to do, especially when you were John's age, nineteen, and wild with the blood inside you which said, *Go, see!*

John had tried to explain: Somewhere out in the West there lay a part of himself he had to go and claim, a whole new side of himself he knew nothing about. He *had* to go. Maybe Mason Raymond had started the idea, but now it was he, John Buttes, who was on fire to go. Out there in the West was a whole new world where he could be anything he wanted. While he plowed and planted, he kept his mind filled with the myths and legends that he had pilfered from cheap books and pamphlets, from newspaper accounts and hearsay, from a few guides which, he discovered, made more vivid than anything Mason Raymond could say that wide country beyond the Missouri, and probably, too, when he was honest and admitted it, from the memory of those marvelous names Mason Raymond had repeated to him like magic words that spelled the whole new world where men could become big and powerful and legends in their own right—Laramie and the Platte, the Plains and the buttes, and most of all Mason Raymond's dream of The Sweetwater, the river that meant the end of the sterile, alkali desert and the rise into the mountains and the great worlds of Oregon and California that lay beyond. Maybe the word *buttes* had caught in his mind, too, because of his name—John Buttes— and that was stuck there without his ever knowing it, so that it stayed like a beacon that said, *Come, see!* There's some of you out there, because of the name.

In some ways John felt he actually had been to some of the places; he had lived them so often in his imagination that they were vivid as anything he knew back home on the farm or in the little town across from Federation Lake. "The land, this land," his father said in that voice that joined pride and awe, standing in the slip of morning—they were late, and they had come out into the first grease of light, standing a little sheepishly in the early-morning rebuke of dawn. The Buttes way was to get up in darkness, dress in darkness, descend to duty in darkness, he and his father coughing as they went by lantern out to the barn; they did the milking before breakfast, the cats swarming from their nests in the hayloft of the barn for the warm milk. Sometimes John turned an udder and sent a stream right at them and they leaped and clawed trying to catch the milk in midair, then squatted down, lapping the white stream off the bare earthen barn floor.

Horses stamped in the stalls, impatient for their grain. As the light increased, roosters crowed. In spring he heard the bleating of hungry young lambs. Occasionally, walking down to the barn, his father made some comment about the coming day, but more often than not his father was silent, an inward man who said little and did much. Show, do not say.

His younger brothers were at their own tasks—in winter the wood, in summer the pails of water for washing and putting up. Encircled at the table they ate, semisilent, his mother the only chatterer in the family; grace was never said: John Buttes's father said God had abandoned him or he Him, first in the cornfields of Antietam and later—just to prove the point —in the Depression of '73.

"Cob," John's mother would say, rebuking her husband, "you shouldn't talk that way in front of the boys."

"You mean you want me to leave them to find out for theirselves?"

"Oh, Cob"—exasperated—"when will you ever *stop?*"

"When the world stops walkin' its way over the dead." And his father pushed more mush upon his spoon and fed it to his mouth.

His father had nearly gone under during the Panic of '73 and he wasn't in much better shape now, three years after; nor did it look as if he were ever going to pull up and get back where he'd been in the green years before the War. Nothing had ever been the same since the War—that's what John's father was always saying. For him it was true. What happened was not so important as how you saw it. And John saw the future as great—with the gold that made for greatness.

"This is a *Buttes* place and you're a *Buttes* boy and don't you never forget it." Hot with anger and rebellion, John would look down, stubbornly silent in his denial of any obligation. If he made no vow, how could his father hold him accountable for a breach of trust? He was going, no matter what. There was no one, not even his father, in this whole wide world who could hold him back. He did not belong to the past, like his father, but to the future because he was going and he had his whole life ahead of him.

What John could never explain to his family because he was trying to protect them, he didn't want to hurt their feelings, was the endless sameness of life in the country was what was driving him away. Hard work didn't bother him, though he thought he had sense enough to question why farm work should be so unending, day in, day out, twelve, fourteen, sixteen hours a day seven days a week; there surely were easier ways to make a living, but people at the Landing—his father, his grandfather in particular—were always trying to make "living next to the land," as they called all that backbreaking imprisonment to the soil, some kind of virtue city people lacked, as if the prisoners of the soil were really a special, provident breed of people city people could never be.

Maybe, but things were happening in the city, things were going on, exciting things, all the way across country; there wasn't the same endless eternal monotonous grind of these mindless chores—there was *change.* That was the key word: change. I don't want to stay the same all my life. That's not living to me. I want to go out and see what's out there. I *know* what's here. I want to know what's out there. And I want to be rich, not dirt poor the way they are and beholden to the bank.

"You'll grow up to be just like your Uncle Clyde," his mother would say. "You want to be like a Raymond the way your Uncle Clyde wanted to be a Raymond because the Raymonds are city rich and the Buttes are plain and land poor. You want to be a Raymond like your Uncle Clyde, is that it, John?" she would demand, her hands on her hips, teeth flashing half in laughter, half in derision. "Raymond's a grand rich-sounding name, isn't it? I guess that's what your Uncle thought, too. *Clyde Raymond* sounded a lot grander than *Clyde Buttes.* Easier for Clyde, Lord knows, he was married to a Raymond. Course he was nice about it—I mean, he went easy. First he just started callin' himself Clyde Raymond-Buttes, and when we all got used to that, he was goin' to drop the Buttes part and just be Clyde Raymond. But he went and got full of debts and the wrongs he done started comin' home, so he never had the time to make the change before he went and hanged hisself."

"Ma, I ain't gonna get full of debts or go hang myself. I ain't plannin' on doin' nuthin' but a little travelin'. What's so all-fired bad about that?"

] *12* [

"You wish you was Mason Raymond, left with all that money—free to come and go as you please with no responsibilities to no one, that's it, isn't it? You'd rather be Mason Raymond and rich than be John Buttes and dirt poor. He killed that man," she said, shaking her head in puzzlement. "That poor boy who wouldn't hurt a flea, he had to go and shoot Hart and put him out of his misery. Because he knew it had to be done.

"And he's never been right in the head since," John's mother went on relentlessly. "Poor soul." The complexities of people seemed to John summed up in his mother's contrary views: Never count on consistency. "He takes after Ardis, his mother. She got it from her father. Strangeness runs in the Raymond family. I know it's not his fault," she said. Well, Clyde was pretty strange too—and he was a Buttes, John thought, but he had sense enough not to say so. "The Raymonds, they—" Words failed her. She understood something fundamental must be the matter with the Raymond blood, but she couldn't put her finger on it. "That boy was gentle as a lamb and he went and blew that old man's head right off. Never even left half the face."

All right, John agreed killing wasn't maybe a good thing but there were times when there was no choice, you had to do it, the way Mason Raymond had to. There was no use shredding cloth over it: You couldn't go on punishing yourself forever for what had to be done.

You gotta be *practical*, John said to himself now. And that's jest what's the matter with Mason Raymond. There ain't a sensible bone in his body. He'll be praying till the day he dies, over somethin' he done that had to be done—and holdin' *me* up.

He squinted, holding in the horse, trying to see Mason Raymond or his horse, that old nag that was as crazy as his cousin riding it, a big dumb-looking mare bent in with spavins and windpuffs, whose back sagged and whose head hung down in the same permanent look of abject dejection Mason Raymond's head had. When that splayed horse and his splayed cousin ambled along, walking side by side, they looked like two creatures out of the Last Judgment who'd been told to turn to the left. Nobody, not even God, was going to save shattered souls like that. Because they won't help themselves, that's *why*, John thought.

He's been nuthin' but poison put in the well ever since we started out. He can't ride a horse, he can't find his way out of one room into the next; he can't even eat straight, but the Lord had evened things out by giving him money. There it was again: God favoring a fortunate few.

Nobody ever give me nuthin'. Everythin' I ever got I had to rustle up on my own, whereas *him*—

Goddam it, why was he always losin' himself and goin' off and gittin' lost? If he's gonna git lost, why can't he git hisself permanently lost? I wanna git into Independence—

A little dot bobbed up and down against the limitless blue. A bird maybe, flying low; or Mason Raymond, plodding along, in that slow, meandering way that drove John crazy.

In a rage of energy John grabbed hold of his horse and commenced hollering and bobbing about, but of course Mason Raymond—if it was Mason Raymond—didn't pay any attention. He never did. John couldn't really take his absent-mindedness personally; it was so evenly distributed. Once that dazed dreamer had even run into a post; he'd been flopping about in some field looking, John presumed, for a suitable praying place, romping around, all turned inward with that glazed-over look John had come to identify as Mason Raymond Ready to Receive the Spirit, when he'd bumped right up against a big upright fence in this field in Illinois. For a moment Mason Raymond's eyes had at least focussed long enough to identify what had hit him; he looked at the post attentively as if he were scrutinizing its cracks. He even leaned forward and studied the grain of the wood. Then he shook his head and moved on. Apparently there was no cosmic outline of the omniscient in that oak.

Dumb dumb dumb.

John semaphored his arms and yelled. Deaf, dumb, and blind—he's just going to be the death of me, John thought. And it's all my own fault. I kept quiet when I shoulda said *No*, and he was smart enough to take advantage of the fact I was embarrassed at how he was carrying on, pleading with me to jest let him come along as far as Independence, he *had* to atone. What are you going to do with someone who talks to you about penance and contrition and the seeds of salvation?

He suckered me in; that's what he done. I'm the one that's dumb.

But one thing he could admit: Mason Raymond had at least taught him the lesson of commitment—what you don't say can also be held against you.

The horse up ahead was in too good a shape to be Mason Raymond's, and—as John got closer—he saw the short squat black figure couldn't come anywhere near passing for his tall gaunt gangly cousin. The living end, the absolute living end: a goddam nigger cowboy out in the middle of nowhere. Where the hell was Mason Raymond? "You seen a kid back there wanderin' around—maybe lookin' a little lost?" He had been about to say "prayin'," but there were limits to what John was willing to spring on a stranger.

The nigger reined in, looking edgy. John felt the need for explication. "He don't hold on to his bearings too well. He's from back East—"

"They're all from back East," the nigger said wearily. "They're all from back East and they're all headin' for the Hills and they're all gonna git rich and there ain't one of 'em know a pick from an axe.

> *"This is the man of whom you've all read,*
> *Who left with the others on the big stampede;*
> *Now he's returned, all tattered and torn,*
> *From lookin' for gold in the Little Big Horn."*

It was too much for John: Mason Raymond off praying somewhere, a goddam nigger spoutin' poetry like that, and he himself so tired and thirsty he was about stove in.

The nigger was stuffing his mouth with black tobacco, looking at John as if of all the ignorant, raw dude Easterners he'd ever seen this was the worst. He held up the tattered pouch. "It's what give me my name," he said. "Pepper Tom. You got one of them good back-East names, I bet, Ethan or Eben or, like one I took up with for a spell, Jonathan," he said. "You know what that Jonathan said to me? He said I was the *whitest* man he'd ever knowed, so I took up my gear and got me my animal and I left him standin' there still askin' what he'd done wrong.

"Old Pepper's gone and died, went to the Great Divide,
Rustled where the good niggers are sometimes let abide.
If they check his brain like I think they do,
They'll see he was 'white' through and through."

John looked at the man and thought, Everyone knows niggers got no sense. This one ain't no different than the others. The black man was half turned in his saddle taking in John and the prairie and the dust, looking everything over and sizing it up as if to get a handle on it. He looked sure of himself, John admitted, a man used to long hours in the saddle probably, and the hard life of the trail.

John just wanted him to go away and leave him alone. He had problems enough. He could maybe handle the nigger on his own and he had learned pretty well how to manage Mason Raymond when there weren't other people around making Mason Raymond do crazy things; but he didn't think he could take on both the nigger *and* Mason Raymond and save much of his own wits.

"You plannin' on ridin' that horse the other side of the river?" The nigger didn't bother to wait for an answer. "That horse ain't gonna last you more time than it take for its feet to wear down, mabbe a week, mabbe a little longer. Eastern horses ain't born to forage on buffalo grass and cactus and weeds. Between his feet and his stomach he'll founder in no time flat. That saddle's nice work though. Who done that?"

"My Pa got it from a man had it in the War."

"Army work—clean and neat, and strong, fixed to last. Nice horse, too, mabbe got some age on it, but clean, hardly a mark on it, and you come some distance at that, but it ain't right for where you goin'. Where you goin' you need a cow pony or mabbe a mule. That animal of yourn ain't no good to trail nor pack nor go across plains, and you ain't gonna git much of a trade 'lessen you find some other greenhorn don't know no more than you and thinks he's scalpin' you instead of you liftin' his hide. That saddle's serviceable enough, but the horse has got to go."

John looked at the black man standing sucking black tobacco into his mouth, a nigger know-it-all he'd picked up out of nowhere—why should he listen to him?

"Mules is better even than horses," the nigger went on. "Plenty of men has got real attached to theirs. Mules, they's tough; they can survive right well where a horse can't make do. A horse, it eats—it gits distemper, it dies. Mules live longer, they's stronger stomached—"

"I don't want no mule."

"Well, do what you want. Git a horse if you want, but git yourself a decent one. Seen a couple of good Indian ponies comin' in. Might try sellin' your animal and seein' what you could git for it, but I'll tell you right now it won't bring much." He poured tobacco in a steady stream between his hand and mouth. "Here, cut that out," he said to his horse, who was crowhopping about. "He got some kind of bug at him?" he asked. Oh, god—" he said, looking into the distance. It must be Mason Raymond.

The truth is terrible. Nothing is ever what you first thought. How could he explain Mason Raymond? He was the sort of thing you just had to take on faith. "He come with me," he said finally. "He's my cousin. So he come West with me."

John watched apprehensively to see what Mason Raymond was going to do. There was never any way to predict. John just hoped he wouldn't start giving his money or clothes away again. Mason Raymond seemed taller and gaunter than John remembered, terrible really. He was only twenty-four or twenty-five, not much older than John, but he looked like maybe a hundred. He had the worst-looking eyes John had ever seen. Even when Mason Raymond's mouth moved to smile, as it did now, his eyes stayed sad, the eyes of a man just come from a hanging. John was struck again by how much of a fool *he*'d been ever even to go down to Albany. It was his mother's doing. She'd got him to promise he'd stop off and see how Mason Raymond was getting along. So instead of heading cross-country the way he normally would have, he'd detoured down south to Albany. Right from the first, he supposed, he'd been resentful because that detour was costing him time, and now he was finally on his way, leaving Buttes Landing at last, in a fever to get cross-country as fast as he could, but a promise was a promise, and he'd told his mother he'd go see how Mason Raymond was. Strange stories about his behavior were floating back to the Landing, and they even got a letter from an old teacher of Mason Raymond's—that one at the Academy with the sleepy name, Morphus, Morphis, something like that—saying he thought maybe the family ought to come down to Albany; he wasn't sure Mason Raymond was eating right, he was just skin and bones, and the big house where he was living, well, it looked deserted, as if no one were inside, that's what the teacher had written.

And he was right—the house did look deserted, but that was because there was no one else there except Mason Raymond; all the servants dead or let go, the furniture covered with sheets and the drapes pulled closed so that there was an eerie tomblike atmosphere to the place. Mason Raymond was holed up in a single small room in the back of the house, bare except for a narrow mattress on the floor and a little niche he had fitted out with some saint with large staring eyes circled in black, eyes that looked as lost as Mason Raymond's. He burnt candles too. The room reeked of incense and tallow.

Mason Raymond had opened one of the big bedrooms for John, beat the dust out of the bedcovers and made the room look if not comfortable at least usable. He smiled and tapped John on the arm and said, "See you at supper," though it was only one o'clock in the afternoon and John had not had anything since breakfast.

"What about my horse?"

"Put him out back in the barn. It's open. Everything's open. Help yourself to anything you want. Anyone can."

John had wandered around the dusty deserted barn getting the horse fixed up and then he had gone into the bare, deserted kitchen trying to forage a little food for himself. He'd had to settle on bread (crusty and stale) and milk (starting to turn). Everything looked scrubbed down to the bone, bare bare bare. He went upstairs after he ate and slept just to get away from the feeling he was inside someone's grave.

They went out to eat. Mason Raymond (at that time), he discovered, only ate once a day—some fruit, a little cereal, occasionally some cooked vegetables. It was mortifying to John for them to go to a big shining restaurant and have Mason Raymond tell the waiter he'd just have an apple and a little oatmeal. The waiter's expression flickered ever so slightly, but he wrote apple and oatmeal on his pad as if they were the most natural things in the world to order for supper.

That was bad enough, but it wasn't as bad as trying to talk to Mason Raymond. He didn't talk at all at first. He just sat hovered in on himself with his eyes glazed over, as if he were in another world, oblivious to the fine men and handsome women dining all around them. The bubbles of chatter and balloons of laughter rose around the room, but Mason Raymond seemed to take in none of it.

Crazy as a coot, John decided. God knows what will become of him. I don't care if he is blood. I don't ever want to see him again as long as I live. He ain't my responsibility. I'll write back and tell Ma and she can figure out what to do. Privately John had concluded his cousin should probably be locked up, though he seemed harmless enough.

Never in the world had he thought, that first night, that he would bring West a grain eater, a man who believed animal blood inflamed the brain and made a man do violent passionate unnatural acts. He et meat before he killed the old man, John thought. Mabbe now he tells hisself it wasn't his fault he done the shootin'; it was the beef made him do it.

He blames hisself all right. He ain't never stopped blamin' hisself. That's his whole trouble. He's prayin' all the time to pay back for what he done. And yet there ain't nuthin' to pay back—why can't he see that? He just done what anyone would have.

Mason Raymond had told John how he'd tried to atone up North by living out in the middle of nowhere, eating roots and berries and things like that, but of course he'd never shoot nor trap no animals, that was against his principles, trying to repay blood for blood—to atone, Mason Raymond said. "I'm trying to atone; there are ways to atone. It's very hard to explain," he said earnestly, leaning over across the table and for once fixing his large grave eyes on John, "but I thought if I got away from everyone and just lived all by myself, I might be able to piece things together, to make sense of what happened, to be able to explain it to myself, because, you see, it all happened so fast that I don't think I even thought about what I was doing, I just picked up the gun and fired.

"No, that's not true either. We were running, chasing the bear, me and Hart and Lite, and then somewhere Lite dropped behind, and it was just me and Hart and the dog; the dog was running like mad, I'll never forget the way that dog just kept going and going. Hart was so proud of that dog. It was everything he always said a Plott hound should be—everything he went looking for when we went to Carolina—and more. That Horatio was the greatest dog maybe I ever knew."

Mason Raymond was talking very rapidly, the words tumbling out of him now as if once the door that crammed them shut up tight inside was forced open there was no way ever to crowd them back in. "We heard Horatio baying up ahead and we knew he'd got the bear treed or cornered or something, and then we came into the clearing and Lite was somehow with us. The bear and the dog—I don't know, it all happened so fast—they ran at one another and the bear grabbed the dog or maybe ran between them; all I remember was hollering at Lite to fire, and he didn't, he just stood there a minute, and then he turned and ran; he dropped his gun and turned and ran and I picked the gun up. There were Hart and the dog all tore up and Hart was trying to tell me something. He was saying—" But Mason Raymond couldn't go on; he was like one seized in the paralysis of some terrible insight as he hung across the table staring no longer at John but inside, into that grim, grisly insight that suspended him in midsentence, a man hanging on the cross of his own guilt.

Mason Raymond's suffering was so intense that John put down his fork and stopped chewing. A moment before he'd been so hungry he felt he could eat his way through that whole menu; now his throat closed tight and the very thought of food made him feel sick. He could think of nothing to say or do; in a way he was as bad as Mason Raymond, John realized. I'm suspended in my own kind of paralyzation, he thought.

That was the first time he got to me, John thought, and then later when he started carrying on about how he *had* to get West, maybe The Sweetwater would purify him, I felt guilty, as if I'd taken his ideas and feelings and kind of made them my own, and finally I said I understood, I'd had the same feelings myself, and then when he mentioned the money, the money he'd be willing to lay out if I took him, that was what done it. Greed—goddam greed, that was what done me in. I got nobody but myself to blame. But that's cold comfort. Please don't start your acting up now, John thought silently, as Mason Raymond lumbered up to them. I only got so much patience and you used up most of that in Ohio. My god, who could ever forget Ohio?

"He don't look none too strong, your cousin," the nigger said. "He don't look like the kind who could pick up on the plains, but then again he don't look like the kind could mine in the mountains neither."

"He ain't aimin' on neither," John said. "He's goin' to the Indians—to atone."

"Is he *crazy?* This ain't no time to be foolin' around with them redskins. Them Indians is bad now. Don't they tell you nuthin' back where you come from? Indians out here is all fired up and jest lookin' for trouble. Don't you never read nuthin' in your papers back home about what's goin' on out here?"

John was hot and hungry and tired, and his horse needed to lay up a bit; of course he read the papers and of course he had more than a good idea of what was going on, but you couldn't explain any of that to Mason Raymond, or if you did he wouldn't pay any attention; he didn't see the world the way anybody else did, that was his whole trouble, but Mason Raymond's problems were too long and complicated to try to explain to a stranger, let alone condense in the short time left while Mason Raymond made it the maybe quarter of a mile he still had to come to catch up with them. So what John said was, "He don't seem to git the picture very straight. He thinks 'cause he's part Indian—"

"Part Indian?" The nigger looked up in surprise.

"He ain't, you know, real Indian—I mean, it's hardly there at all. But he"—nodding at Mason Raymond—"he thinks it's like because he's part Indian they'll all jest run out and be happy as spring to welcome him in; he don't see he's so white them Indians ain't gonna be able to detect some little bit of blood maybe is Indian buried deep inside; he thinks they're gonna see him like all Indian and jest take him in like he was one of their own." John could see the nigger couldn't follow what he was trying to explain, but that was to be expected: Who could understand the turns and convolutions of a mind like Mason Raymond's?

He watched Mason Raymond tumbling toward them, his face expressionless, not a hint of doubt or dismay in it. He looked almost like an ordinary person passing over the prairie, a little thin maybe and, if you looked close, something odd around the eyes, but there were no real visible signs of how mixed up he was inside because a walk didn't count. Lots of men had accidents made them walk a little funny. He just looked tired, not crazy.

"We best go and give him a hand," the nigger said. "He don't look like he's got the wherewithal even to git the little bit to Independence, let alone hike up into the Hills. I seen some strange critters in my time, but he's got to be one of the sorriest-looking instances a man can put eyes to. You kind of lost your bearin's, son?" he asked Mason Raymond.

But what he don't know, John thought, is what I didn't know neither, that that poor scarecrow crawling toward us is like iron inside. I know. I spent a thousand miles finding out you can't judge a horse by the color of its hide.

II

Mason Raymond fingered the scar that ran like a crescent over the ridge of his head. Over the years it had settled in so that it was only a fine small edge where the hair would never grow back in. The scar was his brother bond with the old man who had been more father than friend, Worth Hart, who had had an almost identical, though thicker and wider, scar that traversed his own scalp. Hart's scar had come from goodness and Mason Raymond's from stupidity, one of the many signs of the major differences that divided them. All worth and heart like his name (names were so often symbolic of the people who had them, like Miss Crank, the old-maid librarian at the Academy, or Mr. Dearlove, the minister whose views were too charitable for the conservative little church), Worth Hart had once taken in an idiot boy, fathering him for years, and the thanks he got was being hit over the head with an axe. Mason Raymond's folly had been falling in with a bunch of thugs in New York City —a large difference in scope any way you looked at it.

Hart's scar had pained him—headaches crackled inside his skull without warning or the weather could set his head throbbing with all kinds of warning—but Mason Raymond's scar barely ever troubled him. He would forget about it for weeks at a time until, absentmindedly, he rubbed at his head and suddenly came into contact with the little bald ridge of remembrance.

A great man, Hart, and who ever thought of him now save Mason Raymond himself and Mabel, his wife, his two children? Mason Raymond had powerful convictions about acts of remembrance (he had named his horse Mabel for Mabel Hart), of bringing back the dead; and he said now, over and over, Hart, Hart, and Rivers, Rivers and Hart, willing them back to life, one more of Bartholomew's views he could never sever himself from.

Like Bartholomew, who lived alone in eternal speculation in his cave back in the Adirondacks, Mason Raymond believed you call the dead back from nothingness by remembering them, just by thinking their names. The dead were waiting out there in space for you to bring them some kind of life by calling them back.

Hart, Bartholomew, Morphis, Rivers, all so different, but he carried their beliefs, like no one else's, inside him as if they had been engraved like ancient laws upon his heart. Hart, the old hunter, Bartholomew, the spiritual quester, Morphis, his teacher in school, and even Rivers, his mother's servant, more influential for him than his parents. It was to their wisdom he was always turning, like a lost child needing a parent's hand to lead him out of confusion and despair. The books, too—he mustn't forget those, especially the *Iliad.* If he had only the ability to divine its great messages, he might make routes to the major crossroads of a man's life.

"Power comes from the words that are handed down from civilization to civilization," that's what his old teacher at the Academy in Albany, Morphis, was always saying. Most men believe power lies in force, but the greatest power is in the word. And love, Bartholomew reminded him, love is more powerful than pen or sword. But if this was so, why had Bartholomew been living alone all by himself in his cave? Perhaps not exactly alone—he had stuffed and taken along with him those he had cared about, the animals of this world which were to Bartholomew more open to emotion than the people he had known. Because love—so powerful—was also so dangerous. With people, Bartholomew had once said, loving and hating come so close you can't know which is which, there is no way to separate them. "I learned never to start loving because the beauty of it in the beginning was always thrashed out in the end by the hate, and love, with people, you know, gets to be more than you can stand—all the demands.

"But animals, you know"—he leaned down and touched the stuffed dead dusty dog tenderly—"they don't expect so much. They just want something to eat, a little acknowledgment now and again, like a pat on the head, a run to make them feel a little free, just the comfort, the companionship of being beside you, not asking anything, just lying comfortable and quiet and glad to be near you, just glad to have you there, not making any demands; they don't want to eat and drink you up alive, just so as you can show them you care about them. They never let you alone, people, never; day and night, it's show me you love me, show me you care; and if you don't show them enough, and it's never enough, no matter what you do, it's you don't love me, you never loved me—at you and at you and at you until pretty soon all the love's gone, it's only ugly and brutish and vengeful and wanting to do spiteful things to get back for the hurt, the desire to dominate the other person, to be the one to do harm, instead of having the harm done you.

"Oh, I've wanted so much to love, boy, and tried so hard," Bartholomew had cried out. "And none of it ever came to anything but that driving need to have the top hand, and that's not love, that's not love at all; it's like a crazy desire to control part of the world, even if it's only one small part of it, to show you're better than anyone else, *stronger*," Bartholomew said with great anger and pity at the same time. "The whole awful story of people trying to care for one another in this awful imperfect world and never really being able to do it, and so much of the hate, I've come to think, comes just from that—there is no way to get the hate away from the love because we're all so uncertain in ourselves, and we keep thinking other people can give us a feeling of being loved, of being important and special, and so we keep trying to love, to make things go

] *25* [

right; we start over and over again, everything's all bright and beautiful in the beginning and we think we've found what we've been looking for at last, and then it starts to turn and go bad, and we're so disappointed and angry it hasn't worked, we can't believe that we've made a mistake again, we're all tied up inside with the terrible feeling of failure, turned back in on ourselves and our own uncertainties and insignificance, and sometimes the pain and hurt just seem too much to bear, we never want to see another human being again, like animals we just want to crawl away and lick our wounds and stay still until we get well, and so finally I come out here, boy, where I don't have to break my heart no more trying. I can be with my animals, and they can be with me and the world then don't seem such a hard and ugly and painful place." It was then Mason Raymond had understood that Bartholomew spun his theories, one after another, in the hopeless pursuit of an answer to fill what Bartholomew was sure in his heart was the bottomless, meaningless void of the universe, that Bartholomew was trying to make some kind of peace where there had never been any, that he was trying to impose some sense on a world that had none.

In what other people would have called "real life," Bartholomew had been a taxidermist. In his cave, which was remarkably like one of those family parlors opened only to the coffined, the minister, or the gentleman caller of an elderly aunt, Bartholomew had rigged up a corner whatnot that held his departed friends—stuffed birds, moles, chipmunks, a raccoon, a marvelous white owl. Near the only chair—an enormous carved-out tree stump—there was a stuffed sleeping dog lying with his head comfortably resting on his paws. Bartholomew talked to the stuffed dead dog, whom he still considered capable of communication and to whom, when he came and went, he gave a friendly pat of encouragement. In the twilight interior of the rock room the little mongrel looked alive except for the half an inch or so of dust which had accumulated on his eyelids and inside his alert little ears.

Things just happened, they didn't have reasons why. But there were some choices. Mason Raymond could stand with eyes closed and concentrate or he could squat and try to fuse all the whirling images into one so that he could pass it on, or he could even lie down and stare straight up into the vast sky and once in a while think things out in the heavens overhead. But this afternoon none of these devices had worked. Hart's wounds were still bubbling blood-bright; Hart's eyes were still like great holes in his mutilated face; Hart was still trying to tell him something, and that something was so important that Hart refused to be sent off to the spheres into nothingness, allowing Mason Raymond to be left in peace. Hart called him and Mason Raymond came; he needed so badly to know what Hart was trying to tell him, but the command never quite got through. Outside messages, which were related, flowed through, but the general directive on how to live was lost in all the side wisdom Hart felt he also had to know.

Hart knew, but he had never been easy to discern alive and now that he was dead the matter was more muddled. Bartholomew was trying, but his mind fragmented as easily as a pond interrupted by the falling of a stone—stones, another of Bartholomew's obsessions: He was always picking one up and looking at it curiously, pocketing it for his corner collection in the cave. The past, said Bartholomew, put stones in a man's pockets that weighed him down. I am like lead, Mason Raymond thought.

The black man poured a handful of tobacco into his hand and sucked it up between his teeth, and his cousin John mopped his streaming face with his hat. You must *love,* even if it's hard and dangerous, Bartholomew reminded him from inside his head. It was like his mother saying, when he was young, Pick up your socks and put them in the laundry bag —and did as much good.

"I guess I held you up some," Mason Raymond said to John, whose mouth went up at the corners in a grimace which replied clearly enough, You always do, you dumb dodo. You don't never think of nobody but yourself.

There was nothing he ever did, Mason Raymond thought, that made matters right. He had gone all the way cross-country on his left foot, so to speak. There was a saying for it back at the Landing, He goes left where he ought to turn right.

You must hold your mind in one place, Bartholomew had told him. *Hold your head in one place.*

"He don't look so hot," the black man said as Mason Raymond closed his eyes and tried to keep his head where it belonged, in one place, on his neck.

"He's subject to spells," John said, his voice filled with that disgust Mason Raymond knew too well.

"I'm jest a little woozy," Mason Raymond got out as his legs started to crumble and he said, desperate to seem normal, "I think it's the heat."

His head was getting ready to explode the way it did when everything inside it got away from him and he couldn't control what was going on. The most important thing in life was to control what was happening to you, and he just didn't seem to have any authority over events.

He gulped water that one of them had shoved in a canteen between his teeth. It tasted warm and brackish and did nothing to stop the thunderous pounding of his head, the signal, Mason Raymond was sure, of some final, fatal attack which would, mercifully, end his inadequacies on this earth. I am glad to have gone West. "Gone West," the synonym for Death.

That girl—she had looked so *nice.* She'd been sitting there in that shop trying on gloves—*gloves,* what could be more innocent than gloves, for crissake? And he'd just come in and asked about where the road to Independence was. He was off the track again, having lost John, who had got ahead and out of sight, and there was this sort of general store in Xenia— Xenia, Ohio, the name would stick with him forever (unfortunately)—and he'd seen this general store, what could be wrong with a general store in Xenia, Ohio, you just go in and ask directions and someone sets you back on the right road, you don't certainly see danger in a nice girl putting on a glove and then holding that gloved hand up and asking, "What do you think?"

He looked around, but there wasn't anyone else within a radius of hearing; she must mean him. His face commenced to burn, he had a burning sensation, sickening, in his stomach, and his throat was so filled with feeling that he couldn't speak. He had never seen anything like the color of her hair, ashen like the bark of the white birch.

She turned her hand over once, twice, still debating. The glove was a dark green, so dark it looked almost black. "I don't know," she said doubtfully. "I think it makes my fingers look kind of stubby." Then she turned her remarkable eyes on him, eyes with a yellowish kind of glow in back of them so that she looked almost like a lion with that ruff of blond-white hair and those odd eyes streaked with so much yellow you didn't notice the brown at all at first, eyes the color of rare trillium in the first spring flowerings under the wet bank of leaves in the woods. "Well," she said, widening her eyes so that fire fell through the ashen silky lashes, "what *do* you think?"

He was having enough trouble breathing without pushing his strength to make his mind behave; yet miraculously a voice came out of his throat and though it wasn't one he recognized as his own he gave it his blessing to speak. "Beautiful," that voice said. But of course it hadn't meant the glove.

The girl smiled; radiance lit up her face. "You think so?" she said as joyously as if he'd told her he loved her, she was the most beautiful thing he'd ever seen, he'd live only to serve her for the rest of his life. "You really think so?"

This time he nodded, smiling, oh god his face was going to split he was smiling so widely, and gulping, ready to throw himself at her knees and beg—for what he didn't know, only that she let him look at her for five more minutes, he'd never seen such hair and eyes in his life; he was sure he never would again and maybe Bartholomew was right, the way back to the world was knowing how to love. If Bartholomew hadn't learned, maybe *he* would.

Now he blinked his eyes and looked blankly at the blue sky; he was trying to avoid the image inside his head of the two of them walking down the street, he stiff and formal, the yellow-eyed girl fluttery and gay, her green-gloved fingers resting lightly on his arm. She thought she'd look around for a matching parasol, she had said, and he had bought a dark-green velvet one that afternoon that had cost—he wouldn't think of how much it had cost. He had bought a lot of things in the next week before she'd let him, as they said back home, "have his way with her."

Have his way with her: All she had to do was throw her arms around his neck and nestle up to him, breathe against his neck, and cradle her head against his shoulder for the starch to go right out of him. He'd been such a ninny he hadn't even asked himself how come a nice girl like that was living all alone with her "cousin," a handsome young cousin to boot; he'd been such a boob he'd never asked himself how come a "young" girl like that wasn't married and raising a family of her own instead of running and fetching for the "cousin"; such a dumb dodo that he hadn't (until the end) even begun to question the "young." But by the time he began to notice a little of the lines under her eyes and to see the the little indentures of age at the corners of her nose, he couldn't look at her with any kind of objectivity. He wouldn't listen to John either, who had come into Xenia to look for him and was mad with impatience for him to come to his senses (John's words) and get going West, he was holding them up; it wasn't even any good for John to threaten to leave him. He told John to go on and go. "If I had any sense, I would," John had said. "But you're such a damn fool you'll turn over every cent you've got to that woman and there won't be nuthin' left for me to outfit myself when we git to Independence. You promised," John raged. "You promised that if I took you as far as Independence, you'd spring me to a kit. You know you did."

"I'll give you the money now," Mason Raymond had said, "if you want."

"And I'll take it, goddam it, but not before I seen you got what was coming to you. I never knowed such a goddam fool in my whole born days. Ain't you got *any* sense?"

God, how had he been so deceived? How? Why couldn't he see right off what John had seen?

Because he was a fool, that was why—a damned ignorant fool, just the way John said.

Don't think about it, let it alone. The pain of that final scene was tightening into a hard hand that squeezed his heart open and closed, open and closed, crushing it to nothingness.

"Haul him up on the horse, son. We gotta git him in town

where he can lie up and rest some. He's done in."

He should not have been diverted by a girl in green gloves —serious people kept their minds on what was important. You didn't find someone like Bartholomew abandoning his cave for green gloves. A serious person spent himself on serious things. Also, as Bartholomew had said so many times, You should learn to love what can love you back.

In the year and a half that Mason Raymond had known him the old hermit had given him over twenty lucid explanations of the origin and outcome of man. Bartholomew was at the point in life where every consideration came back to "Where did man come from and where does he go?" But Mason Raymond, who was younger, had an equally important consideration: "What about in between?"

Bartholomew had finally decided that man was really six seeds that six gods had come up with to see which would grow the best. Bartholomew divided his six seeds up into categories of colors: red, white, brown, black, yellow, and mixed. The six great gods, who Bartholomew said represented six great virtues man was not allowed to know, were watching their seeds assiduously to see which grew the best. When one finally outgrew all the others—that is, probably killed the others off like weeds, Bartholomew said quite calmly—then the six gods were going to decide what to do next. There was, after all, no hurry. They had all the time in the world to watch things work out since they were the ones in charge of the clocks.

My own father never cared anything about me, Mason Raymond thought. But Bartholomew did, Hart did. They were like fathers to me. My own never cared anything about anyone except himself, it was as if he couldn't. He didn't know how to love. He'd never learned. Maybe that wasn't his fault, he just didn't know how to care. He knew how to take, but he didn't know how to give; and then, at the end, people weren't willing to give anymore, they'd given all they were going to without getting anything back.

Mason Raymond's father—Clyde Buttes—was stranded then without knowing what to do because in order for him to survive there had to be a supply of givers, and when that ceased there wasn't any way for him to go on. So he hanged himself. At the top of the stairs. We came in, Mama and I, and there he was, with his bare feet, swinging over the landing. On Christmas Eve. I never knew him or understood him, never loved him, I never loved him, I never even liked him, I never liked my own father, and he's dead now, and I don't think about him, I don't suppose anyone ever does much anymore; he's fading away and won't be remembered at all one of these days. People like my father, like Lite the rifle dropper, fade fast. But not Hart, not Bartholomew.

Lite, again the strangeness of names, Lite was such a dark man and Worth Hart just the opposite. Mabel Hart used to say, half laughing, half not, that Hart thought a store more of Mason Raymond than he did his own blood. "It's like he'd spit you out," she'd say, "and the others is jest incidentals."

Worth Hart's two children, Miranda and Albert, and his wife, Mabel, had gone up to the funeral place and arranged about his viewing and burying, and then they'd gone to Lite's house—the man who'd really caused his death by letting the bear maul him—and rapped on the door and Mabel Hart had said, polite as you please, to Lite's frightened wife, "You got ten minutes to clear out."

She hadn't said any more. She and Miranda and Albert had just started going around the outside of the house pouring kerosene. It was because Lite had run off, afraid, and let Hart get killed instead of staying and shooting.

Mrs. Lite had come out and started asking what they were doing, but none of the three had answered her. Maybe they figured she could see clearly enough for herself. Finally Miranda had looked up and said, "If I was you, I reckon I'd git out all I could in what little time's left."

Mrs. Lite had got hysterical. "What do you mean, 'what little time's left'?"

"We're burnin' you out the way we burn out bad bugs come and make cocoons in our good trees," Mabel Hart said.

They set the house on fire first, and then the store. Nobody knew where Frank Lite had fled, but Mrs. Lite and her flock of mismatched children were wandering dazedly in the road that dawn, not knowing where to go.

Nobody took them in. At Buttes Landing the sins of the father—and mother—were passed on to the sons and daughters. It was a good Biblical town.

Lite's probably back at the Landing now, Mason Raymond thought. Wait a while and the storm passes over. No, that wouldn't be true in Lite's case. He could never go back because John's father, Cobus Buttes—who was so unlike Mason Raymond's father Clyde—would never forget or forgive. Others would, but never Cobus Buttes. Things got incised on his mind and never went away.

Mason Raymond thought of his Uncle Cobus testifying on his behalf, explaining, exonerating, extolling. "This boy ain't like some who could forgive and forget. He'll carry that shootin' with him till the day he dies. It ain't easy to forget how you kill a man close up," his uncle said. Everyone stayed stone still when he said that, realizing that for the first time Cobus Buttes was admitting he too had killed "close up." In the war, Mason Raymond thought. And if Lite comes back, Cobus'll kill close up again.

After the inquest Mason Raymond had gone off into the woods, to be by himself, to be "serious," as Bartholomew would have said, moving up to a small cabin at Indian Lake where he'd be away from people. He was, but not far enough. Finally he'd gone with an axe and some supplies way up into the Cold River region and begun hacking a small shelter out of the forest, coming back to town every week or so for supplies. Gradually, as he learned to live in the woods, he cut his visits back to town until at the end he only came in twice that last year, the final time learning from a three-month-old letter waiting for him that Rivers was sick and maybe dying.

He owed Rivers much and he had started down, hoping that maybe finally he would be able to say something about how he felt—but it was too late. Rivers had been buried a couple of months before. "We didn't know where to put him," Mason Raymond's Uncle Cobus had said. "He didn't seem to have no people of his own so we had him laid up on the hill," he said, indicating with a nod of the head the family cemetery where all the Butteses and a good portion of the Raymonds were buried.

Rivers would have liked that. Mason Raymond didn't quite know how to frame the next question. Finally he said, "Near her?" meaning his mother.

His uncle nodded.

Some things should end right. Rivers and his mother buried near one another tied things up. Rivers had loved her passionately, though she'd never known. Perhaps she knew now. In one of Bartholomew's afterlives the dead got to have all the knowledge they'd never had while they'd been living.

"You holdin' up all right, boy?"

"Oh, I'm fine, jest fine," Mason Raymond said, trying to sound convincing. "Sun got to me maybe a little bit back there. I had my hat off," he confessed, not saying the obvious, that of course you always took your hat off when you knelt to pray. But he could tell, from the look on John's face, John had made the connection. He would always be making the right connections; that's how it was with one who wanted to be a leader of men. He had to learn right off how to put the unobvious together. I don't want to be a leader of men, Mason Raymond thought, I just want to learn how to get along. Not always be an outsider.

You *must* get well: That was the last thing Bartholomew had said to Mason Raymond, holding out his hand in a formal farewell. He had been sure Mason Raymond could go back where people were and learn how to love even though he himself had tried and failed. "You're young yet," Bartholomew said confidently. "You get out West with those new ways—" Mason Raymond hadn't had the courage to confide his idea about seeking out the Indians; even for Bartholomew perhaps that idea would have seemed too far outside the bounds of reason, so he'd just said he was going West—"new people, a whole new country, a whole new way of looking at things, people are bound to feel in new, better ways out there." Bartholomew had been genuinely enthusiastic about the prospects. "You'll get well," he said, and then he had added, "Do it for both of us."

I'm trying, I'm really trying, but sometimes luck doesn't seem to be running on my side. Mason Raymond was grinning inwardly, though anyone looking at his face would have described it as "impassive," grinning with a gallows kind of amusement at how hard he had tried back there in Ohio, and how little that had come to. It takes more than trying, he could have told Bartholomew now, but of course Bartholomew already knew that. He was a Master Trier, a Primer of Disasters. It was all Bartholomew's trying and losing that had sent him, defeated, into his cave where instead of letting his own human heart be sliced piece by piece in the marketplace of love and consumed raw, he could hide out and embalm the scrapped hides of old friends. "Ain't nobody can do you in like someone you love," Bartholomew would say even while urging Mason Raymond to go out and try and find love. "You trust them and care for them and give them all of the feelings you got inside, and then for some reason sometimes I think they don't even understand, it's jest plain perversity, they go and do you in.

"Listen," he said urgently, "I had me this woman I could have crawled over the face of the earth for I cared so much, and I could have swore to God on a stack of Bibles she was jest as set on me. We was so close there, in the beginnin' that first year, wasn't nuthin' could keep us apart. We was always laughin' and touchin' and jest lookin' at one another, seemed like we could never get enough of jest lookin' at each other or holdin' hands, jest touchin' one another—best year of my life," he said, and he stopped working his hands and was gazing off back into space recapturing the magic and mystery of that marvelous year, he had forgotten Mason Raymond altogether, he seemed to Mason Raymond transported, a look of wonder on his old creased face.

"You always forget there at the first how it's gonna end up. Anybody even suggested then anything could go wrong I'da said he was crazier than a coot. But you know what? It all started gettin' smashed to pieces and I ain't even sure how it happened. I mean, it seemed to me we was fine, we was gettin' along jest like we always was and one day, out of a clear blue sky, I don't know to this day why, that woman got mad at somethin' I said or did and she didn't say nuthin' to me, she jest flounced out of the house and she was gone all day. I was half wild wonderin' what I done set her off so, but when she come back she wouldn't say, maybe she couldn't, maybe she didn't even know herself. Thin's seemed to go back the same, but later, when I got to thinkin' about it, I seen really that was like a crack come between us and it kept gettin' wider and wider till it turned into this big crevice and we was standin' on opposite sides, and I never really knowed how it happened. I don't know to this day. But this big gulf, it was there and there was no way to git rid of it.

"She got mad oftener and went off longer—sometimes two, three days, then a week, and the end jest before the last she was off a whole month, but when she come back she said she'd been thinkin' and she knew it was her, not me, and she was set on changin' if I'd jest be patient with her and give her a chance, she wasn't goin' to go on with the same pattern no more. 'I'm goin' to make a commitment to you like I ain't never made a commitment to no one in my whole life'—I ken still hear her sayin' it plain as day and see the look in her eyes. She meant that, boy, I know she meant that, but she jest couldn't do it. It wasn't in her.

"She took me off to see the room she'd been stayin' in— most pitiable place you'd ever want to lay eyes on, hardly nuthin' in it, jest a bed, still mussed up, and one little rickety chair and a basin for washin' up, wasn't even no stand, jest that basin settin' on the floor, and she opened the door and was all proud, beamin', when I looked down and seen the envelope lyin' on the floor. Someone had shoved it under the door, don't you know, while she had come home and asked me to give her the chance to try and git us back where we were; while she was talkin' to me someone come and shoved this envelope under her door, jest had her name on it, wasn't no real proper sent letter; and when I looked down, she looked too and she seen it and this awful guilty look come over her face and she reached down and snatched it up and tried like to hide it behind her back as if it weren't nuthin' but the bill to her room or somethin' like that, but the whole way she was actin' give her away, lookin' so shame-faced and twistin' her hands in back of her. It come over me like light—she'd been with another man the times she'd been gone and she wasn't plannin' on ever tellin' me, ever; and she was goin' to keep tryin' to deceive me; right then I could see her gettin' ready to lie and I jest felt sick all the way down to the pit of my belly. All I could think of was, 'I'm goin' to make a commitment to you like I ain't never made a commitment to no one,' and this is what it all come to.

"I stood there calm as could be. I remember bein' surprised at how calm I was. I jest kept sayin' to myself over and over, You always said maybe perception was the price of pain. You always said you wanted to *know*. If that's so, then you got your perception, so maybe it ain't so bad after all, jest standin' there calm as could be, not sayin' a word, watchin' her tryin' to hide the letter and lookin' clumsier and clumsier.

"And it was like I couldn't help feelin' sorry for her—she looked so, I don't know how to explain it, but cheap-like, standin' there tryin' to conceal what she'd done after she'd jest come from sayin' all those close thin's to me. It was the cheapness made me feel worse. That was the worst of it, how cheap it all seemed after the big words. Finally I jest turned and went out the door and went back to where we'd lived that whole year and I kept lookin' around and it was like it wasn't true; nobody could look at you the way she'd looked at me and say, 'I'm goin' to make a commitment to you like I ain't never made a commitment to no one in my whole life,' and know all along what had jest been happenin'. I couldn't accept it, I jest couldn't accept no human bein' could act like that, not after we'd been so close.

"I got out my tobacco and I got out some spirits and I poked up the fire, and I jest sat there and waited. I was waitin' for her to come back and tell me the truth and somehow we'd make it all right, there was still so much caring there, and I sit and drunk and looked at the fire and waited. I waited and waited, and you know what? She never come. She never come at all. It was like after all the big words she couldn't face me no more. I waited and waited, even after I knew she wasn't gonna come, and I thought of how that bleak room she'd been stayin' in was jest like her—a bed to break promises in, a place to wash up, nuthin' really of her own, she was jest passin' through, and that's the way it was with her and would always be, a passin' through of other people's lives, but nuthin' permanent, it wasn't in her to make no commitment to no one, she was as empty inside as that room, jest a few borrowed thin's was all her life hung on and all it would ever hang on; she wasn't made for permanence or makin' commitments, no matter how much she might want to. So I sit and drunk and looked at the fire and I finally said to myself, I can't try no more. This is the last one I ken try with. If this is what happens after all we had, I don't want never again to begin what ends like this. I set up all that night and all the next day and waited and she never sent word, she never come; and I went right on waitin', I kept thinkin', She meant it when she said that about the commitment, she'd done wrong and she knows it but she don't know how to come home. If I wait long enough, she'll come to herself and send word or come call. But she never sent word and she never come back, so on the third day I closed up that house and took what I wanted and went into the woods and I been here ever since. If with all we had, we could end up like that, there wasn't no more use in tryin', never again."

Bartholomew looked at Mason Raymond as if he thought Mason Raymond might have the answer. "She never sent word and she never come," he said, but he was really asking a question. What he wanted Mason Raymond to tell him was how was it possible after all that they'd had together that whole year she could do a thing like that. That was the main answer Bartholomew wanted Mason Raymond to go out in the world and find out.

Bumping along the outskirts of Wayne City, the Independence landing, it suddenly came to Mason Raymond that even if he ever did find out an answer, he wasn't likely to take it back to the cave in time to help Bartholomew out.

Wayne City was just a name given to a lot of sheds and shacks; it lay on the lip of the Missouri and, across the river and three miles inland, Independence waited. At Independence Mason Raymond had promised John he would take off on his own. Now, lying like a sack across Mabel's back, he bobbed up and down as the old mare jogged from one shack

to the next. People probably thought he was dead, an assumption not too far from truth if, as Bartholomew had decided,
you could not sometimes distinguish between what was
breathing and yet static and what was breathing and still edging its way along in space. There are so many dead people
walking around, Bartholomew often said.

He was bumped along past blacksmith shops, outfitters,
hotels, wagoneries, saddleries, provisioners, row after row of
wood and brick buildings that led to the Missouri River,
where the great adventure had begun for thousands of people.
Westport, a few miles away, and Saint Joseph were cheaper,
easier, less troubled with mud and sand, but the Independence
landing at Wayne City still held the magic word of Independence, gave rise to all the echoes its name suggested: to be
free, to be responsible to no one but yourself.

There were horses and oxen standing beside sheds while
their shoes were being banged out over open fires; the side
streets were still clogged with harried men and slovenly
women, with carts and mules, with cowboys and tramps and
even some Mexicans; on the other side of the Missouri the
great adventure waited, but the great days of the fur traders,
the Oregon Trailers, the magic year of the Pony Express, had
passed. Mason Raymond thought about how some people are
late for everything, from the big days of the lumbering and
river running back home in the Adirondacks to the legendary
days when a whole new world had opened up here in the
West. It'd be off from St. Jo or Independence or Westport
April 15th, at Kearney a month later, in Laramie a month after
that, at Independence Rock by July Fourth: the old emigrant
schedule. All the big things had happened before he was born.

He was just passing through, just the way it seemed to him
he was always "just passing through." Things would happen
to John, big things; no doubt he would strike gold in the Hills,
but there was nothing in Mason Raymond that cried out to
create, to subjugate, to bend others to his will, to get rich, to
make legends that left his name behind alive. He just wanted
to know how to live right a little.

The nigger had pulled up and was shading his eyes with one
grimy hand, gazing downstreet at a bunch of ponies being

herded into a corral. "Stole off the Indians," he said, "or stole back. You never know whether you're gittin' Injun or Army stuff. Don't matter where it comes from, I suppose, so long as the horse is sound." He got down off his horse, watching the scene in front of him. He looked over at Mason Raymond and screwed up his face, studying. "You think you could git offen that horse if it was for somethin' beneficial?" he asked. When someone asked a question like that it really meant, Git down.

"They see the two of you with 'back East' writ all over your faces, they gonna empty your pockets, make off with both your britches; but some old nigger come in off the Trail, he don't raise suspicion none. You two go on up to the square and wait there and I'll see what this old nigger can work out. Now what you waitin' for, you think I'm gonna make off with your gear and leave you with nuthin' but the shirts on your backs?"

That was exactly what Mason Raymond did think, but he was bound up by the rules of politeness his mother had instilled. Inside his mind a voice echoed: "And the last I ever saw of him he was going downstreet with my horse and going to get me a good trade and come back with a proper pony for the Plains. That's what he said. Got away with John's, too, and that good saddle, and all our gear. Stripped us clean except for the little hard cash I had strapped on me."

"Boys, you take this," the nigger said. "It ain't much, but it's all I got." He was holding out his tobacco pouch. John shook his head. "There's money in there, at the bottom," the nigger explained. "Good gold from up in the Hills."

"I don't want your money—"

"I don't think you aim to run off with my money no more than I aim to run off with your horses and gear, but the point is you'll be less reluctant if you have somethin' of mine."

"How do I know there's money enough in there to cover our stuff?" John demanded. He was so smart, John was. He'd survive; he wouldn't get taken just because he thought he had to be polite.

The nigger sighed and leaned against his own horse. "With that attitude on you, you're gonna go far, boy—but not with me." He put the tobacco pouch back in his pocket and ambled along, towing his horse, the animal looking collapsed in on itself, head hanging down, knees buckled. "Feelin's like that spill over. And they run back in on you yourself. You the one achin' in the end. And my answer to that is, *Be my guest.*"

Maybe he can teach us, Mason Raymond thought. He looks honest. They all look honest, Hart said inside his head; the ones that are really going to fleece you look the most like God.

"You'll be all right," the nigger was saying to John. He knew Mason Raymond didn't amount to a hill of beans; there was no use bothering with him. "But you got to git yourself a little education 'fore you go off 'cross that river. On the other side you can't make it without bein' leastwise somewhat exposed to advice. But advice can't cost you nuthin'. I ken see your point. Advice don't cost and horses do." He looked at first one, then the other. "I'm gonna play me some cards and drink me some shine, and you ken resuscitate yourselfs the best way you see fit. I know a place to bunk down—plain, but not too hard on the wallet, good enough food to keep you goin'—give you both a little time to think thin's through. Whether or not you know it, you got *problems.*

"With loafers and bummers of most every plight;
On their backs there's no clothes, in their pockets no bills,
But every day they're starting out for gold in them there Black
  Hills."

Good god, he was a poet. Disbelief revived Mason Raymond; the energy of it ran through him like adrenalin. The man's blackness had been a little startling, but nothing truly unsettling, but a black cowboy who came out in verse, that was another kettle of fish.

You got to git used to all kinds of thin's in this world, Hart was always saying, an old man patient with the young. Hart had even given in on Hector, that dog Mason Raymond had wanted, though he knew its color meant bad luck and its disposition was (as he would have put it) unreliable. Day after day he had worked, showing Mason Raymond how to run the dog and, even when the dog proved, just as Hart had predicted, unlucky and unreliable, he never once said "I told you so" or lost his temper or gave up into the hopelessness that

Mason Raymond considered the core of his own personality.

I wanted him to be proud of me, and he was, too, when I found my way in the woods, even if I was only a summer boy at the Landing, when I took that coon alive, other times too. Hart, he never lost faith. And in the end I had to go and kill him.

Mason Raymond thought of Bartholomew in the cave talking about how the best of love ended in betrayal and loss and terrible pain, and for the first time he saw the whole precept quite clearly—it was true that what life handed you with the right hand it rescinded with the left. Bartholomew couldn't face that calamitous paradox, but Hart had learned it and left it behind in the blind faith that things had to get better. He had been a believer, one whose hopes were all founded on the firm faith that what was good that was put in the world stayed there, it could never be taken back. Bad went on certainly: The Lites of the world never diminished; but it was up to the good to take in feeble-minded boys who might hit them over the head one day with an axe or befriend the outcast who in the end would kill them as an act of mercy.

A good man: that's what I want to learn to be, Mason Raymond thought, a good man, no matter what the consequences. You can't hide in caves and close the world out; you carry with you wherever you go the pain that's been. Bartholomew didn't escape; he's holed up there all alone, he thinks, but that woman's right there inside him still hurting him. But Hart—wherever he is—he still thinks of the good that idiot boy did and maybe even he understands and forgives me. I know he does. I can get well if I just try. It's the pictures you keep in your mind make the difference. I don't want to end up thinking that down deep inside me there's only an old rumpled bed someone lent me and a rickety chair, a basin on the floor 'cause there's no stand.

He sat up and spurred his horse on, agitated to catch up with John. When he pulled up beside his cousin, he said, very quiet, but firm in his conviction, "I think we ought to trust him."

John turned in his saddle and looked at Mason Raymond as if he had given the final proof of his craziness, shaking his head in absolute and total incredulity. "You been took once back there in Ohio, ain't that learned you nuthin'? How's come you're always ready to hand over everythin' you got to the first stranger comes along who's got a good word for you? Ain't you got no discretion atall in you? Mason Raymond, when you jest goin' to learn some good plain common sense?"

III

---

*N*eed *a jenny for carryin',* need provisions,
some whiskey, shootin' powder, want to
travel light, but you got to have the basics—jerked beef, a little
dried pumpkin, tobacco, some coffee and sugar, a couple of
oilcloths for ground cover, a poncho for the rain—we got to
have good whiskey for the cheerin' up and the cleansin' out.
That ain't no little stake no way you look at it. You git in the
Hills, prices ain't what you been accustomed to back East—
you reckon when you left home on paying twelve dollars a
barrel for flour?" Tom asked them.

John had read enough to know grub went dear, but he
hadn't been counting on something like twelve dollars a barrel
for flour. He thought of the measly amount of money he'd
scrimped and saved to put together for the trip and he felt
disheartened; then he remembered Mason Raymond's promise of money for a real outfit and he was cheered again, even
though there remained the nagging feeling he oughtn't to take
the stake, it wasn't somehow right. All the way from Albany
he'd been plagued by pangs of conscience, trying to suppress
his doubts that it was really all right to take money from Mason
Raymond by telling himself, Well, he'd never have made it on

his own and one thin's sure—nobody else would have put up with him.

But indecision remained nevertheless. He had a right to the money. He didn't. If Mason Raymond hadn't been "blood" (his mother acting internally as moral advisor again), John didn't think he'd have had so many questions about how justifiable it was to make a trade like that. But the taking of money always put ethical questions on acts.

"Thin's pretty big-costin' out there, are they?" he asked the nigger.

"You won't even look at sugar it don't cost you jest to smell. A man don't jest want the necessaries neither; he likes a little comfort now and then, and comfort out there is a powerful weapon against a man's pocketbook. You got no idea, no idea at all what layin' up a good stake means. I used to run with a Chinaman give me some insight on how to git along in a world where it costs you jest to ask for a glass of water. The cards kept him in comfort like no man I ever laid eyes on. Learned, he said, layin' out track on the Union Pacific. Used to brag how he'd been at Promontory Point when the two ends met up and they drove in that there silver spike. He was the most braggin' Chink I ever seen about the places he'd been and the thin's he'd done, but he could lay down a winnin' hand of cards like enough to make a grown man cry.

"Put away his pick and shovel,
He will never prospect no more;
Death has sluiced him from his trouble,
Panned him on the other shore.

"Got hisself shot layin' down hands like that, that Chinaman did. Laid down this little full house and the first thin' you know *he* was lyin' on the floor, ventilated through. Don't look like that, son," the black man said to John. "We're gonna make it. Where there's cards, there's coins." He put down his hand and looked at John expectantly. For more than an hour he'd been trying to teach him poker. A man don't know cards, he had said, don't know nuthin'. He ain't nuthin' but a green-britched boy till he bluffs his way through some rough spot he's jest got to git his money out. And this here hick town is the best place in the world to learn. Across the river, in Independence, they got men who know how to play cards.

"Oh my gawd," he exploded when he saw John's hand. "You can't play cards if you can't keep the sequences straight. You gotta learn order. Here, boy, repeat after me—one pair, two pair, three of a kind, straight, flush— And you ain't playin' it slow enough. Play it slow, slow and easy and smooth. No rushin', no givin' nuthin' away. Act like you can't make up your mind, you're thinkin' it over tryin' to decide one way or t'other. Nuthin' gives a greenhorn away faster than bein' too quick to lay his money on the table." He began dealing out a fresh hand. "Don't spread your cards out like that. Someone'll git a peek and a peek is better than a guess any day. Now, put that hand down and let's give it a try agin."

John tried to keep his mind on the game, but the alien room, the coughing and scruffy men wandering about noisily, grumbling and knocking into things, the sight of Mason Raymond lying on his bunk fingering the pages of that book he was always reading, spitting on his finger and turning a page, reading slowly down the page and then spitting and turning again, were enough to distract anybody.

John had a seething contempt for what he thought of as Mason Raymond's "schooling," for Mason Raymond's bookish ways—Mason Raymond had carried that scarred copy of the *Iliad* on a trip like this where for crissake every single ounce of weight might make the difference between survival and extinction—and he was always quoting that fat, forty-year-old teacher he obviously admired from his Albany school, a man whose name, Morphis, would put any normal person off; he sounded dead, and all his facts, facts, facts from the past— what good were they out here where your hands and brains had to work overtime improvising and adapting? Schoolish, bookish, a dreamer—what good were *those* kind of people? Yet there was also no denying, a source of unbidden irritation that nevertheless shamed John, that when Mason Raymond said something about some event or person he took for granted that John knew about and John looked at him blankly, a flash of disbelief swept across Mason Raymond's face, as if he were thinking, But *anybody* knows that. He couldn't put two sticks together and get a fire. No matter which way you headed him, he went the wrong direction; and there he lay now, close enough to the firelight so that he could read the print of that ridiculous book of his, not paying any attention to all the commotion around him.

The nigger talked on, poker, poker, poker, but John wasn't listening now.

All right, so maybe I didn't have so much formal schooling but I got all I needed to do sums and read what I need to read; all the rest is folderol. What a man needs in this life is *practical* knowing—how weather works and what will grow where and how to cure a sick animal or put one ain't gonna make it out of its misery and not fuss over it; a real man's got to be strong and know how to handle his women so they don't give him no grief the way that one in Ohio run all over Mason Raymond and he didn't have sense enough to see it; a man's got to *command*. Who's he ever gonna give orders to? The prairie dogs and coyotes? A lot of listening they'll do.

Even up in them woods where he hid out Mason Raymond never really learned nuthin' like you *need* to know, running around with some religious nut who lived in a cave and believed he'd seen God in Warrensburg, New York, and God had winked at him because they were the only two people in the world who knew God was in Warrensburg, New York. — What could you *do* with someone so turned around in the head?

Mason Raymond turned a page, wetting his finger. That book must be all spitted up. What Mason Raymond needed was to get his head down out of the clouds and plant his feet firmly on this earth. But he never would, never in a million years, though to be fair some of his hopelessness was hardly his fault—he had never asked to be born into a family like that where the father was such a trial to everyone—even if he was John's father's twin—and the mother had gone loony in the end.

The miracle and mystery of Mason Raymond's father and John's father being *twins*—an impossibility for John to accept and yet there was no way to dispute the fact of it. The two were

] 47 [

so different, John thought now, as he'd thought he didn't know how many times before, as opposite as night and day. Pa, he's disciplined and works hard and takes life hard but Mason Raymond's father, it was like he run the opposite direction from responsibility as long as he could and when it finally caught up with him he couldn't face up to it so he went and hung hisself. Both of them came out of the same mother's womb and yet they was so different.

John pondered again his Grandfather Guthrie Buttes marrying a half-Indian woman and bringing breeds into the world —*his own father,* though in his heart he denied the truth of this, no matter how provable it was, thinking stubbornly, He ain't got no *real* Indian blood in him and neither do I.

Mason Raymond licked his finger and turned another page. The Indian blood went down *their* side of the family, John thought, and not ours. And the proof of it's I don't want nuthin' to do with no red Indians, but he (looking at Mason Raymond's moving lips silently reading some passage) can't wait to run out and "Hoaw" them to death.

"It's like—like I was meant to go there. I don't rightly understand it myself," Mason Raymond had explained, making an appeal for understanding. "It's as if after what I did, I have to go and be with people who could understand that."

"Ain't nobody ever held what you done agin you," John had said, embarrassed at having to talk about such an intimacy. "Truth of the matter is most people, they think you done a real good thin', havin' the will to put Hart out of his misery, especially after the way they all knowed how you felt about guns and killin'."

John hadn't said that to make Mason Raymond feel better, but because, grudgingly, he had to admit it was true—people back there in the Adirondacks, where a lot of life was just naturally lived by the gun, hadn't been able to figure Mason Raymond out, that was true, but over the years they'd come to have respect for the kind of boy who didn't hold with killing anything and yet as an act of mercy had killed a man who had been like a real father to him. John's own father Cobus admired Mason Raymond and even seemed to understand him, another source of annoyance to John. He puts up with—even seems to admire—in Mason Raymond things he wouldn't tolerate two minutes in me. "You two ain't cut from the same cloth," John's father had said once. "You got natural-born survivin' instincts built into you, and it's like that boy was marked from the start. He's got a head could be full of all kinds of important ideas if it hadn't got shut down so early on his feelin' guilty about what happened to Hart. He jest can't accept it *had* to be done. He keeps feelin' responsible, as if he had to pay for it."

Sullen anger had flared in John over the respectful tone Cobus Buttes had taken as he talked about Mason Raymond; his father never used that kind of solemn wonderment when he talked about him. More likely, the tone was reproachful: "You left that scythe blade lyin' ground down agin," or "I thought I told you to do up that back gate; the heifers was in the corn agin." John's father's tolerance for weaknesses in Mason Raymond he would never have stood for in John wasn't fair.

"You was meant to go one way and he another." It was all John could ever get out of his father.

"He's speakin' the truth," John's grandfather said, "whether you like it or not. People don't all *have* to be the same. Too borin'," he said after a moment, "if they was. They's doers and they's dreamers. You might say you was a doer and Mason Raymond, he's a dreamer. Bein' he's so opposite, it's bound to rile you at times. You get older, you get more patient—more patient and deafer," Guthrie Buttes said, grinning. "They let you git deaf to shut out a lot of what you don't want to hear no more anyway. The world's full of clamorin' comes to nuthin'. You figure on bein' with us for the krautin'?"

His grandfather knew very well he wasn't. He was just trying to make John's going harder.

John leaned forward and picked up his cards and stared at an ace and a king, but he could not concentrate, thinking of home, with the warm sun lying in square patterns on the kitchen floor and his grandfather at the table sorting apples and leaning forward, his hand cupped to his good ear, saying

"What? What's that you said?" Like his grandfather, John loved fall best, when the apples came in and they made the cider, fall when they gathered the cabbages together and krauted. Krauting represented everything best back home, and it seemed so far away that John was swollen suddenly with loneliness, gripped by it so fiercely that the whole of him went sick with longing.

The cabbages from the back garden would be sorted, the larger, better ones buried in a miniature mountain of rich black soil in one corner of the down pasture, to be uncovered, a head at a time, for the family Saturday night boiled dinner. What remained, the lesser, imperfect ones, John Buttes's father and grandfather made into the best sauerkraut in the county.

After the cabbages were heaped high in splint baskets by the back porch, John's grandfather got out the oak barrel that he said the Butteses had always used for pickling. It was big with a hand-fitted top and it had the same rich dark marbled patina as the kraut maul and the kraut cutter. The cutter was large enough to lie flat across the top of the barrel. Next to the barrel Cobus and Guthrie Buttes placed their seasoning, thirty pounds of rough salt.

The two men took turns running the cabbage back and forth across the cutter, watching the light green ribbons fill up the barrel until a loose layer of shredded cabbage lay, a foot deep, on the bottom of the barrel. Then Guthrie Buttes sprinkled salt over the cut cabbage. He did it by "feel." A man got the feel, he said, for how much salt ought to go in only after years of tasting and acquiring a knowing tongue. As for the maul, the maul was John's job. Up and down it would fly, bruising the cabbage until the juices ran and a frothy surface appeared, the cabbage juice assimilating the salt. "The good brine," John's grandfather called it.

When John's grandfather was satisfied the first layer was sufficiently bruised and stirred, he allowed one of his grandsons to take over and repeat the cutting until another foot of shredded cabbage lay at the bottom of the barrel; then he sprinkled the slivers with salt again, he pounded the maul up and down for a moment before he turned it over to John, who worked until once more a lacy surface of salt and juice bubbled up.

All morning the cutting, salting, and bruising went on until the big barrel was almost full. The width of a man's hand from the top, Guthrie Buttes stopped the cutting. He took a clean white cloth and laid it over the top of the kraut. This would keep out dirt. Next he fitted the oak boards he had so carefully cut into their proper place, a perfectly fashioned lid for the barrel. As his closest grandson, John was always sent to find three granite rocks, "the size of your head," his grandfather specified. "Mind," he always said, "granite, *not* limestone." Limestone would react with the acids during fermentation and spoil the flavor. The rocks served a double purpose: to keep the top boards in place and to press down the juices and encourage fermentation. The kraut was good to eat at any time, a few days later when the fermentation had just begun, or months later when the strong pungent brine had permeated each sliver.

To be back home safe: that was the message his heart beat out in a steady painful tattoo. Maybe he had been wrong to come—

"Close to the chest, close to the chest, you got to play your cards close to the chest," the nigger said in exasperation.

"I can't do no more. I don't care how necessary it is, I jest can't look at one more hand."

"He's near ready," Pepper Tom said to nobody in particular, just giving a general announcement to the public at large so that they could be on their toes. "Let's look to the horses and then rustle us up some grub and git out on the town. This here teachin' sure thirsts you up."

A big thick lamp with pieces of glass hanging all off it spun around in the long room, prisms of light dancing in different colors on the walls. Girls, all of them looking tired and indifferent, drooped on purple plush chairs along one wall. They looked up when John and the black man came in and they pulled themselves up a little and there was one blinding moment when all the women opened their mouths and the spinning lights of the chandelier sparkled on their exposed teeth. John felt dazed, overwhelmed.

Pepper Tom was haggling with a large woman in a purple tentlike dress who puffed on a cigar; she was saying that Polynesian Polly had been took since the last roundup and wasn't available in the premises to the gentlemen, but there was a nice new shipment in from Chi.

John sat down on a purple velvet chair in a corner and let them negotiate; what they decided he would do his best to fulfill but in the meantime he could rest, which he did immediately, closing his eyes and dozing off so deeply that a moment later he woke himself up with his head banging against his chest.

"Gorgeous frame to work with," the woman in purple was saying. "Makes you glad to know a good carpenter can still git ahold of an adequate workbench. I'm gonna give you a special rate, you're such a steady customer."

"I'm dead," John said aloud. "Dead, dead, dead. The hog is died." Pepper Tom had been dragging him from one lily palace to the next, "showing him the sights," as he put it. But at some point all beds look the same.

The nigger was behind a big bar laying out different sizes and shapes of glasses, lining them up in a long slender column by size and shape; first came a small thimblelike sliver of crystal on a short squat stem, succeeded by a glass that was slightly taller but a good deal stouter, ranging right up the line to a huge fishbowl schooner that dwarfed everything around it. He turned to John and said, "All you got to do is relax and enjoy yourself a little."

"Relax and enjoy myself? I'm wore clear down to the bone with all you put me through, strung out from one crisis of cards to the next, never knowin' when you're gonna go and make a fool of yourself on some hand or bluff your way through and rake it all in, draggin' me from one purple palace to the next—relax and *enjoy* myself? My legs shake and I can't git anythin' solid to sit on my stomach because you got me so 'relaxed' and now you want me to—" Words failed him for a moment. "It's not to be believed," he said. "You're jest not to be believed. I wish to god I'd never hitched up with you.

I can't *stand* all this, I'm jest not up to it. We been up thirty-six hours straight. You been playin' cards and puttin' me through womanizin' for *thirty-six hours straight.*"

"You're jest a little tired—"

" 'A little tired'? I can't even flex my fingers—"

"Here," Tom said, holding out a slender shining goblet on a long thin stem. "Slim," he said to the fat nigger behind the bar, "give me the best Chablis you got in the house, none of that fightin' stuff Ada lays in for the regulars."

"We run out last time you was here and Miss Ada she says don't order no more till you done drunk the other up first; it jest hangin' 'round waitin', she says, all that other stuff you talked her into orderin' last time is jest layin' 'round waitin', and 'lessen you drink it up it's gonna go on sittin', this ain't Independence, it's only the landing, you know, so she ain't orderin' no more of nuthin' till you drinks what's here." He trotted down the bar and rummaged around in some bottles in the back.

"I'll do the decantin'," Pepper Tom said. "And while you're back there git me a good red—dry—and some champagne, and the best Jerez you got, some Madeira—"

"You come 'round here and git what you wants. How come you still hangin' round this town anyway? I thought you was goin' back down where you come from."

Tom was picking up bottles, examining their labels, selecting some, rejecting others. Once he said, "This ain't that aggressive wine she got on consignment, is it?" Finally he glanced downbar. "I *been* there. I know all that's in between here and there well enough not to be itchy about it no more. Every seven years I make a change jest like some snake sheddin' its skin. The fifth year I git restless and the sixth I git agitated and by the seventh I'm on the move. Been that way all my life. I wish she was a little more selective—" He uncorked a bottle, carefully wiped the rim, and began to pour the golden liquid out through a piece of cloth from his own pocket into a strange-looking bottle. "Not too early in the day for you, Slim?"

"Never too early for me. You gonna go back soldierin'?"

"I done my time. I don't reckon now on bein' no Brunette

to white soldiers any more than I do on bein' no Buffalo Man to Injuns. *Put that down*," he said harshly to John. "Only a dumb ignorant son of a bitch would put Chablis in a glass like that or raise his glass like you done, like it was drinkin' water and you was goin' to gulp it down."

Pepper Tom lifted his own glass carefully and held it under his nose, sniffing. "You pick it up like this. You test the bouquet—then you take a little on your tongue like this—" John watched him roll the wine around in his mouth, gargle, make a little moaning sound, then swallow. "Slow 'nd easy. Smell it—git your nose right down in it and smell it. Then roll a little around in your mouth—don't make such a face—lean your head back and let your mouth git it full. You're gonna git drunk gulpin' the way you do," he said in absolute exasperation. "You're gonna git poleaxe drunk takin' your liquor in that way."

"You're the one who's been pourin' all them different thin's down me." His head was swimming and for the first time all trip he envied Mason Raymond. He was back in his bunk reading his everlasting book, safe from this madman. He groaned. The room was going around; he felt swozzled. Chairs swayed up at him and the walls fell in on him. His head was split by shooting stars. He shot up into the stars and then plunged down and was caught and swung; he was on a giant swing, the universe turning, turning; he wanted to get off and couldn't; his stomach rolled and dropped.

He felt a cold sweat break out all over him. He was going to be sick, oh god he was going to be sick.

"Give me a hand with him, Slim." They took him by the shoulders and shoved; his feet were skidding along, and his temples flushed and hot, his eyes shot through with all those stars shining out of the chandelier and then suddenly he was outside and they were throwing dippers of water over him; he was soaked, absolutely soaked, shouting at them to leave off, he was going to come around, leave off; the water running off him like it did a dog, what were they trying to do, drown him?

He gasped and flayed and sank, rose, sank again, stayed on his knees, begging, until at last they hauled him up and between them they shook him out, water flying off him the way it flew off a dog when it shook itself, and then they hung him up between them as if they had pegged him out on a line so that the wind could run through him and dry him out, and he shouted, "What the hell do you think you're doin'?" and the nigger said slowly, quietly, "He's been through so much it's enough to make a grown man cry, ain't it, Slim? Let's wring him out and pull him back in shape. There's other thin's left in this here night."

From downroad laughter flowed up toward them; somewhere tinny notes vibrated and plucked at the night; some people could even sing, it seemed, in this topsy-turvy world. A stray cat ran out in the road, turned around, and ran back behind a dilapidated building.

Pepper Tom was hauled up under a rectangular patch of moonlight. "I got somethin' to show you," he said. "I been holdin' back." He was grubbing about in his pockets. "Here," he said, holding up a shiny circle that gleamed gold in the light. "It's my lucky timepiece. Don't work much, but it's got mineral value. It was the first real good-feelin' thin' I ever owned—years ago," he said, "the night Jonathan and me, we went out and got so drunk we couldn't walk and we was knocked down and beat up and all our money took and Jonathan he went hog wild and said he wouldn't never trust hisself agin with anythin' of value, he wasn't worth trustin'. Made me take this here timepiece because he said he didn't deserve havin' it.

> "I am sittin' by the campfire now,
>   On wild Dakota's Hills,
> And memories of long ago
>   Steal o'er me like the rills
> Adorn yon canyon deep and dark,
>   Steal through the leafy glades,
> A glimpse, a murmur here and there,
>   Then vanish in the shade."

A star shot across the sky. "Me, I been short on luck all night —mabbe most of my life. Ain't no sech thing mabbe as a lucky nigger." A pause. "Not in this world, there ain't. It's time you tried your luck."

"I ain't ready—"

"Always got to be a first time you throw the cards down on the table," and John's mind began to chant one pair, two pair, *three of a kind . . .*"

Under the circle of lamplight five men sat at the small table and dealt and received cards, each man closed in on himself, the players making bets, slowly, deliberately, moving coins with a clinking sound out to the center of the table, laying cards down, covering them protectively with their hands, their eyes hooded, watching, then picking cards up, opening them out one at a time slowly, slowly, looking carefully and critically at each, closing their cards together and laying them on the table again, moving the coins—*clink, clunk*—out toward the center of the table, resting hands possessively a moment on the money, then withdrawing protection and leaving their money, unattended, in the middle of the table. Under the lamplight the little stacks of coins glowed. They were playing with good hard cash, not the greenbacks that could be discounted ten percent. They were using silver and gold which was the only real money out West. Back East those people could play around with paper if they wanted; here a man wanted to hear the clink of his coins.

John felt hypnotized by the gleam from the coins. He had seen so little real money in his lifetime. The Panic of '73 had been a disaster, nearly wiped them out altogether, but even before that there was never what you could call hard cash around. The Buttes had always got along—they raised good stock and the earth threw up bounty crops along with the rocks, the orchard gave up apples, fruit, and cider aplenty— and so there was never any question of going on rations; there was always even enough left over to make generous trades, and until '73 nobody in the family had much thought about money as such, even though now and again John's mother or grandfather could complain about how dear things had been during the war when John's father was down in Maryland and Pennsylvania fighting for the Union; but in general their life had been that of the self-sufficient farmer snug in his own invulnerability. No one had ever really given the banks or the gold-greenback question any thought. That was city maneuvering, nothing really important for a farmer to think about. Look what happened to Mason Raymond's father, Clyde, when he tried to get in on that city stuff—ended up hangin' hisself.

Everything changed in '73 when things got so bad, it wasn't even barter and trade anymore. The bottom fell out of prices and for the first time in his life John had seen his father scared. The situation was so bad that Cobus Buttes was going, hat in hand, to the bank, and he felt the humiliation of it so keenly that for weeks he had been unable to bring himself to make the trip. "It's like after all these years I gotta go and be a beggar," he said bitterly.

Finally John's mother had got up after breakfast one morning and said, "I'm going upstairs and dress—" They had all looked at her in astonishment because she was dressed and when she saw their looks she said, "No—*good* dressed, and we're going 'cross-lake this morning, Cob—it's a good day for it—and do what has to be done."

John's grandfather and the three boys had gone down to the dock to see them off. John's mother was in the bow of the boat with a great gray hat pinned to her head and a heavy sweater wrapped around her against the morning chill; John's father sat in the middle, with the oars in his hand. Clear, clean light honeyed the lake. Birds were restless with the loveliness of the morning, skitterish and twittery, unable to light and settle down to their normal duties because it was the kind of morning that made ordinary work seem onerous even to humans, one that promised pleasures instead of chores—you got maybe six or seven days a year like that. Perhaps it was the greatness of the morning that had prompted John's mother to take on the meanness of the day. He could see them moving away from the dock, his father gently plashing the still gray waters as his oars rhythmically sliced the water on either side of the boat. His father rowed so proficiently that he scarcely ever even made drippings off the end of his oars.

But he had been different ever since he'd come back from

the bank—shrunk into himself more, his pride wounded in its most essential place. Cobus Buttes had always walked a man who owed no one, and now he was forfeit to the bank. He was no longer independent and his own man, and he knew it and it poisoned all his pleasure in his land. It was no longer *his* land; it was his and the bank's. But he was a man who never complained or discussed his feelings; they were all held inside, and somehow, after a time, that was worse because, John felt, if his father could have voiced his resentment and anger he might have got rid of part of his unhappiness. As it was, it lay submerged inside, festering.

Thus, while no one spoke openly of money, it was on all their minds; it became the major preoccupation of all the older members of the family, and while no one ever said *money* or *mortgage* or *debt,* the word that came to signify all these was "means." There was not the "means" to do this or that. There was no "means" to fix the roof or do the repairs on the barn or go holiday and birthday shopping in the old way. They had to watch their "means" when they went over to the Landing to do even the essential shopping.

They were poor, at least to his father's way of thinking, and after that sufficient would never be enough; there would always be the fear that sufficient was borderline and at any moment they might be toppled over the line into the hopelessness of not owning land. To John's father land meant freedom and self-respect and being able to say goddam to any man.

And now, as he watched the coins winking under the green-shaded lamplight, he suddenly felt a great swelling inside, an overpowering desire to rake that pile of coins in, and he saw at last how Tom could go from game to game, his eyes glittering, just to get the chance to grab up that pile of "means."

Cards came, in that moment, finally to have real meaning for him; they could give him "means"; they could provide a real stake, more than just a sufficient one; but a backlog as well, if he were wiped out once, to reach back on his resources and start all over. The gold and silver under the lamplight meant he could be his own man; he could write Mason Raymond off, say grandly, "I brung you out, you're here now and now you're on your own and I don't want your money, keep your money, I don't *need* it." He understood at last what people meant when they said, "Money makes you free." It was a powerful weapon for a man's own place in the world, and if there was anything he wanted at that moment, it was the power to be free and shut of obligations to any man.

He came to grips partly, too, with the gnawing anger that burned so often inside him. That anger came from a sense of his own impotence because he wasn't free, because he didn't have the "means" to make any decision he wanted; money had limited him and hemmed him in and made him a prisoner of the number of choices he had over his own life; but the rich, they had endless opportunities open to them because they had the wherewithal to back up their schemes.

You ain't got a dime in your pocket, he thought, you ain't got a right to look anyone else in the face. Money's what makes you free to live your own life the way you want, and I ain't goin' to be poor and beholden to no man when there is ways to be free. I'm goin' to do the callin' and make the rules —*me,* not no one else.

The table was so small that it would only hold five; he stood watching, calculating how he himself would have played each of the hands, trying to size up the players. To be able to play cards—really play cards—was part of being a man. Tom had said that, but John saw it now. The man across from him, whose hands he couldn't see until they were laid out, was close to being wiped out; only a few coins remained beside his arm; and he had the look, set and restless, of someone angry and frustrated who was trying to hold back his feelings. A man wasn't allowed to be a poor loser: He wasn't supposed to walk on the weak or go against his word or not pay his debts or run in the face of danger, but most of all he was supposed to swallow his anger and put a good face on defeat. So the loser sat, sucking on a long cigar, never lifting his eyes to look at the other players, watching intently every card that was dealt, nervously reaching out to get his with an impatience none of the other players betrayed, an anxiety that branded him a loser, John thought.

He caught Tom's eye. Tom took out some tobacco, began fooling with a cigarette paper. The moment they'd come to town he'd started to take on airs, buying a little packet of papers and rolling out long elegant-looking cigarettes instead of chewing and using snuff. A cigarette-smoking nigger, if that wasn't putting on the dog. Most everyone chewed and a lot snuffed. Oh, maybe a few odd ones out were addicted to pipes, but Cherry Ripe and Winesap and Uncle Sam were the standbys. John couldn't think of one real cigarette smoker he'd ever known. Wants to be the gentleman in here, he thought, too elegant to spit.

The loser rose, stomped out his cigar, though it wasn't more than half finished, and, wordless, went through the rough canvas curtain that led to the main room where the music, the drinking, the women were; card men played apart, a special breed who didn't want interference, just the opportunity to find like of their kind.

John took his place and carefully removed half of his money and laid it down on the table. The man across from him, large and beefy and a big winner, began counting out cards. The cards spun by, but he left his untouched. Maybe if he didn't look until the very last card he'd grab some luck. Slowly he lifted the five cards and looked at the first, a nine; then an eight, a seven, a queen, another eight. A pair of eights: not good, not bad, the kind of hand Tom said you hang in there with to see how the draw goes.

The bet went around, an opener that was moderate enough and no raise to John, who put his opener in feeling a little easier; no raises to the opener all around would be an encouraging sign saying no one had much, a hang-in-there hand all around. Then suddenly the last player said, "Raise you one," and there was a shuffling around the table as the players reexamined their cards. One of the men threw his down; he was bowing out, but cautiously each of the others inched money out on the table.

Maybe I should have dropped, John thought. He was sticky under the arms with apprehension. He took out the nine, the seven, and the queen, discarded them, getting three cards back. He picked each one up slowly, hardly breathing—a seven; if only he hadn't thrown his other seven away he'd have had two pairs, not a bad position for straight five-card stud; a ten, no good at all; he scarcely breathed as he picked up the last card. His heart dropped; his stomach went whoop; he felt as if his whole insides were sliding away—he had another ten.

The two pairs were okay, but just okay, nothing sensational, again a holding position basically, nothing to feel aggressive about; he'd have preferred another eight, a solider position, especially considering that initial raise from the last man which indicated strength, a pair of kings or aces, something strong to come on with, and he watched carefully the discards all around the table; the others had drawn three cards apiece, too, so that meant that no one had had more than an initial pair.

"Check." That caution came from the initial opener. The strategy would be, he thought, at least if everyone had wait-and-see hands, to check around to the man who had raised, a big red-faced angry-looking man whose hands had rope scars all over them and the tip of whose left middle finger was missing. Now he looked angrier than ever and a voice inside John said, He didn't get nuthin'. He's goin' to try to bluff.

"Five," the scar-handed man said, pushing his money to the center of the table.

The others began to fold. John carefully monitored his five to the center of the table. "Call you," he said, thought a moment and then—what the hell, you gotta take the bull by the horns—"And raise you five more."

Now the man across from John, the big, beefy, angry man, began to fiddle with his coins, lifting them up, letting them fall back with tiny chirruping sounds. John waited. Finally, with pursed lips, he counted out the extra five. "Call you," he said.

"Two pair," John said, laying down his hand.

The man threw down his hand in disgust. "Openers. I didn't get a damn thin' on the draw."

John began to rake that beautiful money in.

"Christ, I had bettern than that and folded," a small, weasely-looking man across from John said, the conservative kind, one who didn't bet if he wasn't absolutely convinced he had it. John's sweating was calming down; he had begun to breathe with less pain; his heart was more normal and his stomach didn't feel as if it were going to heave up three days' worth of beans. He could now think of chicken-hearted Mason Raymond in his bunk with contempt. He don't never do nuthin', John thought, except lie around and moon and read.

He dropped the next hand because he had nothing to work with, not even a pair or the possibility of a flush, didn't cost him more than the opening ante to get a look at those cards and decide no dice, and what was more important, to take the opportunity to study the way the other men played. They were heavy and stolid and looked uninspired, but you couldn't really tell right off the bat, you had to suffer through the nervous intuitions of the game itself to get any true insight, for the indisputable fact was that each one had sizable winnings at his side, a sure-enough tipoff that none was without luck or skill.

Betting on the current hand was going placidly, keeping pace with what was; hard to tell what any one of them had, and that, John saw, was their secret: They never exposed anything, even a winning hand, by raising; for as the cards were laid down one man had three deuces, one two pair, and two men came up with straights, one lower than the other, but straights nevertheless and straights were a better-than-even odds for at least one raise. Cautious, conservative, and utterly (in a way) unpredictable, because you would never know what they had —the worst kind to deal with. The bluffer John would be able to figure out; if he raised and looked as if he were breathing a little hard, then he probably had the goods; but if he just called, you could probably figure on a bluff. The conservatives would only bet a sure thing; if they opened or raised, the message would be clear and direct: drop unless you had a powerhouse.

His tension began to come back; he picked up his new hand and sucked in air, recognizing immediately that was a give-away sign. Tom had warned him to keep careful control over his breathing; anything at all, even the slightest intake of breath, might indicate to other players the nature of his hand.

Never draw to an inside straight, he heard Tom saying in absolute emphasis. He had a seven, eight, ten, three, and jack.

But god, he felt lucky. A man had to grab at his luck when it came; he had to *act,* that was Mason Raymond's whole problem; he didn't know how to take any action. He was imprisoned inside his head; instinct and intuition and action were all foreigners to him. Throw that three and pick up a nine —nothing to it if you were riding high. And why shouldn't he ride high? Wasn't he getting rid of Mason Raymond—my god, think of it, getting rid of him at last—and he was maybe going to be able to go on to the Hills with this nigger who knew his way around the land as if he were a blind mapmaker. The two of them—what they could do! On the first pot he'd raked in quite a bit. Now, with a little real luck, he could pick up money for a real stake, not just the pickings he had.

The bet was to him and he started to put the money in when that inner voice which was Tom's said, emphasizing every word, NEVER DRAW TO AN INSIDE STRAIGHT, and he laid the cards down and said, "Fold," thinking, I'll never *know* whether my luck was on or not. How's come I listen to a goddam nigger?

He was furious, absolutely furious; he would have liked to pound his fury out on the table. You're tough, you don't rely on *nobody,* only yourself. That was the only law to live by. Don't lissen to nobody but yourself. It's your money, bet what you want. Don't lissen to no nigger. Don't lissen to *nobody.*

He put his hands on the edge of the table and gripped; even his palms ached—I got no business here, he knew—he didn't think that, he knew it—if I don't trust in my own judgment —I never should have dropped; that was just plain cowardice, playing it safe—the way Mason Raymond would. A *man* don't play it safe. A man takes chances. I could have pulled that nine, I know I could, but I chickened out. I lost that pot 'cause I chickened out.

He opened the new hand of cards that had been dealt to him and stared, because there before him were five hearts, five lovely hearts, a flush dealt him straight out without his even having to sweat one card out.

Luck is riding right with me, he thought. I *could* have had that nine. I let myself listen to some nigger gives advice all over the place on how to play cards, but you don't see him do nuthin' but fold or throw his hands in. I ain't seen him rakin' the money in.

"Well?" Impatient, officious, impossible. "How much?"

] 63 [

"Five," John said.

"*Five?*"

"That's what I said, five."

Coins began to pile up in front of him. Others besides himself apparently felt that luck lay with them. Give me a sign, he prayed. Show me my day's on its way and it ain't no time at all until that lunkhead cousin limps out of my life. Show me I'm on my own.

"*Well?*"

"I don't want no cards."

"You don't want none, no cards at all?"

"That's right."

The other four were all looking at him. The cards he had drawn lay in front of him. John waited while the others drew —two or three, each one of them. The beefy sunburned man across from him hesitated. He had only taken two. If he raised, John knew he was in trouble. He had maybe a full house, which would beat his flush. "Call ya," he said. John felt a moment of absolute exultation, an exhilaration so complete that he might have made the same cry he gave at the end of the ascension of the ladder of love. He opened out his flush.

"He done it agin," cried one of the other players.

"You ain't leavin'?" the beefy man whose money John was scooping in demanded. "I'm entitled to git a chance to git back some of that money you took. Ain't that right?"

"Ain't no rule says I can't shut up shop whenever I want and call it quits." A voice inside him had just warned, Don't push your luck. Your luck only runs so long.

"You sure are a little snot-nosed badger," the cowboy said, rising in his chair. "I ain't gotta take that offen no snot-nose ain't even wet behind the ears, likes to think of hisself as a man."

"You lay a hand on him," John heard the familiar voice behind him warn, "and you'll have this nigger to deal with."

"I ain't afraid of you, no more'n I'm afraid of him."

"You want to try yourself out," Pepper Tom said, "you be my guest. You bigger but I be more willin' and—I be willin' to bet—smarter."

"No nigger gonna talk to me like that."

The big beefy man stood up across the table and looked at them as if he were ready to breathe fire and burn them into the next world—and then I'll know, John thought, either it's there or it ain't. Won't need Mason Raymond's Bartholomew in a cave to tell me. "I reckon I got the right to git some of my stake back. I reckon I got that right. What you mean tryin' to tell me what my rights is?"

Glee seized John; he went giddy on it. He crackled and spit with power. He glanced across the table and looked at Beefy Face, looked at the agitated raw-red face across from him, and he knew that he could stand up to a showdown and face him down. The man was full of nothing but air. Because he was big and looked strong, he could act that way and scare a lot of men into backing down; but he wasn't going to do that with John. I'll kill him if I have to, John thought.

He put his hands on the edge of the table and got ready to tip it up against him and throw him off balance. I'll take whatever's handy and reach out and beat the hell out of him. I'm gonna git me a good gun, not jest a rifle, but a good straight-killing shooting iron, and there ain't gonna be one man in this territory can stand up to me.

In the beefy man's excitement the broken veins in his cheeks had darkened to purple; high on each whiskered side of his face a regular network of purplish veins crisscrossed his cheeks. The man's eyes were glittering with excitement; he was flushed with expectation. Out of his mind with anger, John thought. Didn't have much good sense to begin with and now he'd done jettisoned what he had.

But he was going to back down. He was afraid—because there's two of us, John thought in contempt. One he'd have taken on, but he's afraid of us two. *Afraid of two?* he wanted to taunt the man—fraidy-cat about more than one, that it?

Abruptly the beefy man sat down, his eyes on the table. "Deal—go on, deal," he said impatiently. "So he's got a flush. That ain't no great historic event, is it? Deal."

He had backed down. John had never felt more elated in his life. Even the sensation of sex had never given him such a sense of supremacy. If anyone had asked him why he had come West at this moment, he would have been able to answer easily: to feel like this. Worth the whole goddam trip cross-country, he thought, even dragging dumb dodo Mason Raymond along.

"You done right well. You got pants on you, boy. Man's pants," the nigger said as they walked out; he was hitching up his own britches. He felt the way John did, John was sure; the arrogant way he walked, the arrogant way he shoved his cigarette between his teeth—a man not to be messed with. "Now, it's *my* turn," he said, swaggering. "I feel like we got luck runnin' right down into our joints. I kin jest feel the flow." He stopped for a moment and looked John over. "How's come you quit? You was doin' fine. How's come you decided to bow out? You could've set yourself up a tidy little stake with luck runnin' like that."

"Well, it's like I felt the luck givin' out." He paused, seeing the nigger couldn't get the sense of it. "You know, a man's only got so much luck comin' to him, and then the wheel turns."

"The wheel *turns?*"

"It's like there's this wheel and when it goes up, your luck, it's with you. But then the wheel comes to the top and starts to go down, then your luck starts runnin' out on you."

"I ain't never exactly heard it put like that before." He shook his head. "Luck don't run like that. You git a streak, you gotta go with it. You can't pick and choose when you think you're goin' to want to take advantage of it. Even if there was a wheel. *You* don't know when it's gonna turn. How's come you didn't keep goin' until it actually started to turn, until you seen it was tipped over?"

"I'm wore through."

The nigger stopped and lounged against the side of a building, looking casual. He's up to somethin' sure, John thought.

"Why don't you go on back and git yourself a little shut-eye?"

"Yeah, that's what I'd like to do. I ain't used to all this runnin' around."

"But before you go, lissen—" Now it's comin', John thought. He's goin' to put the bite on me. He folded his arms

—the action had almost been automatic, as if securing the money he had inside his pocket. "You aimin' to go up to the Hills, you say—you aimin' to git there and you ain't got no more sense of what's goin' on out there on the Plains than—than I don't know what, some young babe in the arms. You and me, we join up forces—" John waited. It was what he'd been hoping for, but he hadn't counted on it costing him money. This was going to cost him money sure. "I mean, the two of us, we was to hitch up forces—I'm a little low on funds right in through here," Pepper Tom said and John thought, I'll bet, "but the thin' is, you mabbe see your way clear to back me in a little loan—jest for a couple of hours, you'll be gettin' to the Hills 'fore you know it."

John didn't answer; the nigger shifted uneasily. "I mean," he went on, "we could be pardners—like I got experience—"

"And I got cash," John said.

"Somethin' like that," he admitted. "Somethin' like that." He said that with such finality that there was a great sadness that swept over the darkened streets, as if the black man were confessing all the defeats and failures of his life. I had a hard time, he might have been saying, you know, with what most men git and then bein', you know, black on top of it. This wasn't a good time or place to be born.

It's not *my* fault, John wanted to say at him. He stomped about, fighting fatigue and anger and the urge simply to give up. He was so goddam tired with the drinking and the women and the card playing and now he was supposed to concentrate on making a deal that would maybe influence the rest of his life. He sighed, sighed so loudly that the nigger laughed. "You remind me of my mama," Tom said. "She was always sighin'—sigh so long and so loud you could hear her in the next town, and then if you say to her, 'How come you sigh like that all the time?' she get real mad and sass you right back. 'Because I got work done writ right on my bones,' she say. 'That why I sigh. You sigh too if you had to do all I do every day. It's a *re-lease*,' she say, 'jest to sigh.' People they come to call her The Sigher. Nobody gonna call her that to her face. She a big woman and got a lot of madness in her. 'Here come The Sigher,' they say when they see her come, and laugh and laugh. Once she say to me, so I know she keen to what goin' on behind her back, 'Day I die I want you to have them carve on my tombstone, 'Gone where she don't have to sigh no more.' "

All right, all right, John wanted to tell him, you don't have to pour it on. He stood, stubborn, looking at the waning moon and trying to hold his head up; it felt so heavy that it seemed it would fall down and lie on his chest. "I'll give you some," he said at last. "What I won. That's fair," he said. "I mean, if you lose it, then I ain't really out nuthin' because I didn't have it before and it's fair because I wouldn't have it now if you hadn't taught me how to play them cards." Still, it was a hard decision for him to make, and done grudgingly.

The black man pursed his lips. "You got some fair reasonin' there," he agreed. "Can't find no fault with it nohow. How much you win anyway? I was so busy keepin' my eyes on that big baboon I didn't see you take in the pot."

"It was good enough," John said. He began getting the money out. I'm a fool, he thought, but maybe it ain't really like real money I'm losing if I didn't have it before. That logic reassured him. But more than the logic was the backup he had in Mason Raymond. It wasn't like he was really putting himself out on a limb. He thought of how he used to go way up in the trees and swing. There wasn't another kid who would do that—too afraid. Mason Raymond would say admiringly, You're a swinger in the tops of trees. And I am, too, John thought. I lose what I give him, I can win it back. He felt full of confidence. There was nothing like a run of luck to make a man's life look up.

I ain't takin' from Mason Raymond no way, he thought. I made up my mind on that. But it was him—looking at the nigger—give me the know-how to git this money in the first place, so by rights he's got some claim to it. I give it to him now, I don't owe him nuthin'. And that's how it's gonna be with me—I ain't ever gonna owe no man nuthin', then nobody's got a claim on me. That way you're really free. I come a long way lately, he thought. Wouldn't be many who'd take me for jest nineteen.

"You traded my horse for that? What do you mean you traded my good horse for that? My horse was in the barn. How could you trade my horse for that when it was in the barn?" He was leaning out the window looking at the sorriest-seeming nag outside of Mason Raymond's Mabel he'd ever seen in his life and a ratty-faced girl dragging her feet in the dust. The nigger was standing grinning lopsided, looking up at him from the street below. The girl was struggling with a crazy outlaw of a horse, a horse that had killer written all over its face and danger vibrating from every bone in its body. "Don't look like that," he said. "It ain't as bad as it 'pears. There was this little game goin' and—" He looked away from John, unable to face him. "And I got wiped out early, you know, goddamest hand you ever saw. It was a shoo-in and then this robber, he come up with a full house agin my straight. But I seen a chance to get him back. Laid my horse on the table first," he said, as if that made it all right, that he had lost his own mount before he'd lost John's. "And then I went and 'borrowed' yours," he said, "and I laid the horse on the table and this fellow he put up the girl first and then his piebald, and—you're not goin' to believe this—but I won 'em both."

"I don't give a damn about them. All I want to know is, where's my horse? If you won them, you didn't lose mine, so where is it?"

"I lost it, son. I thought I was hot and ought to ride my luck. So I laid that horse on the line agin—a big pot, take us in style to the Hills—only this time I was outmatched, I lost your horse to two pair agin three of a kind, how could that happen?"

"You bet my horse *twice*? Why didn't you bet that, *that* crazy horse?"

"Who'd want that there Indian piebald?" he asked, looking at the hysterical little mustang running around the girl. She was trying to hold it with a rope, but it had ideas all its own. It wasn't going to listen to anything that smacked of good sense. "Nobody in his right mind would want that, holy mother of god, any fool can see that. I mean, I tried—I said,

'How'd you like the girl and the horse back?' and they all commenced laughin' and there I was, stuck; it was either them or yourn and I couldn't drop out, I had it made, so I bet yourn, and I laid down the hand—" He was looking up at John again, appealingly this time. "And I got took," he said. "But I hung on to the saddle," he said, as if that made it all right.

IV

*B*enjie," she said. "Benjie Klomp—"

Clump? *Nobody* in this whole wide world could be called Clump, Mason Raymond thought.

"My pa named me after him. He was goin' to have a boy and when I come he didn't have no other name to hand out so he give me this here *this* name and I been explainin' it ever since."

She had *this*ed this and she had *this*ed that; for a fact *this* was just about her favorite word; she used it as often as she had freckles on her face and there was a rainstorm of them running over the skin from the forehead to where the neck disappeared into the tattered dress. For a time Mason Raymond had had no idea what she meant until he figured out *this* really meant something like *shit* said sideways. She could be polite and still give vent to her feelings. Put on the table in a poker game and still hankering after gentility. Well, why not? Bartholomew once said that people had really been made inside out. That might certainly be true of her. She certainly looked inside out, standing beside his bunk—torn in flesh and clothing, disheveled from head to foot, dirty, distraught, coughing her lungs up in despair, covered over with freckles as though she had been stricken by some rare disease Mason Raymond had read about back at the Academy in Albany in those thumb-marked books which were passed out and retrieved as if they contained the Secrets of Life, but which gave back only deadly dull figures of population variables, sizes of cities, annual wheat and rye exports of insignificant little countries nobody cared about; while here he observed firsthand the instance of some deep well of human suffering that made the dark freckles pop out all over the girl's face and the bare parts of her arms exposed by the torn rents of her dress, if you could call such a sack a dress.

What kind of woman would end up as part of a poker stake? It came to him with a quintessential dropping of his heart: The kind of woman who would end up jabbering her head off at me. She's latched on to me, he thought, because she sees I'm even worse off in ways than she. The others are men, him and John, Mason Raymond thought, but I'm jest some weak shipwrecked thing cast off in the midst of nowhere same as she is.

When the black man had first brought her up, great loops of noisy wails had wound round her. "I won't stand for this, I won't," she had hollered at them. "I been through more than a mortal's bound to bear, and I'm not takin' any more. You can't *make* me."

"We ain't makin' you do nuthin'," the black man had said. "Nobody tryin' to stop you from doin' nuthin'. You want to run, you run. Be my guest." So she had run. Then she had come back. "I ain't got nowhere to go," she had protested passionately, scratching at her elbow. "Nowhere. Won't no one have me—not after what I been through. I ain't considered—I ain't considered in no way. And none of it was my *this* fault. It was never my fault, none of it. I couldn't help bein' left like I was. I couldn't help none of it, not one single solitary *this* bit of it, but I'm blamed jest the same. It ain't fair. None of it's fair! I never asked for any of those *this* thin's to happen, never done nuthin' to deserve them happenin', but they happened anyway. How could I help it I was took sick?"

The freckles were popping up all over her face from the force of her excitement; they looked as if they might bounce off the skin, hit the floor, and rattle round like rain. "You need somethin' hot, somethin' like a little soup, somethin' don't tear up your insides," she said to Mason Raymond now. "A little soup, somethin' like that. You're so weak." Weak isn't the word, he wanted to say. It's more like worthless, and you know it. Worthless—the two of them, like the clocks and castiron stoves and chiffoniers that littered the Oregon Trail because they were holding the wagons back. People got rid of what was troublesome to them or what they no longer needed or was overloading them. Someone had once told Mason Raymond the West was made up of those who were driven there or those who just drifted out. But nothing had been said about those just thrown out or abandoned there.

He looked over the girl's head to his cousin John, who was as surely driven by inner energies and greeds as the nigger was just as obviously one who had drifted out, and now he's hitched up with us, Mason Raymond thought, because he probably hasn't anything better to do, maybe he even feels some kind of responsibility because it's only too obvious how green we are; and some people cannot resist the call of responsibility, no matter how much it does them in—so there you are: John, driven, and Tom, the drifter, and the girl, a castoff. And me?

He himself didn't even understand all the impulses and reasons that had brought him West, though he was of the nature, he recognized, of the tinkerer who can't help taking things apart just to see how they were put together, only it was not a machine but himself he was dismantling piece by piece so that he might one day understand the intricate operations that made up his own actions. It would be such a help to know why you acted the way you did.

To other people his behavior must seem senseless and irrational, probably bizarre, especially his determination to go and cast his lot with the Indians, people who probably—not probably, certainly—didn't even want him, whose language he didn't speak, and whose customs and ideas would certainly be entirely alien. None of that mattered.

What he learned was that the pool was neither clear nor cool; inside he burned and churned with feelings so chaotic that there was no way to sort them out and make sense of them; he was being consumed by grief and anger and bewilderment and a growing sense of the ironic injustice of what he had done as opposed to what he planned to do. He had never wanted to carry a gun. He did not believe in killing. Yet he had broken every law that he had set up for himself. But the core of his whole questioning assumed there was a reason for things, and maybe there wasn't a reason for anything. Maybe life just happened, and it didn't happen according to cause and effect in any sense a man understood the workings of those two relationships.

There are some things no one (at least here in this world) is ever going to know, Mason Raymond thought, hearing the girl's outraged voice go on and on, and one of them is whether there is a reason for things or not. She was so furious because she was asking for logical answers.

He should say to her, there are walls out there—you can't see them but they are stronger and thicker than any walls you will ever see here on this earth—that you cannot break down or tear through and get on the other side of to know what's past them. Possibly—but he himself mainly discounted this although he knew Bartholomew was counting on it with all his heart—after death, the answers to what was on the other side of those walls would come, the answers to everything. But that presumed a hereafter with some kind of reasonable director who would allow explanations, and Mason Raymond did not believe in a reasonable, logical God; he was not sure he believed in any God at all (never mind Bartholomew had seen him in Warrensburg), and therefore it was hard to believe in a hereafter where they gave out answers, any kind of answers at all. All he could see now was blankness. There was no logical reason why he'd been orphaned young, why his friend Hart had been killed, why he who hated killing had had to kill a friend like Hart. No reason at all.

But she was insisting now on some kind of ordered answer out of him for something she'd been asking, plucking at his arm with insistent fingers and demanding, "Well, what do *you* think?"

I don't think anything about anything, Mason Raymond

wanted to say, yet I *think* all the time; it is not the thinking that
will give you the answers, it's the questions, but he couldn't
say that to her of course. What he told her instead was that,
yes, soup was certainly what he needed (being the dispensers
of food seemed to cheer women up), good rich broth—and
then he had to begin the whole tiresome explanation that it
couldn't be *meat* broth though, because he ate neither the flesh
nor bones of animals, while she sat there, defeated (perhaps
she didn't know how to make a soup without animal parts),
and he was sorry he'd tried even that small subterfuge to cheer
her (he had never felt less like good, rich broth in his life)
because now that he had begun to explain the first of his
oddnesses, that he did not eat meat, she would be curious
naturally to uncover the others. She'd pester him, and then
John, and that would vex John more than ever, she'd probably
even badger the black man, she was the kind who didn't know
how to take *no* for an answer. Keep to your own business and
others won't meddle in yours, there was sound advice for you;
but this girl couldn't have sense enough to listen, she'd make
a crusade out of finding out all the weaknesses and aberrations
that were the matter with him. And she had that kind of raging
energy that never ends; when everyone else was worn through
down at the knees and panting for help, she'd still be running
around hollering as if the day had just begun. He understood
very well how she had survived all alone in the midst of a great
desert with nothing but coyotes and wild Indians. She was a
born survivor if he ever saw one.

Across the way from him John had managed to rouse the
black man and get him to sit up on the side of his bunk. He
sat, head hanging down, looking as if he would never raise and
revel again. It was sad to see that kind of resignation in a man,
and he was pleading. "I'm jest tryin' to lie down and rest my
eyes some," Pepper Tom said. "They both put in a hard time,
they need some rest." He looked at John apprehensively.
"Suppose we jest give ourselfs a little time to mull thin's
over," he suggested, "think about the turn of events for a little
while before we start gittin' heated up over them? My head
feels like lead." He stretched out on his bunk and covered his
head with his arms and lay there alternately groaning and

snoring. Occasionally he made a muffled noise that sounded like someone pleading to be blindfolded before they put him before the firing squad.

The girl had deserted Mason Raymond and tried to attach herself to John. In a pecking order of authority, second-in-command was better than the caboose that came along after the cannon. But John was having nothing to do with her. He had a way, John, as long as Mason Raymond could remember, of holding women at arm's length with a cold, distant look; curt, monosyllabic words; complete disinterest and disassociation. In despair, she had turned again to Mason Raymond, standing by his bunk, distractedly massaging the back of her neck. There was nobody else to whom she could appeal, and even the worthless can occasionally make adequate sounding boards.

"How about a little soup?" she asked again.

John was trying to rouse the black man, shaking him and lambasting his groans with his own worries. "You're the one who won her, you're the one that knows it all, you been all over, you're so smart, you figure it out. It ain't my problem. I don't want to git involved."

"Nobody ever wants to git involved. You could make that the motto of the world: I Don't Want to Git Involved. Ain't too bad when she quiets down," he said, groaning. He was talking over the girl's and Mason Raymond's heads as if they didn't exist. "Good musclin' in the back for my money. And her size don't go agin her. She's small, but she ain't too small. You don't want to count size in women the way you do in horses."

"Listen," John said. "We got to do somethin' about her. We can't carry no girl along with us—"

"She's free, like I told her, to git up and go anytime she wants. No one holdin' her back."

"But supposin' she don't go. Supposin'—"

"She don't go, then I say we got a problem. She can't come with us. I ain't takin' no woman—"

"Then you tell her. Explain it to her so she don't feel bad—"

"I don't care whether she feels bad or not, she can't tag

along with us. That's *hard* country up there."

"We could give her some money maybe, you know, to help her git on her way."

"I ain't got no money. You know that. The cards took all I got—"

The girl stood up. She's forgotten all about me again, Mason Raymond thought, because they're the ones that count, not me. She started tucking up her hair, making a round ball of it and jamming it to the back of her head with a large curved black pin; the ball stood out like a dark doorknob. She was going to try to make do, Mason Raymond saw, because there wasn't anything left to try. But what did she have to make do with? She didn't even seem to have a sack to her name. Came picked clean as a whistle except for the clothes (if you could call them that) on her back. He had never known a woman who didn't have things. But this one didn't have anything at all, nothing, just that old tatty sweater and dress she came in with, tagging along with the black man, desperately trying to explain. "They didn't jest up and leave me. I mean they didn't jest put me out on the prairie and go. They took 'nd raised a shade over me and give me a blanket to cover me and they left me some biscuits and water afore they went. They didn't want me because I was took with the same sickness finished the rest of the family off—my brother, he went first; and then my ma, and finally pa, and then I got to vomitin' 'nd had the sore throat and the rest 'nd they was afraid, so they left me. They put a red flag up," she had said, as if she were proud of such consideration, "to warn off others," she explained, agitated, scratching at her elbow again.

"I laid there tooken with the fever 'nd the spittin' up—and all the rest," she said. "And I waited to die the way the rest of my family done. I didn't know what there was left to git up 'nd live for—my family, they was all gone; they buried them in the dirt and run over the graves with the wagons, beat the dirt down so slick no Injuns nor coyotes couldn't never tell there was bodies there so they wouldn't, you know, dig them up. And that was right, I know that, but then, too, how I'm ever gonna know where they're laid up? The whole line of wagons went over the top of them and there ain't no way to tell where they was put under 'cause there weren't no marker left neither. I was so sick I jest lay in the wagon when they all went over them and I ain't got no idear at all where it was.

"After that, I guess I musta slept or gone offen my head or somethin' because the next thin' I knew they was stopped and puttin' me out and then it was night and dark and I was all by myself, and that's when I commenced to git scared. I was more scared of the dark than of the dyin'.

"I was so scared some coyotes or Injuns or somethin' would git me I set up and commenced hollerin', but my throat was too sore to bring up much so finally I jest lay down 'nd bawled 'nd bawled 'nd when that was over I set up 'nd et a little 'nd drunk some 'nd then I jest give up. That's what I done, I give up. There weren't no further down I could go so I jest quit tryin'. And that made me feel better 'cause if you can't go no further down nuthin' worse ken happen to you. And so I went to sleep 'nd in the mornin' I woke up 'nd I felt better 'nd the first thin' I done was to git up 'nd take down the flag.

"I laid there all that day and then some of the next, and this here *this* Injun party come along and they seen me. They seen the sickness right off, they knew what it was, they wouldn't come near me, they jest held their horses off and looked, then they went off. Weren't nobody goin' to help me, me bein' down with that sickness killed off so many.

"I drunk some more water and et a little of the biscuits and I slept. There weren't no place for me to go, not weak and alone like I was, so I jest laid there and slept. And that night, jest as it was gittin' dark those Injuns, they come back; they didn't come up to me, they jest stayed off a ways and threw me some spitted meat, and nuthin' ever tasted so good as that there *this* warm meat. I et and et and that got me a little strength up. The next day when they come I set up and every day I set up and waited until they come back and give me some meat till I was well agin, and then," she said, pausing, letting a little breath go out in a gasp, "and then they took me off with them, back, you know, up to where they was tribed out. I was eight when they took me and I was with them," she said, her face rigid, no emotion showing, as if she were reciting someone else's history, but standing there massaging the back of her neck as if to relieve a deep internal pain inside her head, "more than fifteen years. I got two children up there," she said without a flicker of emotion, "but when the soldiers come in and burnt us out and drove off all our horses and put them in a corral and shot them down, they give me back—

"Not right then, not till later, when thin's was quieter. They thought if I was put back with my own, thin's 'd go better with them. So they give me a horse, a good horse, a fine horse, the best my man had," she said, "and they sent me in. The soldiers at the fort, they took my horse and put it with theirn, that's why I ain't got nuthin' now. They took all the thin's I come in with. I had one of the best ponies off the Plains," she said without betraying any emotion, "and many fine thin's they give me when they sent me in, and the soldiers they took all of them away from me and give me this dress and these shoes," she said, looking down, "because they said I was white and couldn't go around no more in skins. That's what they called the good thin' I had on, *skins.* But it was all beaded and quilled and beautiful, soft like a feather, but they took it away from me.

"This here *this* white captain he kept at me, sayin' he'd teach me white manners. The soldiers was all nice to me at first till they found out about the boys. They didn't send my boys back with me. Girls, maybe they would have let go, but not boys. They kept askin' me, those soldiers, and especially that captain, how I could let an Injun be with me, and then they started treatin' me—you know—like I wasn't white.

"That *this* Captain, he was always at me. I took his horse and tried to run off—twice—and was picked up and that *this* Captain he come and put a bit in my mouth with wire on it and he said if I pulled somethin' like that agin on him he'd let me know how he handled runoffs. He come up in back of me and bridled me jest like I was a horse—you open my mouth you ken see the scars yet.

"You ain't like the others," she said to Tom. "You ain't no more like them than I is, those white folk." Tears had started pouring down her cheeks. "Then this *this* soldier man put me up for cards," she said, "and they abused me bad and carried me back here. If I was to git near them Hills again, I could find my boys, I know I could. Wouldn't be nuthin' for me to find them. Bone Hand, he'd give good thin's to git me back," she said, looking at Tom, then at John. "Well," she said, and then stopped. "Well, it wasn't no idea, you know, it wasn't no plan. It was jest, you know, like a thought."

If there was a garden of peaches, she would come out with a pit.

Tom—resuscitating himself from a brown bottle—and John paid no attention to her, on their bunk upstairs in this boarding house—if you could give such a clapboard wreck an auspicious name like that—and why not? Bartholomew asked inside Mason Raymond's head. A cave can be a castle, and don't you never forget it. And the forgotten of the earth—that's what they remain, the forgotten: Bartholomew could be a hard man at times. He used to get terribly angry and stomp around flinging his arms out in agitation. "God doesn't *want* you to be sad," he would say in a shout. "I don't know *where* you got the notion you got to be all soured up to be good. God wants people to be happy—at least I *think* He does." That must have been one of Bartholomew's more orthodox periods, Mason Raymond thought now, one of those times where he more or less thought like other people, hopeful. Sometimes he could be very bitter, alum bitter.

Mason Raymond was bone weary and saw no hope of sleep, the place a rumble of men snoring, belching, grousing, or— like their own black benefactor—aggrandizing themselves up into importance. Drink had swelled Tom up once more and until it threw him down again he was full of himself. He was talking like there was no tomorrow. "Adventure jest got hold of this here nigger and moved him all over the map," he said, while the girl looked up, sniffing: Nothing, but nothing, he could have done, that sniff said, could hold half a candle to what had happened to her. "The thin's I done, the thin's I seen," the black man said proudly, while inwardly Mason Raymond groaned. There would be no stopping him; the signs were sure and steady, a man at the mercy of his mouth. First the girl, now the black man, and all he wanted was to lie down and go to sleep. He could only expose himself so long to people until the electricity between them began to make adverse responses and he said or did absolutely the wrong thing.

"I been a contraband in the war. I been on the Chisholm Trail from San Antonio, Texas, to Abilene, Kansas, with nuthin' more than a horse, a bag of beans, some dried beef, and a good coil of rope. I been to Abilene and back some six, seven times. I been shot at in the War and a couple of times in places I had no business bein'. I been hit once and I been down sick like to die, but I ain't never give up. A man he can be down on his luck a little, but that don't mean he's got the liberty to be a quitter. It's all out there for the takin' iffen you only give yourself half a chance."

He would now, Mason Raymond thought, run through the Great American Dream. He closed his eyes and asked Bartholomew how to talk about other men who dreamed themselves heroes and ended up sweeping the back rooms of places like this. For once Bartholomew had no answer. Perhaps there wasn't one. But a continent, Mason Raymond thought, had been put under wagon ruts on the assumption that hard work earns gold, and a whole people driven out of their homes and up into the hills on the notion God favors those who sweat, and men like these even still believed, down and out as they were, that if you will only work hard you will end up in mansions covered with gold. But Mason Raymond believed there were other kinds of worlds. He had seen them for himself, up there on the Cold River flats. Men who lived in caves carved worlds also worth looking to. Love, he heard Bartholomew call out, you must learn to love one another and yourself.

"Outlaws, ranchers, horsebreakers, wanderers like myself, I seen them all and more. There's a place they call 'Nigger Hill,' near Deadwood," the black man said, "takes its name from us niggers who staked out claims up from the creek. You need water to separate gold from the rocks and dirt, and those white men, they sent us'n up from the water as a kind of joke, puttin' us on, but we wasn't onto them yet, we thought they was squarin' with us when they said there was gold to be had in them rocks. It was hard work, too hard for white men, and we thought, we was sech fools, that's why they was good

] *81* [

enough to put us'n onto it—because it wasn't white men's work, but it would do for niggers. It was a dry claim, don't you know, one where you had to carry all your water to do the pannin', and I soon seen the sorriness of it and give it up, but some fools, they stayed on.

"Indians bad up there now," Pepper Tom said. "Bad bad bad." He looked briefly over at the girl, as if for the first time recalling she was there. "Well, they *is*," he said stubbornly. She looked down at her lap not saying anything, but Mason Raymond saw the balky, obstinate set of her mouth. She may not have much, he thought, but I wouldn't cross her if I was you, he wanted to tell the two of them, but they were too preoccupied to pay attention to a mite of a girl and a dodo of a man. That's all we are, Mason Raymond thought, two people no one has to pay any attention to. Yet he could not feel sorry for the girl. He had seen the survivor side of her in her, and he felt sure of it.

Benjie Clump (a name Mason Raymond still couldn't bring himself to believe) was made of strong stuff. So, too, now that he was beginning to look at the facts less emotionally, was that girl back in Xenia, Ohio. There was no doubt about it—you would have to call her a survivor.

Mason Raymond thought of the dry-goods clerk looking up as she tapped on the window, smirking; she was laughing and waving her parasol at Mason Raymond to hurry up, and Mason Raymond heard the words from the dry clerk, from between that great set of deadly white teeth, a meat eater all right, a devourer of the animal flesh of the world, saying, "Easy, *that's* the word for *her* kind."

Mason Raymond stared at the man, at first unable to feel anything, even pain, while his hands disengaged themselves from whatever it was he had been holding and he stepped back, empty of any sensation at all, though he had managed to move, was even at the door where he stood frozen in the doorway until she came, smiling, happy, unaware anything was wrong, and grasped the latch on the door and yanked away the barrier of wood and glass between them. "You comin'?" she asked brightly while he stood rooted where he was, suddenly engulfed in pain and grief and anguish; he felt

] 82 [

for one moment as if he were going to die, that his heart had actually stopped functioning, and yet she didn't see, didn't see at all, chattering on, sopranoing how he must come down-street and see the cutest, the dearest . . . her voice trailing off, crying, "What is it? What's the matter? What is it, love? What's the matter?"

She got him out onto the sidewalk where he went through the motions of walking, putting one foot in front of the other, step after step, moving his body about first under the dappled light of the trees, and then out into the open sun again. She turned him in at a gate and got him up some steps and through a door into the "cousin's" house where, in the dark room off the front hall which they called a good parlor, his body went down on to a chair and remained there, a bone skeleton propped up in the sitting position on which the flesh felt to him as if it were on fire, for heat and shame and lust had run in where the pain of a few moments before had been. Burning. Yes, of course, the sins of the flesh. The punishment of fire. Lust and fire and the flesh. It is better to marry than to burn. School knowledge that his teacher, Morphis, back in Albany at the Academy, had explained. The notion was from John (or so Mason Raymond remembered, that marvelous saint who had wanted to pull down and smash all the "idols" of the Acropolis because they were pagan execrations). "School-teachers burn," Morphis said, reaching over and laying a plump white hand on his podium.

Mason Raymond's hand raised the glass she had got be-tween his fingers and he drank broth, strong, meat-based, presumably life-arousing. At that moment he did not care that he was consuming the other animals of the world, he didn't care about anything. Then he stopped drinking. He could not take his brother's blood to survive. Yet he had had to kill Hart. God is a paradox, Bartholomew told him, it is the only way He's a possibility.

He had never known love before so that he had been totally unprepared for its pain. He knew—oh god, how well he un-derstood—that she of the green gloves had never loved him at all, that it had all been an act, a means of manipulating him out of his money, and he couldn't bear this knowledge nor the

] 83 [

fact that John had known all along and had been impatiently trying to bring him to his senses.

Then the "cousin" had come in, hearty, jovial, racing along in some anecdote about a drunk loose in the streets who threatened to— Then the "cousin" stopped, and there was the limp straggle of a final line, some empty phrase which rose to the "cousin's" lips and lay there in the dawning realization the whole jig was up, the country sucker had at last caught on. Those were exactly the phrases Mason Raymond saw on his face ". . . jig up . . . the dodo's wise to us at last . . ." The "cousin's" voice was ironic with exasperation. "What did you expect?" he asked. "The romance of roses?" But it was the wrong question: Mason Raymond had been a runner after roses all his life.

They commenced jabbering the whole squalid truth; of course he wasn't a "cousin" at all, wasn't even a husband, not even a lover; leastwise in any real sense now; they were simply, in their phrase, "trying to get along," which Mason Raymond took to mean they used their graces and their indiscretions to keep them afloat in a precarious world where *nothing* was as it ought to be. "Surely you can understand?" they kept asking, and in his pain and embarrassment and (John's oh-too-accurate word) stupidity he kept standing there shaking his head no, he did not understand.

Their exasperation was so terrible because it totally excluded him. More than anything else he feared being turned out permanently by them. He fell on his knees and clutched her around the legs, crying out he didn't care, it was all right, please, just let things stay the way they were.

It was the girl who asked, "Are you mad?" and the answer, of course, was that yes, of course he was mad. He had been certifiable for years, everyone knew that. But he was harmless and—more important—had money, so he was allowed to run around making messes like this.

He was down on his knees—down on his knees—with his arms wrapped around her legs, clinging to her through the bulky folds of the expensive garments *he* had bought her in all those stores in Xenia, Ohio, where the clerks must have been laughing their heads off at him.

She was trying to pry his hands loose and, when she and the "cousin" had finally dislodged his fingers by blows, seeing inside his mind the picture of himself being pummeled and kicked by the one whom he had seen, yes, as a rose, a beautiful fair rose that would flourish forever on the sweet waters of his love, he stumbled to his feet and—

Oh, once I had a sprig of thyme,
I thought it never would decay . . .
Thyme, it is a precious thing,
Thyme brings all things to your mind. . . .

The song was still there inside his mind, from a long time ago, in the mountains in Carolina, perhaps because he thought now of the lines about the rose:

This sailor he gave to me a rose,
A rose that never would decay,
He gave it to me to keep me well reminded
Of the night he stole my bonnie thyme away. . . .

In the hills in Carolina, with Hart, where they went to bring a dog back—Horatio, the dog Hart had loved so much—there had been another girl, his first girl; he saw how she looked as she lay on the straw pallet, a cup held to her face, her lashes trembling as she lowered her face and blew into the cup. That time, long ago, Mason Raymond had been uncomfortable, standing over her looking down because he had realized he hadn't done right by her and he wasn't going to in the future either and he didn't know how to make it right with her at the end like this. He *couldn't* make it right with her because there was no way to do it; if—as was true for him at the time—you did not even understand the differentiation between lust and love, how could you explain to a wild mountain girl that her wildness had been like a call that you had answered and now, in your shamed, civilized way, you didn't want mountain and city to meet.

But she had known all this long before Mason Raymond, with the wisdom that comes early with living around animals

—all kinds. "You ain't so smart, let me tell you. You ain't got so much to brag about," she had said, sneering. "There ain't a man in these mountains couldn't best you beddin'. Little peanut thin' on you ain't even worth mentionin'."

He looked down at this girl snuffling at the side of his cot. She could hurt him, she was capable of doing him great harm. All women could. He must be very careful. John understood about women, but he didn't. John didn't get himself lost or wouldn't fall for a hand turned toward him in a green glove. He would go into a card game and *win*. He would go into the Hills and find gold. He would be rich and reckless and someone to be reckoned with. He would hold power in his hands and make women fall at his feet; he would be feared and reckoned with and remembered. But I'm not ever going to be any of those things. People see it right off. It's like I'm jinxed and they're afraid some of the bad luck will rub off on them. They just want to get shut of me. I should never have come West with him. I have imposed, and that is not right.

Go and get well, Bartholomew had told him.

I want to get well.

The faint hope in those words glowed with hope against the immense darkness of the rest of Mason Raymond's mind. He concentrated all his energy on gathering his feelings for the future around them; he wanted that simple sentence to flow to every single cell in his body and become the central core of its survival.

In the midst of the vast dry hot desert with its scrub cottonwoods, its brown, rusty-looking sage and dead scaly cactus, he lifted a vision from back home, from the East and the Lake, of the Lake waters rolling in to shore. And then he thought of the ocean he'd seen in New York City when he and Hart were on their way to the Carolina hills to search for the dog. He was standing on a cliff looking out to sea; below him where the sand had been scooped away by endless tides there was a steep drop of fifteen or twenty feet. Where he stood, a few blades of coarse grass were bent back by the steady sharp wind that blew in from the water. The waves were high, the tide coming in, crest after crest breaking just below him and the aftermath of the swell rolling in onto the sandy beach and disappearing down into its depths. Little bubbles burst out of the sand as the water seeped in. Small creatures might be under there breathing in and out.

Here on the hot, dry desert Mason Raymond heard the rhythmic flow of the tide coming in. He could smell the salt of the spray, almost taste it on his lips as the sea mist blew in. He was standing on the high sand bank and the wind came in strong with the smell of salt and chilled his face and hands. He began to feel cold, but it was very important to stand very still and concentrate on that vision of the faraway sea and to lock it in his mind with the thought *I am going to get well.*

All right, you are going to get well. That is fine. I am all for that. But tell me one thing: How do you do that? How do you take the first step back to what you might call "getting well"? Mason Raymond's head was light, almost dancing with the shock of the thousands of holes in the sky where the stars would burn through, thoughts inside his head pouring through him like the gases with which those stars exploded, even though there was still a wall between him and the world outside; yet, he seemed for a moment poised in the trembling of the spheres and, under the influence of those internal lights, he was overcome with a sense of his own smallness in comparison to the great size and significance of space. Many things could happen out there, Bartholomew had promised. But we are very limited here. Haven't you felt that? He was petting his dead dog absentmindedly, stroking away some of the dust.

John was talking about grasshoppers, explaining how he would have left home sooner except for those four years the grasshoppers had been eating over the Plains, how he'd heard that insects lay on top of one another three, four inches deep, there were so many of them that they blotted out the sun, a hundred-acre cornfield vanished in an hour, the trees were so swollen with insects that they cracked and splintered under the strain; trains couldn't run because the bodies of crushed grasshoppers made a layer of grease so thick that the train wheels just kept spinning, was that true?

Wasn't anyone ever going to go to sleep? John talked about the wagons that came back East with GRASSHOPPER painted on their sides, about the panic three years back, in '73 at the Landing, how it looked like the Butteses might lose their place, how he would have been here a whole year earlier if the Laramie Treaty hadn't given the Sioux the Black Hills and kept the miners away, not that he thought the Government was really serious about any long-range plans to keep the miners out for good; the Army couldn't keep the miners out permanently; they were too determined. The miners were going to go in, and if they ran into trouble with the Indians sooner or later the Army was going to have to intervene and it was sure going to be a day of pardoning and partying in hell when the Army intervened on the side of the Indians.

The girl squatted tense near Tom's and John's bunks, the set of her jaw determined. She was trying not to speak out, that must be it. Obstinate. Yet upset—you could tell that by the way she was alternately scratching an elbow or rubbing the back of her neck.

At one time Bartholomew had been very big on Indians (he went through religions and races like days of the weeks) and when Bartholomew was in his Indian period he said that since Mason Raymond was part Indian he must go out West and take his place with his brothers. "I'm not Sioux," Mason Raymond had tried to explain, but of course a little thing like tribal affiliations made no difference when you were trying, as Bartholomew saw it, to bring mankind to the cornerstone to build a new temple in the desert. But as Bartholomew bent over his fire and breathed life on it and talked about atoning, about going West where the last of the natives were and devoting his (Mason Raymond's) life to them, there seemed to be some logic in what he was saying. Mason Raymond began to be persuaded. He had spent a whole year reading and thinking about Bartholomew's notion that the set of his life lay with the Sioux, and finally it had seemed a kind of sign when John had appeared in Albany to announce he was going West and had come to say good-bye. Mason Raymond had seen this was a call to him to go West and become, as Bartholomew had said, the red man as opposed to the white. Then you will have two sides to your soul. He himself had been ready, Mason Raymond realized, for a long time; he had just lacked the way to begin.

People back home were mad at Custer, John said excitedly, and at Sheridan and Crook, too, for going into the Hills and driving the miners out. You ought to be plenty mad about what they done to you, John said to Pepper Tom. He gave no answer, but made a kind of assentive gurgle. John didn't blame any miner for sneaking right back in, didn't blame the soldiers (he would have done the same) for deserting to go with them. The Hills were the future—

"Run you out before you can even stop and explain," Pepper Tom said. "Lose your stuff, lose your work. Other men, they come in and take over all you've done, git the benefit of all your effort. It ain't fair, I tell you—the thin's I seen, they jest weren't fair. Not that I got anythin' personal agin them Injuns—but let 'em put their tipis up someplace else, they don't need them Hills—"

"Yes, they do." The girl interrupted, very firm. "Them Hills is sacred. *Paha Sapa*," she said. "They's sacred to the Injuns and they was give to them in their treaty."

"They can go someplace else. Ain't nuthin' so special about them Hills. Lots of places I seen is—"

"They don't want to go noplace else."

"It ain't as easy as that, girl. It ain't a question of what they wants or don't wants—"

"The Hills was give to them—"

"They maybe said somethin' about it," one of the men in the room agreed. "You know, to git them out of the settlers' hair, but they didn't know there was gold there then—"

The whole room began to come alive with a sudden stiffening of backs, of angry men arguing that those worthless redskins ought to be given a good hiding; it was up to the Army to do that, not to run their own people out. If there was gold in the Hills, then the Indians would have to go. They didn't know nuthin' about the importance of gold, they didn't know nuthin' about the importance of anything. Mason Raymond wanted to say he had Indian blood and so had John, it ran in their family, but to remind John of that wasn't going to win any argument. John didn't want to be reminded he was an eighth Indian. What didn't show, what others didn't know, was something he could ignore. He won't deny it, Mason

] *89* [

Raymond thought, but he won't volunteer any information either. The moment to stand up and be counted had come; someone repeated the Sheridan saying, "Only good Injun is a dead Injun," and Mason Raymond stood up and announced "I'm part Indian."

There was a moment's silence; the black man was bent double laughing. "If he don't beat everythin'," he said. "Every time you think he's gonna go and cash in his hand, he slaps down an ace. I gotta give you one thin'," he said to Mason Raymond, "ain't nobody gonna come up with no easy wins where you're around." John glowered at him and looked away, denying they were related at all. Mason Raymond lay back on his bunk contemplating the raw, unfinished ceiling overhead in which busy spiders were spinning intrigues. His outburst had done no good at all. Somewhere out in the blind spaces of the spheres for a month or so Bartholomew had believed—for a while—that the soul of every man who ever lived possessed an inch of the sky. His theory was that when you died you dried up and shrank down to the size of half a pinhead; that way your inch of space was plenty of room for you to be safe in. You lived on air so that you didn't need any work to survive. Since there were limitless amounts of air, you never had to worry about an end.

Only one thing had puzzled Mason Raymond. What did all those millions and billions of pinheads do out there in their inches of space? They thought, Bartholomew said. They thought about everything that ever was. Weren't there some pinheads—half a pinhead, Bartholomew insisted, a whole pinhead would be too big for an inch—all right, wouldn't some half a pinhead decide his inch wasn't enough and try to take over someone else's? No, said Bartholomew, absolutely certain, they got love up there. It's what keeps the inches apart.

Mason Raymond had got to seeing Hart all dissolved down to the size of half a pinhead squatted down in his little inch of space, thinking away; but there was something not quite right about the picture because Hart wouldn't want to be in his inch all by himself. He'd want his dogs with him. If a man shrank to half a pinhead, how small was a hound?

Nor could Mason Raymond imagine Hart being satisfied

with just one dog. The inch Hart had would be all crammed full of dogs, no matter how small they could be shrunk to. Those dogs would be barking and running around and carrying on, wild that they were confined in such a small space, frantic to get out and get on the run. There'd be all that noise and confusion, and pretty soon Hart's neighbors would start complaining; they'd want a little peace and quiet to do their thinking in; before long a bunch of them would start gathering at the corners of their inch-wide spaces and shouting for Hart to shut his damn dogs up—no, it wouldn't work. Even out in the outer reaches of space there were bound to be troublemakers like Hart, and all the love in the world couldn't deal with them. Hart wouldn't be there ten days before someone would start getting a committee together to deal with the public nuisance and curtail his freedom. Some people always had to be freer than others.

Mason Raymond had tried once to explain to Bartholomew the problems some people in their inches would provide, but all Bartholomew had said, impatient, was, "You ain't got no *vision.*"

When Mason Raymond brought his eyes back down from the ceiling, he saw John and the black man getting ready to go out. He wondered how long he'd been transfixed out there in space. Time for him didn't exist in a single place or at a single time; he could come and go and live separate lives inside and out all at the same time. People didn't understand that and he had given up trying to explain. If some men wanted to be freer than others, other men lived in different worlds from their neighbors—and those who were different were always a menace in one way or another. But that was very negative thinking.

He was backsliding into his old point of view, had been immediately ready to reach out for the nearest painful part of his mind and pull it out so that he could pour his pity over it; he drew himself up abruptly and put a stop to the action. I am going to get well, he told himself. I am going to take pride and pleasure and comfort in saying yea instead of nay. I am going to get well and learn how to live the way other people do instead of always being a running sore; I am going to be well

. . . I am going to be well . . . I don't care how hard it is, I am going to learn to live with some of the confidence and courage of other men.

Behold the turtle. He makes progress only when he sticks his neck out.

V

At home back in Buttes Landing the days
almost always ran as smooth as the quietly
lapping water that washed up on the shores of Federation
Lake. Now and again a storm blew up waves, lightning
cracked across the lake, thunder raked the hills, a reminder of
the larger events outside that could burst in and disrupt the
isolated quietness of the community. It was a place in John's
eyes of almost absolute stagnation, and that was the principal
reason he had been desperate to get out, to burst beyond the
boring trinity that John's mother said was life—Birth, Mar-
riage, Death; that's the triangle, she always said, that makes up
people's lives, and when she said that she nearly drove him
crazy because it seemed to him if that was all there was to life
who would want to be born in the first place.

He knew, absolutely, she was wrong. Outside of the stuffy
smugness of this little Adirondack hamlet lay great adventures
and high tests of courage and magnificent deeds of bravery—
just look at some of the stories of these men, he would say to
her, trying to get her to read some of the cheap thin pamphlets
on Bridger and Glass and the Sublette brothers, but she always
turned up her nose at anything that fell outside the confines

] 93 [

of what she knew, suspicious to the end of the alien and the strange, viewing everything different as dangerous and a direct threat to her home and happiness. You couldn't argue with a closed mind, and John gave it *up,* but that complacence only hardened resolution to get away from what he thought of as the "small peanuts" of Buttes Landing and head for the great untapped experiences outside. They had a saying in the Landing: "Couldn't wait to shake the dust from his heels," and that's just the way he felt. Women set a lot of store on marrying, of course—more than men; but even in the Landing the men didn't have much more vision, most men would most probably have gone with birth, death, and work. War, his father might have added, as if violence had the true significance of rounding off a generation's existence. It gave John pause, thinking of destruction as one of the fundamental forces of existence.

People's lives seemed so strange to him. Why, when you had so many things you could do with your life, so many possibilities to explore, would you stay put in a dried-up little place like Buttes Landing or rot out on a farm like his father and grandfather and the Butteses before him? At first John thought it had to do with age; his father and grandfather were old; but soon he saw age had nothing to do with it because his two brothers were perfectly content to stay put. He was the only one in the family, it seemed, born with the wandering itch. Maybe his mother had been right. Maybe he was a little like Clyde Buttes, Mason Raymond's father, who had also not been satisfied with Landing life, who had seen bigger things than a rock-crop farm and a barn full of cows.

And yet just getting out didn't guarantee success. Look what had happened to Mason Raymond's father. Look around this room. In this room you saw how tentative success was. A few had power—some maybe come by it naturally, some given it by their father or father's fathers passing it along; some grabbed it, but only a few, only a few of those; but the main force of men foundered; luck blew them around like chaff on the wind. They were no better off here out West than they would have been back home. Look at the girl, look at Mason Raymond, even look at the nigger, who seemed to have more control over his life than most, but he hadn't come to much, still trying at his age to win a stake to a new life. I'm not like *any* of them, John thought, anger rising in him, the anger of potential power looking arrogantly on impotence. I'm gonna *control* my life, he told himself fiercely. I'm not gonna be broken by a couple of thin's come up I got no control over, that make me afraid to take chances anymore. I'm not like Mason Raymond, broke by one bit of bad luck. You *gotta* be strong, he thought.

"Trouble is, some jest seem to be more marked than others," his mother said. "It kinda looks sometimes like it runs in families." She was trying to make excuses for Mason Raymond; she felt sorry for him. To her way of thinking he had been too young when his problems came on him. But somehow she seemed to think that it was everyone else's responsibility that Mason Raymond was only fifteen when he ran up against all his bad luck. John couldn't go along with that; he had a private theory that most people brought their bad luck on themselves, almost as if God shoved it off on them because He didn't think so much of them as He did of other people. He had tried to go into the theory with her that some people were kind of chosen and some were sort of left behind, but his mother could be a very stubborn woman when she wanted. She said no God *she* knew played favorites like that. "Well, jest look around you," John said. "Don't it seem to you there is some people more favored than others?"

"It may *seem* that way, but no one knows what's the end scheme of it all."

He groaned. There was no use trying to have an intelligent discussion with her, she always fell back on those awful old warhorse sayings of hers like "Penny pinchers pinch themselves" and "Fair is as fair does."

Her stubbornness was her wall against accepting what she didn't want to own up to. First she refused to accept the fact that he was really going and then, later, when she saw that nothing any of them could say would change his mind, she had said, "All right, go if you have to, but I want you to stop off in Albany. I want you to stop by there and see what's going on with Mason Raymond. He worries me."

When John had argued Albany wasn't on the way, that it was way out of his way, she had set herself to do battle. "You're not like any of my others," she said, "and you're gonna do it because *I* ask it." The force of her feeling was proven by the fact that he had done it. In a sudden insight now he understood why: What she had been saying to him was, You are my firstborn, I love you best, but I can never say that because a mother is not supposed to love one child more than another. Perhaps some vague inkling of that had been in him when he'd agreed to let Mason Raymond tag along as far as Independence. In some way he was doing penance to his mother for leaving in the first place by taking Mason Raymond along.

The agreement between them, and Mason Raymond seemed to accept that, had been Independence; still John was uneasy. People who had no real drives of their own always wanted to join up with someone who had a strong notion of where he was going. It's goin' to be the devil's own work gettin' shut of him, John thought as he watched Mason Raymond fussing with his bedroll, trying to get some of his things in order—the few, that is, that were left. All the way cross-country he had been giving his possessions away or leaving them behind as if they were encumbrances he was goaded to be rid of. He had no sense at all about money and even less about the material things a man needed just to survive in this world. But he was blood and John's mother loved him ("He has a special place in my heart," she said in that terrible cliché of hers) and that, John supposed in the end, had really made the difference.

The girl was a terror, too, just the kind, like his cousin, who had a special ledger all her own at the store of disasters. *Won in a poker game?* he asked himself for the hundredth time in disbelief. How I'm ever goin' to git rid of either one of them?

He certainly wasn't going to get any help from the nigger, who lay in his bunk hunched up, bleary-eyed, trying to sleep out the alcohol. Tom looked up briefly and said, lying right between his teeth, "I ain't never gonna drink one more drop of that poisonous stuff if I ever git my head back on my shoulders straight." Some help he was going to be.

They had to get supplied, start gathering together all the stuff they'd need on the trail and in the Hills—flour, bacon, coffee, sugar, salt, yeast powder, the basics like that. A hundred fifty pounds of flour per adult—and flour twelve dollars the barrel, my god, the cost; twenty-five of bacon and pork, fifteen of coffee, twenty-five of sugar, a good amount of salt and yeast powder; pemmican, too, stored in a hide bag and covered with melted grease to keep it; on the trail it was mixed with flour and water and boiled up, leastwise that's what all the guides advised. And they certainly weren't going to be able to carry stuff like that themselves, they had to have decent range horses and a mule, a mule sure enough for storing the stuff. And horses—what horses did they have beside that outlaw piebald and Mason Raymond's Mabel. Some horses!— since Tom had gone and lost the decent ones they did have; that showed you how much help he was going to be. Decisions, decisions, decisions. And the nigger laid out flat. And that girl, for godsake, and Mason Raymond. Hogs in the corn again.

The girl can take Mason Raymond, John suddenly thought. The brilliance of the idea overwhelmed him. My god, it was so simple. He could get rid of both of them at the same time. Why hadn't he seen it before? Probably because all the simplest, most straightforward ideas were the most difficult to stumble on; their very simplicity ruled them out. Anything easy was suspect.

The girl was cooking beans—it was beans, always beans— over in the communal corner, and once the nigger raised himself up high enough to say with a sick start, "Food?"; then he lay back and went on dying. He'd been up in the night laying water to his head, complaining there was a crack across his skull through which air was pouring in and his brains couldn't take the pressure. Once he went up to one of the bare walls and leaned against it, resting his head against a strut. "I can't stand it lyin' down," he said and closed his eyes and slept that way, standing, for maybe an hour before he slid down and squatted on the floor, his head buried deep in his arms. "I'm gonna die," he announced. "You threw your poison up," he said to John. "Mine's still down there inside killin' me. No, don't come near me," he said to the girl. "I'm so hurtin' I'll come apart if you so much as give me a touch. Head couldn't stand the jolt." He made a sound like weeping.

Toward morning he crawled back to his bunk and threw a blanket over his head. "I jest can't take no light," he announced, and there he lay, stretched out, the blanket wrapped around his head, the other men moving all around him, laughing and coughing and hollering to one another. Every once in a while he would rise up and pronounce the arrival of that Final Rider in the Sky, give a death rattle, and fall back groaning he would never ever touch another drop of liquor so long as he lived if only the lead in his head would go away.

> *"O, the beefsteak's of leather,*
> *The pies are put together with tin;*
> *Bread you can't cut with no sword,*
> *Butter with wide-whiskers, and coffee that's thin,*
> *Way out yonder where we're goin' one day,*
> *To the Hills, to the Hills where we're on our way."*

Craziest nigger probably on the face of the earth, poetry-quoting (even in his present state!), wine-guzzling, card-playing son of a bitch—imagine trying to write home about him or, for that matter, the girl, "won her right across the table in a poker stake, Ma"; or Mason Raymond, "lays down in gopher holes and prays his heart out and all that happens is he's sunstruck. You ought to see what happened to him in some hick town called Xenia, Ohio, Ma; he was robbed blind, and I do mean blind, by a woman musta been forty years old. It's been a great trip."

The girl handed him a trencher of beans and he looked at her and he thought, What an ugly girl. Indians didn't think like whites; maybe to them she had been real good-looking. She must have had a different name, too, among the Indians; it was impossible to think of Indians calling her Benjie. What did they call her? He was curious, he really wanted to know.

"Pte-san win," she said. She looked away, holding the second trencher of beans, Mason Raymond's, in her other hand. "White Buffalo Woman," she said.

White Buffalo Woman? He shook his head.

We rode West, Ma, Mason Raymond and me with White Buffalo Woman and a nigger cowboy named Pepper Tom. We was quite a show in our own way.

In spite of what Tom had said about his puking up his poison, there was still an excess of alcohol in John's blood and the depression that came with it as an aftermath. Writing imaginary letters home was surely a form of this, and of homesickness. He looked around the ugly room, at all the ugly men and thought of the warmth and comfort of New House back on the other side of the Lake from the Landing. He thought of his father, smiling that rare once in a while when he said, "God, how your Ma could ride. Never seen nuthin' like it. Jest born to the saddle, horses bred right in her blood, her bein' a Morgan and all. Still can take a horse and outrun any ordinary man I know, but in the last years she's slowed some." John's father would laugh. "Got more staid, too, ain't you, Cam? She don't see it as proper now to run around wild on a horse the way she first done." His mother would give a snort. She knew he was teasing her, but she had never quite learned how to react to that kind of affection. If they were eating at the table, she would get up and start fussing with things on the stove.

Yes, he missed them, but he was still exuberant with the idea of being here—and when they got on the other side of the Missouri, once across the wide Missouri and into the real Independence and rid of Mason Raymond and the girl—

Mason Raymond rose, sepulchral, from his bunk and lumbered over, tall and bony beyond belief. So it was beans again. Mason Raymond only ate once a day; what did he care if it was beans, beans, beans. Mason Raymond probably *liked* beans. After all there was certainly no meat in these beans, just good gassy beans, not even a mean little strip of salt pork for flavoring. Beans probably make Mason Raymond feel more spiritual, like roots and tubers, elements of the earth. No animal flesh would pass his jaws and do unclean things to his insides. "You catch more flies with honey than vinegar," his mother said inside his head. "Sit down," John said to his cousin. "Might as well eat together as alone. When I come

West, I thought I'd be eatin' buffalo meat and beef. You remember how I used to brag I'd be eating bison steak for breakfast?'' An unfortunate allusion, John decided, considering Mason Raymond's feelings about animals. John floundered trying to find a way out of his predicament, stabbing about in his beans. Hung-over Tom reared up to the rescue, always willing to be a wealth of information on the range. "Bison all run off from these parts, you shoulda knowed that, killed off long ago, big white hunters, railroaders, those titley sportsmen from foreign parts, men got no sense at all. You see one once in a while, some stray, but the only real herds left is up in the north, where the Injuns is. Little further along the trail, you come on the pronghorns though—and they make mighty tasty eatin', I ken tell you. No beans for me," he said to the girl, rolling over. "I got a head on me the size of a bucket.

"A man with a big mouth and a bigger head,
Ain't got nuthin' more to expect than to be dead."

Mason Raymond was looking at his plate of beans abstractedly, a look—or rather the absence of one—that signified Mason Raymond had drifted off into his own world and was probably talking with one of his dead friends or concocting some woolly scheme where he could go about bringing all the quarreling countries of the world under one big umbrella that kept the rain away.

"You're goin' north," John said to him, trying to get a handle on his attention. "You'll see plenty of them pronghorns," he explained, "up there." It was no use. Mason Raymond nodded, serious, as if he were committed to the proposition that he would see lots of bison and pronghorns up north, but in reality he hadn't heard a word John had said. John turned his attention to the girl to see what he could work with her. "And you're goin' north," he said. "So how's come the two of you don't hitch up and go together since you're both goin' north in the same direction?"

"Well," she said tentatively. It was a *very* tentative "well." She looked at Mason Raymond, who was dwelling inside himself probably doing his visualizing and adorizing, and she took hold of him and gave him a shake. If you want a mule's attention, John's grandfather had once explained to him, you go out to the barn and you take this two-by-four and you slam him one over the head. And when the mule looks up, you say, "Now I got your attention . . ." Mason Raymond did not look up; all along John had known he was far worse than a mule. "You there," she said to Mason Raymond, "you there . . ."

"I been a trial to you," Mason Raymond said to John, suddenly shaking himself awake. "All along the way, I've been nothing but a trial to you and trouble. The whole way, I've held you back—one way or the other. I was a bother. I never pulled my weight. I held you back. I know that."

What was he supposed to say? Stubbornly John held to a half-truth. "It ain't your fault. It's jest the way thin's is."

"Tell me something," Mason Raymond said in that dead-serious way that drove John crazy. "What could I do to make things go—you know—go better now?"

Mason Raymond was hitched up right in front of him, but the picture John had in his head was of Mason Raymond standing out in the middle of the flats looking around in bewilderment about which way he was supposed to go. He was the kind who was always going to have trouble knowing which direction was the one to take. What could you say to someone like that how you made things go better?

"One of the reasons I know I'm so much trouble," Mason Raymond confessed, "is because I feel that about myself—that I'm a trouble to myself. I'm always a trouble to myself, always thinking about myself; I can't seem to get outside myself and forget about what's going on inside me and start thinking about what's happening to everyone else. The way I see it, the sign of a good person is one who can get outside, who can forget about himself and think about other people. But I don't know how to do that. I try and try, but I just don't seem to be able to do it."

The girl's face was all screwed up, intense and eager, ready to butt in, like she was a regular wealth of information on how to get along with other people—her, John thought—but Mason Raymond wasn't even looking at her—she might just as well not have existed—and as far as John was concerned personally, he sure as hell didn't care what she had to say. The nigger lay booze-blasted, quivering every once in a while and muttering he would never again mix the grape and the grain. What did I do to deserve these three? John asked himself, and then decided with absolute finality, *Nothing.*

Someone in the midst of unburdening himself of an obsession, Mason Raymond rattled on and on. "So I figured if I could get myself out here, get with people who were worse off than I am—not really worse off, but, you know, people other people thought were worse off—then maybe I could get out of myself—*atone,*" he said, using that awful word again. "Do you maybe understand?" he asked anxiously. It made sense the way he saw it. "The Indians are different, they don't live the way we do, they see things differently, they don't put their lives together the same way we do—it's as if they were looking for something else and understood other things than we do. They might understand, they might be able to help," he said. "And since I was part Indian—"

The girl was not to be denied. Some women just never learned their place. "The Injuns know *lots* of thin's white people don't know. You go up there," she said eagerly, "I bet you could find out lots of thin's you never even thought of, thin's other people, white people, don't see because they ain't learned to. You got to train to see the way the Indians do or you ain't never goin' to see what they see. But you got a start, bein' part Indian and all. You stand a chance you might be able to learn, but you can't jest go out and do it right off the bat."

"Well," John said enthusiastically. "There you are. I mean, it's jest like it was meant to be, you and her gittin' together. Here the two of you got the same aim in mind, the same determinations and destinations. Couldn't be more fortunate iffen you'd planned it out. Jest made for one another, jest as if it was all laid out."

They looked at him, perplexed; didn't seem to see. "You can both go off together," John explained. "You can both go up north to the Indians together." He was getting excited. The possibility of ridding himself of both of them so easily—

so logically, morally, guiltlessly (oh, the glory of it)—was like a reprieve from prison. He began to race through reasons. They both wanted to get to the Indians, right? Well, then, there you were. What could be clearer? They could go together. *Together?* they asked, turning and looking at one another and making instant inventories and evaluations, ones that obviously did not inspire inspiration; but John wouldn't let them off on the mere excuse of incompetence; he plunged on, no longer needing even to prove an absolute faith in efficiency; the pretext was good enough.

Of course they would get through. Nothing to it . . . just a matter of a little confidence. Why, with a couple of horses . . . and here his voice dropped and died. It wasn't as if they could all just go down to the stables and help themselves from a large assortment of finely boned steeds. There was Mason Raymond's old nag Mabel and the piebald outlaw of the range that had come along with the girl in the card game, and that was that. The damned nigger had let the decent horses go on a draw. My fault for giving him the money in the first place, John thought. Drunk-assed thing to do. Niggers ain't any of them got any sense of responsibility. Easy come, easy go.

Yet an uneasiness arose in John. His father, had he been able to read such thoughts, would have looked at him with contempt, and John respected his father's opinions because he thought of his father as a "good" man; yet he could never agree with his father on niggers or Indians. To John's way of thinking they were just plain inferior, no matter what his father thought; women, too (his mother of course excepted) —weak, willful, spoilt and spoilers: Well, the girl had come with the piebald, she could go with it just as well. "You got Mabel," John said to Mason Raymond. "Mabel's a good trustworthy animal. And her, she's—she's got that there animal that come with her." From his bunk Tom groaned. John ignored him. "With a little trainin' that horse would probably work out real well," he said optimistically.

Mason Raymond put his plate of beans down and looked at John. He was going to be bone honest and dirt-farm sincere and ruin everything. "I know I only asked you to bring me as far as Independence, that you got every right in the world to go off on your own now. You don't have to make any excuses. You've been more than fair. And I don't intend to impose anymore, I really don't. I don't want to hold you back no more, and I want you to understand that. And you get your stake, fair and square. Don't worry about that. You fulfilled your part of the bargain more than your share. You got a right to do what you want now—leave me go on my own, for instance, that's only fair, but I don't think you ought to saddle her with me. It wouldn't be fair to her to shove her off on me. She's got rights, too—all she's been through, she's got a right to more than me." He stood like a dumb, stricken animal. "I don't want to offend," he said to the girl. "I didn't, did I?" he asked anxiously. "But I'm no good on the road. I'm no good at all. I always go wrong. I try—I really do—and I'd be glad to have you come along—it isn't *that,* but I just think I'd be a thorn in your side. You'd be better off without me— much better off, the way I see it."

"Let her lead. She knows where the Injuns is. Let her do the directin' and you jest follow along," John said desperately. "You got to go," he said. "I got to git to the Hills. Every day I ain't on the way is a day gone, a day lost, a day wasted, one that someone else might be findin' the gold that might be mine. I can't spend a lot of time traipsin' around lookin' for some Injuns who's movin' this way and that all the time their-selves. You can see that, can't you?" Mason Raymond's head dropped forward; his eyes seemed to have lost all their color; his skin looked as if it had no blood beneath it. That pale skin said to John, No, I don't see. What good was gold? was what his face said plain as anything. Oh my god, what could you *do* with him?

Frustration and a sense of futility flowed through John as they had ever since he'd set out from Albany. He took hold of Mason Raymond (a trick he'd learned only a moment be-fore from the girl but one which he had recognized immedi-ately as productive) and shook him until he felt Mason Raymond's bones vibrating beneath his hands. "You gotta go! You gotta git off my back!" He was shaken by the feeling of his own violence but he also felt strangely relieved, as if in the sheer physical protest he had made he had at last forced Mason

Raymond to listen. All the rational explanations in the world didn't sometimes add up to one good blow.

"Hold off that yammerin'," the nigger yelled. "My head's stoved in enough without all that yammerin'. Ain't no need to argue anyway. We're all goin' across the River. Let 'em hang in with us till the Trail divides and then they kin go their way and we can shove off for the Hills."

John could have killed him. Why did he have to butt in? What business was it of his? The girl, okay, maybe she was some of his affair, but Mason Raymond was none of his business. He's jest a nosy old nigger, always sticking his two cents' worth in where it isn't wanted. Why can't he just be quiet and have his hangover on his own and stay out of what don't concern him? If he hadn't reared up and butted in, I'd be shut and free of the two of them. Even in this year of the centennial there were still apparently plenty of times to try men's souls. Not just the nigger but that damn girl, too, because the next thing she said was, "The Injuns is in the Hills. We's all of us headin' for the Hills, you know." There was absolutely no justice in this world. She should have died at eight under that canopy or been killed by the cavalry on that Indian raid or run off elsewhere with deserters or been won by some other sucker in a poker game, but—no—she had to go and get herself hitched up with them. No justice at all, *none.*

He was so angry with Tom he would have liked nothing better than to rattle his bunk until Tom's hung-over head burst but, incongruously, all he could think was—and a nigger shall lead them.

"That horse, that there piebald, it ain't so bad as it might let on. It's come along some," the girl said cautiously, "since it joined up with us. I mean, down to the barn when you're messin' around with it, it ain't so spooky and rackety as what it was."

"I wouldn't exactly say there was a radical change," John commented drily.

He watched while she turned away from him, obviously displeased, but holding her temper so that he wouldn't have any excuse to get rid of her. You'd have thought all those

] *105* [

negative experiences she'd been through would have weakened her will a little, but there was a powerful residue of conflict left in her, John saw. Nuthin' but trouble and expense, that's what she was goin' to be. It's what all women were. "Horse like that ain't good for nuthin'," John complained, "except kickin' up trouble." What he was implying was that she fit the same category.

Her eyes flashed for a moment; then she started scratching her elbow, a habit she had when she was agitated, but making an effort to keep her voice even, reasonable. "What if I was to tell you that in a day—maybe two—I could git that there horse so as you'd never want another one in your whole entire livelong life? What if I was to tell you I could git this here *this* horse so marvely that you'd come crawling on your hands and knees jest to thank me. What if I was to tell you that?"

"I'd say you had rocks in your head, that's what I'd say."

"You want to make a little bet? I heard you so lucky with cards, you want to make a bet with me I can't do that? Maybe I got a little learnin' you don't know nuthin' about inside this skull of mine. Maybe I got some ideas you ain't never even thought of; maybe I know a few things even you ain't cottoned to. You sayin' I'm willin' to make a bet on it and I'm sayin' if I do you kin have that horse—on one condition. We make it even odds."

"What do you mean 'even odds'?"

"I break that horse so as even you say it's broke right and you stake me to the Pass, and iffen I don't—"

"And iffen you don't?"

"Iffen I don't then I'll go away on my own and you'll be free and shut of me. You won't never need to see me one more thankless mile."

Strong persuasion, but he looked for the hidden snare behind it. Things were never what they seemed. She was looking apprehensively at Tom, who grunted, took his tobacco pouch and, pouring, gave a short laugh. "Way you feel," he said to John, "it's a bet I'd take any day. You reckonin' on tamin' that outlaw in *two* days, is that what you're tellin' us, girl?"

"That's what I'm sayin', yes, though I don't know it'll even be two."

God, the pride they put into women, it was something to see.

"Well," she said. "Ain't no time to start like the present." Even Mason Raymond was with them when she started down toward the barn. He appreciated maybe the crazy, though, more than anyone else, it came to John.

The piebald was backed up in a corner of its stall pawing, its eyes rolling, ears flat back against its head, teeth bared. "You're sure you're going to be all right?" Mason Raymond asked uncertainly. "That horse doesn't look any too safe to me."

"Jest fine," she said, as if she were going to prove to all of them she understood the law of the Trail as well as any man: Those that can't keep up are left behind.

Still, at the stall door, she paused, as if thinking over things for a last time. John went to the tack wall and got a bridle and started to hand it over to her. But she shook her head, no, she didn't want a bridle. She reached up and took a coil of rope off a wooden knob over the stall door.

"You ain't even gonna use no bridle?" John asked her.

"I don't need no bridle, jest some rope. You got some rope you can spare, this don't look too holdin', that is if it ain't puttin' you out too much to loan me a little rope?"

He got the rope, feeling like some kind of criminal. She took it off him without so much as a thank-you. John waited for the nigger to come up with some smart-alecky poem that would show who'd been put in whose place, but the darky was too wine-fogged to fudge around for poetry, it seemed. He leaned back on the far stall and rolled his eyes, then closed them, resting them, John supposed, waiting for the good parts but not expending any energy on the in-betweens.

She opened the stall and went in, closing the door behind her. Quick as a wink she threw the rope around the piebald's nose, then flung that back around its neck; she had fixed a loop, John saw, so that when she gave a strong pull the rope would cut off the mare's wind and bring it to a halt. Still, she must not have been all that confident because she said, "I may need a little help gittin' it out of town." She paused. "Best not to let her go through town. You could maybe"—she turned to John—"take the other horse, *his* horse"—nodding toward Mason Raymond; even she knew enough not to ask Mason Raymond to handle a horse in a difficult spot—"and iffen you'd crowd me to the outskirts I'd be much obliged for that."

"That weren't in the bet—"

"No, it weren't."

"I can't see no harm in a little help like that. That don't *break* the horse," the nigger said, and John was doubly furious at him; this was the second time he'd butted in where it was absolutely none of his business. I should have followed my first instinct, John thought—you can't trust a one of them. I'll never think of him as nuthin' but a nigger again, he thought. I'll be damned if I'll even call him by name. Why does he have to go and butt in where it's none of his business? But that goddam nigger just went right on interfering where he had no business being. "I don't mind fendin' for you atall," he was saying. "As a favor—to a lady," the nigger finished, smiling, only he wasn't being sarcastic, John realized with a start, just amiable and interested to see what she had in mind to break that miserable piece of horseflesh and maybe casting about for some diversion to take his mind off his stomach and head.

John watched in a helpless fury as the nigger went down and took down his saddle and headed for Mason Raymond's horse. The girl gave the rope on the piebald a jerk and swung the pony, unexpectedly, around toward the stall door. "Open up that door!" she commanded and even Mason Raymond jumped. John swung the bar back, and she came out at a fast clip, the piebald trotting along beside her. Tom gave a little whistle of appreciation and started working faster on getting mounted. The girl and the pony ran down the center aisle of the barn, the girl leading the pony or the pony leading the girl; it was hard to tell which. They sprang into the early spring sunshine—a beautiful day really for a girl to git herself all busted up. But it was her that made the bet, John reminded himself, not me.

Mason Raymond ran after the girl, though what he could do in a crisis besides pray was beyond John's ability to conceive, and from John's experiences he had never seen that prayers much changed animals, minerals, or men. And even if there were a God and He was listening, such supplications must only annoy Him. The faith of mountains had not moved men; why should a few small words on the wind? Wasted wind, wasted wasted breath. He'd been pointing that out to Mason Raymond ever since they left Albany, but maybe his prayers were a kind of magic to him. Other men nailed up horseshoes and carried rabbit feet; Mason Raymond lay down in gopher holes and made a tent of his hands.

As soon as Tom shot by him on Mason Raymond's horse, John panted after on foot; they were headed for the water, the great divider. For a flash he remembered his early optimism that once at the Missouri everything would be better. All men, it came home to him, had their superstitions.

The pace was terrible. He was sweating and sucking for air as they careened down the last shabby streets of Wayne City before the tie-ups and the wharves; the girl must be absolutely exhausted because she was running harder and faster than any of them to keep abreast with the piebald (and of course the nigger couldn't have done it at all on foot with his hangover and god alone could keep track of Mason Raymond), but the girl yanked and tugged and turned the piebald away from the busy part of the piers. She was heading for open country. John had to admire her determination, but that admiration was a grudging emotion inside him, angering him, making him feel smaller in his own eyes, as if maybe he didn't know as much about people as he thought he did, and if that were true, he didn't have his life wrapped up as tight as he thought he did —a flaw so bad, if it were true, that it frightened him. Most people only lived from day to day, trying to deal with dangers as they appeared; but smart people had strategies that foresaw the hazards of the future and made plans to avoid them.

They had reached the end of town, but the girl kept going. John didn't understand what she was hunting for. They were out in the open now; why didn't she start schooling the horse?

She's goin' to swim that mare out, he thought suddenly, remembering he'd heard stories of how the Indians broke their horses by letting them fight against water, letting the water tire them out. It was hard for a horse to fight a strong current and if it tried to buck or rear, the water held it back.

Even if a rider got dumped, the water acted as a cushion to the fall.

She ran along the wide bank taking in the lay of the land, the depth of the water, the strength of the current, checking everything out until she was satisfied she had found the right spot. She jerked the pony's rope to get it stopped, took off her ratty sweater and threw it down, the piebald rearing and plunging and kicking against restraint as she stripped off her broken shoes and torn stockings and tied up her dress around her legs (exposing thin white freckled limbs); then, grabbing mane, she hoisted herself up on the piebald's back. The pony braced itself and rocked back on its hind legs, ready to rear. The girl was talking a blue streak and hanging on for dear life; but the little mare spun around and bolted, galloping off in a cloud of dust. Tom was sitting in the saddle watching, but they'd lost Mason Raymond somewhere back in the rush.

John saw that the piebald was one of those hard-hooved animals that dig in and pick up momentum, dig in again, get going real fast, stop and dig in more, and then run in sprints, digging in and increasing speed and going full force until there was no stopping the runaway streak; racing like that was born in the bones, no way on this earth to teach it, more some inner vision that horse had and was running to, something it saw no one else did, than anything learnable.

"My gawd, what a pair of runnin' legs that little black-and-white has got on her," the nigger said.

John was still too mad at him to answer.

The piebald suddenly stopped, went down on its knees, then up in the air, as if a bee had stung it, then plunged sideways and spun in a circle, a dazzling display of quick movements all calculated to unseat the rider; John held his breath.

The girl slid to one side and threw her bare legs around the belly of the little mare, clinging like a burr; the pony went up in the air again and came down with a crash. Tom kicked Mason Raymond's horse and John ran forward. "Git back, git away," the girl screamed at them. The little mare righted herself and bolted out toward the far end of the sky. In back of him John could hear what sounded like sobs or sighing or maybe even singing, noises so queer no normal human being made them. Mason Raymond must have arrived.

A circular cloud of dust revealed the whirlwind path of the pony who seemed, if you could trust the patterns of dust, to be galloping round in small, concentric circles, but John knew that circling meant the girl was gaining control because if she could get the animal to confine its dash within the limits of a circle, she could slow it; eventually she might even get it stopped. And she would have winded it bad and taught it a fundamental lesson it needed to know: that she was smarter than it was strong.

He watched and waited and presently he saw the little pie-bald slow, steady, almost stop—then break free and bolt again. The next view he had was a small puff of what looked like smoke disappearing down the long lonely stretch of prairie, vast and empty and stung by sun, with one lone shadow, a smudge from an overhead cloud, making a small hopeless thumbprint on the awful emptiness of a land that seemed to run on forever to nowhere.

Mason Raymond was caved in on the ground, holding himself together with his arms, awful racking sounds rattling him around inside the protective circle of his arms. One thing you could say for Mason Raymond: He took things hard. On the other hand, the nigger sat, stoical, on the horse, staring off into that particle of space into which horse and girl had disappeared as if everything that happened was inevitable and emotion, any emotion, a waste of energy. To get through life, his inert posture suggested, you had to be totally disengaged from all involvement.

John sat down to wait, staring at the muddy river—the rivers of the West, it seemed, were all muddy: the muddy Mississippi, the muddier Missouri; he longed for the clear, rustling streams of back East instead of these stagnant brown holes called creeks or the wide long lanes of moving mud that were named rivers, marooned in the monotony of the dust and dirt, the endless dryness of the air and the buzz and throb inside his head from bugs and heat and dust; and the mud, everywhere the mud and slop. Buzzards and bobwhites dipped and dropped in the endless open bowl of sky overhead, a porcelain cup on which, for a moment, he imagined one of those signs he had seen on the trail, signs someone had pasted up as a reminder that the human hand could try in its own small way to imprint itself on this vast landscape, tacking up an irregular little square that announced

THIS
IS A
ONE-HEARSE
TOWN

The hinterlands: the hunter lands where John Buttes from back East squatted down on his hams in the lengthening sun and thought about what it was like to think about going on a trip and what it was like to really be on it. God alone knew where she had got to—or, more accurately, where the horse had carried her off to.

But she'll be back, he thought. Any fool knows that you don't git rid of the people who give you troubles. Still, he was uneasy. She had been gone an inordinately long time; hours, it seemed to him. "What's happened to her?" John was so agitated that for a moment he forgot his anger with the nigger and his voice sounded friendly but then he remembered the nigger butting in and his voice got cold and he would in no way call him by name.

"I don't rightly know. I don't rightly have a handle on that one." The answer came a moment later when she roared up out of the horizon and headed straight for them. Mason Raymond stood up, gaping, but John gave a shout at him to run and began making time himself. He didn't know what the nigger was going to do and he didn't care since whatever happened to him he had brought on himself, but he himself was going to get the hell out of the way.

The mare smashed toward him, trying to kick him with its hind legs as it thrashed past. John tried to shrivel himself up as the pony and girl made a sharp turn back on him and he watched, disbelieving, as they began to circle, going round and round as if they could wind him up in an invisible cord. John was trying to run away from them, going in circles himself, dizzy, but running with all his might, with only one thought in mind, to get clear of those two, but the piebald was faster than he was and he was going to be cornered; just as he turned to strike out at the mare, he heard the girl yell; but she flashed by him and into a thicket of brush; the pony sailed over a hurdle of fallen trees and careened between two thick standing trunks so massive and close together that the space between seemed made for elves. He screamed "Jump!" but the girl and horse got through; possibly they passed, like shadows through solids; anything was possible, John had decided, in a world where he would end up with a nigger, a lunatic, a squaw woman, and a maniac of a horse.

The girl screamed and the piebald went airborne, suspended over a tangle of brush and wood at least five feet high, hanging motionless over the debris, then crashing down on its knees, the girl somersaulting over the mare's head, the horse lying on its side. Both of them had to be dead. He scrambled toward her.

She was not only living, she was thriving on the intensity of her rage, hanging over the horse and beating the shit out of it. There was not to be any more genteel equivocation of *this*. "Git up, you mangy godforsaken critter," she shrieked. "Git up before I skin you alive. You know better than that."

Reluctantly the animal, mud-encased, rose, the goddamest worst-looking sight John Buttes could ever remember laying eyes on. The girl jumped back on and the pony stumbled forward, limping, looking as if it had suffered a major injury in its spill. "Don't give me any of that there *this* shit," the girl screeched. "I know you, you goddam faker." She reached overhead and grabbed a half-broken branch and brought it down with a resounding *crack* on the little mustang's flank. The mare left off limping and went briskly into the rapids. "Oh my god," Benjie Klomp shrieked, "this water is jest freezin'."

The horse looked worn out and the girl done it; they seemed to float free on the current, the mare spinning this way and that and the girl lying dazed across the mare's neck with that tacky dress plastered wet against her, hair tangled and matted, arms entwined around the horse's neck, hanging on for dear life. John hollered to her to give it over, she'd made her point, but she was either too ornery to answer or too tuckered out to try.

She was leaning over the horse's neck crooning endearments. "Good girl," she was saying. "Good girl." Having broken the piebald, she was now trying to give her back some semblance of spirit. One thing John had to admit: that showed a good heart.

When the girl finally rode the horse out of the water, she said, "This here *this* horse ain't gonna trash on us no more. I'm goin' home—oh, I'm goin' up to the Powder and home—" and she slipped down and flung her wet arms around John's neck. He was horrified as she clung, sobbing out her gratitude; he was engulfed in the smell of wet horsehair, wet human hair, an odor so acrid that he gasped while she hung on, half strangling him, the horse hopping around with what little energy it had left, John desperately trying to extract himself from her stranglehold because he might not be smart about much but one thing he knew for sure: The least response you made to anyone, especially a woman, the more that meant you were willing to take on responsibilities. And he wanted nothing, absolutely nothing, to do with her. Period. End of argument. Finish of the affair.

Two

The Start

I

Tom's grandfather used to say: The year is composed of a thousand seasons. He might better have said, There are a thousand seasons to a man's soul. Tom thought about that a moment and then decided it was only true for some men; probably most men were more even-dispositioned than he was; he hoped most men had less sadness in their systems than he did and less of his restlessness. Maybe part of that sadness and impatience came from being black; he didn't know, there were so many things he didn't know. But he did know that to survive you had to take one bad thing at a time and try to deal with it; you couldn't try to deal with everything at once or you got overwhelmed. Take the matter of the horses, for instance. There was a problem enough for you without even beginning to speculate about what was going to happen to the girl and that Raymond boy. Concentrate on the particular and let the general take care of itself.

The Buttes boy over there was fussing and fuming because he had to walk while the Raymond boy rode his nag. Tom had lost the Buttes boy's horse at cards, but by rights of Buttes's bet with the girl the piebald now belonged to him, but he

wouldn't ride. You had to give him credit for that. The girl
had broke the horse, it was in a way then her horse, Buttes had
said, stubborn, absolutely refusing to ride, even though she'd
traded it off; yet mad, too, because Tom had told them horses
would be much cheaper the further on they went. Marysville
would be about right for buying, but they'd be gouged sure
in Independence. Trading and tricks were a way of life with
Tom. But boys didn't know that yet. Well, life was tricking
and trading. They'd learn one day.

She and the horse come with the cards and now she done
a trade on Buttes and he don't know how to handle what he
won. That little mare, it's his but it ain't his 'cause he didn't
break it. She got him there, Tom thought. So there was Buttes,
sullen and resentmentful, driving the mule they'd bought with
their poker winnings, a good solid-backed animal that could
carry four people's gear—though the girl certainly didn't have
any possessions worth mentioning—the Buttes boy mad as a
hatter about tending a mule and going on foot; but there were
other problems as well, ones Tom hadn't anticipated, and
though he didn't want to have to deal with them, there was
no way to put them off because they were immediate; you
can't ignore what's pummeling you right in the face. The
Buttes boy worried him, not just because he was mad about
walking but because he was restless and agitated; he'd been
talking excitedly all along about crossing the Missouri, but
when they got there and he saw it was just a big muddy river,
no different really from any other big muddy river, going
across had seemed to have been a big disappointment to the
boy; he was sulking about the fact, Tom was sure, that there
hadn't been some big monumental difference between one
side of the river and the other. Tom could identify with that
let-down feeling, the disappointment that comes from having
your heart set on something and then not getting it because
what you got was so small it didn't count. All of which made
the girl's feat with the piebald an even bigger thing.

Yet there *was* a difference: Across the river meant the defi-
nitive line between East and West. The trans-Missouri country
was a land that stretched from the bend of the river to the
headwaters of the mountains like a giant thumb that stood

from the Missouri up to Canada, down deep into Texas to all the places Tom had been and seen and the many things that had happened to him. Though Kansas and Missouri had been states since 1860, they were still mainly wilderness and wildness. Only the Eastern part of Kansas was what you might call civilized. Out beyond lay the territories. Things *were* different on the other side of the Missouri, but the boy just couldn't see that yet.

I could set you up such a list of future disappointments they'd last you twice a lifetime, he wanted to say to the boy, but he kept his mouth shut, having, he thought (for once), enough sense to know the young don't want to hear from the old how bad life's going to be on them.

They don't believe it anyway, Tom thought. Each and every one of us at the start thinks we're special, we're going to get what everyone else doesn't. Well, a few do, he reminded himself. Damned few. And who chooses those? he wondered.

For a moment he was overwhelmed by looking back, seeing the bare outlines of his life, with failure after failure and disappointment after disappointment chalked up against the score of his life—right from the beginning, born black in a slave shack already empty of the father who'd sired him, grown up in the fields stealing education where he could—laws against niggers even learning, and all his reading and writing had been because his mother and grandfather had been determined even if he wasn't a house nigger, he was going to get what he could. It was the fierceness of their determination, not his own native drive, that had got him the book learning made such a difference later; but then, right from the start, he must have been a disappointment to them; he had to be prodded and forced toward something he should have thirsted for himself; then later, the Army years and the Trail, and two or three women he had cared about, but never really with enough self-discipline to get himself in harness to settle down; drifting from one thing to the next, with no sense of an outline to his life, just letting things happen, seeing how they'd work out instead of trying to shape life himself.

The very fact he was a bachelor seemed to him a symbol of his inability to grasp hold of the events around and try to order them; he was content with the chaos, the drifting, the bobbing about without direction. Women were trouble; they tried to tie a man down and they had this drive to make objective their feelings, to put a name on love with children, as if only in bringing that new combined flesh into the world could they satisfy their need to know their love had come to something.

Having this Benjie along was going to mean the kind of trouble only a woman could bring—grumbling, organizing, forever tidying up—he didn't like it at all.

Lord help me when a woman catches me by the hair,
Ain't nuthin' after that ever goin' to be straight and fair . . .

A good woman, a good bottle of wine—the wine first, of course, so that it made the blood rise, and what you did after came natural with the woman you were with. Some women liked it straight but some had real strange notions inside their heads, and for Tom these were the most interesting. Still, it wasn't like you wanted a woman around all the time—any more than you'd want wine around all the time. Anything you got accustomed to lost its specialness. And those demands—those needs to tidy up life. He wasn't made for that.

But, god, he missed his horse. Gone in the gambling, like so much else in his life. He was getting old, missing a lot of the good horses he'd had in his life, the horses, and a few of the women, and most of all Jonathan, he ought never have taken so much offense at what was most probably just an innocent little remark—after all, all Jonathan had really said, and that off-handedly, was, "You're white clean through"; he probably even hadn't meant it the way Tom took it— but the young are quick to a sense of slight, hotheaded, so either/or. You get older you get more reasonable, you're readier to excuse, to forgive and forget. Still he felt sad about the loss of some of that pigheadedness of his youth, all those temper storms when he'd felt he had to prove he was as good a man as any, black or white. But the young were always too hot-tempered. It cost them a lot they regretted later in life.

Forty-nine. That was old for this country. The West had always been a young men's country—rough young men who could ride. He considered the tragedy of a man like Greeley who'd run for President and lost, whose wife had died, and who'd ended up insane, people said, a man who'd had greatness in him and it had all gone for nothing in the end. Even the ones that seemed singled out for some significance looked lost and lonely when you looked at them in the end. The grief of growing old was in the increasing ability to see how life left you with so little of what you'd hoped for when you started out.

He looked at Mason Raymond. No one in the West could really get along who couldn't sit a saddle right, who didn't learn how to get legged up properly. Raymond was hopeless until he could learn to ride, and if he hadn't learned to ride in a thousand miles, Tom had pretty well concluded he was never going to. He had no business out here at all really any way you looked at it—he couldn't ride and never would; he didn't carry a gun and would be useless in a fight. You had to be able to ride and you had to be able to fight out here in order to survive. And Mason Raymond couldn't do either and never would. But there was something about him, a kind of courage Tom couldn't put his finger on. In the old days that kind of courage would have been meaningless, useless, but everything was changing; maybe a new kind of man was needed. He didn't know, he truly didn't, since he was from a different time, before barbed wire, when the range was open and the cattle runs went for hundreds of miles unhindered. Before barbed wire, before sheep, before windmills, before the Plains could have water dredged up and farms fenced in and cattle kept out. Barbed wire stopped the drives and the windmills made puny little gardens grow out of the sod. Two little inventions had changed the whole Plains; it was as simple as that.

Hard winters and dry summers: that's what he remembered of the drives. The cattle, of course, that went without saying because in those days all their lives were really tied to the cattle and to their horses because in such a vast, uninhabitable land there was no place for a man on foot; so with the cattle went the horses—cows, horses, courage. Lots of men came in, but an awful lot of them didn't stay. Something fundamental was lacking in their makeup; they couldn't get along because they just couldn't make do with so few things, they couldn't adapt or change or fit in—Tom wasn't quite sure which, maybe a combination of all three—but the country could only tolerate a certain breed of men; the others were weeded out by a natural process.

A sense of loss and a feeling of dread for the few months left in his forties haunted him, and watching those two young bucks and that girl didn't help—it was like it was all ahead of them, maybe not so much for the girl, but even she had a lot left to go on; but the two boys, he knew how they felt—that they had all the time in world to make mistakes and correct them. That's the way they probably felt, and he felt as if he didn't have any time at all. He knew too much and they knew too little and both were bad, but Tom didn't know any way in the world you struck a delicate balance where the world seemed just right—oh, a moment or two, yes, but nothing lasts. What was it the Buttes boy had said about the wheel—it went round and you with it; on the way up everything went with you, and on the way down everything was against you; but what the Buttes boy failed to say, and what Tom saw, was the way up went by with dizzying speed and the way down went slowly and interminably. Life seemed so far oftener down than up.

Maybe he oughtn't to have joined up with them. They were too young and eager and underexposed. He would never truly be with them in anything, some part of him always detached and observant, ironical of their youth, but jealous, too, heartsick with the feeling of loss.

Up ahead the two horses went side by side down the trail, Raymond out in front wobblily saddled to his horse and the girl bareback on the piebald swinging her legs as she went, happy and chatty, as if once she started talking there was no stopping her. A real free spirit, as his grandfather would have said, and his grandfather set a lot of store on spirits being free; it was a shame he didn't live to see the day a nigger could ride a good horse and not get hanged or shot doing it.

The two riders seemed all right in their way, but the Buttes boy was sulking, tramping along tugging at the mule. He was still put out about their buying a mule and not horses, but a mule was an absolute essential for hauling gear, and for the time being he and the Buttes boy could walk and wait on the horses. That horse the Raymond boy had wouldn't hold up on the prairie, but it would do for now, and the little piebald— he grinned—a real tough little mustang if ever he'd seen one. Tom had an eye for a good horse, just as he prided himself on knowing wines (learned that off the Captain he'd served with during the War, a Boston man who said no gentlemen ate his dinner without the proper wine nor courted a lady without the proper rhyme); he'd been horse conscious all his life, got it from his grandfather, who would say how those devil overseers could ride all day long on one of their good plantation walkers and it wouldn't even work up a little sweat on the horse. Niggers had reason to hate those horses, but most of them couldn't help admiring them. Tom's grandfather had stole one right out of the boss's barn and took off—he was going North, he said; he didn't care, he was an old man, he'd waited long enough. Didn't take no time at all to catch him up, a nigger on a good animal like that and out on the road without a proper pass. They strung him up right off the horse; leastwise that was the story that came back, and Tom had no reason to disbelieve it. Certainly it was the kind of economical nigger killing white men went in for. Wrap a rope around a black neck, give the horse a smart swat, the horse went forward and the black man hung behind.

He knew, that old man, when he set out he wasn't going to git nowhere but git caught. What he want to set out to such surefire finding for? Maybe he was ready to go. He was old and tired and wore out, a field nigger who had never done nothing but bend back in the cotton rows, and now he was slowing down he was constantly being prodded and harassed to keep up, consumed with a scathing bitterness at the injustices that had piled up on him one after another all his life. He had only held out one hope, one vindication, for all his misery, and that was that one of his blood would be born light enough to get out of the fields and up to the house, to be a house nigger instead of a field nigger, and he'd watched first his children and then his grandchildren come out "black," as he said bitterly, "black as the ace of spades."

I took after him in more ways than one, Tom thought, but I don't think that was no source of pride to him. He jest seen I was gonna have one long list of trials for a life same as he had. But at least mine's been varied and what you might call in-ter-rest-ing while his was jest plain mud. Like the river back there, he thought, grinning, looking at the sulky boy prodding the balky mule along, one as bad as the other for stubbornness.

It's the river all right made the boy so mad. And the mule ain't been no help. The mule was irritable, but that was constitutional with mules—

Oh, cows is lax, and horses come dumb,
But in all this wide world you plumb
Any animal you know for the fool
Harm a dang-blasted ordinary mule
Can do . . .

The winter cold had deadened the long prairie grass and in the old days at the height of the Trail in the forties and fifties wagon trains could not set out until new growth came through or there would be no feed for the stock, but everyone had to be out of Independence by mid-May to get through before the bad storms hit in the mountains and could catch and keep them there, like it did to the Donner party, and kill them off with cold and starvation. He thought of Donner, so confident, going out with forty thousand dollars strapped to a money belt around his waist and not having any idea he was going to get caught in those mountains.

Tom'd been over the trail up from San Antonio to Abilene so many times he could close his eyes and feel by the jolts and ruts where he was, but this trail to the Sweetwater he'd only run once there and back and he had to keep a sharp eye out; there were all kinds of troubles and dangers to be avoided or circumvented. He wasn't worried about Indians, not around here leastwise; the only red gentlemen left here weren't likely to have it in their heads to do a little molesting of his scalp; they were too demoralized, dirty, and lazy for more than some petty thieving; up North in the Hills where the Oglala and the

Brulé and Hunkpapas were, that was a different story; he'd have to take the proper precautions to keep campfires small during the light hours and move around as noiseless as possible, keep the fires doused at night, and muzzle the horses and mule, but he'd worry about up North when he got there. You got plenty troubles every day, his granddaddy used to say, not to borrow on into the future. Anyway, the things you worry so much about up ahead ain't usually the bad ones lying in wait. You think back on the last year and all the things you was afraid of and you consider all the bad things really did done happen, you see most of the time there ain't no connection between the two. But people always ready to shake hands with the Devil before they meet up with him.

The first three miles after the river till they got to Independence itself were full of expectation and the city itself a wonder, laid like a checkerboard with its big brick courthouse with the conical roof and the park all around, the big hotels and fancy stores (and some of the most rascally-looking people in the world), but then the next seven or eight miles had been rocky and hard going; now the trail flattened out—they weren't really at the plains yet, but the land was leveling out flat and even the smell of the air felt different; they were really West, whether John Buttes saw it yet or not; that was the way Tom felt, slapping the mule on the rump and trying to get it interested in moving on. Mules had a way of disassociating themselves from people's plans; they didn't seem to take much enthusiasm in anything asked of them. They understood they were beasts of burden and not objects of affection, and they had sense enough to learn the prime lesson men never seemed to absorb, that you should only invest your love in that which will love you back.

Tom was content just to walk along, as if the walking itself were a proof he was better on his legs than most men his age, but there was a concern in his mind that kept nagging at this pleasure, intruding to tell him that there was going to be trouble. For one thing, those two boys, they were too different, the one too passive and without sufficient interest in his own survival and the other blazing with excessive arrogance in his energy and competence. And to complicate matters there was the girl—a combination that spelled trouble no matter what angle you looked at it from. Somethin' in you jest *takes* to turmoil, you ole coon, he said to himself, couldn't even help chuckling, thinking of all the scrapes he'd been through and then it was almost as if he had deliberately set himself up for one more, hitching up with these three. The kid there had wanted to siphon off the weak and let them flounder for theirselfs and if he'd only kept his mouth shut, why he and the boy could have gone off to the Hills probably with no trouble at all; but, no, when the girl spoke up that they was all headed the same way, he jest couldn't keep his gums shut, he'd spoke up for her—too many possibilities for high jinks, so here they all were trudging into the Shawnee Mission, eight miles from Independence, a large handsome complex of brick buildings that looked almost Southern in design; if they'd been white instead of red, Tom could easily have pictured them back down South. He had a momentary stab of what could only be described as homesickness. No matter where you were born or what happened to you during your early years, "home" was back there where you grew up.

The Shawnees had donated two thousand acres of land for their boys to be taught blacksmithing and brick masonry, for the girls to learn to spin and weave and sew and cook the white way, living upstairs in the long attic dormitories of these elegant brick buildings now baking under the Kansas sun. But you had to hand it to the Methodists; they weren't throwing up second-rate missions, even for Indians. The blacks had never done near so well. What churching and learning they got they got on their own and most often against laws saying they couldn't learn to read and write; blacks weren't supposed to be Christianized because Christians could be saved, and you couldn't have a saved slave. He thought of Sherman's march to the sea and the great beautiful buildings so like these burned and looted. Well, he was never going "home" again. Freeing the slaves had only made things worse for them in many ways. Where, for instance, were the forty acres and the mules that were supposed to go to the freedmen?

People who lose wars never forget, he thought. Years from now—god knows how long—the hatred will still be there.

The Mission had been sold off fifteen or twenty years before, closed for lack of students, the Indians let loose to roam around the prairies unbaptized; Civil War troops had been quartered in its beautiful buildings; now the property was privately owned and the owners would put you up for a price; the once-beautiful grove gone—a watering place all the prairie pioneers remembered, and now it was no more than a fading memory of the great days past. He mourned greatness gone even as he stopped with the others and bathed his swollen feet in the little stream that ran by the red brick buildings, admiring the first spring flowering here that was in bud, red clusters of maple, Indian apple, and the first prairie wild roses he had seen; later, he knew, there would be whole fields floating in rose. A pair of eagles hung free in the empty air over the farthest building of the mission, and he heard a hidden spring purl softly somewhere in the midst of the few trees left.

It was a moment of quiet and loveliness, and he took it in greedily. Nothing lovely lasted long. A moment later the mule, which kept winding itself up in its rope and moaning in a high querulous way, commenced seesawing and putting its rear end out and laying back its ears ready to kick. There was no way to talk to it in any real friendly way because it didn't even have a name. Tom was tired and would have liked to lay up a bit, but he knew the Buttes boy was edgy—his disappointment crossing the river and his irritation with the mule had made him ready to pick a fight—with his cousin sure enough, Tom thought, if I don't git them all on their feet and movin' agin. You keep busy you don't have time to think. You keep movin', you don't have time to pick fights.

The road scalloped around some rickety-looking scrub and a sick-looking stand of trees and came sharply down a slope past the narrow stream that ran through the Mission. John was still having problems driving the mule, and snatched up a stick and set to beating it belligerently; and the Raymond boy, even though he was riding, looked tuckered out, but the girl rode happy and carefree, as if she didn't have a worry in the world. Tom smelled the mule and John and then a new smell, just as bad, himself, the sweat of his own armpits and crotch and feet coming up in the blazing high overhead sun. Last year in the Hills there had been sixty-seven consecutive days of rain, the winter had been one to set a record, and the wet, snowy spring a mud springer; now this early spring heat—so unseasonable —would bring out the bugs sure. They needed coal oil or bear grease to keep the insects away—but that would make them smell worse, too.

The road was so crooked that old-timers used to say Satan spit it down that way, and the little column lurched this way and that over the rough road until Mason Raymond let out a yell as he began to ford Indian Creek and the cold brown chocolate-colored waters came up and splashed about his pants, and Tom shook his head: a goddam country where you were either too hot or too cold, too wet or too dry, muddy or dusty, but never anything in between.

They were making their first stop at Lone Elm campground, the usual stopover for the first night past Westport. The pioneers had taken two days after Independence to reach the spot, but that was because they had long, disorganized columns of wagons, people, and livestock, and they were all overloaded and right off the bat they started experiencing the first problems of the trail; the emigrants were ignorant and overeager and that combination was a sure invite to calamities.

Someone had long ago cut down the lone elm for firewood, and Tom took the mule and tied it up, hobbled the horses as slowly, surgingly, the plains began to sink away into the encroaching darkness. The far hills grew faint, dimmed into shadowy purples, disappeared into the engulfing darkness. The whole horizon seemed to sink into the watery twilight; it rippled and rose and sank before Tom's tired eyes. The boys had begun arranging their gear, an occupation which was, he thought later, to become the single unifying theme of his trip with them. They were always packing or unpacking, repacking in order to try to get a new or better arrangement for things. They could never accept what any experienced trailman knew: There was no best arrangement. Reorganizing was a way of life along the trail, any trail—that and the feeling of earth and dust and grit flying up in your face.

They ate cold. He didn't mind so long as he kept a supply

of tobacco on hand, but the others would probably have liked the comfort of a campfire and something hot. Even with guns, the game was gone, as he had told them back at the bunkhouse. The emigrants had killed or driven the game off early, and by 1850 most of the bison had disappeared from the Platte River Valley. When they disappeared, they left the emigrants —and those who came after—not only without meat but also without the precious buffalo "chips," the manure that could be used as fuel on the long stretch of the trail, and their presence would have made building a fire no problem. But all along the trail now fires were going to be a difficulty because there were no chips and long ago the wood had been picked clean.

Even when they got to pronghorn country, there was going to be trouble with Raymond, who wouldn't touch meat. What kind of man only ate once a day (when he could get more) and lived on fruits and nuts and would not even touch animal fat?

Talk came hard—not just because they were tired but also because they were so unalike. In one way, Tom thought, they were almost like a miniature world all their own—all the problems of their differences, their jealousies and fears, held them apart. He took down his bedroll and lay down, looking up at the black sky and getting ready for his last smoke of the night. He still had a few treasured cigarettes left. All small children, even black children, were afraid of the dark. Light was good. You felt safe during the day and afraid at night in the dark. The dark boded evil, a piece of knowledge that troubled him often. Now it came again, that uneasiness over color, as he looked up into the almost starless sky. It was too early for the moon, for most of the stars. To be born black posed so many problems. He knew well enough to be born at all posed problems, but to be black made whole new dimensions. He felt the old hollow nameless unhappiness, the old wonderment of what it would be like to be white, the fear and the superstition that were among man's oldest: that the black was bad.

The girl looked up from a scrappy little fire as he woke up and her eyes widened and she began to wring her hands as if he had given her a bad jolt and she was going to start feeling funny all over. The fear was real enough even if the reason wasn't.

He didn't know, he didn't know. People were all so afraid of so many things. And of course they were right. There were so many things to be afraid of. But he was just surprised and pleased to see she'd got a fire going. He wasn't mad about it.

The mule and the horses were nowhere in sight. Run off, Tom thought. Well, that's one way to begin the day. No day begins fresh, his grandfather used to say. They all come in with the pus of the past. A black bitter man, his grandfather, no two ways about it—but with reason, with reason.

"The horse needed a little working," the girl said modestly, casting her eyes down. "So I run her some to let her git rid of her morning spirits. And I found some good new grass over there so I drove them up that way. And a little wood. So I thought I'd git a fire goin'—it's good to start the day with somethin' hot," she said, all flamed up with the heat of pride, her cheeks burned red with it. She'd shown them, she had. All Tom felt was relief. He was glad enough not to have to run around looking for lost animals out in the middle of nowhere what with everything else there was to do. And he liked to "start the day hot," too—coffee lifted the soul.

"You like johnnycakes?" she asked. "Likely you're wolfish after all that walkin', nuthin' real proper put in you last night. You didn't eat enough supper to satisfy a mosquiter."

"You ever walked for a cake?" he asked. She looked at him. "Niggers, they strut all the time back down South for a big fancy cake. Don't tell me you never done heard of a cake-walk."

"Not up where I been," she said drily, and he wanted to laugh. She'd almost made a joke—things were looking up. When people began to joke and laugh, the tensions went away. Them two, Tom thought, looking at John and Mason Raymond, they ain't *never* gonna let down and laugh together. That's one thin' I can count on.

He felt depressed again, then brightened, thinking of the girl taking him to task for thinking there were cakewalks up in Indian camps. She was grinning a little so she'd got up out of the right side of the blanket this morning. "I weren't so done in in the joints I could show you a thin' or two about struttin'," he said. "I done walked some in my day, I can tell you. Before the War," he said, and felt deflated again thinking of it. He wondered what it was wars won. Certainly not forty acres and a mule. Won me the right to come out West and let the Indians and the Army mo-lest me, and he started grinning again, cheered up. Forty-nine wasn't *dead*.

"Old man like me can still eat johnnycake though." He crumbled part off and ate. "Not bad," he said. "Not bad atall. What other wonders you got up your sleeve 'sides good horse sense and some fine fire cookin'?"

She turned away, a sulky look on her face, offended. She thought he was joshing her, making fun of her Indian training maybe; he didn't know, who did with women? But one thing sure—her dignity had been injured. Tom let it go. They had a long day ahead. Better to save his strength.

And a moment later he needed it.

"How's come you never do your share?" John Buttes demanded. He was standing with a skillet in his hand. He had been giving the girl a hand with the cleaning up, scouring out the skillet with sand; everything seemed quiet and orderly, and then suddenly the Buttes boy was standing in a towering rage saying to Mason Raymond, "You haven't done shit's share of your part of the work ever since we started out."

Tom had expected a flareup between the two boys, but not this soon. After a while dust and dirt and monotony and fatigue caused a certain kind of craziness on the Trail that was familiar to old-timers, but this was too early for that reaction to have set in. So it was something else that had triggered the Buttes boy's anger. Then Tom thought, It's 'cause *he's* got a horse and he ain't. He thinks he's downrank because he has to walk and look after the mule and he's all boiled up because Raymond's got a horse and ken ride and *he* can't.

"You're a menace to everyone—everyone walkin' around on this goddam earth. Can't you see that, for crissake? Jest look around you. You wouldn't survive five seconds if it wasn't for one of us, and yet you ain't even got the sense to try to do your own share of the little bit of the work you can do." The Buttes boy flung the skillet on the ground with a great crash. "*You* clean it up. *That* ain't too much to ask is it, jest to sand out a little skillet."

Mason Raymond picked up the skillet and started scouring it out. He didn't say anything, keeping his eyes on the pan, not even following the figure stalking off to where the horse and mule were staked out. "Goddam fuckin' mule," John Buttes raged. "Goddamest fuckingest mule in the whole of this goddam fuckin' existence." Tom sighed. He would have to do something right now or matters were going to get so bent out of shape that he might not ever be able to set them back where they belonged. Well, it wasn't as if he hadn't had plenty of practice on the trail in situations like this. But you never got used to dealing with murderous rage no matter how many times you ran up against it.

Tom got up slowly. If you moved too fast when a man was this mad, you enraged him more. He lumbered over to where Buttes was stomping about in an effort to work out his anger in exercise. When Tom's mother was mad, she used to move furniture—what there was of it. She would steam and storm and lather up and then suddenly she'd collapse in a chair and cry. He knew a lot about frustration himself, but he had come to appreciate that no one probably knew as much about it as a black woman. He'd never known his father; traded off before Tom was even born.

As Tom came up to the boy, he had a sudden insight that he had perhaps taken up with these boys because he cast himself in just that role. He was at the age for fancying such foolishness, that was sure enough. Crazy old coon, he said to himself, your head's all turned around. You're goin' to father these boys?

He didn't try to speak to the boy; he just began fussing with the mule, shifting weights around, testing straps, adjusting ropes. "Awful pesky animals, these damn mules," he said at last.

The boy was incapable of answering, so choked by rage that there was no way for him to get the words up out of his throat. Tom pretended to take no notice of his not answering. He went on fiddling. He wet his lips. He had a craving for tobacco but put it down, concentrating on the matter at hand: Speaking, not smoking, was what was needed. "Listen, I know you're all riled up about havin' to walk while he gits to ride, and I don't blame you. I don't blame you no way atall. He's got some strange ways that git to you, I know that, too, but—" But what? "But," he went on, licking his lips, how he wanted a smoke, the need was overwhelming, "but we're gonna git ourselfs horses. It won't be long now, jest to Marysville; that ain't far now, a day or two at the most," a perfectly logical explanation which Tom somehow felt was weak nevertheless.

"Why don't *he* walk?"

Tom couldn't think of how he might account for this, but while he was fumbling about in his head for a proposition, the boy said bitterly, "He could at least have *offered*."

True again. "Mabbe he never thought of it," Tom said at last.

"He never thinks of anythin'."

"You want me to ask?"

"There are some thin's you shouldn't have to ask. People should jest *know*. They should offer. You shouldn't have to ask."

"But it takes time for people to learn that. He ain't exactly what I'd call experienced." Fatigue was building up in Tom. He just wasn't equipped to dispense all this wisdom, he decided. And he *had* to smoke. He took out the tobacco, considered a minute, and then passed it along to the boy who, surprisingly, took a handful and waited for Tom to pass him a wrapping paper. Smoking the peace pipe, Tom thought. Them Injuns had something with their ways after all; they'd understood a long time ago tobacco could clear the head.

They stood there smoking, looking at the mule. The mule, however, wasn't interested in them. It was wigwaggling around trying to do ornery things with their equipment. "You're the one that agreed they could come along with us. They could have cut off on their own if you hadn't said they could come with us. I brung him all the way from Albany, but I never told him I'd take him no further than Independence. I got him to Independence, and you ain't got no idea, *no idea at all,* how hard that was, and now I got to help drag him along near another thousand miles, and it ain't fair, it ain't fair at all. I don't care what he does when he gets there—but whatever it is maybe he ought to practice doin' it on his own." He stopped, winded, furious, helpless.

"They couldn't make it on their own, not him and that girl. You know that."

"Maybe so," John argued. "But that ain't *my* responsibility. There is other ways to go—stage, trains, wagons, I don't know—"

"They's with us now so they's our responsibility."

The boy's anger was building up again, harder and firmer this time, fanned by the feeling of the injustice done him. There was nothing like self-righteousness to make a man pigheaded. "You never even consulted me," he said. "You jest went ahead and said they could come. That wasn't right *nohow.*"

Accurate again, Tom conceded, tired to the bone, and they hadn't even started out on the trail yet, but he felt as if he'd already put in a long full day of hard work. I'm too old for all this emotional upset, he thought. I took on more than I ken chew, an old man too full of himself to admit he isn't as handy as he once was. The War wore me out. Work's wore me out. Jest plain livin's wore me out.

The boy was looking at him, expecting him to make things right. The young got in over their heads, they expected the old, whom a moment before they'd pushed away and despised, to swim out and save them. They didn't even expect to say thanks; they just figured that being saved was their due —because they were young and had a whole life ahead of them and the old had used theirs up getting in and out of bad waters and ought to have got enough valuable experience to do lifesaving. And, all things considered, the boy was probably right about that, too. He did owe him rescuing.

Tom took a long drag on his cigarette and cast about for some answer to the unanswerable. He had had no right to make the decision that affected both of them all by himself. He knew that, but he'd had to because—because there wasn't anything else he could do, considering those two. "Well, I done wrong, I guess. I shoulda consulted you and I didn't and you got every right to be riled up. So, you got some suggestion as to how I could make thin's right with you, I'll lissen and see what I ken do."

The boy looked flummoxed. He didn't want to have to present solutions; he wanted Tom to do that. "Well, what's done's done," he said finally. "Ain't nuthin' we can do about it now, but I'll be glad to git me a horse, I can tell you that."

A truce. For the time being. But one thing was sure: that boy had a powerful amount of anger stored up inside him. He was fairly on the griddle from it. What would make a boy with all his natural abilities so apt to rage the way he did? Something else he would have to take into account: Good lord, he was bone tired and they hadn't even started out. One day on the trail, *one day,* and any way you viewed it the trip ahead did not look promising or providing.

II

There comes an April day in January and a
March wind across August, you just never
know. She thought this in Indian; then she translated the idea
into English—somewhat uncertainly because the two lan-
guages were so different.

That there *this* Buttes shouldn't have lit into his cousin like
that; it wasn't right; but of course people who were strong
walked all over the weak and never thought twice about it. It
was the weak who did all the thinking, trying to figure out how
they could do better and just get along, not even hope to
succeed, just try to make do.

Just the looks of that there Buttes made her feel inadequate
—you could see right off he was going to get on in this world,
but anyone who took a look at her knew right off she wasn't:
Benjie Klomp, who'd come out of the dirt ribs of Kentuck,
one of the Klomps who couldn't make anything grow where
everyone else only had to spit on the soil and it bloomed.

Her Pa had loved her though, *really* loved her, the way no
one else ever had, even if he was a failure, setting out to
homestead after everyone else had got the choice lots, so
broken-down in spirit he didn't even expect anything decent,

"Jest someplace I ken git thin's growed to keep my family's stomachs full," the family being Benjie; her mother, Lydia Klomp, aged twenty-eight, looking one hundred and twenty-eight; and The Boy, as he was always called, four, whose birthing had put all those years on Benjie's mother and picked the weight off her slick as a whistle. "She ain't got *no* meat on her atall," people said, clucking disapprovingly, and gray-eyed, gaunt, giving-up Lydia Klomp said back, "God made fat and God made lean. Guess he put me on the left when I went through."

The Boy wasn't much for fat either, just like a straggly weed sprung out of a brown cottontail when he commenced with the desert sickness. Took him less time than the rest to go. Her whole family dead of the desert sickness, which she found out later white people called the cholera, gone before you could count off the days of the week on one hand. "Honey," her father had said through the cracked lines of his lips, slits between the black stubble of his beard, "don't look like none of us is gonna make it, but you knowed I loved you best. You knowed that, didn't you?" Said it feverishly, determined, the one thing he wanted posted behind him,

BENJAMIN KLOMP
LOVED HIS DAUGHTER BEST

so he said it and said it (every time she leaned over him he said it) while his wife, still breathing and able to hear (the ears, they said, were the last of the senses to go), lay on the bed of quilts right beside him, hearing him say over and over what she'd probably suspected all along, that she was the poor soil in which he'd spit his seeds and got one bloom to grow at least. He died holding Benjie's hand, and the wife, the mother, the last one to go, a day later.

Benjie couldn't remember anyone who'd held her hand with such a feeling of desperate love since. Men had yanked her, pushed her aside, grabbed hold of her and thrown her down, but none of them had ever taken hold of her hand and held it because there was any caring. The whites threw her out and the Indians weren't going to gather her in—not the Indian women at first, no, not the men neither; she was a stray, they'd accept her for that, a white brought in and raised among them and could have been adopted by them but there was something wrong about her, she never fit in, she was never really one of them.

It's jest been one long casting out—cast out of Kentuck (though rightly speaking that weren't no fault of my own); cast out of the cart, sick and dyin'; then the Indians made me go back, they cast me out; and them white soldiers laid me down on the card table, jest like I wasn't white atall, but was no better than China Polly, that Chinese slave girl sent over to be the wife of some Chinaman made his money probably on the railroad, card crazy, willing to sell his own kind, and then lost her in a high-stake poker game. "Bring the girl," the Chinaman had said. And they brought her and when some white man won her he didn't know what to do with her. "Now I've got you, what am I goin' to do with you?" he'd asked. That woman was set apart just the way Benjie was. White Buffalo Woman. White Buffalo Woman: China Polly. And now *he* (looking at John Buttes), he'd like nothing better than to cast me out, but I broke that horse and he give his word, so he can't jest go and take a stick and drive me off like I was some kind of stray dog come cringing in on my belly begging favor, he gotta keep to his word if only to save face with the others, so I'm here and here I'm gonna stick till we git up to *Paha Sapa,* the "Hills That Are Black," she thought. The Sioux called them black because they were so heavily forested with dark-green pine that from a distance they looked pitch dark. The *Paha Sapa* were the refuge of the sacred gods of the Sioux. They had been safe there before the yellow metal came up from the earth.

But the Indians knew a curse lay on the *Paha Sapa* because long ago white men had come into the Hills and helped a tribe of Indians who were dying of some sickness they could not cure. The white men had tended the tribe and helped make the sick well, and when the sick were well again they rose up and slew the whites. Rain and thunder and hail and great winds rained down on the Indians and finally drove them out, and over the place where the whites had been massacred great clumps of wild roses sprang up and spread over the Hills. The wild roses ran through the Hills; they were there now as a reminder of past treachery.

Under the red roses lay the yellow metal that would bring the whites; Father DeSmet had warned the Indians to keep silent, but there was no keeping that kind of secret safe from the whites. All the Indians knew that maybe in their hearts.

It was Custer two years before (maybe two years, she wasn't good on time) who'd found the gold up on French Creek and brought the soldiers and miners down on them and the massacre that sent her back to the whites who didn't want her either.

She tasted death inside her mouth: smoke and grit and something spoiled, something that fouled her whole insides. When she thought about the wagons going away and leaving her all alone, she had that taste and smell in her mouth; and when she thought about the ride after the Indians took her with them there was the same bad taste; they rode day after day through country so barren and bleached that it looked like the end of the earth, so dry and dead that great scars had opened the earth up in fissures and deep caverns of sand; rocks, red angry rocks, jutting up solitary to the sky; long ledges of yellow sandstone bluffs streaked with blues and greens; ravines and gulches and brown, greasy streams where when they cupped their hands to drink they could see tiny little tails of life wiggling about in their hands; she was sick, sunstruck, sun-dazed, the parched earth so white that it blinded her at times, went into the bad taste in her mouth which was like alkali and dust and the other half of death: Young children were buried in white instead of black.

Then, at last, cresting a hill, she saw the village, near the curve in a river, a cluster of tipis with smoke hanging over them like frail feathers; men and women mingling as they went about their chores, and at the stream children rooting for crayfish, their tunics pulled up, their legs bare; dogs barking, horses snorting, someone singing or keening, she couldn't tell what kind of sound it was, and the long single ride into camp as the people poured out to meet them and a cry went up, but when they saw Benjie they just stopped and stood and looked. And looked. Very quiet, looking.

She had two distinct pictures juxtaposed in her mind—the quiet village of that very first day and the charred, black bones

of what was left after the surprise raid. Years after, she saw the
smoke, the debris, the twisted and wrecked tipis, torn buffalo
robes, dented cooking pots, dead bodies, bloody skin and
clothing, mutilated children, howling dogs, splintered lodge
poles, shredded coverings, trampled grass, all burning, smoldering, or dried stiff with blood, and the smell . . . it was like
the bad taste that fouled her mouth. She gagged now and
swallowed, forcing bile back. She had got through that and she
had got through what came after—April in midwinter, she
must remember, the spring winds that come quick and melt
all the snow, the warm southern chinook that raised zero
temperatures in an hour or two and turned the frozen ground
to mud and slush. That kind of quick change could come to
people, too. So you said to yourself, Well, I got through this
day (or week) (or month) (or winter) (or year), a philosophy
that seemed vaguely assigned to the tall, pale woman who had
been her mother and who was so colorless that she had be-
queathed only one major memory to Benjie: Lydia Klomp in
the doorway of the rundown Kentucky clapboard that was
little better than a slave shack, standing there, looking out at
the rickety wagon Benjamin Klomp had loaded with their
belongings to go West; she had looked first north, then south,
finally slowly from east to west, shading her eyes against the
sun, taking a final look round the land she knew so well and
had worked so hard and which had paid her back so poorly,
ungrateful, it seemed, for even the largest sacrifices, for the
three small bodies buried under stones in a weed-strangled
rectangle over the other side of the vegetable garden; in the
beautiful bounty of Kentucky where the blue grass was so
green it was said to be blue the Klomps could not even grow
good cabbages; worms ate down even into the heart of them
and when you opened out the leaves they mocked you with
their message from an unknown malignant world which sent
silent signals of the forces of evil at work everywhere, the kind
of people on whom even the minister quit calling, there was
so much disaster and death. At that last parting moment Benjie's mother had tried to smile, she whom Benjie could
scarcely remember ever smiling and certainly *never* laughing,
being brave no matter what doubts crushed her down, saying,

as if to impart to them all her useless courage, "Well, the Lord never closes one door but He opens another." She was right, certainly, but not in any way she could have hoped or foreseen, all the family bones save Benjie's now bleached into some sort of gravelly dust that wouldn't even help grow anything in the vast deadness of this desert. No, the Klomps were not growers.

The forms of death resided everywhere inside her head—in the skulls and bones of the animals the Indians had killed, in an abandoned battle site where unknown bands had tried to count coup, those reckless acts of bravery against an enemy where the most important thing is not to kill him but to *touch* him, but in which many were killed in the trying; death she saw in the bodies of animals suddenly encountered stiff or half-eaten or bleached by the sun, the hollow holes of their eyes turned up to nowhere, in the bare bones of the very earth itself, the long gray procession of land into nowhere, death everywhere.

Tiny tufts of dead fur, slabs and bones of dead creatures rose and fell before her eyes; she seemed to smell, too, the dried blood on the Indians, the death sickness that had been inside her; the memory of her ride back with the Indians was so much a part of her even if she had tried and, to an astonishing degree, succeeded in fighting back all but the bare outlines of that part of her life, suppressing those details that, when they did suddenly surface, were so painful that they sent her heart storming up in an anger of anxiety; her heart went so fast that it changed beat and her head felt light; even then she remembered it all, there was no way to forget; she would try to focus on the moment, the hour at hand, just to get through that day, because the past was painful beyond endurance and the future so fearful there was no sense in trying to look ahead, you could only say to yourself, Well, I got through that (hour) (day) (month) (time). But this was not winter with the hope of a chinook; this was the first hot spout of a summer which would bring a long trek to a people who might not *want* to take her back. She was white and had brought trouble enough down on them.

These people don't want me, she thought, and you can't

blame them none: What is there to want? A long stalk of a girl looks like her ma, came out as unlucky as her pa; probably it wasn't caring even that brought Bone Hand to take up with me but the use of another pair of hands to do the meat and skins and carrying, and I was white, in those days there was some honor to having a white in your tent; back then at the first a white girl was something to prize, even though he was not one of the ones who had brought her in, to show you were a great man. Bone Hand got the white child because he was so strong that no one wanted to argue with him, the strength in his hands was as strong as the hardest bone, it was said; that was how he had got his name. But he was strange as well— in the matter of dress, for instance; he didn't want to paint and decorate or even wear eagle feathers for the coups he'd counted; he didn't care about beads or quills or fancy bone work. All his passion was centered on one thing: his horses. Every morning he went to the corral and stood amongst his spotted ponies, examining them carefully for cuts or swellings, puncture wounds, unsoundnesses, standing fierce-eyed in the midst of the restless horses, who thrashed their tails and stomped nervously, hard, on the ground in irritation. Bone Hand's horses were noted for their feet. They could race on the hardest ground and never damage their hooves. He rubbed a secret herb into marrow and fat and then rubbed that across each horse's hooves every morning.

Indians loved horse racing, but with Bone Hand it was like a fever threatening to burn his life away. He was only happy when he was racing and betting. He won so often no one wanted to make a match, and so he raced seldom and was most of the time silent and displeased. His was known as one of the quietest tipis in camp.

But with his horses Bone Hand was an altogether different man from the one who sat, silent and stern, in his tipi. He talked and laughed and joked with them, and his face shone with pleasure and happiness. This was Benjie's first insight into the fact that some people were easier and freer among animals than they were with other human beings, perhaps (she came gradually to believe) because the obligations were clearer and the responsibilities less complex, perhaps too because the human was always in charge. It was good to feel in control; harm came from being in the power of others.

She would go down in the bright early morning light before the bathing and stand off, watching. Bone Hand took no notice; she might just as well have not been there. She was a woman and the horses were a man's province except during the long marches when danger appeared and the women had to stand with their hands clamped over the animals' nostrils gagging them from making any sound. Men walked with parallel tracks; women's feet turned in: The difference between the two was all in that. One rode a splendid horse and went to count coup; the other walked with heavy burdens or with straps balancing the bundle from the head, and this turned her feet in. The Indians saw no difficulty with this division, as if one were the arrow and the other the sheath; but Benjie remembered her mother and her father, and her parents' life had been different. She identified with their life and not that of the Indians. Even after Bone Hand began to make little exceptions for her (perhaps because of her whiteness or her interest)—to teach her and let her try things with the horses other Indian women might not have expected, though many were expert riders and handlers of the family mounts since for them the horses and hides were the sum of all their wealth; still, they had not the same privileges as the men and they did not *own* the horses—even then she never really rid herself of the belief she had a right to these privileges simply because she was white and white women should be treated differently from Indians. Bone Hand's indulgence was a joke; everyone teased him and said he was blinded by the light (white) which had come on him, but he paid no attention; perhaps he scarcely heard, he lived so much inside.

Indian life lapped around her, but it was as if she stood in the water only up to her knees. She did not love Bone Hand; he was too stern and aloof. And then, too, he had those strange scars on his chest that made her uneasy, little knotted fissures of flesh where the skewers had been pulled through in the Sun Dance. She knew the visions and courage of the Dance were the most important part of the camp life, and yet there was something in her that held off, that saw the scars as symbols of other cruel, inhuman practices she could never come to accept—the self-mutilations at times of death and intense grief, the vicious tortures and tauntings of an enemy, the seeming indifference to life as a stationary solid thing rooted in one place, the changing of one name for another, as if none of them felt the need for fixed centers of themselves—he who was Curly one day could become Crazy Horse the next, just as some of the people later stopped calling him Crazy Horse and began to call him Strange Man. My name is Benjie Klomp, she would tell herself, and I was born near Lexington, Kentuck. Let these people call her whatever they wanted, that didn't change who she was.

The constant moving, the putting up and pulling down of tipis, the packing and unpacking unnerved her. She could never accustom herself to it. Always there remained with her the idea that travel—moving—meant danger. In Kentuck, poor as they had been, they had been safe as long as they stayed still; it was only when Benjie's father had decided to go West that the real bad time came.

People who kept breaking camp and moving about the way the Indians did seemed to her to have little more than a temporary claim on this earth; she could not understand their faith that the land belonged to all and man was only a moving moment on its surface. Their troubles, especially with the whites, she was sure, came from their not being able to stay put, never ever being able to define what was theirs. The incessant breaking of camp was a reminder that these people really had no real home, not like the little farm she remembered back in the Blue Grass State; she could picture the straggly hollyhocks out by the privy and see the little patch of garden she and her ma worked over next to the graves. Poor as they had been, she had had her own room, not sleeping all together the way these people did, grunting and snoring and jerking around under the skins and making rude noises, the most private parts of their lives public.

Nor could she bear the little babies and old people deliberately left behind to die, perhaps because they brought back once more too vividly her own abandonment as the wagons went by and she was left all alone under the little canopy.

The Indians hated the white man's punishments of whipping and hanging, considering them degrading; yet many women hanged themselves, especially the old who became too weak or sick to go on and who asked to be left behind; most preferred the noose to the wolves, so though hanging was disgraceful to the braves no one said it was wrong for the old women. Children who were born crippled or deformed were often abandoned; these the wolves or weather got.

In the beginning, because Bone Hand wore only the plainest clothes, he seemed to her a man of no account. The Indians, she decided, had thrown her off on some weak man who had little power and hence would not be able to protect her from real dangers. She felt insulted as she was brought before the silent, stony figure, and she didn't even know how to plead her case. English was no exchange language here and the only Indian word she knew was "Hoaw" and she wasn't even sure that was a real Indian word; maybe it was just a white corruption of some word of some Indian language that sounded like "Hoaw." And yet she was so young and shy, even in her own language, that she could think of nothing to do but stand, staring down at her feet, with the strange-looking moccasins on.

The Indian was working with a knife, turning it back and forth in his hand. He didn't even look up when she stood before him; the whole of his attention was turned on that knife, as if it were a strange and mysterious instrument with which he might turn many marvelous movements in the world. He brooded over it, his cold impassive face suspended over the gleaming blade as he drew it back and forth against a long conical stone.

The set concentration and dedication of the man to the knife encircled her in its intensity and drew her up into the action, as if she were that blade being scraped and sharpened against the stone; the Indian would move her precisely back and forth against the stone until she glittered and gleamed and cut to the bone.

She had come under his care like the knife, an instrument that was to be fashioned to his use. The knife might go dull or be stolen or even, in some moment of carelessness, be broken beyond repair. Everything one owned, even the most useful things, was a responsibility and a cause for concern. In that way there was never any genuine pleasure in ownership, only the overriding worry about what might go wrong—also, with the white girl, the very real possibility that if she ever became the envy of another, one who was stronger (and everywhere there is someone stronger), then there would be trouble. The knife could bring pleasure and be of use, but it was also a concern. So, too, was it with the girl. It wasn't until she'd begun learning a little of the language that she came to understand Bone Hand's plain clothes as a mark of great distinction, a sign that he scorned the ornaments others took so seriously. His courage was said to be so great that he could not keep count of his coups and when Crazy Horse, who was in some ways as strange as Bone Hand, wanted someone he could count on he would call for his Cheyenne friend and they would sit in council and smoke and talk of the visions of horses they both saw inside their heads. Like most chiefs both Bone Hand and Crazy Horse spoke more than one dialect, and all Indians could understand one another through their intricate sign language.

She did not understand Bone Hand or any of the other Indians, and she looked down on them; they were dirty to her way of thinking, and they smelled, threw their pups into the pot, greased themselves with animal fat, disfigured themselves with knives and paint and dye, ran around with their oiled skins exposed, had no common sense and even fewer moral codes as she understood them. Taken in a group they were cold and hard and forbidding, cruel even and unfeeling; their mahogany skin stretched so tightly across the bones that any instinct or feeling underneath seemed unable to break through. Their arms and legs were pocked and sliced by scars; their clothes filthy and, to Benjie's eyes, slovenly; but they stood tall and straight and—most important—they looked down on her because they knew things that kept them alive and she didn't.

She grew tall, though still like a stalk; she was thin and her fair hair turned dark from grease and smoke; even her skin stopped looking white; continual exposure to sun and dust darkened it to the color of cottonwood bark. She looked as Indian as any in her leggings, tunic, and flat moccasins, her hair paired into greased braids and walking the characteristic pigeon-toed walk of the women.

She gathered fruit and nuts and bark, carried wood, learned to sew with porcupine quills, and she struggled with the language—with its clicking and gutteral sounds, its high nasal whines—she learned to eat raw animal organs and to drink the first warm blood from the cut throat of the buffalo; she could fish with a hook made from the rib of a mouse, and hoot, when there was danger, as well as an owl to give warning that something strange was near.

Bone Hand did not raise her himself; two sisters, both his wives, gave her instruction. She was as close to them as a child or a sister; she fit into their tipi life smoothly and without any sign of rebellion as she grew older and was initiated into the more difficult women's work—the making and shaping of the tipis, the fashioning of the all-important buffalo skins into parfleches that carried the dried meat and pemmican, or the special parfleche that held the war bonnet; she could make pointed needles from buffalo bone and sew with buffalo sinew; she handled cooking stones with skill and could pound and dry meat and make it into pemmican, mixing it with fat and chokecherries; she became a scraper of skins, one who could peg and work with sharp stones to clean the inner hide; she learned to mix cooked buffalo brains and liver in order to tan and roll the hides; she could wash with sandstone and soften; she could stretch a hide and cut it and sew it and keep it soft. She wore and slept under such hides. She ate buffalo. As much almost as the Indians, the buffalo became a part of her life. She was a curer of its meat, a tender of the fire of its chips, a tailor of its hide with porcupine quills. Dressing and eating and living as an Indian, she never stopped thinking white. Yet she had to survive, and to survive meant three things: to endure suffering, to suppress her own sense of superiority, and to keep a small flame of hope going somewhere deep inside. She was not White Buffalo Woman; she was Benjie Klomp.

The first eight years—the most important ones in her life—

had been spent in another world, the white world where whites had formed her; the red world was like a skin around her she could peel off at any time. It showed her red on the outside, but that skin was so thin that it was like a membrane that the smallest fissure could crack completely and curl away, the red skin that covered much that was no more than emptiness. She knew what many whites would never know, that life was not just either/or, that it could be both/and—but she was in a sense stranded in the "and," waiting for the "both."

There never seemed to be any doubt that she would become Bone Hand's third wife. There was no anger or jealousy on the part of the sisters; they welcomed her as additional help —they were getting older and she was young and able to do more than her share of the hard work—and they chatted with delight about the possibility of a baby as if it were their own, particularly the older sister, Dark Hair Woman, who had lost two of her children to the white man's coughing sickness and who seemed to go out to the menstrual hut every month and weep as she went, though Benjie awaited her own flux in fear that it might not come. She believed she would be rescued one day and go back to her own people where she belonged. To have a child meant having ties with the Indians she could never escape.

Her first pregnancy came when she was fifteen, months of retching and a boiling feeling of burning eating up her heart; she had dragged from day to day in an endless despair of nausea and heartburn and the desolate realization that with a half-Indian child she could never now return to white life as if this Indian one had never existed. Of everything—the endless months of vomiting and being so weak, the long difficult labor, the wrenching, tearing act of the birth itself—the most bitter pain was the final acceptance that she was now permanently Indian, marked in a way she could never erase.

The baby's breech birth, with much loss of blood, left her for months after weak and helpless. She only wanted to close her eyes and be left alone, but the child was always squawling and being taken up by one of the sisters and pressed against her where it rutted and suckled with such energy that her breasts pained her. Both became swollen and sore from nursing, more perhaps from the inner pressures of her aching heart, which resisted and tried to reject the baby by consciously trying to stem the flow of milk. But nature was stronger than her will. It seemed to her she never closed her eyes and sank into the deep escape of sleep but someone was stroking her awake and the howling little face was being guided to one of her cracked and oozing nipples.

In six weeks, when the birth-blood flow ceased, Bone Hand was back, fumbling his calloused hands over her slack belly and fingering her rudely to part her legs and let him come in. She endured him like the child; both of them always seemed at her, at her, at her.

Other Indian girls her age seemed to have happy, carefree times, even the ones with two or three little children; they were always laughing and splashing one another when they bathed in the streams, or running to giggle and gossip; they sang and played games and made jokes over the endless tedious rounds of work; the constant packing and repacking of the tipis never bothered them; it never even seemed to occur to them, as it did to her, that they were uselessly repeating the same tasks again and again with no end ever in sight. She sat listlessly with her infant son beside her, staring out at all the chatter and activity with such sourness inside it made her whole mouth taste rancid. Death had the taste of blackness, and she knew that taste only too well, a taste she identified with the dark moss that grew on the back of rocks where there was never any sun. Yet everywhere around her there were talk and excitement, quarrels and arguments and violent differences because this was the year the great chiefs went to Washington and signed the peace paper and there were those who believed they had done the right thing and those, like Crazy Horse and Bone Hand, who said, No, it was wrong, the whites would never keep their word, they would come and take the land they said they would keep sacred for the Indian.

The next year was the bitter winter that made conditions in the camp so terrible, and it was during this time Benjie's second son was born. This birth was easier, perhaps because she was becoming more resigned to the knowledge that she was going to have to accept being White Buffalo Woman and leave Benjie Klomp behind. She had two children now. She was an Indian wife. She went without feeling, submerged in the many tasks that she set for herself, trying to wear herself out in work so that there was no time for thought, but even when she lay exhausted under her buffalo robe wondering if Bone Hand would come to press against her, she would suddenly be overtaken by a great sweep of emotion, the green-bile taste of despair would flood her mouth and she could not control the terrible waves of bitterness that rolled one after another over her, so that sometimes sleep was impossible. She would lie dry-eyed and hollow, reverberating to the emptiness inside, feeling as if she had lost some hold on herself that was absolutely necessary in order to keep control; for even when she slept at last she would awaken an hour or so later in a violent spasm of anger, the residue of her dreams, dreams which were haunted by the despairs and disappointments of the day, dreams dark with dangers and threats.

She fought back against these emotions and these dreams because they threatened her and when she was overwrought she was afraid she would burst out some truth that would cut her off forever from Bone Hand's forgiveness. She knew that he was, like all Indians, quite capable of casting her out completely, leaving her in the midst of a winter landscape to freeze, or abandoning her in the hot bleaching sun to starve or die of thirst. She choked back her real feelings and tried to make the accommodations and compromises necessary to thicken the red skin around her so that it would become so tough and fierce it could not be removed without surgery. She watched the abandoned old ones left behind and thought, That might be me. . . . I must be careful, I must be careful. She nursed her new baby with toughened breasts that did not ache nor pain nearly so much as with her first child and this time she willed the milk up—I must be careful, I must be careful, I must give milk, I must make a good mother, a good wife, so that I am not cast out. She lay next to Bone Hand and she thought, I must be careful, I must try to please him. . . . She was so tired that every single action seemed an immense effort and she was sick with the sense of a hopelessness that knew no end, but she tried to hang on, to pretend affection for her two boys, to feign admiration and appreciation for her husband, to be kind and considerate of the two sister-wives. In time she learned to accept the little boys—at first a detached feeling removed from the heart of her, which, as they grew older, became a kind of disbelief that these two active healthy little bodies had actually come out of her, a feeling that turned almost to a proud recognition of their strength and handsomeness. She would say, There comes an April wind in January, the chinook, the chinook. . . . Do not feel. Do not let yourself feel. Block off all thoughts that make you feel. If you do not feel, you cannot suffer. You have to care to be involved; you have to be involved to have response. But it was as if the water had risen so gradually before she realized it that it had lapped over her and she was being submerged and she could no longer help herself.

That year in the middle of the Cherries Blackening they went to the Hills to hunt and to visit the warm springs that cure sickness, and it was there in the *Paha Sapa* the soldiers came, and later the next year when Crazy Horse and his band were in another fight, this time with Long Hair, the white man who had given Black Kettle and the Cheyenne so much grief, Bone Hand's band was attacked, and a little time after that she was sent back to the soldiers.

Bone Hand gave her his handsomest horse and a smooth white skin dress with much fine embroidery and intricate quill work. She went to the stream and took stones and tried to scour the grease out of her hair; she even used stones on the face, trying to peel away the dark outer layer of skin so that the white would show through, but no matter how hard she scoured it seemed to her the Indian membrane remained. Yet she was so filled with excitement and expectation that she could not eat or sleep; she trembled even at the thought of going back and, when she was told the boys would not go back with her, she felt no grief or sense of loss, only relief because if she did not have her two little Indian sons with her, then maybe she could return after all and be white, Benjie Klomp, the little girl who had been left out on the desert because of the desert sickness and who had somehow miraculously survived and now, after all these years, was returning back to her own world.

Word had been sent ahead; word had been sent back: Soldiers were coming out to meet her, and she got up on Bone Hand's beautiful spotted pony and smiled down on the two little boys, on the two sister-wives, on the whole backdrop of Indian life that now, as if she had pulled a window shade down very quickly, she could obliterate forever—she was going back, going to be white the way she ought to be; the impatience to get away was wild inside her and yet she had learned how to hold herself in check, how to go through all the long necessary boring Indian formalities that drove her insane with impatience, enduring each obstacle to her departure with a savage patience that kept threatening to snap, until at last, just at the point where she was sure she could not playact one more moment, Bone Hand raised his arm in the final salute that meant she could go down; and she started out over the faint green rim of the hill, her heart singing in her so joyously that it threatened to explode in an actual hymn out of her lips, a white song she had remembered from long ago—"Praise God from Whom All Blessings Flow"; but she held the pony in, moving very slowly, very stately, afraid still they might run out and grab hold of the pony and drag her back.

She was to ride over the rise and down into a long dry gulch and around another hill, and there the soldiers would be waiting for her. She did not look back, but she was sure her family was watching from somewhere up on the rise as she went through the gulch. It was filled with boulders and loose rocks and the horse had to pick its way very carefully. So many years had passed devoid of hope that when, unpredictably and unaccountably, her release had come she could not actually believe in her good fortune. Yet around the end of the gulch, the soldiers waited.

They were very polite, stiff with respect, as she came around the curve in the ravine and went toward them. Later she remembered them as saluting, but she wasn't sure of this; perhaps that part of her return to the white world was something her imagination had conjured up so many times that she believed it a part of the panorama whether it had actually occurred or not. But one memory she was sure of—and that was the ride down the gulch.

All the important events in a person's life are like landmarks, which eventually make up an individual legend. One of Benjie's most important memories was the solitary ride down the gulch, because at that moment she became a girl again, blotted out all the years in Bone Hand's tipi, first as child, then as wife; she went back to being Benjie Klomp, a little girl of eight, left on the desert; and though now she was a young woman of twenty-three, nothing had come in between being eight and twenty-three, nothing she would recognize except that she had grown from a girl to a woman, but all the changes were external; inside she was still the young shoot of Kentucky grass gasping to grow tall and straight, a dazzled girl who was filled with dreams of sweet safeness, of gentle men and comforting women, of towns built on goodness and mercy; she believed, riding over the rocky bottom of that gulch that separated her from the white and Indian worlds, in love and honor and fidelity and courage, all those virtues which the young see as turning the world into a good place; that there were just beyond the next turn soldiers waiting to escort her back to a place where the new habits she would learn would be those of happiness.

She looked down at the Indian moccasins she wore, turned in, pigeon-toed from all the walking and carrying she had done. I shall walk straight and tall and have silver buckles on my shoes, she thought.

Silver buckles on her shoes: that was how she saw the white world—shining, precious, pretty, a place of value. The Indian clothes, the Indian pony they took from her at the fort; and she was glad to be rid of them, grateful for the white women who were all of a rush to rescue her—putting her in a tight-fitting dress and sturdy shoes (you do not wear silver buckles on an Army post) and a bonnet that made her look like the kind of woman who would send her husband and children into the streets by the sharpness of her tongue. She could not recognize herself in the mirror that showed her in this tight muslin sprigged cloth, any more than she could feel herself inside the binding waist of the long dress or the painful pinch of the heavy shoes. The white language fell dead upon her tongue; she could not follow the rapid chatter of long strings of white words. She could not eat with a knife or fork nor sit easily on chairs nor kneel in pews. She did not understand how she was supposed to act or what she was expected to do or where she was supposed to go. She seemed like someone wandering about the fort with no place to go, no plans for the future, and when she tried to ask, no one seemed to know. She was, first, an interesting oddity who had shown up and made the dull enclosure life lift with the thrill of gossip; then a kind of misplaced person whose years in an Indian camp had obviously made any real place in civilized white life an impossibility; and finally, she became a kind of hybrid, a freak whose sudden, spontaneous actions—squatting on her heels (before she thought, for Indian women never sat cross-legged like the men) instead of sitting; dragging her blankets off the bed and sleeping on the hard floor; seizing her food with her fingers and making odd, slurping sounds as she ate—turned her into a crossbreed who was both distressing in some inexplicable way and a source of shame. *White* women simply did not act like that.

Yet she was white. She had been rescued. For a time she had been a heroine, but that lasted only until the novelty wore off and the strange habits alienated the other women; and of course, there remained the pertinent question of what was to be done with her.

She could not be sent back to her family because there was no family. She might have been married off, but with her odd Indian ways who would have her? Within a matter of weeks she was a problem to everyone, an encumbrance, an embarrassment, an expense.

And then it had come out about the two boys. She had let that out herself, a slip, done in an instant, which could never be altered, when she had been trying to be "nice" to a flustered woman she had encountered at the parade ground, a young agitated girl with two wild children driving her to distraction, a little boy and girl running and jumping and throwing themselves deliberately in the dirt; and the final exasperation, the absolute last straw so far as the mother was concerned was when the smaller of the two, the boy, had flopped up out of the dust on his knees and spread his arms wide, crying, "Let's play church. You be Mary and I'll be God."

The mother had been unable to stem her rage. It was bad enough her youngsters had been boisterous, ill-mannered, and dirty in public, but to be disrespectful to the deity on top of it all was too much. She had grabbed the little boy, smacking him first and then shrieking into his face; and it was then, out of identification and compassion, Benjie had said that one small sentence that was her undoing: "I know just how it is because I've got two myself—" She knew, even midsentence, that she was doing herself in, but it was too late to stop the rush of sympathy that had sped the words on their way.

The young mother had stopped and stood, silent, blinking in disbelief. "You *what?* What was that you said? You have *two* of your own?"

From that moment on she ceased being a trouble to everyone's conscience. A white woman who had— Within an hour there wasn't a woman on the post who didn't either go out of her way to avoid her or who didn't look right through her as she went past. There was also the matter of the embarrassing interview with the Captain who, until this time, had shown her an elaborate, almost grotesquely formal respect; now she was summoned into his office and cross-examined at great length about what was, as the Captain called it, "her private life."

He was one of those men who doted on details. "And how old were you when this Indian first—you know—lay with you?" "How many times did he do that—was it often or just once in a while?" "Once a week—oh, more, how many times would you say—on an average?" "Right there in the tent?" "He had *other* wives?" "You mean you were just like a"— pause—"just like say a concubine?" That word he had had to repeat for Benjie and, when she still didn't understand it, he had tried to explain. She knew very well that whites had only one wife, unless that one died, and then a man might take another; but the Captain ought also to know, if he'd been out here on the Plains, that the Indians had more than one, that was their custom; there was nothing wrong with it, as Benjie saw it, it was just different; but the Captain did not view matters in that light—white was right. One wife was right. Look at all the troubles the United States government was having with those Mormons who wouldn't obey that law. But Benjie Klomp did not know who the Mormons were; their example fell on blank ground for dispute.

The Captain tried to get her to describe if the Indians were like the whites and, again, she did not understand what he wanted from her; and then it came out he meant that he wanted her to explain how Bone Hand had come under her robe and left his seed in her; he wanted to see if this was the same way whites did; but since Benjie did not know how whites made their children, but just naturally assumed it was the same as Indians, she was of little help to him—"Too general, you're being too general," he would shout at her. "Be more specific."

He was excessively heated up, his face crimsoning with anger and impatience, while she stood—he kept her standing —and tried with as much honesty as she could to explain the situation to him. "There wasn't any choice," she would say over and over. "You see, I grew up in his tent and—" But he would never wait for the end of her explanation; an explosion of indignation would rock him right out of his chair onto his feet, so that, leaning across the desk, he shouted, "Do you think my wife—do you think *any* of these women—" But Benjie had no way of knowing; she didn't know the Captain's wife except to nod to, nor any of the other women really on the post, so how was it possible for her to predict how they might have acted if they had been brought into an Indian tribe at the age of eight and been raised as Indians? It seemed perfectly logical they would have done the same as she, but of course she had no real way of knowing, only that there must have been someplace at some time a similar case, did the Captain know?

He sat down and grunted, shuffling papers. "They never told us when they said they were sending you back that you had a couple of papooses up there," he said in a voice which clearly accused the Indians of treachery because they had with-held this very vital piece of information. "I can tell you this.

We would have looked at things very differently—*very, very differently*—if we had known that."

He was baffled and angry and out of sorts, sitting behind his big crude desk moving things about. "We'll have to move you," he said at last, abruptly. "It's not the same, not the same at all, as it was. You can't stay where you are, and yet—"

And yet no one knew quite what to do. She was white. She was not really white. She was something else, but what? Not one of those Indian women who lived with a soldier and had her own special category as squaw woman. Nor was she a white woman who had been with the Indians but "unharmed," someone who could perhaps be civilized enough to pass along to some frontier farmer who was not too choosy. She was a white woman who had let an Indian get children off her, and Benjie saw that to the whites on the post this was a sin far surpassing a white man getting children off an Indian woman, though the results were the same, half-Indian, half-white.

She had committed some sin *no* white woman should ever even contemplate, a sin so basic and so damning that no act of penance nor any form of contrition could ever elevate her to grace again. This was most forcefully brought home to her when the Captain had her moved out of her pleasant private visitor's room in the officers' quarters into a small storage area adjacent to the enlisted men, a kind of no-man's territory where she was informed she could stay until they decided what they would "do." She would not eat in the officers' mess; she certainly could not eat with the men; she would be given her food alone in her room, the Captain said in his last interview with her before she tried to take her horse back and run off to the Indians again. She had not run off directly; she had sat a whole day in that little cubicle in a numb state of bewilderment, not knowing what she should do. Breakfast had been watery coffee, a roll; lunch, some greasy soup, the same kind of roll, a little stale; dinner, the same soup, the same roll, staler. All that day she sat very still, trying to think through what she should do. The whites did not want her; they would let her hole up in this dirty little cubicle, however, eating the leftovers from the mess until she decided what she would "do." There was no one to talk to, but she didn't want to talk to anyone anyway; she was in such a state of humiliation and despair that talking could not possibly have helped, only action, some kind of strong, affirmative action that would put at least a part of her life back in her own control.

She had no idea what had become of her Indian clothes; that didn't matter. She could ride if need be in this dress. She would go to the barn after dark and get Bone Hand's spotted pony and she would ride out as fast as she could for the Hills, *Paha Sapa,* the holy Hills that would protect her. She did not think the soldiers would follow her, they'd be just as glad to be rid of her, and this might have been true had it not turned out that something had happened to Bone Hand's spotted pony, it had disappeared; and she had taken the best horse she could find in the barn—not to Benjie's way of thinking an animal as valuable or handsome as the one Bone Hand had sent her in with, but a good solid bay, strong and sure—the Captain's horse, as it turned out, and that was why the soldiers had come after her and brought her back.

The Captain was livid over the theft—"took our good hospitality and spit in our faces for it," he shouted at her. "No better than a lyin' Injun; there's nothing white left in you, but you are white, and I'm goin' to teach you some white ways, by heaven. I'm goin' to give you some lessons that'll teach you to act white even if you can't think white. You're not goin' to turn out like that Parker girl, her son Quanah gave us all that trouble with the Comanches, let me tell you that. I'm goin' to learn you some lessons you won't forget."

When she had tried to run off the second time (this time making a point of taking the Captain's horse), he had commenced the bridling: A brute animal, he said, needed brute treatment. When the word came down the line (rapidly, as all such news traveled in a small, inbred outskirt post) of the Captain's approach to the returned captive, the regular enlisted men knew all restraints had been lifted. Benjie knew that, too, as she stumbled back, between two guards to her room, her mouth raw and still bleeding. Perhaps the Captain might let her walk back. Why had she not thought to ask him that? But she would not ask, she would somehow get past the guard and go, barefoot (certainly not in these stiff shoes; she remembered in bitterness her vision of the silver buckles), as far and as fast as she could, that night. He'd take her in now and let her scrounge for food herself in the mess hall, one of the guards said.

Benjie shook her head, she wasn't hungry. She opened her mouth so that he could see the torn flesh.

"Suit yourself," he said, shrugging.

She thought that if she had been beautiful instead of so plain then she might have made out better, but the plainness perhaps went the worst against her; it worked together with the babyings from an Indian; in her mind she saw what she believed the Captain linked together, that only a plain girl would do such a thing because she probably thought she wouldn't get any other kind of man, even if she got the chance to get back to civilization, so she had laid up with an Indian.

But they didn't think that way, these people, when I first was brung in, she argued with herself. What people first think and what they think when they know you more always turns out, it seems, to be less in your favor, she answered back.

That man (looking at the guard) don't mean to do good by me. There's more of a chance with lots of men around; one or another of them might not let bad things happen to me.

She was not quite sure what she meant by "bad things" because she did not really remember enough about the white world to have more than a few images left, the principal one being the wagons going over the graves, and that was not appropriate to the possibilities at hand. Yet snatches of things she'd heard in the tipis and the anticipation of what was feasible (she had a vivid enough imagination to picture all sorts of indignities) when a woman had no protection prompted her to smile at the guard and try to get along as best she could by agreeing he was right, there was no use starving yourself to death, she said, though she knew that for Indians that would have been an honorable alternative to what might happen to her. I'm goin' tonight, she told herself, one way or the other. I jest git through until tonight and I'll git out of here one way or another, ain't *no* way they can stop me, and I'll git back, I don't care I have to walk the whole way on my bare feet.

Others have done it before me, done worse and got through. I can do it. When I tell Bone Hand what they done and show what's in my mouth, he won't send me back.

She sat on her heels in the corner with her back to the wall as a form of protection, keeping a careful eye on the guard. If he came at her, there were things in the room—a washbowl, a candlestick, the chair itself—she could use to protect herself, and all the time she crouched in the corner she kept telling herself, I'm gittin' out of here tonight. Don't fret. Jest hold yourself still, and rest because tonight you'll be out of here and free. Don't pay no mind to your mouth. It will heal up quick enough. It don't hurt that much.

That's how she thought, keeping her spirits up, all afternoon, squatting in the corner, swallowing saliva mixed with blood, picturing in her mind the long journey over the desert up, miles away, to the *Paha Sapa,* the Hills that cure, thinking about how good it would be to be off by herself, all alone, with no one, Indian or white, to be at her, just solitary and safe out there on the Plains making her way up to the holy Hills.

Benjie choked back the tears, lying on the straw pallet out by the scullery, the one she'd found as she ran, not understanding what a sack of bedding was doing in an Army scullery and then thinking the cook probably likes to lay down sometimes hisself, it's tiresome work; and she had pulled the shutters on the window and the two great boards that made up the door and crouched, up in the corner, hearing footsteps moving about outside, frightened one of those soldier men might open the door and find her. Too terrified to breathe for fear someone might hear her, she lay on the dirty horsehair mat listening to men walking around outside, talking, sharing a smoke, occasionally laughing; remembering everything, from the first one who'd grabbed her—there were three of them come in the room and hauled her to the door of the mess hall where they'd stopped, blank, as if they didn't quite know what to do, standing with her in the doorway and all the men hooting, so that finally they'd pushed her through and there in the smoke from the sooty lamps and the smell of bad food and the jeers of men wanting to know what was going to happen next, she'd tried turning first one way and then the next, looking for an avenue of escape—that first one grabbed her with that look—alcohol and the male feeling surging up and disgust, all there together in his eyes—"Been with Injuns, why you don't know nuthin' about white meat, honey," and as she shrank back, trying to pull free, but not jerking, not wanting to agitate him, get him more worked up, one of the others—one sitting down on one of the long benches—had said, "Don't pay him no mind. It's the liquor talkin'," but no one had really lifted a hand to stop the first one or the other two, the three of them standing in a semicircle around her, moving slowly, backing her up toward the wall; and it was then the thought came to her, They'll have to *git* me outside though 'cause outside no one will have to take notice. They can do what they want outside. She could hear that same man who'd blamed alcohol saying complacently, believing it, but superior because he wasn't one of the ones acting from it, "That's the way it is with drink. It's the liquor does it. That's why I'm so against drinking"; but then later, outside, after the three had got her down and then a couple of others had come and done theirs in her, too, she recognized that voice again, this time it was saying, "I'll go gentle, honey. I won't hurt you none, you'll see. Don't you worry none, I won't be rough like the others."

Even when those men were on top of her, she was never as frightened as when she'd been left on the ground and had finally got to her knees and scrambled a little ways, holding all sound still within so that no one would hear her; she didn't want to remind anyone she was anywhere around; and finally she'd got to her feet and made it to the little scullery and hid behind the shutters, hearing men outside walking around— that's when she'd been afraid she'd really break down.

She tried to imagine her father enveloping her in comforting arms, concentrating all her strength on seeing that image, but even as the arms enclosed around her and she felt a rush of relief, suddenly the sound of footsteps would come, the rough brutal bite of a soldier's boots on the pounded earth outside, and she would lie breathless, waiting, wondering how it was some people, like herself, came to lie, terrified, on rough sack mattresses and others smoked and laughed, creaked in their well-oiled boots under the pointed ends of stars to safe beds?

She lay very still in the hollow hour of the night when the male noises had at last been put up for a few hours, there in the dark with her eyes wide, going to the bottom of her where there was such an emptiness and terror that she thrust her hand in her mouth and bit down on it to keep from crying out; tears poured, noiselessly, down her cheeks, a half an hour, an hour; it seemed they would never stop.

For years she had lived waiting to come back to the whites, despising the Indians and their brutish ways, and yet if at this moment Dark Hair Woman had been near and Benjie could have crept next to her to sob out the whole story from the moment she went off on the spotted pony down the dry, rocky gulch until this one, where she lay, frozen with apprehension on the pallet, she would have been all right. Dark Hair Woman would have known what to do; she would have held her, would have pressed scented herbs and sweet grasses in the sore gap between Benjie's legs where, like her mouth, open wounds bled.

I hated the Indians and despised them and never gave them a tinker's damn; they did bad—cruel—things and they were maybe dirty and did strange things, but *they would never have done anything like this.*

She lay bleeding, trying to think what to do. Light would end the night and then where could she hide? She could not run. She was too sore and sick. To whom could she go? She lay on the pallet waiting, but she didn't know for what. The pain between her legs was bad, but worse were her feelings down deep inside. It was as if part of the heart of her—the quick, strong, responsible heart of her—had been cut out; and the loneliness, the terrible loneliness, lying there with that feeling of violation and bleeding badly.

All these years she had been living with the belief she was Benjie Klomp who belonged to the white world, and now in the void of the night that dream was gone, finally finished once and for all—it had been a deception; and the girl who had conjured up that kind of life, the girl who lived a white life, was even more unreal. She was White Buffalo Woman; she belonged back with Bone Hand and her two boys and the sister-wives and the herds of horses that could run swift and fast and safe away from the whites.

III

Queer ducks, those two boys, to be traveling together, even considering they were related: Tom couldn't picture them coming all the way from Albany to Independence without John going completely crazy somewhere along the way and murdering Mason Raymond. Mason Raymond—the name itself seemed to suggest so much. Got to be somethin' there below the surface I ain't explored, he thought. Always somethin' below the surface, that's what kept you so dadrat busy in this life, looking below surfaces. Tom just wished once in a while the pond were clear and clean.

I don't hardly know what to think myself, he thought, but somewhere in the tangle of things there's got to be reasons and needs, mostly needs, that's what cements people together in the first place, not the A B C logic of why they should get on, but strange powerful exchanges in feelings that come over them that no one else can see.

So, he reasoned, there's some private bond I don't see must have got them boys all the way from Albany to Independence. Don't pry, he reminded himself, you're always pokin' and pryin'. Mind your own business. Tryin' to be father, are you?

he asked himself sardonically, relivin' your spring days agin through them boys, that it? Even while Tom hurrumphed in disgust at the notion, he recognized it as having some foundation in fact. All right, so that explained part (not all, no, not all) of the attachment he felt for the boys, but there was the obligation there—he did feel a duty, even though he didn't know why, to see them through what he didn't think they could manage on their own.

Somethin' I jest feel, Tom thought. My ma, she used to have an old saying about it: My heart just reaches out to them, talkin' about some family come on hard times. We was all on hard times, but sometimes people went down to rock bottom. Hard as she worked—sigh, sigh, and he almost burst out laughing, and yet there wasn't anything really *funny* about all her sighing, I ought to be whipped for even smiling, he thought, smiling all the same—he could picture her right this minute leaning against the plank board ran along where she fixed food and then cleaned up after the fixings, hands in the enamel pan she washed up in, pausing, sighing, saying, "Poor old Uncle Dan, he's so lame he cain't even git down to the still to git his poison to help take the misery out of his poor sick old soul. My heart jest goes out to him."

Women brought me up all my life, he thought, made a difference, I suppose. What would it have been like if my Daddy hadn't been sold off? No way of knowing, just another of those unanswerable questions you asked yourself every once in a while. What would it have been like if . . . ?

Brung up by women and yet never felt really close to them; women have it so hard; men have it hard, but women they have it harder. You see some of them (he was thinking of his mother again), you jest wonder how they can go on. But they are trouble, too. She (looking at Benjie) goin' to bring us trouble sure, mark my words.

Two or three miles out of Lone Elm camp the trail divided on the other side of Bull Creek. They had come to the junction of the Oregon and Santa Fe Trails; in the old days at the height of the emigration—from the 1840s on—thousands upon thousands of emigrants and adventurers had plodded the two thousand tortuous miles between the Missouri and the Pacific, leaving a grave every ten feet; now it was the turn of the gold hunters, all of them scrambling across the Great American Desert in search of The Better Life, or, as the crude sign pointing out the northern fork said, THIS WAY WEST. THIS WAY SOUTH. So simple a sign, someone had pointed out, had never before announced so long and momentous a journey, which Tom conceded was true—in more ways than one. Now there should be a sign that said THIS WAY NORTH, or maybe something shorter and simpler, just an arrow and the one word: GOLD.

Mason Raymond was a distance ahead on his horse, the girl lollygagging behind on the Indian pony; Tom walked and John brought up the rear with the mule, which they had finally named Caboose because it always came in last. Tom dropped behind deliberately, walking side by side with the Buttes boy, who kept trying to coax the mule to move along a little faster. He was in a hurry to get to those gold fields. But those boys had told him they were going to South Pass and *then* north. Why that? Tom had asked. We gotta git to The Sweetwater, they said. He looked at them. The Sweetwater? *The Sweetwater,* they said, nodding their heads in unison. He was going to ask, Why The Sweetwater? And then he thought, Stop pokin'. They want to go to The Sweetwater—they ken go, can't they? You got some place better you want to run to? You *been* in the Hills, remember? And they run you out of there. What's the matter with The Sweetwater? It's got a pretty name. Still those two boys were odd ones, all right. We gotta git to The Sweetwater. Tom shook his head. "I jest can't put it straight in my mind," Tom said.

"What's that?" John asked, relaxed, off guard.

"Well, how it was you come to hitch up with that there cousin of yourn—you did say you was cousins, didn't you?"

"Yeah," John said belligerently. "My pa and his pa was twins—"

"Twins?" First The Sweetwater and then their fathers was twins. What next? Tom couldn't picture their fathers as being born out of the same seed. Obviously the boy didn't want to talk about it, but Tom was fascinated, kept pushing for more

information. "You mean look-alike twins or the kind that's different?"

"They wasn't *like* twins—they was, you know, twins, but they didn't look alike—nor act nuthin' alike neither."

"Was they close?" He pushed. John shook his head. He kept at him. "Was you and that boy brung up close?" Prying, always prying, you old snoop, he said to himself. I don't care, he thought. I want to know.

"They jest saw one another now and agin, summers mostly, when his folks come up from Albany—they had a big place down in Albany they lived most of the time, but summers, they come up, leastwise Mason Raymond's mother, she did; his pa, Mason Raymond's pa, wasn't too keen on the place." He stopped, as if he weren't going to go on, and Tom said, "So then you didn't see much of one another growin' up?"

"Well, along about the War, I think it was Pa said about that time," John Buttes said, "she come up for good, Mason Raymond's ma did, and brung Mason Raymond with her, but Uncle Clyde—Mason Raymond's pa—he stayed on down to Albany. They didn't git on too good, Mason Raymond's folks." John sighed. Obviously he didn't want to go into the whole thing; but the girl, who had been falling back to eavesdrop, a curious one all right, nervy, too, spoke right out and asked the question Tom had wanted to ask but had almost decided was really too pushy to bring up. "But if you wasn't brung up close, how's come you made such a long trip together all this way?"

"I axt myself that same thin' I don't know how many times," John Buttes said in disgust. "Jest seems like I let myself git roped in." He was holding back something he didn't want to tell them, Tom could see; the reluctance was so obvious that it was painful to watch in the conflicting expressions crisscrossing his face. He leaned forward in his saddle to show he was sympathetic, and the girl said, "Well—" Finally John apparently made up his mind there was no getting around at least partial truth. "Like he said, he's—we's part Indian—not much, nuthin' really *counts,* but Mason Raymond, I guess it kinda preyed on his mind, and after he shot that man—

"It weren't his fault, nobody blames him; this friend to him,

Worth Hart—he was an old hunter—was all tore apart by a bear, no way in this world he coulda lived through a maulin' like that, Mason Raymond was jest puttin' him out of his misery, like you put down an animal who's all played out and sufferin' and they ain't no hope—nobody blames him," John Buttes said. "Matter of fact, my pa thinks real highly of him for it, says somethin' like that takes *real* courage when you are set against killin' the way Mason Raymond is—he's so set agin it, he won't even carry a gun. He wasn't carryin' one that day —used another man's, one who *run*. My pa, he *admires* Mason Raymond"—but Tom could detect in John Buttes's tone now not an admiration of his own but resentment—"and he stuck up for him—my gawd, he never stops stickin' up for him— stuck up for him at the inquiry, worried about him all the time he was off that crazy way in the woods"—and the boy's voice was rising in anger and disgust, as if he couldn't understand how anyone, particularly his own father, could find so much to admire in Mason Raymond—"gone up in them woods *years,*" he went on, getting more and more agitated, "lived part of the time with—or at least knew—some crazy old coot lived in a cave with *stuffed* animals, animals he skinned and cleaned and put back together, and who kept *bees* because he said they sang—you ever hear of anything crazier in your life?" He paused, breathless, looking at them for confirmation, "To keep bees in your backyard because they *sang?*"

Then all in a rush, he said, "Finally come out of the woods and went back home, down to Albany, and my ma, she made me promise to look in on him to see he was doin' all right, and he offered me this money, for a stake to the Hills, a proper good stake, if I would let him come along—" He stopped, embarrassed, Tom could see, about the money part.

"Well, I mean, it was only right," John Buttes argued, though no one had accused him of anything he'd done wrong. "I mean, he can't find his left foot from his right. It was jest like I was a guide—anyway that's how come we teamed up."

"But what did he want to come for?" she asked. Leave it to a woman to keep putting her hands in the dough, there was never enough kneading to satisfy a one of them. "I mean, he don't seem—well—exactly suited for this kind of life."

] *168* [

"He's got his head full of religious thinkin'," John Buttes said abruptly, not wanting, it was obvious, to talk about Mason Raymond anymore, he'd had more than enough of Mason Raymond. "Axe him. He can tell you better than me." His voice warned them to be still.

They forded Captain's Creek and started West toward Wakarusa where, Tom was hopeful, they might run into a little luck and put the piebald up for some racing. We run our pot up a little, we ken git a couple of real decent mounts and all the equipment we need. The idea of a race excited him. He loved a good gamble more than anything in the world—even wine and women.

> I was born with a pistol ten inches long,
> My haunts is with women, Red Eye, and song;
> My parlor's the Rockies, my footstool the Hills,
> Lissen, you short-armed bastards and broad-beamed bitches,
> I'm spotin' a race of buckskins and riches,
> A mixture shits nuggets of gold and spits buckets of bills . . .

The rhyme was off somewhere. He got the lines wrong sometimes now, used to be able to rattle off reams of poems without missing a beat. Maybe his memory was wearing out like everything else.

There was more water up ahead, and the crossing was not going to be a happy one because the mule had begun to get ideas of its own and because already the others were beginning to have the old Oregon Trailers' appreciation of water. Treacherous currents, quicksands, panicky oxen, recalcitrant mules, rambunctious children, nervous horses, meddling adults—all these could easily end in drenchings, drownings, loss of livestock, upset equipment, and—in almost every case —an end to the early patience of Independence, that easy attitude toward the trials of the trail that was the earmark of the greenhorn: The longer people were on the Trail, the more they understood its treacheries, whereas in Independence, in their innocence, they had started out looking on the long journey, in many cases, as if it were a lark. Innocence, he thought, is back there on the other side of the Missouri. But they don't know that part of what it means to cross the big wide river yet. They'll find out quick enough.

Caboose had decided to drink. The mule lowered its head and slurped greedily at the dark muddy waters, making sounds that reminded Tom of the wine tasting in Independence when he had tried to teach Buttes some of that Boston Captain's fancy knowledge on wines. A waste of effort, he thought now, the more he knew that boy the less he expected him to take to refinements. He was the kind who would walk off in a huff and never stop to discuss why he was mad because deep down inside he was afraid of words. Tom had known a lot of men like that—stubborn, bullheaded men who had left half their lives behind in unnecessary angers because they were afraid to stand up and admit their errors and try to deal with them. It was always easier to run away. But they were only running from themselves and caught up with the enemy inside in the end.

The water swirled around either side of the mule, and John Buttes took off his hat and bent over and scooped up a brimful, pressing it against his face and guzzling as greedily as the mule. "Ain't exactly The Sweetwater," he said to no one in particular, his face smeared brown and wet from the water, "but it wets your whistle."

The mule began to go down. "Yank up! Pull up the head!" Tom hollered. "He's gonna roll!" The Buttes boy was grabbing wildly for the pack, which had begun to slide; the girl heeled her pony around and drove the little piebald right up against the mule, bringing her arm up and giving the mule a crack across the head, the boy full of rage, eating his insides up in nameless anger because a girl was showing him what to do. He's so muleheaded hisself all the time, Tom thought, and jealous unto death of what others can do he can't, a big strong boy on the outside but inside he ain't growed up yet, he's always pulling against himself, like his own worst enemy. But Tom's uneasiness didn't just come from his nervousness about Buttes; there was an undercurrent in the air of things not right, something out of kilter that he couldn't put his hands on but which he felt keenly—a premonition of some danger waiting for them, not the ordinary hazards of the trail; something that was off, strange. It troubled him, but he couldn't track it down. Getting old, he thought. Otherwise I'd know right off what's amiss. It wasn't just him. The girl's pony knew something was wrong, too. It had been acting odd all morning. An Indian pony didn't act on edge that way unless there was something cross-threaded. Indian ponies had instincts for danger bred in the bone. They were always keyed up for an enemy raid, like they'd developed a sixth sense about what was normal and what was off. Don't gallop to grab hands with the Devil, as his grandfather would have reminded him.

John struggled to regain control of the mule, and the girl whooped and hollered as she and the little Indian mare plunged this way and that in the water. Then John started shouting and taking his hat and using it to throw water at her. They were frolicking, for godsake. Well, they were only kids really. He shouldn't be impatient with them. He'd done some frolicking in his own time.

Finally the Buttes boy headed the mule landside and in another minute they began to stagger through a muddy bottom up the incline to the creek bank on the far side. The mule slipped and knelt, rose up and slipped back, then began to founder in the thick mud.

Tom had sloshed up the bank and was standing waiting for the others to catch up, trying to suppress an unreasonable irritation—why the hell couldn't they come on?—when he saw the glint on metal in the far brush, a reflection from the sun. He wheeled around and plunged back down, dropped a good cigarette as he hit the ground. "Git down," he hollered at them. John jumped down beside him, letting go of the line to the mule; Caboose struggled on alone toward dry flat land. They would lose the mule sure; it would run off or get shot, but Tom hollered at the boy to let the mule go, it was expendable, he wasn't.

"You always said they was so valuable, them mules—what is it? What's the matter?"

"Git down!"

The mule made an awful bellowing as it floundered about in the mud and tried to lurch over the hill, the pack on its back —which was anchored to John's good saddle—slipping side-

ways and hanging at an awkward angle, the mule kicking and
thrashing.

"Don't make no movement, jest sit tight and hold this here
horse of yourn," he said to the girl. "Never mind the mule,"
he said to the Buttes boy, who was starting up toward the hill.
"Git down—git down like I done tole you or I'm gonna knock
you down." He turned on the girl again. "*You hang on to that
horse!* Don't you dare let loose of that horse, you hear?"

He looked around to see what Raymond was doing, but he
seemed to have disappeared completely. With a sinking heart
Tom thought that he might already be on top of the hill and
in the line of fire. That kid's so darn dumb, Tom thought, that
—well, there was nothing to do but go after him.

Tom moved slowly along the bank making no noise at all.
The nigger in him, white folk would have said. What did they
know? They hadn't been in black skins. I know darkies who
can't even *sing.*

He crouched down, ahead nothing but scrub and sand and
those funny hunched-down bushes that dotted the whole
damn West and big sandstone humps looming up, defiant,
against the sky. That crazy kid was standing daydreaming, not
even looking around, just leaning against his horse starry-
eyed, too green even to understand that in a strange place you
had to keep your eyes open all the time. Past the Missouri only
dead men dreamed. But there he stood staring into nothingness. What was he staring at? Hadn't he seen the glint from
the gun? No, none of them had, only him. They'd carried
their innocence right across the river; only he was armed with
the rudiments of knowledge and that came, of course, with
age. They were young and untried; that's what he was holding
against them and yet that's what held him to them.

Tom crept through the sharp sunlight, fell in the mud and
slipped down and sank, crouched, stone still, for a moment
not even looking around, in the ramrod rigidity of his back
the message he wanted the girl and the boy in back of him
to understand: *You-all shut yourselfs up still, you hear? We in
trouble, bad trouble. You keep down and keep still;* and behind
him the girl and John must have understood because they
didn't even seem to breathe in that sucked-in stillness in

which Tom jumped up and fired—*whang*—and Mason Raymond dropped as if he'd been shot and his horse bolted and ran.

The mule went, too. Tom scrambled to his feet, bent over for a moment undecided, looking first toward the fallen figure, then down the road into the whirl of sand into which the horse and mule had disappeared, thinking, *Well, the mule's done run off with the horse. We done it agin.*

But it wasn't so much "we," he considered, as whoever it was that lay in wait hidden over there in the brush, probably more than one because sure as God made losers and winners in this world, whoever's gun had caught the glint of the sun, opening Tom's eyes to the dangers ahead, wouldn't take on four if he was all alone. Even for a surprise ambush, that was too uneven odds. Two or three of them over in the brush, Tom thought—*at least.* Oh, Jesus, he thought, and though they's four of us it's four mighty slim pickings.

The whole desert had clattered awake at the sound of Tom's gunshot; small animals bolted for safety, birds whirred around in the air, insects were humming and hollering out alarms, and Tom thought, Injuns probably or runaways, deserters mabbe, or outlaws, but somethin' bad sure enough. *We're dead goners, leastwise he is if I don't git that kid out of there and git him and me back down under that bank.*

He leaned forward and grabbed hold of Mason Raymond's foot and started to yank him back. Mason Raymond let out a yell, sounding as if he had been struck by a rattler. I took him by surprise, Tom thought with some satisfaction. He increased the pressure, dragging the boy back.

Now he could see Mason Raymond's horse up ahead, standing not too far off, its ears alert for threats. If they's more than four, Tom thought, they'll come out and git that horse now. God knows where the mule run off to.

He felt the lip of the bank as he inched back and he fell over, pulling Mason Raymond with him. The kid was the color of greasewood, he was so scared, but at least he wasn't dead, and neither am I, Tom thought with a surge of relief. Now all we got to do is wait and see, and if they come out after the horses, see if there's more than one, and if they don't come out, it jest that one I got and maybe two or three more, but one way or the other we still ain't in the clear.

He waited, the gun ready in his hand, nothing moving in him save his eyes which traveled furiously right and left seeking out the enemy, the sunlight deepening and the greasewood motionless, no sign of movement, no sound, nothing, not even animals and insects and birds making any noise now under the sharp sunlight except the increased breathing of Mason Raymond as he crawled toward him.

It was hot and the mud made crouching down wet and oozy, but under the cover of the bank they were fairly safe. "That horse answer to you?" he asked Mason Raymond. "You call him, will he come?"

"I don't know. Maybe. It's a mare," he said. "Mabel."

"Jest call the damn horse, never mind its sex."

If the horse started to trot back to them and it looked like it was getting away, Tom thought, and if there were lots of other men out there, surely they would come and make a grab for it, using it as a shield.

Mason Raymond's voice sounded more like an echo than a real voice. "Mabel," he called. "Mabel . . . here, Mabel." They waited; then Tom could hear the horse coming, a steady tattoo of hooves on the hard ground, the hoof sounds getting louder and louder. That meant no one had run out to grab it. The animal stood on the ridge of the stream bank and looked down at them, expectant, waiting. Mason Raymond started to get up and go for it, but Tom yanked him back down. He can wait a minute, Tom thought, won't hurt him none at all. We got to be sure.

Mabbe they went after the mule. No, they'd git the horse first and then worry about the mule. In this country horses were riches, worth more than mules, leastwise to outlaws. Still, all that gear, that real fancy saddle they'd put on the mule, were something to consider besides just animal flesh. Mabbe those critters would elect for that saddle instead of the horse.

He waited. The horse began to get impatient; it whinnied, wondering why it had been called if no one wanted it. Tom crept up toward the top of the bank and looked out from underneath the horse's front feet. The horse put its head down and began to rub against his head. Jest like I was a goddam scratching post, he thought in disgust.

Nothing moved, nothing.

He crawled up and crouched behind the horse, using it as protection, scanning the landscape for any telltale sign of danger. Nothing moved, nothing. Yet something was wrong. He didn't know what it was, but something was wrong, and yet everything *looked* all right. But they wouldn't run off, not if they had cover and we had to come out in the open to git at the mule and the horse, he thought.

But if I killed one that quick, mabbe that put them off. Mabbe one dead for the day is enough. He waited, watching. He just wished he could see what had happened to the goddam mule. Mabbe that's where they were, after the mule.

He tried to think it through. Out here you could never just make one assumption because more likely than not no other man was acting from the same kind of values you did. So you had to search for different ways around a problem. One, they could have had a bellyful with one killin' and could have skedaddled. Two, they could be laying low and waitin' to even thin's up (a more logical bet). Or, three, they could be doin' any number of thin's his mind was too undernourished to imagine.

We can't crouch down behind this bank forever, he thought. On the other hand, there's no sense in venturin' out and gittin' shot. We ain't in that much of a hurry. I could do a little reconnoiterin' though.

He kept Mason Raymond's horse in front of him as he began to reduce the distance between the bank and the inert body he now saw up ahead, moving slowly, measuring every leaf and rock. Nothing stirred, and yet something was wrong; he felt it. He stopped, scanning every inch of landscape. Nothing out of place, and yet— Old and flighty, overimaginin', overreactin', ain't nuthin' out of place. Yet he moved forward, wary.

Tom toed the body over. It was an Indian, the face and the long greased braids and the bear grease smell and the clothes made that sure enough, an Indian with half his head blown away.

Tom knelt, keeping his eyes alert, fumbling with the Indian's shirt, looking for some piece of evidence that would explain why he was out here all ready to help take on a party of four; his hands got stained with blood and brains, and he wiped them once impatiently on the Indian's pants, then went on rooting around in the dead man's clothes. He didn't know quite what he was looking for, just some clue as to why he was out here getting ready to kill them, willing to get killed himself in the attempt.

Mason Raymond suddenly jogged up beside him. That kid ain't got no sense at all, he thought in exasperation. "Git back —git back and take cover." The kid didn't move; he was staring at the Indian's head, or what was left of it. He seemed paralyzed. Tom grabbed hold of him and shook him, remembering the girl's example, You gotta git his attention first and then let him lissen to what you want. "Git back."

Mason Raymond rose like one in a trance and trotted toward the bank. At least he does what you tell him, Tom thought, if you ken wake him up.

There was nothing on the Indian that was of any interest. Probably jest out general thievin' and stealin', Tom thought, and figured to take us by surprise. A couple of good shots could do it. He would have killed us he could, and took what we got, but there was still the matter of how many others had been with him and where they were now. But they let the horse get away from them. If they was any sizable number, they wouldn't no way let that horse git away.

He was perplexed, standing in the middle of the plain over the dead Indian, with Mason Raymond's horse as a shield, wondering why they'd let Mason Raymond's horse trot off instead of grabbing it. That must have meant that they had run off. Yet something in him was working, and what it boiled down to was those two questions that kept repeating themselves over and over, How many of them was there and where did they go and git to?

Old days, he thought, I'da come up with an answer right off the bat; might not have been one hundred per cent accurate, but it would at least have been an answer. In this world you gotta come up with some kind of answers quick or you ain't gonna run far.

Something was moving a little ahead—the mule, grazing on dusty green rough-looking needlegrass. Been significant number of those fellers in the brush, they'd have got their hands on that mule sure enough. Mabbe there were only two or three and they reckoned on takin' us by surprise, only I see the glint of the gun and got one and now they don't want to take on four of us.

That would have been the ideal solution so probably it was the furthest from the truth. Still, leaving that mule free like that didn't make any sense at all unless there were only a couple of fellows left in the brush and they were scared, so scared they were going to try to lie low and bluff it out.

He inched his way forward, still keeping the horse in front of him. He just hoped the girl wouldn't get one of those spells women went into when things broke down inside them and they went out of control. What *was* she up to?

She was screaming her head off, that's what she was up to, shouting Tom had no right to go and fire like that, he'd killed that Indian without even finding out what he was after; shoot first—so long of course as it was an Indian—and find out later why you'd pulled the trigger.

Then something moved, only a small part of a bush, but that wasn't the way a bush moved. Tom turned and fired and grabbed for the mule, and Mason Raymond's horse broke loose and bolted. Oh, Christ, he'd gone and fucked things up now. Well, the horse was gone, there was nothing he could do about that, but he hung on to the damned mule.

Caboose was as uncooperative as ever. "You're goin' to git us both kilt," Tom said to it savagely. Bullets began to fly and the mule leaped up in the air bellowing; behind him the girl was hollering to hold off, she was almost Indian herself, she had been up with Bone Hand. Shot puffing up the dust all around, dust flying and bullets whanging against the ground. It seemed to Tom as if his whole life had dropped into a void and he would never reorganize it again under the old tenets. He had known from the beginning something was wrong, but his eyes and ears hadn't been able to detect anything (they would have once not too long ago, he thought bitterly) and even when his mind had been cautioning him something was the matter, he'd gone out in the open, something he'd never have done normally—and that meant he was slipping, he couldn't trust himself the way he once had, getting old and unreliable and not wanting to face up to failing.

The girl had run right out in the open—screeching first in Sioux, Tom recognized a word or two, and then in some Indian dialect he didn't know, probably Cheyenne since it was them she'd been up with; he didn't care at this point whether she got shot or not, she was such a damn fool and she made so much goddam noise; but the mule they had to have, and he thought, They shoot it, we ain't got a pot to piss in.

He ran, dragging the mule with him, the mule hanging back and trying to resist, the saddle lopsided, the gear all coming loose, Tom half crazy with exasperation; he finally got that damned animal abreast of her, and he took hold of her with his free hand, trying to drag both the mule and the girl along with him, but their uneven weight threw him off balance and he slipped and went down, let go of the girl and started heaving about to grab her again, but she was set on berating him—would she *never* shut up—and then he seized her and got on his feet again and started tugging both of them toward the riverbank and safety. He could not understand why all three of them weren't down or dead; they seemed to him such prime targets, but maybe in the confusion and with all the lurching and falling, luck had saved them. Anyway no man in his right mind would shoot the mule—the man and the girl, yes, but not a mule or a horse. They were worth something.

The mule started kicking and thrashing, its aim pretty good, Tom jumping this way and that, letting out a stream of obscenities that even he was proud of. He thought of what a spectacular target he must make, black as a bull's-eye in the murderous white glare of the noon sun, hauling the mule and the girl, both of them kicking and beating back, toward the bank, the girl fighting him, the mule fighting him, he fighting both of them.

Let them both die of lead poisoning, he thought, because it was obvious he wasn't going to get both of them over that bank. They ain't worth my hide, he thought, even though it is black.

The girl was half as valuable as the mule and mabbe twice as ornery, but she was human and for the moment, though he wavered about which one he would save, he stuck with the girl. Her sex probably went with her. A man so dumb and so obstinate could have probably taken his own chances and Tom would have opted for the the mule; but women, well, you couldn't expect too much of them in the brains department, you had to make allowances. He grabbed her harder, letting go the mule.

She squealed and kicked and thrashed about, screaming at him to let go, he was nothing more than a no-good *this* Indian killer, Tom paying no attention, just hauling her along by the hair until they were both back under the cover of the bank, next to the two boys, then throwing her down and flinging himself on top of her, holding her anchored while she squirmed and kicked and clawed at him, and god alone knew what had happened to her horse because it was gone, too, and after he *told* her to hang on to it. That great runner who could have made all their fortunes, gone. We're jest a hard-luck bunch, he conceded.

Silence: The shooting had stopped. Not a bird, not an insect stitched sound. It was as if he could hear the energy the sun used pouring down to bake the sod. Even the girl was momentarily mute, lapped in as they all were by molten gaseous gold.

"He weren't no Injun, that there feller over yonder. He was breed and them there fellers over past in the brush is white. I jest seen them as you set off hollerin' off your head. They sent the Injun out and let him git kilt."

She was furious, bloodroot red in the face with hostility. "What they want offen us?"

"Our rig, the horses, that danged mule, all the stuff we done laid up, the whole kit and kaboodle. Ain't everybody heading out here to work they way, you know. Some people ken see quick money in they pockets if they put a mind to it and it don't trouble they consciences none how they come by it. You let that horse run off," he said, furious, to the girl.

"Git offen me—you nigger."

Niggers could call themselves niggers, and some white people used the word and got away with it because there was nothing a nigger could do to stop them, they had power on their side; but trailmates, they could never ever under any circumstances use that word. For a moment he went blank and nothing in the way of feeling ran through him, and then he began to take hold because the word *black* had stayed in his mind, and with it he came back to himself.

The heat, even end-of-April heat, was horrible; he felt heat- and sensation-sick, a murderous gorge in the back of his throat.

Some movement had begun over by the boulders—a flash of metal in the sun, the high whinny of a nervous horse. "Can you shoot?" Tom asked the Buttes boy. "I mean shoot straight and kill."

"I kin shoot," he said.

"Then git ready."

"I can't."

"What do you mean you can't?"

"The gun's on the mule."

"Holy mother of God, don't you none of you never do nuthin' right? Can't none of you hang on to a horse or a mule or a gun?" From under him the girl mumbled something, but Tom paid no attention; he was eyeing John getting ready to try to work his way back out into the open and over toward the mule, which stood blankly inattentive to all that was going on around it. It wasn't grazing; it wasn't twitching insects; it wasn't even moving. Expressionless, it stood in the middle of the prairie brush and endured.

"You can't go out there," Tom said.

John looked back at him with one of those challenging looks which said, *You* gonna try to stop me?

I can't fight them all, Tom thought. He watched the boy crawl over the bank and flatten himself against the dust. Being lean was certainly in his favor, but he was an amateur and amateurs sooner or later fucked things up. You jest done one yourself, Tom reminded himself, you let that Raymond boy's horse git away from you; and you can hardly call yourself an amateur after all these years you puttin' in learnin' the little lessons of how to and how not to fuck up.

The mule stood stolidly planted in its obstinance about a

hundred yards ahead. A hundred yards could be a hell of a distance. The boy kept crawling. Whatever else you could say about him, he was not short on courage. The gun was not on the exposed flank side of the mule; that meant the boy would have to work his way in back or in front of the animal, a tricky business. The problem was complicated by the fact that the mule didn't like being monkeyed with and if it weren't tied it might shy away and trot off. Shots were ricocheting again, a sporadic firing that meant the men in the brush were trying to turn John back.

In a burst of courage that was more demented than determined, John suddenly shot up, ran forward, grabbed the mule, and jumped to one side, some protection in the fact that the mule would go down before he would. He groped for the gun, working awkwardly with the ropes, his head ducked down, his fingers all sixes and sevens. There was now quick successive firing from in front of him and Tom thought, They really goin' at it. The exchange of shots was steady and emphatic, signifying the serious business of killing.

He wouldn't even let himself contemplate what would happen if a shot got ahold of that boy. He would be responsible. I knew somethin' was wrong, but I couldn't sense it through. I'm the one got him in this mess, got them all in it—

John yanked the gun free and ran for all he was worth. Tom raised up, the girl coming unpinned from under him, grabbed hold of her, and fired out into the unknown. Whoever was firing at them either had bad aim or wasn't taking careful sighting; a good shot could have got both him and the boy easy. But there was something else saving them: Mason Raymond's horse. Hysterical, it plunged over the bank right on top of them and for a moment there was a tangle of animal and people.

"No wonder they weren't aimin' so good," Tom said. "They was tryin' not to hit the horse. Where the hell did the horse come from?"

Mason Raymond had hold of Mabel and was talking low and quiet to her, but her eyes were bulging and her sides heaving in panic. "You got any idear how many of them's out there?" Tom asked John. The boy was panting from his run.

"Too many," he said. "Four, five, maybe more."

"How's come they don't rush us then?" Mason Raymond asked. But at least he was hanging on to his horse. At least they had one animal left.

"How the hell do I know—maybe they will. I can't tell you what's goin' on in *their* heads." He was nervous, that's why he was so touchy, thinking, You gotta come up with somethin'. You ain't that old and done in. September, some say, is the best month of the year.

Mabbe someone'll come along and help.

Sure.

Stay and fight or sneak out. Couldn't sneak out and if they stayed and fought they probably weren't going to win. The odds were too much against them. But it was funny, he wasn't so heat bothered. For a fact, he felt cool—*cool?* He glanced up into a huge angry cloud swallowing up the sky in purple jaws; a sudden spurt of wind flew up in his face and a great roaring seemed to lift up the hinged dirt of the earth. The sky went black without warning. There was a sound as if an enormous array of cannons were being fired; the skies poured down molten fire, torrential rains, zigzags of lightning, hail as round as a man's thumb and heavier; the roar of wind flung pieces of earth and vegetation into his face; the wind ran and tore and bit and clawed; the creek bed in back of them suddenly seemed to run in a wild tide of tumbling rocks, sage, white water; wind beat down the grass as firmly as if a thousand buffalo had passed over it.

The mule's tail was flying up against its back, out there with all their equipment, and when the rain really hit the food would get a soaking from which it might never recover.

Tom heard three tremendous roars of thunder, then a rip of light again, clap after clap of crackling lightning, some a hundred feet high, and the rolling thunder, the trees whistling and bending and giving in the wind; he was stung all over with rain and hail. You didn't get no ordinary storms out here on the Plains; that much you could say for the weather beyond the Missouri.

The wind beat bits of greasewood around like terrified birds; dark and winged, they sailed through the sickly-green sky, then crashed, flapping, to the flooded ground. The rain was freezing; he felt numb all over. The creek bed suddenly flooded. He was in the midst of one of those fierce storms for which the Platte River Valley was famous, one of those maelstroms which could occur unexpectedly anywhere from Independence to Fort Laramie, where hailstones could be five inches thick and dent the pots and pans and kettles with which the earlier emigrants had tried to cover their heads in protection.

"Git back across the creek," Tom screamed at them.

"Back across there?" John asked, stupefied by the command. The torpid creek had suddenly become a raging torrent.

"It's the only way. In another few minutes you won't be able to make it, the water'll be too high; but if we go now, we'll mabbe git across and we ken git ourselfs far enough back so as they can't git near enough to us to do no real harm. Git up on his horse," he ordered the girl. "At least we got one left—no thanks to us. And don't give me no lip. This ain't the time for lip."

He hoisted the girl up on Mason Raymond's horse and, dragging against wind and hail, tried to get it going. He kept beating the horse across the rump to force it down to the water, and the horse kept standing stolidly, refusing to move. It had been through enough. Tom was impatient; it had to get through that avalanche of water before the creek rose any higher, but he couldn't get the horse to move; it was afraid of everything now. Cold, wet, miserable, Tom stood in the downpour and strung together profanities. Then he gave the horse a crack with the reins that resounded even through the noise of the storm, and the animal got going, but at the water's edge it balked again. Water poured like the eruption of a volcano past them. "It ain't no good," the girl kept saying. "We ain't goin' to git across. There is no way in this world we is goin' to git across that."

"Hit him, hit him hard from behind," Tom shouted and John, dragging Mason Raymond along with him, got up near enough to give the horse a violent blow. "Harder, hit him harder."

John took the gun he had just risked his life to get and brought it down with all his might against the horse's rear, and the animal plunged ahead into the whirlwind of water. It was like a piece of prairie brush whirled first one way, then another, spinning in circles as the water tossed the animal about. There was no way in this world (as the girl had pointed out) that it looked as if the horse would make it saddled as it was with the weight of the girl, and Tom looked at the two boys, who were bigger and weighed more, with despair. Whatever muddleheadedness had made him think he could control things and get them all across this country?

Tom plunged into the water himself and grabbed hold of the girl, holding her fast to him so that she couldn't be swept away, reins in one hand, the other anchored around her waist. Both of them were plastered wet from the rain and the river, the wind throwing their sodden clothes up about them, wet lumps of rag.

They made it midstream but then they began to be dragged downstream, and as the horse was drawn downriver it was also being thrown back; they were losing ground, might even be toppled and carried off. Great crashes of thunder sounded; enormous columns of lightning flashed; Tom fought to keep the horse upright, leaning so far forward the girl was stretched flat along the horse's neck. Now or never, he told himself, and tried to drive the horse through the roaring waters. Nearby lightning hit something with a dazzle of brilliance and a splutter of electricity. The terrified horse tried to break loose but was sinking like a stone. If Tom didn't move it immediately, he would never get it to the other shore.

Water rose over his back and swept over the girl's head. She rose up shrieking and Tom held on, trying to right the horse. White foam, white bubbles blew up in a thick spray all around them; they looked sudsed. He worked feverishly.

Meanwhile the horse found its footing again and was plunging on. Suddenly it rose and scrambled, fell, rose, and scrambled again; it had reached shallower ground. They were across, limp and exhausted, but across. But the two boys were still on the other side.

Tom stood, blank, in the howling gale, bleak with the pointlessness of everything. He felt cold enough in the eye of the wind to perish, and what difference did it make really whether he froze to death or was plugged by a bullet. There must be a poem somewhere for all this, but for the moment rhyme failed him.

On the other side of the water one of the boys was screaming incoherently into the gale. Tom didn't even try to understand what he was saying; just words thrown into a wind that swallowed them alive and spit them out miles beyond. He stumbled a few steps forward and sank in the mud; it made queer slurping sounds as it grappled up at him, and for a moment he found himself laughing, wild uncontrollable laughter that rose from the picture in his mind of the Captain sloshing wine around in his mouth, admonishing him to savor the sensation of the grape. When he was being swept away by the river, swallowing great mouthfuls of brackish water, what had his taste sensation been then? A drowning man was said to review his whole life in a flash, but what was there worth reviewing? He would go out of the world as powerless as he had come in, a nobody, a nothing, a nigger who never got anywhere in his life. Black skin, black life. It seemed to him as simple as that.

IV

Claps of thunder fell down on John, an announcement, it seemed to him, of the end of the earth, Armageddon, as those fiery-tongued preachers back at the Landing were always predicting. The parting of the skies through which lightning flew in great silver arrows was perhaps an opening for Mason Raymond's avenging angels; they would come forth and flourish their golden trumpets and proclaim the final battle between good and evil. John was half expecting Mason Raymond to rise up and shout "Hallelujah!" but Mason Raymond, like himself, only stood shivering, watching the terrible storm that poured down on them.

Tom had got the rope off Mason Raymond's horse and was uncoiling it and looping it around the horse's belly. But it didn't look to John as if there were going to be enough left over to throw across to the other shore. It's too short, he thought, it's too goddam short, but maybe he can throw it out partway and we can git in the water far enough to meet it and he can use the horse to help drag us across. He looked at Mason Raymond and felt somewhat reassured; Mason Raymond looked calm, and even, in a strange way, capable. John had been expecting him to be down on his knees waiting to embrace The End.

Tom threw the rope. It fell into the water, sucked under, and disappeared; the tug of the current was so powerful that Tom was pulled straight out of the mud and out toward the powerful mouth of the water. He dug in, sinking again in the mud, and tried to loop the rope in, fighting the fierce determination of the water. Mason Raymond's horse panicked, brayed, and danced in terrified hops of hopelessness. Tom was shouting.

John crept out into the water. It rose to his chest, caving it in with coldness. He was yanked free of his footing by a sudden jolt of water and he fell face down, openmouthed with astonishment so that he swallowed muck, retched, flailed about, and then found bottom and scrambled to his feet. He reeled and fought the water, trying to swim, but there was no way to go against such force. The only hope was the rope and Mason Raymond's horse as leverage. "Shout over somethin' to that fuckin' horse," John hollered to Mason Raymond. "Give it some encouragement or somethin'."

Tremulously the call came on the wind. "Mabel . . . Mabel . . ." like he was calling the wife of the man he had killed.

The horse couldn't hear. "Louder, call her louder for godsake, she can't hear."

And there it came again, clearer, but more plaintive, "Mabel . . . Mabel . . ."

On the other side of the river the horse stopped its crowhopping and hesitated. Tom got himself pulled out of the mud; he looked gray instead of black; it wasn't an improvement. "Keep callin' her," John commanded.

"Mabel . . . Mabel . . . come on, Mabel."

Tom urged the horse forward and started to throw the rope again. John forced himself against the freezing waters to meet it. The rope landed ten feet from John, who threw himself out and fell flat on top of it, anchoring it with his whole body. But he had it, he had it, pulling it in and fastening it around his waist. Though he knew his voice was useless in the vortex of all that howling wind, it kept shrieking, "What about the mule? What about Caboose?" Then he was swirling and spinning in the insanity of the current, thrown under, spitting, fighting to surface, submerged, unable to right himself, tossed and turned, rock bruised, rope jerked, waterlogged, fighting, praying, cursing, lungs bursting, somersaulted, catapulted, smashed back under, stung and broken and hauled at last up onto the opposite shore where, spewing black water and rage and impotence, he screamed, "We left the damn mule behind. We left Caboose back there with all our supplies." He never even thought of Mason Raymond, who was also back on the opposite shore.

Nothing was right, nothing . . . and there was nothing John could do to make it right. Worst of all his anger could find no focus. He could not blame Tom or the girl for Mason Raymond, who was waiting patiently on the opposite bank, could not blame them the piebald had run off (well, yes, he might blame the girl for that, but not Tom), could not blame them the mule was abandoned and that there were men waiting to blow them all to Kingdom Come, could not blame any of them for the skies falling in on them, neither for the mud nor the raging river, not for the lashing wind or the cold wetness, not for anything. All these were just things that had happened and there was nothing that he could do to control or order them; as in all other times, his life was getting away from him and his sense of helplessness was what gave rise to his rage; he felt weak and puny and insignificant in a world where he needed desperately to be strong—and would never be strong enough to stem the tide of outside events. He would never have strength enough to get all that he wanted—never, never, never.

He remembered how he had told himself all the way from Albany . . . once you get across the Missouri, things will be better—and of course what he found out was that nothing was any different on the other side of the Missouri. No matter where you went there was no river you could cross where things on the other side would be different. "We gotta go back. We gotta git the mule," he said. "And, if we can, the horse."

Great streaks of green, open welts, festered in the purple cloud collisions overhead; a wounded sun lay behind that green, pressing to break through, like pus, and the raw sky held the breakthrough back, pulsing, like a feverish wound

beating, as if the sky ached and throbbed; and with the throbbing and pain there was no time to trouble with rain or wind
or hail; these died down, and the sun shot a single violent
thrust through the storm; the wind fell back, the rain sputtered
and died to a sullen drizzle; a great throb of red, like blood
coagulating into a ball, glowed on the horizon, and gathered
heat and force, the determination to burst through; pulsating
there above the distant bleak and blown horizon like a cauter-
ized open sore. John could hear Mason Raymond's vagrant
calls now, hopeless, choked, hoarse; he mastered the instinct
to cover his ears. It was wrong to shut pain out.

Under the lime-violet sky the river raged on, a force that
defied the two men and the girl to master it, but already Tom
was doing things with the rope, doubling it up and knotting
it together every four or five feet; his language one long string
of abuse directed at the kind of god who would let his good
tobacco get soaked through. The girl had shriveled into herself, shaking with cold. Tom made a wide loop of the two ends
of the rope and knotted them into a big circle. "Here, you,"
he said to John, "git the horse."

John went over to the animal and tried to get it to move.
It was shaking almost as violently as the girl; we're all going
to die of the shakes before this day's through, he thought. He
hauled the horse up next to Tom and stood, teeth chattering
—lord, what a tune the back molars could play—waiting to see
what happened next. He was fresh out of advice. In such a
sorry situation advice was of no use anyway.

"Only consolation is that they's as bad off as we is," Tom
said. "Guns probly as wet and useless as ourn." He threw the
looped end of the rope around the horse's body and began
making adjustments.

"You goin' back across?"

No answer, just more fiddling with the contraption he was
rigging up. He swung himself up and held out the double-
knotted strands of rope to John. "Git in front," he said.

John stared. Git in what front where?

"In that space at the front, you're gonna swim and I'm
gonna guide you with the horse. Ain't no choice. It's that or
let the boy git bushwhacked." They were arguing when they

heard the whinny, high and hysterical, a horse gone crazy; on the opposite bank of the river the girl's piebald came flying into sight, plastered wet with mud and briers embedded like freckles in its coat (to match the girl, John thought), the worst-looking critter John Buttes had ever seen, crazed, his father would have said, and he would have been right.

Crashing and roaring, the river came down with rocks and boulders, old dead trees spinning crazily in the current, bushes and brush flying from bank to bank. The Indian pony was racing back and forth on the opposite bank, and beside it the mule suddenly appeared, braying; the girl started shrieking, and in all the hubbub and hysteria another figure had started up on the bank in back of Mason Raymond. The girl began to wave and scream and dance up and down, as if finally too many pressures had been put upon her and something permanent had snapped, she wasn't ever going to be right again.

"Christ, it's one of them," Pepper Tom said. "You git one problem it begits another." He got down off Mason Raymond's horse and began stamping around in frustration. "I can't think what I done to deserve all this."

When in doubt, do something—anything—was a motto John Buttes had heard espoused most of his life by people at the Landing. Now he seized on the maxim, desperate, and threw the rope over his head. "Git on," he said, "git on and git goin'." He seized Tom and shoved him toward the horse. "I'm game if you are."

"No, no," the girl was screeching. "Wait—it's one of them Army men, one of them Army men, I tell you."

"Deserters," Tom said. "That's what them fellers were doin' with that half-breed Indian, deserters goin' to the Hills and wantin' our rig to take them in." Suddenly his face lit up. "Let them git the mule out and catch up the horse. Let them do the work and let us reap the rewards." His face was shining. He began to cry his joy into the wind: "Let them catch our animals up for us and then we'll git them—"

Stark, raving mad, John thought; now I've got two loonies on my hands, two loonies and this damn girl. "Git on the goddam horse. We got to git across—Mason Raymond's over there all on his own." If anyone had ever tried to tell John he would take his own life in his hands to go back and get that crazy cousin of his, he would have counted him in the same class as the rest of the insane. But when it was a matter of Mason Raymond's life, there was no hesitation in John; though their ties had never been close, as he had tried to explain to the nigger (he'd be damned if he'd call that colored man by name, this was all his fault), that thousand miles from East to West had forged a link John himself had not even been conscious of: *I'm responsible for him, goddam it,* was the way he thought of it now. I can't just leave him over there to git kilt because he will git kilt—or worse, blind or paralyzed or something awful like that, and then I'll have him on my hands for the rest of my life.

I never thought I'd make it to Independence with him; god knows it's goin' to be hard enough to The Sweetwater; but *the rest of my life?* I can't take that.

John looked across the raging river and thought, Will you jest look at him now? Mason had started up the bank, going toward trouble instead of away from it, just the kind of thing no sensible human being would do. The Army deserter left off hassling the piebald and began waving his arms and pointing. "Signalin' the others," Tom cried in despair. "What's he doin', goin' back so as they can gang up on him?"

Mason Raymond was slipping and sliding in the mud, trying to scramble up the bank. "He ain't gonna let them git the horse and mule," Tom said. "He thinks *he* can hold 'em off."

"Shoot," John said to Tom, "for godsake, shoot, you got the perfect chance."

"Gun won't work. It's all wetted up."

"We got to do somethin'. He'll git kilt." John jumped up on the horse and thrashed it back toward the raging river. Its strength had already been drained in the first crossing and it was tired to the bone, but it tried. Mason Raymond, he don't even worry he's like to git shot, John thought, he ain't even got enough common sense to be scared. He'll jest let hisself be filled with lead without even a decent protest.

John started hollering, the girl started hollering; only the nigger was silent. He's give up, John thought. "What are we gonna do? He can't hear but even when he can he won't listen,

] *191* [

he's so dadblasted contrary. What can you *do* with someone like that?" The anger had begun to take hold again. John felt like beating Mason Raymond's horse in his frustration, but even he, for all his rage, could see the horse was done in. It couldn't get back across the stream let alone make a return trip back again to this side.

Mason Raymond was almost to the top of the bank; he hoisted himself over the rim and then gave a giant lunge and toppled over near the deserter, grabbing him around the ankles. The man hit him across the head with the barrel of his gun, and Mason Raymond lay still. "Well, that settles that," the nigger said. "He's been buffaloed."

"They ain't took the horse and mule yet. Don't you want to wait around and see that?" John asked.

"That boy probly ain't dead, if you's worried about that, jest busted up some in the head. Might as well lay there as here, ain't any of us gonna eat or git warm this night, I ken tell you that."

They fell back to a small outcropping of sickly brush, beaten down by the storm. A fire was out of the question. Anything that might have been burnable—if they could have found anything—would have been too soaked to catch fire. They huddled together, waterlogged and wind-torn. "Night comin' on and the cold," Tom said. He began to strip. John and the girl watched, neither alarmed nor horrified, simply spectators at an event of some interest, but apart, uninvolved. He got down to an underoutfit the like of which John had never seen before, a one-piece shift that looked as if it had been made out of an old discarded saddle blanket. His arms and legs were big thick knots of muscle and his neck, before it ran into his underwear, was corded so thickly that it looked like the rooted ground knobs of some old vine. "You too," he said, but they paid no attention, examining him curiously to see what he planned to do; he was shaking out his clothes and pounding them against the ground. "You, too," he repeated. "We got to beat the water out and then try and dry 'em out. We git ourselfs to do a little runnin', keep up warmer than if we jest stand still and mabbe even we ken git up a little wind, help dry us down. Ain't gonna eat nuthin' this night, might as well git workin' on the guns 'cause in the mornin' I'm aimin' on findin' them fellers and takin' back what's ourn. I never was one to let lyin' and thievin' be."

You were never one to let anything be, John wanted to say. He looked at the thick powerful body in front of him. He thought of how he had neither Tom's well-honed bones and muscles nor his crafty mind. He was just a green boy, wet and out in the middle of nowhere. Jest nuthin', he thought in disgust. There ain't one single solitary thin' I can think of to recommend me.

Weak tea-toned light liquefied the new day. Though the stream had dropped a little, its level was still flood-high and dangerous. Neither the mule nor the horse was in sight, but on the opposite shore Mason Raymond was sitting up hunched over, his head cradled in his arms. They hollered and he looked up once and then his head sank down again and that was that. "Cleared out," Tom announced, "sure as sin them buggers hightailed it out last night with our horse, our mule, our stuff. But they sure as hell weren't goin' to take *him*. We're gonna have to move quick to catch up with 'em. They got that jack slowin' em down; one thin' you can say about that ornery critter, he ain't no runner, not like that little piebald of yours," he said to the girl, real admiration in his voice, and John got mad as a hatter. That horse wasn't hers at all; all she'd done was swim it around a little in the stream. "We git that little mustang back we got ourselfs money in the pocket. I never seen sech runnin' and I seen a lot of good horseflesh in my day. We got to dunk ourselfs all over again gittin' back across that damn water, discourages you startin' the day out like that. We only been out three days and all I got to say is this been some trip. But some of them are."

They trudged, silent, down to the bank, Tom hauling Mason Raymond's horse along beside him. What was troubling John was the fact that when they got across the river all four of them couldn't ride one horse and that meant that three would be walking and even the one on horseback would be held up; there was no way in this desolate desert John could see any way of overtaking the deserters and getting their property back. And even if by some miracle they did catch up, how were they going to get the better of men who probably outnumbered them, were probably a whole lot better armed? If they were Army deserters, the chances were they'd run off with the latest and best the Army was issuing. But the nigger was exuding confidence, scouting back and forth along the bank for the best place to ford, the perfect example of a man who knows things about the world that John hadn't even begun to suspect.

He had found a good place downstream, Tom was shouting, signaling them to come along. To John's eyes there wasn't much difference where they tried to cross the wild waters; any spot was going to be mean going. No choice though—no choice *ever,* teeth or claws. He held the horse while Tom strapped the girl on; she'd get the privilege of riding, of course. And so, it seemed, would the nigger; he was climbing on behind her back. Oh, fuck it, John thought, what's the use of gettin' mad? I'm always tail end, me and that damned mule.

The horse held up well enough in the shallower shoals, but as the water mounted over its flanks, it began to stagger and slide, going down stoically, drowning and death, what did it matter, sliding under the water without flinching, water coming right up around its eyes; and then it took to paddling, bumping and heaving, damn plucky though, you had to admire its guts, swimming against that wild current, an old beat-up nag like that.

John stood watching. After they made it across, maybe they could get the line back to him again and he would have the privilege of being hauled back through that freezing water a second time. Then he looked down and saw they'd left the rope. Uncontrollable anger took hold of him; he thought for one actual moment he might pass into darkness with the intensity of it. Of all the damned stupidity—can't nobody around here do *nuthin'* right?

Wet and triumphant, the horse scrambled up through the mud of the opposite bank. From his side of the river John yelled at them; they didn't even raise their heads to holler back, too tuckered out to care they'd made it. How was he supposed to get back across? That horse wasn't up to another trip back and forth again. They didn't have the rope. And he couldn't swim that water no way that he could see it. The current and the cold would kill him in no time flat. He was freezing enough as it was now—that wind had a bitter bite; in another hour he'd be a pillar of ice. Like one of them figures in the Bible, turned to stone or salt or ice or something because it looked back. You were never supposed to look back, that was the moral John read into that story; otherwise the past petrified you.

But what did they care? They were across—across, exhausted, too exhausted even to look up and see his predicament.

"Let the horse rest up," he was shouting over to Tom, "and when it gits its second wind, I'll haul it back across."

"It ain't goin' back across."

John didn't argue. The nigger was right. The horse was done in. He tried to think what his father, his grandfather, would have done. They wouldn't have made a big issue out of being left behind; that much John knew right off. They wouldn't have got mad or put the blame off where it didn't reside. They would have— The words came to him very clearly: *Show, do not say.*

He plunged into the water. It was like a slam of ice crashing up against him; he was paralyzed with cold, trying to move his arms and legs and nothing happening, swept downstream with a wild whoof and rush around a corner and crashing into a curve of the bank, hauled up on mud, plunging right and left, frantic to keep from being mired, the current sucking him up and lifting him high in the air for an instant, then dropping him out in midstream again; and, desperate, he flailed and kicked and went under, came up again and smashed against something, a broken branch, grabbed and hung on, racing downstream. He was past all feeling when a rock suddenly somersaulted him into midair and he came down with a crash, then went out, spinning, into space again. He fell with a thud, beached in weeds and a pile of brush and debris, thinking, Oh god, I bet I busted my head, and then everything dissolved; he felt as if he had been pulled to the bottom of the river and left there for dead.

When he opened his eyes the four of them—Mason Raymond, the nigger, the girl, and that goddam nabby horse of Mason Raymond's—were looking down at him. The nigger was viewing him with a smile, a glitter of gold from the back of his mouth catching hold of the sun, making a glittery spike as he leaned forward:

"*Who looks upon the corpse with tearful eyes,*
And heaves a deep-regretful sigh?
Ah, 'tis both of us, the last and true,
Who smile so joyfully down on you."

He paused a moment as if in reverent silence; then he said, "Stove in, but not give out. A little bent up, but all in one shape, so to speak."

They raised him up and gave him blows on the back. Water gushed out, vomited or spilled, he wasn't sure which and didn't care.

John coughed up bile and felt his head divide and multiply against fate. They started to strip him. The girl said something, and he said, You want to feel my *what?* but she had her hand on his heart; she nodded to Tom and Mason Raymond, and they raised him, water running out of every crack, there wasn't an empty socket. Where did they get the strength? Especially Mason Raymond. A great knob stood out at the left side of his scalp and part of his face was lividly blue and purple. Yet there he was trying to help drag John about, he and Tom pulling John to his feet where he hung suspended, like freshly butchered meat, his arms making the letter C around each of their necks, mouth gushing water as if it were the badge blood of the slain. *Life was jest too difficult.*

It's my own fault I'm in this mess, he reminded himself when he was able. No one made me come West, nor drag *him* with me. Not true—you were greedy. You wanted the money he promised. Ain't you never heard that hogs that glut theirselfs git sick and die?

Sick, miserable, mad, irritable, angry, weak, and wet, the three men walked and the girl rode. At least that was the way they started out. Even in extreme, at least at the beginning, secondhand scruples were observed. But after a time the courtesy could not hold up. Mason Raymond was so light-headed from the blow on his head that he kept stumbling, and twice he fell and had to be helped up; John came to the point where he simply sank, his legs no longer working, and lay, cursing, until the girl got down off the horse and, with the nigger, helped him up. That seemed to him the last straw: kept going by a ratty girl and a down-at-the-heel nigger.

"We can't keep goin' like this," the girl said, woman-weak, the others ignoring her, staggering and flailing about trying to keep going. Finally the nigger called a halt and they all, even the horse, gave up for a while, defeated cyphers out in the midst of nowhere, a lesson from which nothing could be learned. "We got to take turns," the girl argued, and when no one opposed her the matter was settled, silently. Later, after a timeless interlude, the nigger stood up, swaying, and looked the others over. "You take your turn on the horse first," he said to Mason Raymond. "You look the worst. Then you next," he said to John, "then me, then the horse rests, then we start over with the girl."

They switched every fifteen minutes except for the last fifteen minutes of each hour when all four of them walked and the horse rested. No one had a timepiece that functioned—the nigger's never had and Mason Raymond's was water-soaked and John and the girl had never had one to begin with—so the nigger counted. One, two, three . . . and so on until he went to sixty and he said that was one minute and they should keep track and he kept that up until he hit sixty fifteen times and they switched. The plan was to try to keep going as fast as they could; otherwise there was no hope of overtaking the deserters. In John's private view there wasn't much anyway, but he conceded that, cold, wet, hungry, and thirsty as they were, they had to try something, and this was as good as anything he could think of, though he hardly shared Tom's preposterous prediction that in maybe a day or two they would begin to make the final closing in and get what was theirs. What he wanted to ask was where they were going to eat and water and rest and dry out. The drying out took care of itself under that murderous sun, but he was weak from hunger and burning with thirst and faint with exertion, and there was no way in this wide world they could even limp on if there wasn't some letup. That came, miraculously, from some plant the nigger spied around noon. He hauled them all up and took one stirrup off the horse's saddle and smashed the plant's top off and told them to reach in and strip themselves off some of the insides of the plant and chew that; it would help their thirst and ease their stomachs up. Mason Raymond lay down and closed his eyes, chewing. He had a strange small smile on his face, as if he were actually happy lying there all banged up munching on that bitter stem; yet John envied him that smile because it meant he was outside John's kind of suffering—legs crippled with cramps, head woozy with fatigue, stomach and bowels arched in gas agonies, back wet with sweat and lumped with stings. I ain't *never* felt worse, he thought. He looked at the nigger, who looked as if he were bleaching out under his agony; he'd gone from black to gray; and there was no way to describe the girl, standing there filthy, rubbing the back of her neck first and then scratching at her elbow, so slit up and down at the seams she seemed to John to be coming apart in quarters: He expected to see the partition take place right here before his eyes, another one of the unbelievable legacies of a land that refused to have mercy on anything, even itself. God help us all, he started to think. But it was queer—the words that came out in his mind were To Whom It May Concern . . .

The land over which they had been trudging was flat—flat and hot—a long lonely emptiness of landscape with a yellow sun which lay like a pox on the ground, yellow running sores of sun pitting up odd places in the earth, a place fit only for lizards and buzzards, crows and cowbirds, offering nothing to eat except an occasional root or stalk the girl or Tom pried out of the ground and advised them to chew and small stagnant water holes that were full of alkali and small swimming creatures that tumbled and turned so that they looked like a basin of moving question marks. The sun was so hot that it had soaked up all the moisture from the storm; they were walking over sod so dry and parched that it crackled under their feet, as if that terrible storm and all that rain had never occurred.

"Earth here jest so dry it eat everythin' up," Tom said. "Runs right down through the pores to someplace god knows how far down. Dry as bone," he said. "Seems like it's drier even than before the rain come down."

Occasionally a building, low and lonely, haunted the horizon; they plodded on, lost dots amidst the endless, vacuous earth, the empty sky. There was a message somewhere in all this for John—one which seemed to read *Go back, go back. Git back home where you belong.*

Light-headed, he saw his mother sitting under a halo of lamplight, only it was the sun overhead that made the lamp. "Don't you never git sick and tired of all that mendin'?" he asked her.

"It's got to be done, John."

"Supposin' you didn't do it?"

"Supposin' you didn't milk the cows or feed the calves?"

There it was: the irrevocable law that at least the externals had to be in order because, god knew, few of the internals ever were.

"Your Grandpa told me about the cow dyin'. I'm sorry. It makes thin's hard, don't it?"

"It makes them jest about impossible."

"We'll find a way."

"How? That's what I'd like to know—how do you think we're goin' to find a way?"

"Well, you got to wait and be patient. God provides."

"He ain't been doin' such a munificent job lately, you ever notice that? I mean, the whole country's goin' to the dogs and you can sit there sewin' and say God's goin' to provide."

"Eat your supper, John, you'll feel better." There it was: Food and optimism could cure anything.

"You say somethin'?" the nigger asked. I been talkin' to myself, John thought.

They staggered into the Catholic Mission of St. Mary's, where the Jesuits had run a manual-labor school for the Potawatomi Indians, that, too, now abandoned, the Potawatomi, no more than the Shawnee, taking to white training. But it was a place they had been heading for like the Holy

Grail because there were likely to be people around, no matter how broken-down and outcast, and where there were people there was food and water—and even if they couldn't beg no grub offen strangers, weren't no one could deny them water. They could live without food for a while, but they all had to have water, well water, to douse their insides. All of them had the desert complaint—diarrhea—from the bad water they'd been licking up and probably from those plants the girl and the nigger had gouged out of the ground. They were all weak from the running out of their bodies and they needed purging and a rest—god, I need to lie down bad, John thought, jest sleep. My insides like my outsides is jest done in.

He bulldogged his way along the road, kicking up dust, swiping out at things until the nigger began to mutter under his breath. "Fierce, fierce, oh he's a fierce one all right," mocking me, John thought, stopping in the middle of the road and turning on the nigger and saying, "You want to make somethin' out of it?"

The nigger looked at him and sighed. "Like what?" he asked solemnly. "You mean, like you and me scrappin' here in this dust in this one-hearse burg in the condition we in?"

"What makes you so smart? Jest answer me that—what makes you so goddam smart?"

"Jest tryin' to keep up with you," the nigger said, grinning. "Jest doin' my best to keep abreast of you."

St. Mary's had been the first cathedral between the Missouri and the Rockies, the See of Bishop Miege, "the Bishop of the Indians," as luckless in the end as everyone else. The place was no longer famous for its religion but for the terrible outbreak of cholera in '49 when fifty people had died in one week alone in one of the camps. It's what we gonna git, we don't git some hep, John thought. His mind was fogged. Help, he told himself, not hep. Oh, to hell with it. What difference does it make?

John stood in the lengthening shadows of the old Indian See thinking about all the lost people in this place—most of all of Daniel Boone out here, though it seemed impossible somehow to imagine—yet Daniel Boone's twelfth child (Napoleon, what a name for a child of Daniel Boone and the wilderness) had been the first male child born in Kansas, at least the first one who had been recorded when Boone had been at the Indian agency trying to teach the Kansa Indians how to farm. The absurdity of the whole notion struck John again—that great frontiersman trying to instruct a lot of sulky Indians who didn't want to learn how to farm. Naturally he had failed. Everybody, it seemed to him, was destined to fail out here. Took on more than we could chew, he thought—I jest wish we could chew, I'm so hungry I could eat that dadblasted mule and enjoy every minute of it.

"Look up there," the nigger said.

"Where?" He'd be damned if he'd call that nigger by name. I ain't goin' to, even if he don't seem to take no notice. Sticks and stones can break my bones, but names can never hurt me —another of those old saws that didn't ring true. There were all kinds of names that could crack you right open. People talked about me the way they talk about Mason Raymond, I couldn't stand it, John thought. People back at the Landing used to say I was cocky. Maybe they didn't mean it as no compliment, but I took it that way because what they meant was I wouldn't take nuthin' offen nobody, but they look at Mason Raymond they know they could jest piss all over him and he wouldn't say nuthin, he'd jest stand there in the golden rain like it was all was due him. *"Where?"* he repeated.

"Up there, yonder—settin' in the sun."

He strained his eyes against the sun—an effort that was only rewarded with the sight of another piece of human driftwood, a dried-up length of human leather, a relic of better days, hunched up against a barred-up building, one of those edifices which, like the man himself, had certainly seen better times but was now of no imaginable use whatsoever, a worn-out memento of the past simply waiting to be torn down or razed or burned out.

The nigger trotted over and bent down by the old man, just as if he had nothing more important to do than pass the time of day, nothing more on his mind than being sociable after a long passage over the plains. "You seen some men and a mule go through here—on horseback, like as not in the last day? The mule all strapped up with lots of gear and toting a good-looking saddle? And a little Injun piebald mare with them?"

] *201* [

"Men comes and men goes."

The nigger squatted down in the dirt. "You ain't got any tabacky on you, has you? Mine got all washed out."

"Might."

The nigger was patient, waiting while the old-timer took his time about getting out a plug. He pulled off a piece, passed it over. "Ran off with our rig," the nigger said. "Wiped us clean out—would have riddled us with bullets, they coulda. Thin's ain't like they once was."

"*That's* the god's livelong truth. It all gone back on itself," the old man said. "Gone and soured up, all of it, what was once nice and sweet. Cain't trust nobody no more," he said, looking up at the nigger. "That's why I went and took myself out of it, 'cause there ain't nobody you can put your confidence in no more. Ain't that the honest's livin' truth?" he asked, apparently wanting verification from men he had no faith in.

" 'Pears so sometimes," the nigger said. John was raging. Why don't he axe him for somethin' to *eat*? Stand there chatterin' like that when we're all near starved to death. Chewin' while we're starvin'.

"You reckon they'd go the old ford? I mean, it bein' so well traveled and all. If I was a man took someone else's stake, I'd light out for less traveled ways, wouldn't you?"

"You might, I might," the old man admitted, "But that ain't what you could account proportionable odds. They was headin' straight for the old ford," he said, rising, all gnarled and arthritic and bowed in strange places.

"Thanks," the nigger said. "We're much obliged to you. It was all our gear they made off with. We ain't even got a bone to gnaw on." So now he was getting around to the importants. It was about time.

"Figures. But glad to be of assistance. There's a mite of jerky here," he said, "you that bad off."

John was ready to jump, but the nigger went real casual. "Don't want to disoblige you none." John's stomach was roaring; he could have killed that posey old black.

"I reckon I ken spare it. I lay in a good supply—don't want to be caught short out here on my own. Don't want to have to do and axe nobody for nuthin'. Ain't never done so till now, figure it's too late to start. Some thin's, anyway, man don't *want* to start." He portioned out a little more of his tobacco. "Bad people comin' in now, a whole new crowd. Old days, it didn't used to be like this, you could trust people, leave your mule and gear right out in the open, nobody goin' to touch nuthin'. But thin's is all changed, the rabble, they is all streamin' in. And I been washed up in the tide. Ain't many come lookin' for old Bee Allie Hall no more. Ain't many even remember old Bee Allie anymore. Thin's you done in the past, they ain't of much interest to the present. I used to be knowed the whole length of this here Platte River Valley," he said, pride puffing him up. Let him talk as long as he wants, old windbag, John thought, so long as I git to eat. The jerky was hard to chew, short on saliva as he was, going so long on short rations and bad water; his mouth was prissin' up on him; but, god, it was jest good to have somethin' inside it didn't taste like fungus, he didn't care if the old man never stopped breezin' away.

"Been wagon master back and forth to the Columbia more times than I ken count on these hands"—holding up arthritic deformed fingers. "Ain't many waterin' holes in a thousand miles I ain't drunk at, know what's alky and what passes for pure; know the passes and shortcuts and hard stretches bettern I know my own two hands—you axe any real old-timer, he'll tell you Bee Allie Hall earns his own 'n more, better 'n earns his own, he's a *contributor,* Bee Allie Hall was."

John Buttes's reaction to this litany was to sit down in front of St. Mary's old Catholic Mission and chew his heart out. People come up—men, women, niggers, children, old Irish blowhards—and ask, What you doin' jest sittin' there in the middle of the road chewin' like that? and he'd say, I'm listenin' to an old man ain't never gonna stop and I'm gittin' back my strength 'cause I'm goin' to the Hills, I'm goin' to git me gold, ain't nobody gonna stop me. It was amazing what a little food could do to a man's philosophy.

How come if he was so all-fired great, this Bee Allie Hall, that John had never heard of him? That was what he wanted to ask.

The girl was moving the dried meat slowly around in her mouth, rubbing the back of her neck and turning the toe of one broken scuffed brogue in the dust, watching the pattern it made with the kind of rapt interest usually reserved for major undertakings. The nigger and the old man were chewing tobacco, hawking and spitting, and Mason Raymond actually looked euphoric as if for the whole long fucking trip he'd just been waiting to meet up with an old codger like Bee Allie Hall. He likes all the odd ones, John thought, 'cause he's one hisself.

His damn cousin and that damn girl and that damn nigger would stand there forever being polite while the thieves were getting away with their stuff. We et, John thought. We drink in a bit. Let's git goin'.

How's come he was the only sensible one? Any fool should know they had to keep moving if they were ever going to have any chance of catching up. He began to dance about in his impatience, but just at the moment he didn't think he could contain himself any more, the nigger said, "I don't like to hurry you none, but we got a powerful way to go to catch up, so I guess we best be gittin' along. We thank you muchly for all the help—the jerky, the in-for-ma-tion. Been a *big* help. Saved our lives. Thin's ain't, like you say, the same no more —save for now and agin. It was a *pleasure* comin' on you," that nigger said so gallantly he could have been in some court meeting a king. "But I reckon we gotta git a move on iffen we're ever gonna git back our stuff."

"Don't go empty-handed—" The old man was grubbing about looking for something.

"No, no, you done more than—"

"Ain't many comes courteous no more," the old man said. "Most of 'em"—he paused—"make fun," he said. He wants to give us somethin', let him, John thought, we been on the takin' end so much lately.

A little ways down the road, out of hearing of the old man, the nigger said, "He weren't so bad. An old man but seasoned."

"He was jest a big bag of gas," John said heatedly.

" 'Knowed all up and down the Trail'—who ever heard of him? I ain't and I'll bet you ain't neither and I'll tell you somethin'—I'll bet he jest makes that stuff up to git people to think he was real important, I'll bet he ain't done half of what he claims."

"Mabbe—mabbe not. No way of knowin'," the nigger said, maddeningly complacent. "Here's water. My mouth's bad as that desert. But he was a real *helpful* old man, you got to admit that."

A real helpful old man, that toothless wonder ranting and raving: Yet there was something about the old man that reminded John of his grandfather. His Grandfather Guthrie seemed a great man (well, most of the time), but out here who'd ever heard of him? Who'd ever heard of the Butteses at all out here, and yet back in the Adirondacks they were big people. He could see inside his head as clearly as if he were back at the Landing going through one of his grandfather's spells again (a term his mother adopted for politeness' sake instead of coming right out and saying he was on another of his benders), imagining his grandfather out in the hall, shouting, banging on the door to John's mother's and father's room, demanding to be let in; he could hear, in his own room, his mother protesting, "Go to sleep, Bapa, you'll raise the dead. Go away, stop pounding on the door, you can't come in," his grandfather paying no attention, shouting, banging, demanding to be let in.

John would get up and grope for his pants, his head a thick conflict of the web of dreams from which he had just been wrenched and the action in the hall to which he must attend. He shook his head back and forth, trying to focus his thoughts, muttering, down on his hands and knees searching for his socks. The shoes he could do without, but the socks not. Those halls, even in summer, were cold, and from past experience he knew he was going to have a hard time of it. Only when his grandfather was in one of his really bad spells did he go out into the hall and start protesting he must be let in, he absolutely had to talk to them.

Without wasting time to get the lamp going, John went, one sock missing, to the door and tried to wrest it open; it refused to give. His grandfather, on the other side, was laughing and shouting, "I've nailed her shut, boy, nailed her clean shut, you'll never git out. Not till after they let me in."

This had happened so many times before that John felt no outrage. He went, as he had done in the past, across to his window, shoved it open, and crawled out on the sill. He was suspended over the back porch and with a slight drop he made the roof, wet with dew, and stood, shivering, a moment before he padded over to the edge and swung with his arms from the railing down to the barrel where his mother stored the rainwater with which she washed her hair. There is nothing like pure rainwater for your hair, she always said, standing out in the open, her sleeves stripped back and her bare arms foamed with lather as she rubbed the suds into her scalp. Her long hair lay in glistening strips over her head; she was doubled over, the hair hanging free so that it wouldn't dampen her dress. He saw the picture quite plainly—she even had time to towel up the clean tresses—before he bounced from the barrel to the ground.

Grandfather Guthrie was on the warpath because John's mother had found his hidden cache of booze, removed it from his hiding place, and put it in one of her own. (She was too frugal to throw it out; once in a while she administered a tablespoon of whiskey in hot water with lemon and sugar for the quinsy throat.) Upstairs the old man bawled that he owned this house and he'd just like them to remember that; where was his "stuff"? John trotted down the hall and up the back stairs to find the old man still banging on the door to his parents' room, shouting that he would not have the life drained out of him this way by people who owed him the very roof over their heads, though when he was sober the mere thought that he had mentioned such a thing would shame him into mortified silence for weeks. But when he was drinking, the hidden fears and hostilities of age broke free and surfaced; John saw him as an old man who resented dying, who hated the thought that all his work would mean nothing in terms of redemption on the day of his death, an old man who had few ways of pleasuring himself and the main one, the lethe of drink, was being denied him by his daughter-in-law because she said it was bad for his liver. The liver be damned, he would shout, what difference does it make when you get to be my age?

The great mane of white hair was right in front of John, the dark fiery eyes fixed on his. The mouth was open: He's gonna let go, John thought.

"We got any liquor left around here?" he demanded. "Any real liquor, not that rotgut stuff in the cellar your ma calls hard cider, nobody makes decent hard cider anymore, it's a lost art."

"I think there's some around somewhere."

"I'm an old man, but I know when my blood needs a good dosin'."

"I'm tired, Bapa."

"Well, I'm not. And I ain't a man to drink alone. We lost our best animal today and one we coulda got a good price for. Most people, they think you ought to drink when thin's go well, but I've always been to the mind that the time to celebrate is when they go agin you. The times like these when you say to yourself, 'What's the use?' That's what you're sayin' to yourself these days, ain't it?"

"I 'spect so."

"The use is this, John, the land."

"We don't do somethin' about the bank, it ain't gonna be ourn land much longer, Bapa, it's gonna be theirn."

"And you wouldn't mind that, would you?" turning at the cellar stairs and fixing John with a penetrating look. "You wouldn't mind that at all, you'd be free then to do what you want, wouldn't you? You don't feel nuthin' at all about the double claims you got inside you owe to—you to the land, the land to you."

"A man don't want to be owned when he's nineteen, Bapa. Maybe you don't remember, but then you want to think you can make your own life, you don't want somethin' all set out for you and there ain't nuthin' you ken do to make it yourn. I spent the whole of this year doin' nuthin' but what *other* people want. But now I'm gonna do what's inside me wants doin'."

His grandfather's drinking after that got worse. The more

Guthrie Buttes saw John's resolution stiffening, the more he reached for the jug.

Sometimes he would get so wound up he would bang upstairs and pound on John's door. "I know you're in there," he would shout. "Come out and see what you've all led me to."

"Stop it, Bapa, go back downstairs. I got this door bolted—"

"John, you open up, I want to talk to you. I'm your grandfather, I got a *right*."

"It's too late to talk, Bapa, go back downstairs."

"John . . ."

"Grandpa, I got to git up early—"

"All right, all right." And he would bang back downstairs, muttering and wrangling with himself—he was a great one to talk to himself, argue in one voice, answer in another—John would sometimes come down and look in on him to see if he was all right—well, not all right, but not doing too much damage to himself—and there he would be slumped over, first muttering in one voice and then answering in another. What did he talk to himself about hour after hour all those times— the glories of the past, things he remembered like that old man back there, Hall, that everyone else had forgotten?

He was the hardest hurt when I went, Bapa, remembering the old man standing in the yard looking up at him with misty eyes, but to his credit he had kept himself under enough control so that the tears had not flowed, saying, "So you're really goin'?"

John couldn't speak so he had just nodded; until that moment he had never realized how much he loved his grandfather. He was standing holding the horse, all his gear tied up and laced to the back of the saddle, and he leaned forward and touched his grandfather, a gesture meant to convey how much he was moved. They were a non-touch family; yet his grandfather leaned forward and laid his lined seamy cheek against John's. "Bless you, boy," he said. "Bless you out there in the West."

I never gave him back what he wanted from me, John thought. He was an old man and he made me impatient and I just wanted to get away from him and from the others. His love—all their love—was holding me back. And he knew it, John thought. That's the worst part: He knew how impatient his oldness and his love made me, how much I was dying to get away from the responsibilities all their love put on me. Why is it that we can never love at the time the way we should love right? Why is it that we can only look back on the ruins we have made of love and say to ourselves, Why didn't I . . . ?

Feeling more perky—the girl even skipped once or twice—they made the approach to the old Vieux Ford where the Oregon Trail crossed the Vermillion River and where in 1846 the ill-advised Donner party had started out too late on the long drive to California, started out late and with the worst possible kind of advice, and with that bad luck which seemed to haunt some people in a particular and vengeful way. The Ford had been named for an old Potawatomi chief who had operated a toll bridge, charging a dollar an outfit, which the early users had thought an outrage. Nearby were the fifty graves of the emigrants who had died in the big cholera epidemic of '49.

On the other side of the Ford the Trail was ten to twenty miles wide where the wagons had spread out so that they wouldn't pile on top of one another's dust; where the terrain was rough and a single line necessary they had alternated every day, the lead wagon moving back and the end one shifting to the head of the line so that no one wagon had to eat dust all the way from the Missouri to the Columbia.

Dust reddened John's eyes and made them itch and smart; the brilliant sun blistered his skin and caked and cracked his lips; the mosquitoes and gnats were merciless; he was freckled and rubbed raw all over from insect bites and alkali. And he was hungry and thirsty again just as if he'd never eaten or drunk. The nigger hung on to the jerky, portioning it out in niggardly little bits. Who gave him that right? John wanted to ask, but arguing meant using energy. He panted on, silent. He got his share, and that was after all what mattered.

At the Little Vermillion where the nigger gave each of them a pull of the jerked meat, he said there used to be a marvelous stand of hickory he'd heard about, the last place on the long road to Oregon and California to lay in a good stock of axe handles. It was gone now, hacked away like every other piece of timber the early emigrants could get their hands on. "You drink—careful—here. We got a ways to go till next water. Don't fill your stomachs too full; they'll back up on you."

Under the Kansas sun they plodded on, with the red-headed woodpeckers calling their coming ahead to the sod shanties of the Plains homesteaders, water being sucked out from under the dry hard earth by windmills over deep wells. Droughty Kansas it was called back home where the cartoons pictured huge cornstalks growing way over a man's head, grapes as big as watermelons, and watermelons so heavy that it took two men to tote one of them—before the grasshoppers came. Now the abandoned acres and empty houses dotted the trail; the land ran on, relentless, baked and brown even now in the spring, under the plowed earth of those who had stayed behind. Three days of sun had made the dried winter tufts of last year's grass like tinder. Well, we won't have no trouble gittin' a fire started tonight, John thought, jest use this here burnt-up grass to git it goin'.

"My bet is they's layin' up in Marysville, those deserters," the nigger said. "Always was a good stoppin'-off spot, they tell me. Make repairs, do some washin' up, mabbe even a little lovin'." His face broadened into a smile:

"Pleasures like poppies spread;
You seize the flower, its bloom is shed;
Or, like the snowfall in the river,
A moment white, then melts forever."

John, whose interest in poetry had been mild to begin with, had long ago come to the point where when the nigger began to spout he began to get soured up. The poetry just added to his other irritations—clothes that clung to him as if they had just been burbled up out of the river; he felt chafed raw from where the seams of his pants and shirt rubbed in the moist, secret creases of his body. An hour, an hour and a half on the trail, and he was bathed in steam and sweat; the sun burned everything—man, animal, earth. The sun sucked up every bit of moisture and, while the grass looked for the most part as dry and dead as midwinter, here and there he detected small green shoots that were fighting their way through last year's death to make this year's rebirth of green. Back home there might still be big snowstorms; here he felt encased as in an oven. He pressed on, a physical act of pushing and shoving against the heat, the blue wall of sky, the sun shimmering on the brown undulating slopes ahead, yawning, turning over, burning everything dry as tinder under the molten sky. He could not believe that only a few days before this earth had been so wet that you could wring it out.

A crazy country; crazy, crazy people running around.

The girl was up ahead on Mason Raymond's horse, seemingly unaware that the two men following her had stopped. John slogged along in back, a habit picked up from nagging the mule. When he came up to Mason Raymond and Tom, the nigger's whole face was screwed up in concentration. "Somethin' the matter," he said. "Somethin' not jest right."

In the far distance what looked like a great wall of fire trembled before John's eyes. The suddenness with which it sprang out of the plains startled him and then he calmed. A mirage, a common-enough occurrence in the great emptiness of these parts; it wobbled and floated all the way across the horizon. For a moment though he had even imagined he smelled smoke.

V

*S*he *identified* the smell at once. She had
seen and smelled burned prairie too often,
from when the Indians stampeded game in an ambush, to
mistake the odor. After the buffalo stampedes and ambushes
the whole prairie would smoke for days. Once she had seen
them use the same technique to flush an enemy out.

The sky had an orange halo rising about it up ahead, long
ribbons of red rising and falling like streamers against the
small white puffs of smoke; the whole plain looked alive with
panicked creatures trying to take cover. She wheeled Mason
Raymond's horse around and, as she heard the faint roar
ahead, she knew that even though this wouldn't be anything
like a raging late-summer fire, consuming grass over a man's
head, it would be bad because three days of prairie sun had
sucked the moisture out of the thin new grass, and what lay
underneath was the bone winter-dry tinder that would burn
wildly, with incredible speed. Them men set this, she thought;
they waited for the wind to be right and then they set this here
this fire so if anyone was following they could burn them back.
The only defense was a backfire or dragging a line over the
fire, and those men knew we didn't have any equipment to dig
or drag.

Benjie's first impulse was to reel the horse and gallop back, but the walkers weren't going to be saved like that, not if Mason Raymond's horse had any part in the plans. It had caught a whiff of the fire and was starting to panic. Benjie ridged her back and brought all her weight down in the saddle, holding Mason Raymond's horse steady under her. It was rocking back and forth, frantic, but it still hadn't got the bit between its teeth so that it could take off and run. She leaned forward and drove her hands hard against the bit in the animal's mouth, punishing it and holding it in check at the same time. The animal's head flew up and caught her across the bridge of the nose, an awful blow that felt for a moment as if her head had been cracked apart. Blood spurted all over the saddle, all over her hands, all over the horse's neck. That there *this* horse might be old but it could still be ornery, too. Wasn't a horse put on this earth couldn't be. No four-legged animal without its streak of meanness when you came down to it. Two-legged as well. *You* know that.

Flames flew up in front of her, shooting uncontrolled over the old dry winter grass; towers of black smoke and great open patches, like huge windows, through which she glimpsed the charred remains of the open earth beyond, smoldered and sizzled like the aftermath of a great buffalo burn-out; the horse got away from her and raced, unchecked, toward the line of the fire. Her face throbbed so fiercely that she couldn't do anything but hang on; somewhere the reins were flapping free and the horse's front legs might get caught up in them. She had to pull herself up and get the horse in hand.

The heat was intense, even though the fiercest part of the blaze was perhaps a quarter of a mile away. She felt singed. The horse was emitting high screaming whines; it banged sideways and then ran west on a parallel line with the fire which continued, leaping and crackling, in large bolts across the dry brush, a hopscotching of incredible speed through which open untouched portions of the prairie could be seen.

Benjie dropped down on the horse, groping for the reins, blood streaming down the horse's withers. Her hand closed over leather and she yanked hard, trying to guide the animal slowly in a quarter circle, then easing up; the horse ate up the earth under them as if it were dropping away; she saw nothing solid at all, only thin smoky vaporous air.

She was not afraid and not bad hurt—her nose probably busted up some, but nothing serious—and she felt confident about the horse. She'd fought out enough of Bone Hand's prize stock to know hot blood when she saw it. This was only panic. A real spirited horse, once it made up its mind, could never have been stopped, there just would have been no holding it—the piebald, for instance—but this horse, it didn't have that kind of heart, it was too humanized, too many years on it; you could reason with it with your hands and legs and talk it into something sensible—if you kept your head.

The fire was so close that she could see the individual ribbons of flame, an avalanche of sound and searing and cracklings that threatened to incinerate them all to small gray lumps of bones here on the burning plain.

She let the horse set its own gait. She could begin to distinguish the others, left behind, John the easiest because he was the tallest. John was half out of his mind with exasperation and outrage. He put out his arms and semaphored to her to get that horse reined in. Her head was light from the pain of the blow and she felt dizzy, a spinning sensation that dipped her down toward darkness, but she tried to do what he was pantomiming. Yet she felt herself slip sideways and she almost went off; then she caught control again and the three figures in front of her came into focus and began to enlarge and assume normal shapes.

"Hang on, you dang fool, jest hang on," John Buttes screamed.

What did he think she was trying to do? To Benjie there seemed no possible way for all of them to outrun the fire; it looked as if it extended all the way across the plain, but behind was the Little Vermillion, water, which they had crossed some time back, and if they could only somehow get back there, they would be all right.

The horse was winded; it sagged under her, its lungs weak and ready to give out. She could hear John hollering at Mason Raymond to run, goddam it, run for all he was worth, while behind her the crackling fire increased its intensity. She drove her hand across the horse's rump and it staggered into a game, if stumbling, trot; the nigger was hollering something, but she didn't care; the thing was to get to the water.

Benjie smelled her own singed hair; her face burned and blistered and her nose throbbed incessantly; her lips felt cracked and even her neck was raw. She pulled off her sweater and threw it over her head. Run, she told the horse. Run, goddam it, push your goddam *this* legs and run, run like you never run before in your whole goddam *this* life.

The creek was how far? No way of knowing. She hadn't been keeping track of distance; there was something about the monotony of plains traveling that mesmerized; she had been dreamy ever since a few minutes after they'd set out, visions of roses and hollyhocks interchanging inside her head. First she would see one and then the other. She had been trying to figure out why those two flowers seemed so important to her, why they haunted her dreams as well, especially the hollyhocks. In her sleep the night before she and her mother had been weeding the garden, straightening up every once in a while to ease the stiffness in their backs and looking over the roots and vegetables to the hollyhocks. "One door never closes but another opens," her mother said, and Benjie had seen the outhouse door had been left ajar. But that was not what her mother had meant. She had been looking at the graves. Perhaps in some simple way she was trying to console herself. Grief had eaten away at her until it had even taken away the outer flesh on her bones.

John and Mason Raymond pounded past Benjie, running for all they were worth. The horse jolted to a halt again. I'm gonna die out here and there won't even be enough of me left to know where I went down—jest like Ma and Pa and The Boy, nobody ever knowing the exact spot any of us was buried. Jest like none of us even ever existed. At least there was graves back in Kentuck.

At that moment the nigger grabbed hold of the horse's bridle. In the smoke and glare she hung on and let Pepper Tom try to do something to get the horse moving. She wasn't going to be able to do it herself. And she wasn't going to climb down and leave the horse and try to run it on her own. It was the only horse they had.

] *215* [

Tom held tight to the bridle and pulled, the horse blundering after. Her weight was holding them back and she made herself get down off the horse, and reins in hand, she and the black man ran, dragging the horse after them.

The fire was close enough to keep them going at full speed, but the horse was holding them back, completely panicked again. She could see the river ahead. Her lungs were seared with effort, every breath painful; but she kept forcing her legs to get going as fast as they could. The nigger was laughing crazily and mumbling something—one of his poems no doubt —but they were gaining, they were going to make it. They hauled the horse over the bank and flopped down, gasping, Benjie so relieved to be safe she could have knelt and given thanks with gratitude.

Tom was looking at her face. "You sure is some sight," he said.

On the other side of him John and Mason Raymond crouched, ready to swim out if necessary, but the mud seemed for a moment to have held off the advance of flames. Every once in a while shooting stars of embers would explode over their heads or a single leap of flame would suddenly spook out, flare up, and hiss itself into silence; but the breakline at the top of the bank held; the four were at the river edge, crouched, Tom hanging on to the horse, waiting to see whether or not they were going to have to swim out.

Things had been bad before—nothing to eat, no blankets, nothing but what they had on their backs to make do with— but now it was like they were just plain wiped out. The horse was all heaved up and they were all fire-tinged, but she wasn't the worst, even though her nose throbbed terribly. Mason Raymond looked fried to a crisp. "Well, one thing," Tom said, examining him. "I don't know if you's goin' to the Great Bend in the Big Beyond or not, but there's one thin' I ken tell you for certain and that is you ain't goin' to be doin' much prayin' for some time to come. Them knees of yours is all fire tipped."

John tapped her on the shoulder and motioned to her with his head to take herself off with him a way, he wanted to have a little talk. She looked at him so annoyed that she didn't even try to disguise her hostility. Couldn't he see she was wore out? "I don't want nuthin' but rest, I'm that tuckered out. What's it you want to jaw about anyway?"

"I want you to give me the horse."

"It ain't my horse. Why don't you axe him"—shaking her head at Tom—"or him"—indicating Mason Raymond. "They got more say than I do. Take it for all I care. Where you gonna take it anyway? Out there into that fire? I'm jest bone dead tired," she said. "And my face hurts somethin' fierce and now you want to go and plague me about a horse ain't even mine. You figure to take that horse out single-handed, that poor done-in horse, make yourself some kind of big hero, doin' what, may I axe?" Mason Raymond's mare stood with its head hung between its legs as busted out as the rest of them. "That animal needs layin' up," she said. "Needs it bad. You ain't takin' that horse nowhere—jest look at it, ain't you got no pity in you at all?"

"One of us on a horse might jest catch up," he said.

"One of us on a fresh horse, not this here *this* horse. Anyway, what you plannin' on doin'—takin' them all on single-handed by yourself?" She looked at him, just downright disgusted. No one would carve such a crazy plan.

"Might get through," he said, looking at Mason Raymond's horse. "That horse don't look like it'd make another mile though," he said, finally seeing it her way. He looked down, defeated, but seeking, she divined, some face-saving escape from his foolishness. "You sure done some harm to your nose," he said at last.

"Horse came up and banged me with its head—my own fault, I was leanin' forward and not lookin'."

"I reckon him"—nodding at the nigger—"and me could git it back in shape. Be painful though, you know, while we was movin' it back. Ought to have somethin' to hold it, too—I don't know though, a nose might jest naturally hold. What do you think?" he asked the nigger. Mason Raymond was sitting down staring out at the water, his eyes closed. They ought to do somethin' about him, too, Benjie thought. He got burned some.

"We'll set it and then we ken use this here clay mud to mold and hold it. That mud dries, it'll be hard as rock. Won't look so pretty for a time, clay all over your face like that," the black man said, smiling, the gold tooth at the back of his mouth gleaming. "But you ain't gittin' ready to go to no cake walk so mabbe you won't mind as much as you might under other circumstances."

"I've had worse and got through," Benjie said. "I reckon I can survive this without too much moanin'."

She did not sleep that night, the pain and wakefulness reminding her of that other anxious night back at the barracks when she had hovered, all nerved up, waiting for daylight, determined to start out for the Hills, not caring if she ever finished the journey or not; it was not the end of that trip that mattered, but the fact she had will enough left to go; that would show there was still a small spark of Benjie Klomp left inside, that not everything in her life was determined by events that happened outside herself, that some things—she didn't care how infinitesimal—were due sheerly and solely to her own determination.

When she got up off the pallet, she felt as if all of Bone Hand's horses had run over her; she was nothing but aching muscles and bruised bones; there was a hot, white searing rawness between her legs. She left the heavy (buckleless) shoes behind and went slowly on bare feet across the earthen floor. She was going; she didn't care if she fell every five feet of the way, she was going.

She opened one of the big boards partway and looked out. As she parted the boards the hinges squeaked and the sentries, walking overhead, paused and looked down. They held their guns in the uneasy position of men ready to meet an enemy.

She knew that whites weren't able to sustain a sense of menace over a long period of time; when a strange sound set them on the alert, they would perk up and listen, but if enough time passed and nothing unusual occurred, they lost the sense of danger and went back to their normal routine, reassured. An Indian assumed, once a sound said something was off to him, that that danger was permanent until he himself removed it; an Indian could wait, motionless, hours on end for confrontation and resolution.

Benjie prepared to wait, as an Indian would have waited, until the guards lost interest and went back to their bored, inattentive tramping around the ramparts. There was really no reason for those men to be apprehensive; the only Indians to be afraid of were up at the Powder River or in the *Paha Sapa* getting ready to defend their land according to the Treaty of '68.

No white person or persons shall be permitted to settle upon or occupy any portion of the territory, or without the consent of the Indians, to pass through the same.

They were not going to forage down here, those hostile and antagonistic Sioux and Cheyenne who had put in such a hard winter and needed time to fatten themselves and their ponies for the conflict that would come. They would not waste useless energy just to make a minor skirmish down this far on the white man's fort. The winter had been too bad for that. But the friendlies near the fort had not found it much better, she thought. The stories of the Indian hardships in the camps away from the forts that had been carried back to the Indians tented around the forts had been little comfort. In some ways the friendlies were as badly off, maybe worse, than their brothers —short of blankets, freezing; short of supplies, starving; short of hope, despairing. At least up in the Hills there was the kind of anger and hate that gave hope.

No, there would not be an attack and these sentries knew it. Bad as the winter had been, worse was that the soldier, Three Stars, had come in March and attacked Two Moon and driven his people off. The soldiers had destroyed their village and all their food and clothing, "a lesson," the Captain who had bridled Benjie had said, "that should teach them red niggers who has the power and who doesn't." The Captain had been very confident. He put a lot of faith in Red Cloud and his influence, not realizing, as most whites did not realize, that Red Cloud was old and his power gone. Now the young men listened to Crazy Horse and Sitting Bull, who would not hear about petitions from the Great Father to sell their land or to bargain away its mineral rights. The time of talking was over.

Benjie knew a great deal of this—more than the Captain, for all his boasting—because she had been one of those asleep in the tipis when Three Stars's soldiers came. There were three waves of them: the first firing guns, the second coming at the far end of the village, the third driving off the horses.

While the carbines and pistols were being fired, she had been hurried up into the hills; bullets were flying this way and that, but Dark Hair Woman had been very calm, helping the children who had become separated from their own families. From one of the ledges Benjie watched the soldiers put the tipis to torch and burn all there was in the Two Moon camp. The horses that were pesky were shot, the others rounded up and some of these fired upon too, but some of the young men of the village had managed to sneak back that night and get some of the Indian horses back.

It was very cold and there were no hides to keep out the cold—they all had been burned. There was no food; that, too, had gone up in flames. Two Moon had come and stood by Bone Hand and said, "You were right. There is only one road we can go." That road was a three-day trip to Crazy Horse's village. They had struggled through snow, fatigued and freezing, hungry and heartbroken, the old and sick falling by the wayside; but no one had been abandoned. The long solemn line would halt, immobile, while a few of the stronger struggled through the snow to lift up the fallen, to encourage the weak, and in some desperate cases to shoulder the beaten. The village had gone at a crawl, inching its way toward Strange Man's camp where there was food, warmth, the promise of help.

Crazy Horse had come out to watch them straggle in. Though there was little left for his own people after the bitter winter, he went first to Two Moon and then to Bone Hand to welcome all their people in. It was there Two Moon made the decision to fight and Bone Hand the one to send Benjie back while the rest of the village went on to Rosebud. They would fight now and hold on to the Hills or die and go to the Land of the Great Spirit where there was still an honored place for a man obeying his obligations; here, in the white man's land, nothing was what it seemed, nothing could be held to its word; everything was as water that cascades through the hands and drips and sweats in the sun. She believed—she was as sure of this as anything she had ever believed—that the Indians with Sitting Bull and Crazy Horse would fight a war to the end. But not here, not at the white man's forts where the weight of favor went with the whites; no, they would fight up in the Hills where the Indians knew the spiny ridges and queer crevices, the peculiar stone wedges and the tall styluses, the bottomless chasms and crazily running rivers, and the odds were with the Indians.

Benjie waited quietly, patiently, without emotion—she was past feeling, she thought at this point, letting her mind focus on a central shape, a mountain with strange needlelike rocks, that she remembered from the *Paha Sapa*; that was where she would go, to the winding, treacherous path around the rocks like upright needles, and then to Rosebud where, by now, she believed, thousands and thousands of Sioux and Cheyenne would have gathered, getting ready.

The coming of the sun worried her, however, because the more light there was the more chance of exposure. But she had no choice but to wait, and waiting meant also the necessity to remain calm and confident, to be so sure of herself that no enemy would ever have such faith in his invincibility.

The sky was suffused with pink; lurid slashes of blue would eventually knife their way through, but for the moment the smudges in the sky were the color of a woman who has washed her buffalo-bloodied hands in water and the blood has run into the water into a steady infusion of pink. Looking up at the sky overhead was like a reversal of looking down into a pool of pink-bloodied water. Blood in the sky. Blood on the moon, that was said too. And blood on the earth, always blood somewhere. A violent world. He who denied that denied the meaning of birth. Everything, it seemed to her, came from blood; blood was perhaps the metaphor by which all existed. She thought of her bloody babies extracted from her bleeding body; the red-membraned bloody afterbirth; the buffalo with their slit throats; men scalped in coups—life was so violent so shouldn't its sign be blood? There was blood on her legs now as well.

One of the sentries had begun the steady measured pace of the reassured guard; in a moment the others, emboldened, would follow suit. Most men were like buffalo, if the first buffalo went over the chasm to the valley a hundred feet below, the whole herd followed. The Indians used this knowledge for easy execution. They simply drove the herd toward the brink and let them take themselves over. The first buffalo, in its panicky flight, would plunge over, and all the rest would automatically follow.

All the men on the parapet were tramping in unison; she crept into the colonnade beneath them and began to move silently from shadow to shadow; when she reached the big gate, she was not quite sure what she was going to do. She could not, because of its weight, open it herself. An alternative would have been to scale the wall in a place that was relatively free from constant observation, but her legs were too weak to make the scramble over.

Outside the wall she would be all right, she was sure, so long as she hadn't run off with the Captain's horse again. The problem was how to get outside. For a moment she considered what she felt was a suitable form of revenge for all that had happened to her. She would sneak into the stable and muzzle any cry from the Captain's horse, her hand cupped over the horse's nostrils, Indian style; then she would cut the Captain's horse's throat. There would be no suspicious noise; the horse would simply fall, somewhat noisily no doubt, but hardly suspiciously since all the horses in the barn rolled and thrashed about on and off. Then she would slip away.

The horse meant nothing to her, in spite of the fact she had twice tried to run away with it; the only thing about it that mattered was that it was the Captain's property and what she did to it would reverberate back on him; hence, hurting it would be hurting him, and there was much appeal in this.

She stood, massaging the back of her neck. She had come here with all the goodwill in the world; she had wanted, more than anything she could think of, to fit in. And at first everything had seemed to go well. Then, because of a few thoughtless words, all her high hopes had been shattered and the long downward spiral to her outcast state had begun again. She had become a person with no place to go.

Yet everyone needed a place, somewhere that was safe and where there was love, not much love even, just a little; that, and a feeling that what you did was appreciated, that it mattered—*to be wanted,* she thought, to be wanted and appreciated and loved. The picture of her father came into her mind; she kneaded her hands. The image of the Captain came into her mind; she felt the bridling of her mouth with wire.

I will cut his horse's throat, she said to herself resolutely.

The desire to punish the Captain was so strong that the consequences—*If you do that, they will come after you*—almost did not matter. He had humiliated and hurt her—*deliberately* degraded her, that was the worst of it—and he should be paid back. But you are only going to make things worse for yourself, she argued silently. He can always get a new horse, but you—

She was trapped in indecision; first one alternative, then the other seized her. To get away—that was all she really wanted. But to punish the Captain—that would mean regaining some of her self-respect, and what a sweetness there would be in that. She stood looking up at the blood-red sky, opposing desires so strong that any compromise was impossible, but so, too, was any end to the anger and frustration that swept over her in her feelings of powerlessness and insignificance. She grabbed her hands and wrung them, as if physical involvement with her two distinct separate drives could somehow, in the act of coming together and grabbing one another, lead to resolution.

Resolution seized her from without; a pair of strong hands locked over each shoulder. "Runnin' off agin, was you?" he said, that soldier whose only name she ever knew was Skinner, but whose face she would never forget; it loomed over still, guarding the prize caught at dawn while everyone else was sleeping. He kept her locked in a back shed during the day and took her off under the wagons at night, when he fed and bedded her (once each, daily), for that first week; then the others in his outfit began to catch on, but by that time they accepted her as his by right of possession, the way an Army saddle issued to a man becomes "his," or a man's seat at the table, which he takes every day, becomes "his," not by any real right of ownership but by the mere fact of custom and habit.

After a time there was no need to be secretive about Benjie; he could take her out on his drinking bouts and along to his card games; and then, after a time, he seemed not even to have any real proprietary interest in her, the novelty of "owning" her had worn off, and any notoriety or admiration he might have got from the other men for having his own white woman had waned enough so that it was nothing at all to Skinner to put her on the table in a game of cards.

The burnt-out spring roses of the plains seemed to her now like the burnt-out dreams over which she had walked all her life. The hollyhocks—plain, straggly, homely—represented what she was, a girl come up out of hardscrabble soil in the lush Blue Grass State, one of those born and bred poor and meant to make the best of it, like the hollyhock not even meant to blossom every year, but one who only shoots out and flowers, dusty and bedraggled, every other year, sometimes not even then, no garden bloom that you brought into the house but weedlike, sturdy, ratty around the edges, "poor pretty." Hollyhocks bloomed around rubble and debris, the hard earthy spikes of bad soil; real flowers bloomed in the rich loam of the earth.

You don't know things like that for a long time, she thought. You think you are going to be one of the real flowers. You do what your parents tell you and you don't see that all the dreams of roses you make up on your own aren't going to come to any real flowering. But her father was a farmer and he knew all about the reproductive tendencies of seeds; that's why her father hadn't wanted her to stay put amidst the rubble and debris, probably he hadn't wanted any of them to stay there and be what they were destined to be there; but most of all he had wanted her life to have color and beauty, so he had uprooted them all, yanked them out so violently that hardly any of the native soil remained on their straggly roots, threw them in the wagon and went West, not realizing there wasn't enough earth left on any of their roots to last them through the transplanting—a modicum perhaps on hers, but not enough to sustain more than survival from what she had been; there was not going to be any metamorphosis. So she'd only survived, and then only perhaps because the Indians, with their close ways with roots and herbs, had nurtured her through enough to throw up hollyhocks here in the West, the same sullen backyard flower that grew back home beside battered wood wells and old stone fences and outside lopsided privies.

But her dreams had always been of roses, miles and miles of breathy pink petals floating in the prairie wind, of roses she had seen running across an entire plain, and now her understanding was like one of those sudden scorching prairie holocausts that run wild, burning all the flowers down into scorched powdery dust, a life of dreams that would end in nothing but charred dust.

You had to accept what was. Hollyhocks, she said to herself. That's what I am; that's what I'll be all my life no matter how many other thousands of roses run wild on these plains.

She felt the same pain that she had experienced when she winced under John Buttes's fingers bending her nose back into place. It was pure and simple, physical. Though the anguish was inside her mind, the pain was physical.

Men were not gentle. Lots of people thought they were born hard, but then maybe the tenderness had all just been taught out of them. "Don't look too bad at all," John Buttes had said proudly. He wanted her to praise his work. That was the weakness in men, that terrible need for praise. Every woman knew that need, the need for women constantly to reassure men that they were strong. He had hurt her and because he was a man and was allowed to be rough and to treat her in a way she could never treat him, he could get away with that roughness—get away with it and expect at the same time to be praised for it.

One day I'm goin' to git my own back on all of them, Benjie thought. But to his face she said, "I bet you done a right good job." She also knew she was dependent on these men and had to do what was expected or pay the consequences. It seemed to her significant that a man came *down* on a woman, as if, it came to her, he was down on her in the very way he thought of her—she was inferior and so whatever he did to her was all right, no matter how much it hurt or humiliated.

"Won't no one be able to tell it was ever out of shape," he said. "Maybe a little bit on the bridge," he admitted. "But nuthin' noticeable. But we got to git us somethin' to hold it in place—"

Us.

"—somethin', you know, don't make it come too loose. Them bones don't stay where they should 'lessen you hold them secure. Where's that there clay?"

He didn't even call the nigger by name; he just made the demand like what he wanted was owed him. While the nigger was foraging for the right kind of mud, she had experienced a moment of violent upheaval inside her in which hatred expanded into explosions of anger; she was staring at him, her eyes like the eyes of a snake paralyzing, with its steady stare, the bird it intends to devour. He shifted uncomfortably, not knowing how to react because she wasn't following the pattern she should, wasn't being properly grateful or pulsing out praises to him the way he had expected; and she sat in her anger and rebellion and kept right on staring, thinking, He's not goin' to beat me, none of them is goin' to beat me, I don't care what they do. I will not give way. I will *not* break down. I don't care what happens to me. Nuthin' in me is goin' to give in, I don't care how hard it is.

But her nose had hurt so then that it would have been such a relief to be able to cry. But some people—people like her —weren't in any position to cry. People like her had to be hard like stone. What was the saying? You can't get water out of rock.

Roses had run ahead of her, mile after mile of wild roses. The honey-sweet scent in the hot air was almost sickening; now and again the sky would darken with the flight of thousands of passenger pigeons, pink and blue and sometimes in a certain light so purple that they looked black. It was hot, oppressively hot, and the sweet smell of the roses was like death because it reminded her of the wild flowers that had sprung up over the dead white men after the Indians had risen up and murdered the white men who had made them well in the *Paha Sapa*. Before the end of this day the plains would be black like the burnt-out flowers, the burnt-over grass with the great black bodies of the buffalo dead. The sky would be full of buzzards and her hands red with blood from the fresh meat. She was on her way to her first buffalo hunt and she rode to the ambush with the other women to wait until the killing was over and the butchering could begin.

In back of her, where the wind would be behind it, the plains suddenly burst into flames. The animals would run ahead of the fire into a narrow pass that would corner them in a canyon where the women and hunters waited. There was a small break the Indians had built just before the entrance to the canyon, also part of the trap. In front of the one escape route hunters were also strung out, waiting.

The buffalo came at a dead run, stampeded; there were so many of them that the whole plain looked black where they swept over it. She saw the puff of smoke from Bone Hand's rifle and heard the faint crack of powder igniting. The big bull he was chasing trotted on, paying no attention, its shaggy head bobbing in time to its awkward gait; then suddenly it stopped, surprised, and stood still a second, then began revolving round and round in circles, its tongue lagging, foam flicking from the mouth. Bone Hand gave a whoop and galloped forward, puncturing it with arrows, driving them in with such force only the tufted end showed outside the hide. The big bull began to bellow, still circling, blind with rage. Bone Hand turned his pony and started back. But there was no need; the bull had fallen to its knees; it glared up with savage eyes through the black mud-matted mane, and then dropped heavily over on its side, blood running from its mouth, its nostrils foaming. Still it was not dead. It lay on the ground grunting, pawing futilely to try and get back up, tearing up sod, drenching the thick coarse canyon grass with blood. The bull's efforts to breathe were monumental; its sides heaved, blood spurted from the bullet and arrow wounds. It never ceased making sounds of anger and pain and outrage. Benjie ran toward it, her own heart heaving and pitching with almost as much effort as the animal's; she felt as if she were dying, but it was the buffalo's eyes which were turning white and milky. It was a big strong young bull, good for eating, with a fine hide; its carcass would do for many things—clothes, food, utensils, possibly for part of a tipi—but Benjie bent down beside the corpse and commenced to beat on its sides with her fists. She wanted to beat air and life back into its lungs. She buried her head in the buffalo's filthy fur, feeling the mud and bugs and blood mix with the salty water coursing down her cheeks.

A blow fell on her back, then on her neck. "Cut the throat and get at the meat. Cut the throat and drink some of the blood and get at the meat." He grabbed hold of her and put her on her feet. His eyes were terrible—blank, dull, colorless, eyes that were absolutely devoid of any understanding. All at once she believed all the atrocities she had heard of these men beginning with the Minnesota massacre. "Do as you are told," he said.

Over the years she had become one of the best women in the village to skin down and dress out an animal. The first was hard—the first is always the hardest, she thought, remembering the birth of her first baby. But certain things were expected, like the skinning and dressing out of the buffalo; from these there was no escape. Still Bone Hand had protected her as his woman against many dangers. Only with him had there been a small margin of safety. She had to go back then to him. She would ride into the village and Bone Hand would come out and make the brother sign, touching two fingers to the lips and swinging his hand straight out from his mouth signifying it was all right, she could come back.

He's jest got to take me back, she thought. He's jest got to. I got nowhere else to go. Nuthin', absolutely nuthin', will make me go back to the whites. And I can't no way live on my own. So I got to go back to Bone Hand. The Injuns has jest got to take me in. I got no place else to go.

Three

Alcove Spring

I

*M*ason Raymond's skin seemed to vibrate.

He felt as if someone could reach across and grab a flap of skin at the forehead and give a yank: It would peel away just as a snake's skin is shed every seven years. It had been, it suddenly occurred to him, almost seven years since he had shot Worth Hart.

Seven years since I shot Hart. He had never before allowed his mind such bluntness. He had used devices to avoid direct confrontation; usually what he thought was something like "since Worth died." It was not just his *skin* peeling away from the conflagration; he had altered something fundamental in his mind as well. You stop running around words—going sideways the way that girl does with her *this* instead of *shit*—and you have to face what is. Yet the shock of that statement —*shot* Hart—for a moment had been like an internal explosion inside his mind.

Well, I did shoot him. There's no way to run around that. Never before had Hart come into his head like this and then gone back (to wherever it was he stayed, perhaps his half or whole inch of space somewhere in one of Bartholomew's spheres) without Mason Raymond paying his debt of remorse or the absolute obligation to do penance for the universal law he had violated.

He thought, well, I killed him—I *shot* him—and there's nothing I can ever do to bring him back. He got up and waded ankle-deep, shoes and all, into the freezing stream and commenced plastering himself with large fistfuls of mud.

"My god, what you doin'—you crazy or somethin', coverin' yourself all over with *dirt?*"

Nor did John's exasperation disturb him. I'm not the fool this time, Mason Raymond thought. It's *him* that doesn't see. "Mud is good for burns," he said. "Bartholomew, up there on the flats, he was always forgetful and getting some part of him scorched by the fire and he'd put mud on it, said it drew the blistering out, and he had some pretty bad burns, but nothing ever infected or scarred bad—I'm burned and I'll be damned if I want to get sick or scarred, so I'm putting on mud, just the way Bartholomew used to do. Bartholomew thought a lot, John, and he had maybe some what you'd call queer ideas, but basically anyone who could live out and survive the way he did all those years had to have a store of common sense as well. I just wasn't looking much at the common sense at the time, but now and again some of it comes back." Mason Raymond couldn't help grinning, much as it pained him, at the look on his cousin's face; he's been put in his place for a change, he thought. I must be getting like everyone else, he thought, if I take some satisfaction in the licks *I* get in. Bartholomew would have to stay up in his cave for a while and leave his head alone; Mason Raymond saw he was going to have to attend matters at hand, here in—what state was it they were in? he asked.

"Kansas—bleedin' Kansas still," the black man said, "we ain't even to Marysville yet and we run up a score like I ain't never yet heard of. You best lie back," he said to the girl. "That blow you got takes a lot out of you more than just a whack across the head. Does your insides in, too, churns you all up, in your feelin's too, gittin' a bad blow like that does— you, too," he said to Mason Raymond. "You git yourself all covered over with mud, you ought to git some rest—though ain't that stuff cold?"

"It's freezing, but I'd rather be cold with the mud than on fire with the burns. It's kind of like the cold mud and the hot skin even things out. We gotta go after those men," Mason Raymond said with such violence he surprised himself. Years had passed since he'd felt such anger—Lite, he killed my dog and I would have killed him if Uncle Cob hadn't stopped me. "John," he called to his cousin, Cobus's son, and John looked up, sullen and skeptical, as if to ask, what you up to now?

"Listen," Mason Raymond said, "remember when we had that bet about the coon? You know, the time your father made that bet with Lite about which of us would bring a coon in first, and I brought mine in and it was alive and Lite, he was so furious because he said it wasn't fair, I should have shot it dead, and he shot my dog, he shot—"

"Sure I remember," John said grudgingly. "Who'd go and forget a thin' like that?"

"We were going to kill Lite, you remember that? We were going to kill him, you and me?"

"We was, wasn't we?" John Buttes said in wonderment. "My god, you was so determined wild horses couldn't have stopped you, but my Pa and Rivers, between them—"

"Rivers took the gun," Mason Raymond said. "And your Pa wouldn't let us go. But you and me, we had it in our minds to kill that no-good lying cowardly Lite, and if we had—listen, John, if we had killed him then, the way maybe we should, Hart might be alive today. Lite was a bad, evil man and I *shoulda* shot him," Mason Raymond said, getting more excited, "just the way these are bad, evil men and *should* be got —they tried to kill us, and when that didn't work they set that fire; they don't think *anything* about other people. All they care about is themselves—they'd set fire to the whole prairie and burn us out and craze all those animals out there and never think a thing about it. They could have killed her—" Mason Raymond said, turning to the girl—"or any of us, *all* of us, done it without even a second thought—" He paused, the words all clotted inside his throat. "Those men out there, they never even laid eyes on us, but they couldn't care less whether we were alive or dead—no, that's not true either. They *wanted* us dead. And they're out there now, with all *our* things, probably they're laughing themselves sick because they think they've burnt us all to Kingdom Come."

He looked at each of them in turn—the girl, strange with the clay covering half her face, the black man staring at him in perplexity, John rooted silent in astonishment—it was all so clear to him; how could he get it across to them, but John ought to understand, John had known Lite and Hart. "Don't you see?" he asked John. "If you and me had gone ahead and killed Lite, none of the bad things would have come after. You and me, we didn't do what we shoulda then, but we can now. You and me—we're the ones should track those men down and get our own back on them."

"Holy jumpin' Jesus," the black man said. "What next?"

He'd been really crazy for such a long time that there was no way to present accurately the logic of what he was saying. Anyway, he thought, maybe I wasn't ever really crazy. Grief takes a long time getting over. *He* (looking at John) doesn't know that yet. He's never had that kind of emptiness and sense of loss, the kind that had driven Bartholomew away from people because people had hurt him and, if he wasn't around them, then how could they do him more harm? And yet, ironically, it was Bartholomew who had urged him to go out and hunt love.

It's not love that's going to make me be able to live with myself again, Mason Raymond thought. In *this* world, he could have said to Bartholomew, there are certain things don't respond to love, all they understand is fear because fear is all they know how to respond to. I'm just fighting fire with fire, as the saying goes.

"We can't all go," he said, trying to assume the calm logical tone of a man absolutely certain of his plans and the methods of their execution. "Someone has to stay with her"— nodding toward the girl, who suddenly went furious, anger popping the freckles out all around her clay nose. "I got a name," she said. "I don't know why none of you never use it. I'm always jest 'her' or 'the girl,' but I got a perfectly good name and there's no reason in this wide world why you can't use it."

"You laid up and I ain't," the black man said to Mason

Raymond. "John and me the ones should go and you the one should stay here with her."

"You don't know nuthin' about guns. You ain't even handled one in years," John argued. "Him"—nodding at the black man who, like the girl, John never seemed to address by name, and it came to Mason Raymond he himself couldn't remember using the black man's name, why was that? "You, you stay here with her—and we'll—"

"I got a name, I tell you. I'm Ben—"

"—and we'll go on and git—"

"—jie Klomp and I can't see—"

"—them faster than if you was to go—"

"—why you can't call me that!"

"—and you yourself can see your legs ain't in much shape for traveling," John finished.

All of what John said was true, but it wasn't the pertinent point. The real truth was that John didn't want him to go because he didn't have any confidence in him. He trusted the black man—Tom, Pepper Tom, he's got a name, Mason Raymond said to himself, just the same as she has—and he's got no faith in me either, and I can't blame him or John. They're not going to let me go, he thought in dismay; then, a second later, I *got* to go.

"The truth of the matter is, son," Tom said, "we don't catch 'em before Marysville, we ain't got a Chinaman's chance, as I see it, after that—after Marysville, prairie runs short and you go into desert—barren bluffs, yucca, don't end till you git to South Pass, and so it ain't, you know, like we got all the time in the world to catch them critters—" His voice drifted off; he was watching Mason Raymond's face intently. He sees what's inside, Mason Raymond thought. He's a man who can read feelings. "You want to go bad, don't you? You got any idears how to handle a gun atall?"

"It can't be *that* hard. You load and point and shoot."

"It's the pointin's where the trouble is. It ain't hard to aim close up, but you put some distance 'tween you and what you're shootin' and it's a different matter."

"Look," John Buttes said to Mason Raymond, and he sounded desperate, "he's got years of experience whereas you, you jest ain't even got the feel for holdin' a gun. It jest wouldn't work," he said with finality. Your legs is burned, you got a bump on your head, you don't know nuthin' about a gun, and you ain't goin' to git no know-how jest like that"—he snapped his fingers—"jest 'cause you want to."

Either a lamb or a lion, Mason Raymond thought, no in-between. He rejected such absolutes. I'm going, he thought stubbornly. I can't change other people, but I can change myself. Maybe *they* can't see it, but I know it. He thought of the many metaphors that dealt with passing through the fire and he thought he had some inkling of what they meant. He fingered the copy of the *Iliad* in his pocket, remembering

Proud of his prowess, Hector led them on. . . .

To Mason Raymond, Hector was special. He had never ad-mired the great Achilles, whom Mason Raymond saw as only a sulker in a tent; all his sympathy had gone to the Trojan who had realized right from the beginning Troy was doomed be-cause his brother, Paris, had trespassed the ancient law of hospitality when he had run off with Menelaus's wife; but there was no choice for Hector but to fight and die—and be dragged around the wall three times and left to be licked by the dogs, Hector tamer of horses; Hector, who symbolized to Mason Raymond all the lost right causes that had been de-stroyed and desecrated.

"All the arguments," he said, "are on your side. But if you two want to go," he said, looking first at his cousin and then at the black man, "then she'll just have to stay here alone. Because I'm going."

"Well, I guess that settles that," Pepper Tom said. "We ain't got a lot of firin's to waste, but a practice or two won't bankrupt us. And you there," he said to John Buttes, "don't you go lookin' like that. You come a thousand miles with him, you should know him better than me. Her and me," he said, grinning, "ken sit back and wait while you two go and settle the score.

"Like other horse thieves they had their rise and fall;
From Allen to Curry to Hall.

On yon pine tree they hung until dead,
In Boot Hill they rested in many a lonely bed.
Then be a little cautious how you gobble horses up,
For every horse you snitch adds sorrow to your cup.
We're bound to stop this business, or hang you to a man,
What I say is lynch the whole damn clan.

"You two young bucks probably got more grit in you than an old man like me, but that ain't sayin' I couldn'ta gone and give 'em a good fight, too. Well," he said, handing Mason Raymond his gun, "I'll put up a target and let's see how you shoot. Jest do me the favor though and wait till I'm out the way before you take aim and let go."

John was surly as they started out, setting a hard pace right from the start as if hoping that in the first hour or two he would wear Mason Raymond out and they could limp back and Mason Raymond would admit defeat and John and the black man could then formulate a more practical plan.

John didn't even wait to walk with him, keeping a pace or two in front, pushing a little harder each step so that Mason Raymond couldn't quite catch up, even though he kept forcing himself to move faster and take longer strides. He can't keep this up forever, Mason Raymond thought. Pretty soon he'll be running and you can't run long in this sun. But John was a woodsman; he flew along with the long, powerful stride of the well-honed man of the wilderness.

He began to gain distance on Mason Raymond, at first only a small distance, but then Mason Raymond was forced to stop and rest; John got so far ahead that Mason Raymond had to make himself move out or he was afraid he would lose sight of his cousin completely.

John paid no attention to the insects swarming over them whereas Mason Raymond swatted and flapped. John just kept going, eating up the landscape, getting farther and farther ahead. *You're askin' too much,* Mason Raymond kept thinking, but he kept going on into the heat and dust and blackened grit that blew up off the earth, following the bends and loops of the river, traveling through a devastation so complete that its only tangible signs of life were the angry insects that had escaped the flames by flying high into the blue sky overhead and now dropped back into the smoldering aura of smoke and ash to torment him and cloud the small, vanishing figure of his cousin up ahead.

The earth hissed and steamed, a wonder it didn't burn right up through his shoes. Hard-hooved, Tom was right when he said that about plains horses, the hard-hooved endurance no white man's horse would ever have. He thought of poor old Mabel given out, back with the girl and the black man.

Bugs seized him and pulled at his skin, devouring him. He was welted all over where they gnawed. He remembered reading the emigrants' warnings that the mosquitoes would be turkey-sized and the bugs as big as crows. He believed them now. No wonder the Indians stayed high in the hills, where the wind made a natural protection against such insects, as the girl had told him, and he understood firsthand what misery whites who had settled in to homestead must go through during spring and summer; for the first time Mason Raymond understood what a price those farmers had paid to have a hundred sixty acres of their own land. I couldn't live in this kind of place, he thought. I couldn't stand the flatness or the desolation, nor that sun, these terrible bugs. They got Indians to worry about and grasshoppers and droughts and the emptiness all around them. How do they stand it?

Yet he was being driven by a strange seesaw kind of energy that flared and fizzled, flared and fizzled, his insides raw with hunger and his throat closed up with thirst; an awful driving energy that wouldn't allow him to let up on himself, a driving power he had never experienced before, hammering inside, forcing him forward, as if a giant engine he had never fired before had in some mysterious, unknown moment been set in action inside and there was no stopping it; it heaved and shuddered and beat faster and faster, flaring up in great bursts of energy until it heated itself to such a point that it burnt out; and, reddened and burning hot, died down and shut off— push, shove, thrust, throb, overheat, burn out, collapse; rise, pant, push, drive, and consume itself, then give out utterly; thrusting him down in an exhaustion so empty that he was unable even to think, the mechanisms of his brain shut off as effectively as if they had never functioned at all, a fatigue that was like a tomtom beating inside his blood, slowly at first, and then suddenly and volcanically, the beat unwinding until the machine would begin to hum and sputter, then flare up in a great blast of speed, sending him, startled, as if he were in the midst of a fit, to his feet; and pushing on, the whole impossible process incomprehensible, the long thrust toward what he was now thinking of as "The End" propelled and driven by some strange power inside, a man at the mercy of instincts he could not disobey.

During these furious bouts of energy, he pushed along in a trance of action, until it seemed he was speeding over the devastated earth like a driven demon; then abruptly at the moment that he felt his own powers begin to expand until they would engulf everything around, there came the collapse and he pulled up, lathered and heaving, standing windless and panting, the heart under his ribs heaving so hard that Mason Raymond could feel every beat within his body.

He hung under the sun suspended in desperation, grinding out an agony of fatigue in long noisy sobs of anguish while the day burned on, a glare of red, shards of sun bursting up at him from some queer crystallizations left over in the earth from prehistoric times, white dancing lights the sun picked up and sharded into his eyes in fiery little furies of white, and now and again a dance of green and red and gold. Gold, he would think, that's what John is after, that's all he cares about.

Under the blackened skin of the burnt-off earth, color seemed to come flooding up like a volcanic outpouring. But it was all illusion, some trick that fierce mass of energy glowing red overhead was producing out of what had been buried so long ago, the trembling riches that lay under the outer rim of the earth. For a brief incandescent moment Mason Raymond would think *gold* and an instant after he would feel a small stirring within, the beginning of some rejuvenation that would thrust up in that drive of power that would begin a furious flying over the fired-out earth, forcing him against the sun and heat and horror of the blackened landscape toward a distant horizon where John trudged on ahead and Mason Raymond gasped after, thinking two things, neither connected logically in any way but both entwined in his mind: *gold* and *those men.*

Lymph fluid was running from parts of his burned skin, especially the bad parts on his knees. His hands were raw. He had blistered burns from the fire on his neck and scalp and the hair was all singed off his wrists up to the shirt sleeves, and raw open running sores from the fire were crowded with sucking bugs. He was like a burning bursting blister of pain, but he kept pushing himself, the pain an activator: So long as he kept going and kept John in sight, he reasoned, he was all right.

"Jest keep movin'," he would tell himself, and he would go on until all the will in the world couldn't move him another inch, and then he would stop and die for a little while and watch John going on up ahead, a dot growing smaller and smaller until Mason Raymond wasn't really sure he saw him at all.

They had been driving the day down, wearing it out, and finally the sun gave up trying to wear them down. It sank toward the distant mark of the end of the earth, the purple shadows of its defeat lengthening along the endless stretch of land ahead.

A wind rose, faint but cold. Mason Raymond could sense the tightening of his face in relief; under him the skin went wet and dark, the whiteness drying down to giant sweat-stained ovals that encircled his arms and legs. He felt a moment of exhilaration as his pace picked up and he began to gain a little on the figure ahead; then he saw this was because John had stopped. He was standing very still squinting ahead into the enclosing darkness. A thin lip of smoke hung over the purpled horizon.

Smoke meant men. Mason Raymond tried to remember the name of some spring the black man had said they would hit before Marysville, but his mind was blank of anything except that that half-smile of smoke must mean there were men ahead, more likely than not the men they were looking for, laying up there ahead talking and laughing and sipping their prairie coffee, probably shaking their heads over how easy it had been to make off with those greenhorns' gear. He imagined Caboose, hobbled off a ways, nibbling disconsolately at the poor pickings around the campsite, and the piebald jerking wild-eyed at the hobbles that kept the pony close to camp.

Overhead stars were popping out like bullets, bright quick flashes that burst before his eyes in dazzling moments of explosion, then dimmed to slow, steady pinprick fires, miniature galaxies of white sparks that made him feel once again close to Bartholomew, who crawled into his cave here down below on the vast ruin of the earth. Bartholomew said the stars were points of path prints to other places out in the universe where men were meant to tread. He believed the sky cracked open at night to let these signal lights out.

Mason Raymond dragged himself up to John thinking, now that he's caught up with them he's not going to run on himself. He'll wait for me to give a hand—small as it is, as John would no doubt point out. "I'll lay my bottom dollars that's them," John said. "We'll wait until it gits a little darker, then sneak up on them." He turned and surveyed Mason Raymond. "You look done in. You think you can make it?"

Don't answer, Mason Raymond told himself. It's just a rhetorical question to make him feel better. Yes, he thought, but one of these times I'm going to have to settle with him. He's stronger and better put together and more experienced and he'll beat me, but I'm going to have to go in anyway. Otherwise we're never going to be on any kind of equal terms. You have to settle scores so that other people understand them, and the only thing he understands is a gun or a fist. I'm not going to shoot him so that means I'm going to have to fight him. I'll lose but in a way I'll win. Just the fact I'm fighting will be enough. That's what *men* are supposed to do: fight. That's the way he thinks, leastwise.

But after the anger, Mason Raymond thought, there always has to be a reconciliation. Violence cannot go on forever. It's the means and methods of reconciliation I'm interested in, those things that piece the world back together after it's been taken apart.

"Ain't nuthin' to do but go on," John said, as if to reassure himself. "Got to lay some place this side of that grove, come on them unexpected."

He stood at Mason Raymond's side, gazing up toward the distant smoke. He's afraid and hesitant too, Mason Raymond thought, and yet the fact remained that for someone like John it was probably always easier to travel alone, not to have to make plans with someone else or endure the emptiness of people like me, Mason Raymond thought. He wishes Tom were here, and I can't really blame him, but—

But can't he see I'm trying? Somewhere along the way during the past weeks he had come, without his ever even realizing it, to the conclusion you could despair a while and *think* you had given up, but you hadn't really completely given in. You sank down and you dwelled in the dark part of yourself and you told yourself you had given up, but all you were doing was postponing arising and revitalizing yourself. After a time the giving up began to gnaw because it was so empty and that emptiness, that awful nothingness, grew and grew until it was so unbearable that you said to yourself, *I got to do something: Something—anything—is better than this.* And so you got stirred up. Maybe that was how you got well. Just that getting stirred up was the end of giving up and you started thinking about what you were going to do and finally some plan, any plan, began to break loose in your mind, and you said to yourself, *Well, I guess that's better than nothing. I guess I'll try that,* and so you started putting together the pieces that had broken loose in your brain and that was the end of the giving up and the beginning of trying, of getting well—of being like other people. You came out of the cave.

Mason Raymond didn't feel inadequate or stricken as he once would have; he stood and rested from his fatigue, waiting for John to say when he wanted to move on, the two of them under the black cup closing down on them from up overhead, standing waiting and resting and waiting for some shard in John's mind to detach itself and flow up through the blankness and ignite a little flash of light, like the bursting gases of the stars a little while before, to pinpoint in the darkness an inkling of the direction in which they would be going. But in the meantime he felt the peace and purity of the waiting. *We all need a rest now and again,* he thought. *It's a sweet thing to rest now and again, to rest and wait and know in a while you'll be up to what's ahead.*

There were trees near the smoke, a mile, a mile and a half from the grove. Now that there was darkness they could creep toward the camp. He looked around—a few low boulders, but some distance off, some scrub growth he couldn't identify, nothing at all of use really. He followed John, who was bent over and moving cautiously off a distance into a tangle of burnt-out weeds. Up ahead the ashen prairie extended almost to the grove. The deserters deliberately set fire to the dead winter grass. They didn't care what happened to us. Why should I have any scruples about what happens to them? They were the ones starting to shoot at us, would have killed us back at the creek if they could and when they couldn't they did the next best thing; they made off with our stuff, left us with nothing—nothing at all in the middle of nowhere, left us to starve and freeze and thought nothing of it. And set that fire to finish off what they started.

He felt no hot sweep of rage that runs over a man when unaccountably he is challenged or insulted or demeaned in an unjust way, not the kind of violent anger that purples the face and sends an arm up murderously, while the mouth screams, "I'm goin' to kill you, you son of a bitch." Mason Raymond had witnessed that kind of fury many times; it was a common occurrence in a backwoods area where men were too long isolated from the necessary barriers of behavior civilization demanded for survival, and he understood it and, in some ways, could even condone it. Maybe condone wasn't the proper word; maybe it was more like he could forgive it because he could make some sense of it.

But the cold, rational pounding of his heart and the clear rational ticking of his brain said in an entirely different way, "I'm going to run those men off, one way or another"—that was something he had never felt or understood before. Yet these feelings did not disturb him. They were the first break in the blankness of his mind, the first incipient jarring that would commence the tearing away of that piece of his brain that needed to be freed so that he could think through action. Already beginning to act, he took Tom's gun and laid it on his side. He would use it if necessary. He had made a very clear distinction in his mind: them *or* us. That bleak, bitter, icy resolution was one of absolute clarity. Whatever he had to do, he would do. There was no corner anywhere inside him, neither in heart nor mind, that recommended anything except swift, accurate, deadly retaliation. What you sow, you reap— if there is an instrument for the reaping. And he would help be that instrument.

John stopped and looked at him. Checking me out, Mason Raymond thought. He had the feeling John knew what he was trying to tell him—that he would do what had to be done, without fussing or fretting. They would get back to Tom and the girl, back with food and, if they could find something to carry it in, water. There'd be something there with those men to carry water and they could haul it on Caboose. And there'd be those men's horses. He could ride one of them and rest on the way back.

He stood and looked at John and thought, You don't trust me and I don't blame you, but it'll be all right.

They set off. What John had in mind, he whispered to Mason Raymond, was circling around and coming in from the opposite side of the smoke. They won't be expecting us at all because we was supposed to be burnt to a crisp somewhere way back out there on the plains, John said.

Half a pie of moon lay flat against the sky, just as clean cut as if some woman had cut slivers out and served up the other half. A leftover moon, Mason Raymond thought as he circled with John and went toward the grove. He felt no need at all to stop and rest; a relentless flow of angry energy had refilled that space where weariness once would have hollowed out a place of weakness inside him.

An hour later Mason Raymond was still going strong, maybe stronger than before, the power inside gaining instead of failing, as if he were finally finding out there were places inside himself he could count on that he'd been unsure of before or afraid didn't exist or were not to be trusted. There was not one single part of him that wasn't absolutely sure he couldn't do what had to be done. What mattered was doing what had to be done.

John stopped to load the gun. He told Mason Raymond he didn't want any noise near the camp, not even the smallest giveaway that something was off from the usual night noises of the plains. The gun glowed under the sharp light of the half-moon; it looked powerful and full of menace, a weapon that could be trusted. John patted it in the same way he had patted a horse giving it confidence. *Everythin's gonna be all right; you do your bit and I'll do mine,* he said almost soundlessly to Mason Raymond. *Won't take no time at all if we work together. A few fast firin's 'nd it'll be all over.*

As he moved in close behind John, the timber became thicker; he could hear the sound of running water. A spring, Tom had told them, there's a spring up ahead, but Mason Raymond still couldn't remember what Tom had called it. A spring and a falls. That would probably be the falls he heard. The spring was ahead of the falls, a clear jet of water that poured from porous rock, with a large boulder on which someone had carved the name. There were graves nearby, too, Tom had told them; the names of the spring and the people buried there; one of them had been an old lady who had been part of the Donner party lucky to have died here instead of starving and freezing later in the winter pass where the rest of the party had been taken. One detail remained in Mason Raymond's mind: She had been going to California to see her son who had gone West earlier and one of the party had cut a lock of her hair and given it to her granddaughter. During that terrible winter when the Donner party was holed up in the Pass, freezing and starving, the little girl had somehow survived, walled up in a cave against winter with the others, eating dead human flesh; when the rescue party came she still had clutched in her hand the gray hair snipped from her grandmother's hair from the burying back at this spring.

He stopped, not resting—he didn't need resting—but trying to think through where those men would be camped. He grabbed hold of John and brought him to a stop. It was very important that he and John move carefully, and it seemed to Mason Raymond John was going too fast. He's always in a hurry, Mason Raymond thought.

The two logical places for campsites were either at the spring or at the falls, but some parties—larger ones—might set up a little ways off where the ground was leveler. But the men they were looking for didn't have to worry about numbers so more than likely they would lay up at the spring or the falls. The falls would be prettier, a consideration if you had women with you, but those kind of men wouldn't care anything about how things looked, they'd lay up where there was convenience—the spring. John and Black Tom were the gamblers, but he'd put down odds on it. "I'll bet they're at the spring," he whispered. "Take off your shoes." John looked at him as if he were crazy again. "We don't want to make any sound, and it's quieter in bare feet—if you're careful." John nodded his head appreciatively.

They both sat down and unlaced their boots, pulled them off, stripped off their socks and stuffed them in their boots. The Indian in me, Mason Raymond thought, but I don't dare say that to him. He'd have a fit.

He tied the laces of his boots together and hung them around his neck. John followed suit. For a moment it came to Mason Raymond he was actually the leader. Such a thing seemed impossible, but John was watching his every move carefully, doing just what he did. "No need to have to go back in the dark and look for our boots. There's enough to do without wasting time on that," he murmured. "Go slow," he said, "and think each thing through real careful and it's gonna be all right." John nodded, not arguing.

Mason Raymond began moving slowly, cautiously, one foot precisely laid on each piece of ground he surveyed thoroughly under the pearly light from the leftover moon. In the woods it was more difficult to see than out in the open because the light was partially obscured, but the clear bright night let enough moon through to give him sufficient vision to see he wasn't going to walk on sticks or stones and give himself away. John was close behind him, following in his footsteps. Mason Raymond took his time, often pausing to bend down and pull aside a twig or remove a stone before he put his bare foot down. He went so slowly and cautiously that they took maybe twenty minutes, a half an hour to get close enough to hear snoring.

We've come late enough in the night, he thought, so they're all sleeping. No, they won't all be sleeping. One of them will be up watching. They mighta figured they burnt us off but men like that, they'd be scared someone might sneak up on them, haul off their stuff. Take turns, one at a time, sitting up watching, loaded guns ready. Suspicioning people don't sleep as much as others. They've got more to watch out for.

He crouched down with Tom's gun cradled in his lap. He had to think very carefully now, lay plans out so neat and even there could be no hitch. He was conscious also of smelling something new. Tobacco. Though he didn't smoke himself, he'd smelled it often enough around Tom to recognize the odor almost instantly. The one—or ones—sitting up guarding are smoking, sitting smoking—on the lookout for trouble. We're trouble, he thought. Been through a pile of troubles already. Soaked and banged around back there in the flood and nearly burned alive out in the open.

"You and me," he mouthed to John, "we go slow and quiet and hit the ones that are awake and then we run in and make the others stand up quick." John didn't understand. Mason Raymond leaned closer, mouthing the words again, breathing almost a little sound into them. John looked at him. He couldn't know how many there were, but he'd kind of calculated on five, one or two watching and three sleeping. Five gives one of them a chance though, he thought, time enough if he's quick to get his gun. He'd be fast, too. Those kind of fellows were. "It's going to be hard, but we can do it without any killing if we work fast," he mouthed. John shook his head. Mason Raymond went through it again.

"Too much risk you don't shoot the guards," John said in his lowest voice. "You take one and I'll cover the others—"

"We can *hit* the guards," Mason Raymond whispered.

John shook his head. He didn't argue; he just crouched, shaking his head *no,* he wasn't going to do that.

Mason Raymond bit his lip. If he had to kill, he would do it. He understood that, but he couldn't see how that was a necessity here. "We can sneak up behind and *hit* them."

John shook his head again, no.

John began to move, half crouched, inch by inch, crawling along even more circumspectly than before, making no sound at all, trying, it seemed, even to hold in his breathing. He's the leader now, Mason Raymond thought. When it comes to killing, he's the one who goes on ahead. He himself was having trouble with his lungs, making the same kind of sounds he'd made when he had first put his hands on that girl back in Xenia, Ohio, and he'd felt the soft light skin, so unlike a man's, under his fingers and something rapid and uncontrollable happened to his lungs, a kind of lunging for breath that made rapid raspy sounds, sounds he couldn't control because by then he was beyond himself; he couldn't even think; everything was happening to him; there was no control, he was swept up in what was happening and yet he was a part of it, even though he was helpless in what was happening to him, all harsh, gaspy breathing and fumbling hands and the sharp, hoarse cry at the end when he was suddenly flooded out of himself and he was, for one uncontrollable moment, completely in the midst of the center of himself and yet also completely outside with that involuntary moan coming right out of the heart of him.

No control at all, everything pouring out of him as if he were dying. Like dying, emptied out of yourself, but full of yourself, too. No control over any of it.

But he could control now. He *had* to control now. He stopped and concentrated on his breathing, trying to count and regulate the oxygen, but the breaths were coming too fast and irregularly. He waited, not the kind of numb waiting he had felt these past years but the kind of waiting which meant planning and discipline and the final willing of what would come. What he had to reconcile himself to was that this was going to take time, and now that he was keyed up to do what he had set out to do the waiting was an agony. He saw John going on ahead and he couldn't call out to him and he couldn't move until he had control of himself.

He was filled with a fury of impotence on the one hand and on the other the absolute necessity of control. He made an effort to void his mind, closing his eyes so that he couldn't distract himself by any physical image, concentrating every fragment inside his mind into darkness. He called out to Hart to help him and the image of Hart was clear and pure. It said, "You'll make it, boy," and gradually he felt himself relax; he might almost have slept if he'd let go completely—he *was* tired, but he was tense, too, and he held fast to that small tenseness that warded off sleep. He was all right; the breathing was hardly distinguishable from the faint rustling of the trees overhead where a small night wind sucked at the branches.

He went on, trying to catch up with John, but going very carefully, the gun closed tight to his chest. The smell of tobacco grew stronger; he heard the crackle of a fire. John had stopped again to peer through the knotted brush. Mason Raymond crawled cautiously up next to him. A man sat with his back to them. There were lumps under blankets circled around the fire, five of them. Six men altogether. A lot. But only one guard. "There's only one awake," Mason Raymond said into John's ear. "We can *hit* him and get the others off guard." John sprang up and fired.

II

The man who had been sitting with his back to them fell forward. John kept firing, not counting, just aiming the gun, pulling the trigger, shooting. On the far side of the fire one man jumped up and ran. He got into the woods before John had a chance to see whether he had grabbed a gun or not because John was too busy aiming at a man who had got hold of a rifle and had raised it. At the moment he put his face along the barrel to sight and fire, John fired.

There was a silence of sorts, no human noises but the fire was crackling a little. John ran without caring that his bare feet were being bruised and cut; he found a fallen log and dropped down behind that and began ramming bullets into his gun. His hands were trembling and he dropped two of the bullets and one he had a terrible time even getting in place. He was panicky about the man who had got loose and while he was reloading it came to him for the first time since he had begun to fire that he had forgotten all about Mason Raymond. Why wasn't *he* firing? But of course he wouldn't be. John had known from the beginning he couldn't count on him for anything. That nigger, he'd been around a long time, he should have known that right off the bat. Sending that kid instead of comin' hisself, could have got me kilt, John thought. Somethin' else to chalk up against him.

My god, why didn't he *shoot?* John thought in a rage.

When his own gun was reloaded, he jumped up and ran, his boots banging against his neck, and fired again and again into the bodies lying around the fire. He couldn't take a chance on one of them only being wounded and crawling for a gun and getting him when he wasn't watching. He kept moving while he was shooting so that the man who had got away wouldn't have a steady target.

He could see the glistening water from the spring under the moonlight and his head seemed filled with the dancing lights from the fire—greens and golds and reds flashing up in flames —and an occasional splash of the water inside his mind in between the rapid bursts of firings. His anger against Mason Raymond was stronger and tighter than his feelings about the outlaws; it was this frustration and rage that kept him firing. That damn Mason Raymond, he would think, he didn't even shoot once. He left it all to me. It's that damn nigger's fault, too, for sending him with me. The two of them—it's like they're in league working against me. Whole damn world is out to get anybody who wants to hold his own—more than hold his own, get more than the average.

He dodged back into the woods, panting, and ran with the boots thudding against his neck, his bare feet being cut and punctured. He headed into a thicket where he dropped down, heaving and gasping, loading the gun again. He was out of control and he didn't care, he'd like to have killed all of them, Mason Raymond, Tom; yes, even the girl—but he had to get himself in hand enough to make plans. It was absolutely necessary to plan. He heaved up something and spit it out and heaved again, a dry racking heave, and then enormous hiccuping sounds split open his chest with lightning pains, and his face was so hot that it felt as if all of it had burst, a roasted piece of fruit that had completely come apart; there were lights, like the flames from the fire exploding inside his head. His hands were shaking and he had a chill that racked his whole body. He had never been so cold in his whole life, not even when he'd been submerged in the river and thought he was going to freeze to death from the rushing waters.

Something violent had happened to his heart; it seemed to blow up inside him, and for an instant he thought he had been shot. Then he knew he hadn't been shot at all; he just was sure his heart had given out on him. It thudded up in a great wallop of pain and fell down and stopped and he blacked out; when his eyes opened again, he didn't know where he was, but he didn't care because his heart was leaping and lurching in such a terrifying way that where he was didn't make any difference anyway if he was dying and he just let go and sank down and gave in to death and thought in a jagged moment of final surrender, *I done the best I could, and I never got no help at all from him.* Then nothing happened to him, neither thinking nor feeling nor willing, only the thudding breaks inside his chest and the dislocation inside his mind and a full understanding and resignation that there was no power in the world or anywhere inside him that could save him now. He had done what he could and that wasn't enough and there wasn't anything left inside him and no way to get any more, and that was that. He'd started out to do something and he just hadn't done it. But he couldn't do it all on his own. The nigger should have known that. Him and me would have pulled it off, John thought.

The goddam boots that Mason Raymond had made him take off were the living end, banging against him every time his heart heaved up and he shuddered in return and that shudder sent the boots to banging against his neck. He reached up and wrenched the boots free and threw them on the ground. They hit the gun. It must have fallen from his hands. The gun. His mind focussed on those two words: *the gun.* It was all that protected him and he thought, *The gun,* and then, *Why didn't he shoot?* and the picture of Mason Raymond collected in his mind. He promised himself that if he ever got out of this, the first thing he was going to do was beat the living daylights out of Mason Raymond. A man was loose in the woods who was trying to kill him, and a no-account girl and an over-the-hill nigger were waiting for him somewhere back across the blackened desert, and what was Mason Raymond doing? Lost hisself somewhere probably in the goddam woods, John thought.

His anger was all, it seemed to him, that sustained him. It almost even straightened out the lurching of his heart because his rage burned with such a steady, concentrated flame.

He took up the boots and tried to disentangle the knot that held the laces together. His hands weren't working, not for knots anyway, and he took out the socks and pulled them out straight and wiped off the bottoms of his feet. He had deep lacerations, perforations that were bleeding. The socks soaked up the blood and it still kept coming although the wool was wet all the way through.

What difference did it make?

He threw the socks down and tumbled over and lay on his side, harassed by so many pains and perplexities that he wanted to be dead once and for all. Then, finally, he could say, and it would have meaning, *I've done all I could. None of this is my fault. You should never have sent Mason Raymond.* Because if he didn't die he couldn't give up—that was the awful part of it. Being dead was the only sure way to give up.

You gotta get up and do somethin'.

John closed down his mind or tried to because he *was* going to die, he was in the process of dying right this minute, and he wasn't going to be badgered, not now, not ever again if he could help it, not even by his own anger; but it was so powerful that it wouldn't let him alone. If only he could get his hands on that nigger; if only he could lay his hands on Mason Raymond—

You gotta *git up. Git up and git goin'.*

He lay still and died—or tried to. But even his heart was going back on him. It had stopped bounding about and was steadying itself to begin going the way it should. Every now and again it would pull one of its tricks, but for the main part it was behaving itself and that meant there wasn't anything he could do to stop it dead. He took up his socks and wrung them out and put them back against his oozing feet. Even his feet were against him: They weren't bleeding nearly as badly as they had been.

He began working a stocking over his right foot and it went on fairly well, his foot cooperating, like the rest of his body, in tormenting him by behaving in a considerate way. He got the second sock on with almost no trouble at all, and after that there was nothing left to do but work with the knot in the boots. He used his teeth. They worked well, too—he unhooked the knot, detached the boots, and worked them on over the socks. He had expected the pain and didn't even try to complain against it. All this was part of some plan to punish him and once he had accepted that it would be ridiculous for him to ask questions like *Why?*

He stretched his legs out and flexed his toes. They were *all* working—of course—nothing so broken or so bent up it wouldn't respond. The gun next. In his hands the cold metal was a rebuke for his careless treatment, as if the gun were saying, *I done my duty and now you do yours.*

He smoothed the gun over with his hands looking for dents; he didn't know how hard he'd dropped it. He searched around for the last of his bullets. Been shootin' up a storm, he thought. Wonder there's any left at all. But of course there would be some left because what he was supposed to do was load up and go looking for that last one—that last one who would be hiding out in the woods somewhere waiting for him, laying up probably in some good cover near the camp so that when John came back he could plug him where it counted. Let *him* kill Mason Raymond for all I care, John thought, save me the time and trouble and powder.

Can't go back until I track that man down. And can't go barefoot no more because my feet can't take that no more. Got to go slow and track him down, find him afore he finds me. Hunted all my life, but huntin' animals ain't the same as huntin' a man. We sicked dogs on coon and bear, he thought. Me and Mason Raymond, we had that contest to see who could git the first coon, and he brought his in live. None of us could take to it, him bringin' in his coon live. We all naturally thought he'd shoot same as anyone else. Cuckoo from the day he was born. Lite was so mad he killed his dog. We was goin' to kill Lite, Mason Raymond and me, and Pa, he put a stop to it. That was the beginnin'. I jest never knowed it then. But Mason Raymond knew it. Mason Raymond done his killin' and now I'm doin' mine.

He couldn't handle the idea. It made too many alterations in his feelings, and he wanted them to remain simple and logical. Two things that were true but in opposition could not be logical, and yet that was how so much of life looked to John at this moment.

They stole my stuff and left all of us out there to die. They set fire to the brush so as to burn us up. They got a right to git what was comin' to them. I ain't gonna take on about shootin' a man the way that cuckoo Mason Raymond does.

This ain't gonna do *me* in. I ain't Mason Raymond. I got different thin's inside me.

John got up and let his weight rest on his wounded feet. They smarted almost intolerably, but he had expected that. You could lift yourself above pain. His father, his grandfather, preached that. You don't take no account of pain and it can't count agin you, they said, their faces mountain-rock stern. Like all simplifications, a kernel of truth lay somewhere within. He would pretend, as his father and grandfather had, that there were certain options open to those who cared to exercise them —unworkable often, but an attempt nevertheless to give ground rules under which some behavior could operate. Thus: Do not pay attention to pain. They were strong, his father and grandfather, and it was important to be strong. He was strong, too—because he opted to be strong. *I will not be weak like Mason Raymond,* he told himself.

He held the rifle warily, ready, trying to ignore all the pain, listening. He was woods-savvy in a myriad of ways, lores and signs he'd learned from his father mostly, some from his grandfather, a lot he'd picked up on his own. For one thing, he saw instantly that from the short period involved in the shootings until after he'd come through to himself on the ground a great deal of time had elapsed. The sky told him that, the moon gone and in its place a diffusion of mauve-gray light that meant dawn was not far away. *No good trackin' in light.* He had to use what little was left of the fleeting darkness to his advantage—but was the darkness an advantage? He didn't know this land and maybe that other man did.

Don't press yourself because you're nervous. You've been learnin' the advantages of waitin'. Mason Raymond was smart in one thing anyway, in being cautious. You want to go too fast, settle thin's right off. Sometimes it's better to take your time. He thought about that awhile, looking up at the sky and watching it break loose. A half an hour maybe until day poured down. He lowered himself and put the gun across his lap thinking about killing five men and what that meant in terms of being different from what he'd been before he crossed the Missouri.

Thin's are goin' to be better on the other side of the river, he reminded himself sardonically.

Near a large boulder there was a well-marked path going to the left and John, stooped Indian style, followed it to a big rock where he could make out initials, a *J* and *E,* and an *R* with some letters after it that looked *eed.* There was also a date, *26 May 1846.* He hadn't even been born then.

He was on an incline, a good place to take stock—if someone didn't blow your head off when you raised it to get a good look. From this hill, the guides had said, the old trailblazers had had a hard time getting their cow columns and wagons down half a mile and on to the Big Blue, where many had made their crossing, but there was a fork from the spring with a sluggish trickle of mud and water running at a crooked angle toward the raging river, a backwash of the Blue, he supposed, and as he crouched behind the boulder that had Reed's name and the 1846 date carved on it, he considered the possibilities. Where was the one who had escaped? For him, to go on was to go out more into the open, and that didn't seem a likely thing for a man on the run to do. More likely he'd stay holed up in the grove and take his chances on flushing John out. If he had a gun—that was the big unknown, if he had a gun, and it made all the difference in the world. And maybe he doesn't know there are two of us. Mason Raymond never fired. Maybe he thinks there's only one of us, and for all intents and purposes there only is. What's Mason Raymond goin' to do? Sneak up behind him and whack him over the head a little, enough to knock him out but of course Mason Raymond don't want to *hurt* him.

It's jest him and me, John thought. Any way you size it up, it's jest the two of us against one another.

And he's older and wiser than me, that deserter. He's been in the Army. They teach them real clever thin's in the Army, especially out here where there's Indian trouble and you got to be real smart to survive. I got to think through real careful, map it all out better than *he* can.

I can't do that, he thought. I ain't got the equipment up here, he thought, thinking of his head. I ain't dumb but I ain't a thinker. It's like it's always been goin' on instincts with me, countin' on how I *feel,* and now I got to think.

If I jest knew whether or not he had a gun. Well, I don't know.

He went back in his mind over and over, recreating the moment the man had jumped up and run off, and he couldn't come up with one clue as to whether or not the man had got ahold of a gun.

I'll jest have to bank he did. It's the only sensible way of lookin' at it. Figure on the worst and you'll be pleased with whatever scraps they give you that ain't all that bad.

So he's probably in the woods here someplace lyin' low waitin' me out, reckonin' I'll make a wrong move, and when I do— I can't make no wrong move; it comes down to that.

The rest of them is all dead and all his gear is there in that camp. All he's got, it's there in that camp, but he can't go back to git it till he takes care of me, and how's he gonna figure on doin' that? Two choices: Wait me out or hunt me out. Be better to wait me out. Take time but safer. But if I don't move, if I wait him out, he'll maybe git uneasy—each one of us waitin' the other out. But the advantage is all his 'cause he's et and drunk and had some rest, and, me, I jest been pushin' myself without nuthin' to go on except pain.

So, I can't jest sit here eatin' myself up with wonderin' and waitin'. You gotta. I can't. You gotta. And what if Mason Raymond goes and does somethin' crazy; you gotta figure on that.

Sun was coming up, bugs moving in. Birds coming out, too, some woods animals motioning about looking for somethin' to eat. Everything normal—except two men crouched down waiting to kill one another. And one crazy one wandering around doin' god knew what. I'm so tired, he thought, I jest can't keep my eyes open one more minute. Keep your eyes open, goddam it. He jerked his head up, punishing it, snapping it so violently the bones in his neck made a funny crunching sound. Keep awake, damn you, keep your eyes *open.*

But his head kept falling down and his eyes felt as if they were glued shut, he just couldn't get them open no matter how hard he bit his lip and shook his head to make it wake up. Sun so hot, bugs all over and he couldn't even swat—that'd make movement and noise. Had to do something. No, that's the mistake *he's* waitin' for. Bowels bad, too. Needed evacuatin'.

Everything was wrong. He was falling into drowsiness, couldn't pull himself out of. I shouldn't never have left the Landing. I didn't have it in me for what a land like this takes. Just to sleep— No, he couldn't. The bugs were in his ears, inside his nostrils, all over his face, massed over his mouth. That sun, the dry wind—he was dying of thirst, dying for some sweet water. The Sweetwater, he thought. At Independence Rock you come to The Sweetwater and go into the mountains. You get good water at last and crisp, fresh air, and you climb —you climb out of this godforsaken desert into pure air and high skies and mountain meadows.

His feet were all swoll up, too; they throbbed inside his boots wantin' to be let free. He kept shaking his head trying to make enough pain to keep awake, his head falling down such a relief when his eyes closed. Jest to rest a little. Had got to relieve hisself. His bowels were all tied up.

Hang on, hang on.

The position of the sun indicated midmorning; he had been waiting without moving four or five hours at least, and there was no calculating how much longer he would have to sit cramped up and silent, nerving his opponent out. One of us got to give, John thought. It's jest a question of who's got the guts to sit bein' bitten to death, dryin' up with thirst, tired and havin' to go to relieve hisself and not bein' able to do it. Sooner or later one of us has got to give. I ain't gonna be the one. I'm gonna sit here till doomsday iffen it's necessary. Somewhere out there thin's is bad with him jest as they's bad with me, maybe even worse because he's sittin' there thinkin' about how he was lyin' sleepin' by the fire and all of a sudden shootin' started and he was jest the lucky one got up and got away. He must be thinkin' how he might jest as well be laid out shot up as any of the others, wasn't nuthin' he done spared him, jest blind luck; that kind of thinkin' gits to you, goin' over in your mind how everythin's luck really and now maybe your luck's give out.

Maybe he ain't got a gun. Maybe there wasn't time for him to grab up one as he run. Then he'd be hidin' out tryin' to figure out how he could git back to that camp of theirn and git hisself a gun. No, he'd have grabbed hisself a gun on the run, second nature to a man livin' the way he done: Wouldn't even have to think about gittin' his gun, he'd jest do it automatic.

So it's a question of waitin' him out. Sooner or later one of us has to do somethin' to give hisself away. Or Mason Raymond will give hisself away and that'll let me know where he is. One way or the other the odds is with me if I jest sit still and *wait*.

His bowels were so bad they were all knotted up with cramps, and he tried to bolster his control by reminding himself of other men out here, in the old days Milton Sublette hacking off his own gangrened foot, laid up all alone in the mountains Indian-surrounded and his foot rotting right off him and sawing it off with his beaver knife; Hugh Glass, bear-mauled and deserted for dead by two men left to watch him, Bridger one of them, the great Jim Bridger lightin' out and leavin' Glass for dead because Bridger was a greenhorn on his first expedition, and Glass was so bad mauled there was no hope of his pulling through, and besides there were hostile Indians all around; so Bridger and the other trapper, they left Glass and went back for safety, but Glass hadn't got it in his mind to die; he crawled to water and lay livin' on bark and berries until he finally got enough power together to get up and walk a hundred miles back to help. John thought of John Colter, who'd first enlisted as a private with the Lewis and Clark expedition when he was twenty-eight and had later gone out alone, paddling by canoe down the Missouri to the Platte, and then got recruited on an expedition that sent him off on his own a hundred miles into Crow country, blundering into the Yellowstone country along the way, the first white man to bring back tales of boiling mud and steaming geysers, stinking springs and great smoking pits, the great river of yellow rocks, hot brimstone springs, "Colter's Hell," it was called derisively and the stories Colter told no one believed, "lyin' Colter," he came to be known as, dying a few years later settled down by the Missouri (married, even) of "jaundice," John Colter who'd gone everywhere and done everything, even been caught by the Blackfeet and stripped naked and told to run for his life, and he'd managed somehow to do it, dying settled down and no more than thirty-eight, but old and bitter, saying he'd never go back to the mountains or exploring again, and though one after another of an expedition had come to his little cabin to beg him to come with them, he wouldn't do it, he'd had enough. A land like this asked too much of a man.

The mountain men who had opened the West up with their explorations and then been driven out by the settlers who'd come after, or been killed by Indians or cold or the country itself, the dead ones maybe better off than the ones left who couldn't adapt to civilization, men overrun by the times; beaver hats were no longer in style in London so nobody was interested in the trappers anymore, and eager emigrants were pouring across the Missouri to Oregon and California; the great days were all gone, the great men, too; and John felt in setting the stories in his mind he might recreate some of the strengths of those men. And now, squatted here beside the Reed boulder, gas-cramped, bug-bitten, thirsty, exhausted, miserable, and in pain, he finally faced the fact that in its own way his hour had come, not grand like Glass or Colter or the Sublettes, but a time of testing nevertheless, to see what kind of stuff he was made of, modern and useless and secondhand as it might be.

The sun was low. I been dreamin' awake, he thought, or maybe I been dreamin' asleep and didn't know the difference, I only thought I was awake when I was really down in some kind of sleepin' I didn't even recognize. I been so long without anything to eat, anything to drink, without sleep, I been through so much and am so tuckered out I maybe don't know no more what's real and what's only happenin' inside my head. I got to git myself pulled together. *I got to pay attention.*

He looked around slowly, taking stock. The day was going down. When night came on so would the cold. To crouch silent, not moving, not even shifting a little to get the chill out of his bones, would present more of a problem than lying up during the suffocation of the sun. And he had to relieve himself. He had to. He couldn't hold out any longer.

So much was senseless. What did they go and steal our stuff for in the first place? How come they started shootin' at us? Why couldn't they jest have let us be? We weren't doin' nuthin' to them. They was the ones who come along and started all the trouble. We wasn't doin' nuthin' but mindin' our own business and tryin' to git along as best we could and these men, *they* come along and started the whole thin'; it weren't none of it our fault, but it's all led to this. Why'd they want to start this in the first place?

III

He heard something wrong, not an animal, no small one anyway, not bugs or birds, but something moving through the woods, something out of the ordinary. The noise that wasn't right was coming toward him, moving straight in his direction. I gotta do it, he thought, straining against all the restraints tying him up. John did all the rest. We could have maybe done it another way, but not after he started firing. There was nothing to do but shoot then, and I just locked up, I couldn't do it. It all happened so fast. He was running and firing so fast that I couldn't take it in. Then when it was over—

At least you had sense enough to keep quiet, he thought. At least you did that. At least you just stayed quiet and didn't make things any worse.

Nothing—that's what you did, *nothing.* Not then—you let him do all the dirty work—not after. You watched that man run off and you didn't even raise your gun. You just stood there and watched. That's not maybe as bad as Lite's running and leaving the bear to get Hart, but it comes close to it. You didn't shoot and that man got free and he could have killed John. And then you didn't do anything after—you just waited.

All this time you've just waited. You got to take on responsibility when it comes to you, even killing again, whether you like it or not. Not doing anything in the midst of evil, Bartholomew said inside his head, is aiding evil. The world is full of so much wickedness because most men won't take on the weapons necessary to fight it. Love, he cried out to Mason Raymond, love even your enemies.

There comes a time to shoot, boy, Hart said in a hard voice inside his head. You can't love what can't never learn to love you back.

I can't do it, I can't.

You must. You don't have no choice.

He forced himself rigid, not moving, imprisoned in his own indecision, the insects swarming over him, worst of all the knowledge that he'd let John kill the five men by himself and had let the sixth get away.

The noise of the grove was normal now, nothing out of the way. Whatever had been moving had stopped. Mason Raymond twitched an inch one way, then another, trying to get away from the itch of his clothing. A dazzle of late light poured through the gaunt branches, a beautiful spring day, fair to see, as if to say there's all this glory all around but you take no part of it.

He turned his eyes with their insect-stung lids away from the vast flowing sun and gazed down on the little branch of water that he'd identified earlier as an arm of the spring, and his heart pounded.

A man crouched down below, slowly creeping along through the brush. He was cradling a shotgun in his arms, and he kept looking from right to left reconnoitering every inch in front of him before he moved ahead. He looked like a cripple, doubled over and moving his head, turtlelike, from out of his hunched-up back. Mason Raymond had only to raise his gun and fire.

He's too far away, he thought. I'll miss.

The man stopped. His whole body looked as if it were concentrated in the act of listening. Don't shoot yet, Mason Raymond told himself, you'll miss. Wait.

But the man did not move on. It was as if he sensed some

menace close by and was trying to scent it out. I fire and miss, I'll mess everything up. I didn't help him with the others and if I botch this up—

This is my last chance to make anything right.

He waited. Below him the man remained still, stationary.

Darkness was coming on and already. Mason Raymond had to strain his eyes in the weakening light. In a little while, he thought, it's going to be dark and I won't be able to see straight to shoot and he'll get away from me.

Just wait a little longer.

Five minutes, just wait five minutes. You're taking too much of a chance this far away. If in five minutes he hasn't moved, then shoot; but in the meantime you can give him five more minutes.

He fought himself, staying still. Down below the man stayed motionless. He's waiting for it to get dark, Mason Raymond thought, but doesn't he know he's out in the open?

No, he thought, he thinks John's up in the grove. He doesn't know about me. Somehow that man below had got around and circled back and, Mason Raymond thought, he reckons on coming in from in back—he must have come during the light, the late light, because he didn't know the layout too well. He must have known it some though, Mason Raymond calculated, to figure out how to come this way, but not well enough to do it by dark so he waited all day—all three of us, he thought in wonderment, waiting all day—and then he decided to get bold because he must have thought that maybe was the only way to get the draw on John. He waited all day for John to move, and when John didn't move, he said to himself, Well, he's never going to move so I've got to plan new, and then he decided he'd come down this way, through swamp, late, when dusk was coming on, and when it was dark—

But he didn't know about me.

The five minutes are up, fire.

No, wait just a little longer—

The man below inched his way out and then paused, almost straightening up. For the first time Mason Raymond saw his face—he was an ordinary-looking man, some beard, dirt, but nothing to distinguish him as bad or a killer or even a lighter of prairie fires. He looked a lot like most of the trappers and traders that used to be so familiar at the Landing when Mason Raymond was younger but who, in the past years, had fanned out or died or settled down. You scarcely saw the old-time trappers who used to glide in with their pelts piled high in the backs of their canoes and the skull of some animal, a talisman, nailed to the bow. What Mason Raymond couldn't understand was why the man below looked so surprised. His whole face had a look of startled wonderment on it.

Squinting, Mason Raymond tried to see what had plunged this man into such a state of astonishment. Then he saw, disbelieving, what had happened. The man down below was sinking thigh-high in soft mud, slipping silently down into ooze. He raised one arm, holding the gun over his head, and as Mason Raymond watched, the man threw his arms out, the gun still in one hand, the ground sucking him under to the waist; he was trying to throw himself on top of the mud, as if he were going to try to swim out, but he was beginning to panic, thrashing now, and that panic would undo him because if he didn't keep calm and paddle slowly out of the mud it would pull him under. He was in quicksand.

Mason raised his gun and a voice inside him said, You sure this is right? He'll suffocate, you know. Let him die like that. He didn't wait to listen to any more before he fired.

As soon as the explosion took place, Mason Raymond started to holler. It had suddenly occurred to him that John might start firing indiscriminately and hit him. "I got him! I got him!" he kept screeching at the top of his lungs. He sounded as excited as the girl Benjie could get; he hadn't given a thought all day to her or Pepper Tom, whose gun he'd just fired. They had been completely wiped out of his mind. But that was all right, he thought, we had to get this thing taken care of. Now we can think about them.

John came crashing out of the woods in *back* of him. Mason Raymond was startled; all along he had assumed John was up on the other side of the camp and all along he had maybe been no more than a few feet up ahead. He had just time enough to think, It's a wonder we didn't shoot one another, when John began beating him on the back. "You got him!" he shouted and laughed—pounding Mason Raymond on the back and shouting and laughing and trying to jump up and down. "You got him! You got him! You son of a bitch, you got him!" He couldn't seem to stop dancing about; glee had made him half delirious. He was laughing as if his sides would split, laughing and sputtering out, "You got him! You gone and done it! Oh my god, I jest don't believe it. You got him!"

I did, Mason Raymond thought, I did. I did it. "I did it!" he cried, pounding John back on the back. "I did it." He was hollering and shouting and laughing now himself, both of them like jumping jacks bouncing around the brush, pounding one another on the back, and happy, so happy they couldn't stop themselves from carrying on, or so it seemed to Mason Raymond when John, forgiving him totally, said, "We did it —we said we'd do it, and we did it. We done it, Ray—we done it!" John hadn't used that old nickname in years, and Mason Raymond, sharing that momentary madness of elation, pounded him right back, but he never said "we"; what he said was, "You did, John. It was you, not me," while John, hopping about, would hear nothing of it. "It was both of us," he kept saying. "We both done it. You got the last one. You done it, too," and Mason Raymond didn't know how to tell him he'd pulled the trigger not out of hate but out of the horror of knowing the man would suffocate if he weren't shot.

The falls were clear and cold and nothing had ever tasted better than this icy water. First he drank greedily; then he left his clothes on the rocks and rubbed water over every part of himself, while John stood and watched, shaking his head. "I'da thought you got enough drenchin' back at that there *this,* as that girl would say, creek. I know I did."

"I feel dirty right through. Throw those clothes in, too, will you?" The spring tumbled down over the proscenium of rock and Mason Raymond splashed and purged himself, ducking his head until it pained him. He got out and stood naked in the moonlight looking at the crude letters ALCOVE SPRING carved into the rock, and he thought: Someone came along here and carved that, giving the place a name so that it was special, Alcove Spring; it was a place people would know because it had its own name.

Being shot was better than suffocating. He'd just done what had humanely to be done. But he lacked the courage to tell John that. Maybe John had seen. He would hear the shot. He would jump up. He would see. Mason Raymond didn't have to say anything. So I am a coward, he thought. It wasn't like he could help it. He had deep divisions inside that he couldn't come to grips with. He could know a thing *had* to be done and still shrink from doing it. The part that bothered him right now though was the fact that the man he'd killed he couldn't even carve a name for. A man dead and gone and no one to know how to mark the passing. It came to Mason Raymond how many, like that man, like the girl's family, had died on this trail without anyone making a mark to note it. Life in *this* world, Bartholomew preached, was not meant to mean.

He'd like to have been able to make a proper grave, to leave a marker with something permanent put on it. Yet he wasn't sure he could have shot in the open. The contradictions, the contradictions . . . But still this is one place I guess I won't forget, Mason Raymond thought. The marker's inside my head and that won't ever go away. I'll have to carry that man around, he thought, the way I do Hart and Bartholomew.

Deep night was closing in. There were dry clothes back at the spring on the dead men, strip those men if that had to be done. He had no real feelings about them. They were John's dead. Let him carry them around.

He beat the water out of his clothes and wrapped them into a ball and padded, naked, carrying his wet things and his boots back toward the spring. We have to fix up some story, he thought. It's not right to put on them—thinking of the girl especially—what's been done. No need for them to know there was six, won't help anything, won't change anything. Leave them what little innocence they got left.

Can't dig five graves. Can't dig one big hole and dump them all in, almost as bad as doin' five separate ones. Can't even think. My head aches so. Get me some clothes, fix us some grub, do something about my head, figure out something later on. Can't concentrate on anything, my head hurts too much, cold and empty and all the things that have happened, all the things that have to be done.

One problem provides another. He and John couldn't just pick up Caboose and their gear, gather up the extra horses, and start back to where Benjie and Tom waited. You didn't just leave five bodies lying around. You cleaned up. He might have been tempted in his new hardness to let what was be, except that their own party had to come into Alcove Spring —they needed water and resting up, resting up mostly—and that meant moving the bodies. You couldn't bring live people in to rest up among the decomposing dead.

No sense either in dragging all that stuff back and forth— no, he and John would have to take everything with them. You couldn't trust anybody except maybe a handful of people, like Tom, like the girl, people you knew; and maybe in the end you couldn't even trust them. How far could John go in understanding what was inside him, or how much really did he understand of John? Who could you trust? Maybe only yourself, sometimes not even that. I *know* I can't trust myself, Mason Raymond thought. Oh god, it was all so complicated, everything always moving. Nothing—nothing nothing nothing—staying in place.

I can't think like this, he told himself. This kind of thinking's bad for me. I always think too much. Don't ever be sorry about what has to be done. Just do it.

Do it.

Take one thing at a time. First the clothes, and then a fire, a fire and some food. Good hot coffee, feel better then, I'll come up with some ideas. John will maybe know what to do, how to bury them some way that doesn't use up what little strength we got left. I'm just not up to all the necessary planning now.

I can't remember ever being so tired.

He went into camp trying not to feel any emotion, just the bottomless fatigue that made him so helpless. He'd just had too much put on him and he couldn't cope with one more demand. But he didn't want John to see that. He wanted John to think he was holding up fine. John walked around the bodies like there was no problem to them at all, toeing them over, looking at them almost with disinterest.

Mason Raymond couldn't see the mule or horses; they must be tethered off at a distance. But the bodies were all there. Three were still under blankets. They were the easiest to look at, even though there were dark globules of blood dried all over their coverings. The two men out in the open that John was now examining more closely were crumpled grotesquely sideways, the man who had got his gun and had been ready to fire when John had shot him looked as if he'd been shot five or six times. He was covered with a low cloud of insects. Mason Raymond forced himself to look at the man who had been on watch, gazing down into the open sightless eyes, into the jagged wounds where the bullets had gone through the clothes into the body, opening both cloth and flesh and letting life out. He'd expected less mangling, a cleaner death, having forgotten that John had gone back to shoot again and again to make sure there was no life left in any of them. He just kept on shooting, Mason Raymond marveled, as if he would never stop. I couldn't fire once and he never stopped.

Packs lay in a heap on the far side of the fire and he went around the gray, dead ashes of the fire and stood naked and chilled in the moonlight trying to make himself realize he had killed one of these men and now, if he couldn't find clothes in the packs, he would have to strip and wear their clothes, the clothes of men he and John had just killed. He could feel nothing over this and that in itself was the strangest part, that he had no feeling, he who was usually so sensitive to every situation. It's like I'm gone dead inside, he thought.

He started going through the packs, putting aside bacon, flour, coffee, flint for starting a fire, looking for the whiskey, wanting the whiskey more than anything else. He needed it. Though there had always been cabinets of liquor both at the Lake and in Albany—a very full wine cellar in the Albany house—Mason Raymond had never been what was called a drinker. He would take a little wine once in a while, very occasionally hard spirits. Wine bothered him because it reminded him of the sacraments the body and blood of Christ consumed, cannibalistically, as he saw it, in churches in remembrance of a passion whose meaning he often debated. Why should Christ have died for *him*? For any of them? Why should that even have been necessary? A more experienced god would have worked things out better in the first place.

It is a pagan drama, Bartholomew had attempted to explain. In the old times men ate the hearts of dead kings to get their courage; in modern days unleavened bread and wine (or grape juice) symbolize that same atavistic instinct to share of strength by eating the flesh that had incorporated it.

Now Mason Raymond had a strong urge to swallow powerful distilled spirits, the need to wake his numb body and feel. He could not even call on Hart or Bartholomew and have them come. Everything inside him seemed blanked out and empty, and he feared this feeling of nullity even more than he was apprehensive over the kind of emotions that would rush in to fill that void. Men thought and felt and suffered. They remembered. They anticipated. They were capable of seeing abstract relationship where no pertinent evidence existed for cause and effect. That was the ability that set them apart from everything else in this universe as *he* understood it (Bartholomew had different concepts), and to lose the distinguishing features of his humanity was beyond his strength to cope with. He must wake up. But he couldn't, not by himself. So he would force himself into feeling with the liquor.

They drank it all up, he thought. I'd bet anything that was the first thing they did. He passed over the usual garb of the trail—a flannel shirt, a buckskin jacket, changes of drawers and socks, an extra shirt, an India rubber blanket. The underwear fit, even though it was on the smallish side, and the shirt, while big, was thick and warm and with the cuffs turned back would be all right. He had to try three pairs of socks before he could find anything near a good fit. The right size socks were important so that they didn't rub and blister. I can dry my own pants, he thought. No need to take theirs. But he could not find the liquor—or the tobacco. "I think they took all the liquor," he said to John, who only grunted. "The tobacco, too." Another grunt—he's tired, he doesn't want to talk, Mason Raymond decided.

He was glad, though, to see John gathering some scraps of

wood to pile on the dead fire. Get a fire going, water on for coffee (there was a blackened pot on a stone over to the right of the fire bed), lay out my pants to dry, cook up some bacon and bread, eat, we'll feel better. He ignored the bodies, the swarms of flies (as best he could), the slightly sweet stench (been in the sun all day, he thought, doesn't take long to start to turn), tried, too, to ignore the pulse and throb of his feet as he padded about. He was having trouble breathing because of the stench, bad, but he thought, Put that out of your head, give John a hand with the fire, he's as tired as you are, maybe more so. He did more "work."

He built carefully, helping John make a nest of leaves and twigs, working with the flint so that the spark could catch, watching a small spark catch, smoke, die; he went on striking, patient, almost happy with his task because the ordinariness of it blotted out the numbness inside his head and the notion of what else lay waiting to be done. Finally John took the flint and got a spark going. Leave it to John, he thought.

A sliver of spark, smallish, picked up a leaf and ignited it. John waited for it to take, then bent blowing carefully so that the dry debris around would catch. Little tongues of red and yellow worked their way in and out of the brush, licking it into flames. John stooped, prudently adding a twig here, a slightly larger branch where the fire had made some headway, then gradually added larger limbs until he judged that the fire was going to be all right. Then he stood back, looking satisfied. He'll make his way wherever he is, Mason Raymond thought.

Mason Raymond went to get the coffeepot, empty it, and carry it the few yards to the spring, where he rinsed it out three times before he filled it with water for new coffee. A dead man under a blanket lay directly in front of him. Mason Raymond turned over in his head how much of the coffee-sugar mixture that he had found wrapped in oilcloth he ought to throw in. He wasn't going to be niggardly after all he'd been through, but there was no point in being wasteful either. Supplies would have to be rationed.

He went back and watched John blowing on the fire, sending it up in a flurry of energy. There were stones for the pot and for a skillet he'd seen laying over on the other side of the fire by the guard. It would need scrubbing out. These weren't the kind of men who would be fastidious about what they cooked in. He left the coffeepot on the stone by the coals and got Tom's gun. He had to try to think more circumspectly. John had his gun with him all the time. He was sensible enough to know danger might be anywhere, might strike at any time. He'd been through enough to know he needed a loaded gun beside him, he couldn't take any chances. He doesn't take anything for granted, Mason Raymond thought.

Carrying Tom's loaded gun, Mason Raymond retrieved the frying pan and went up to the spring and gave the skillet a thorough scouring with a rock and dirt, then rinsed it with clean water. He took a hunk of bacon and set it in the middle of the skillet and put the pan on a cooking stone. The fire was so hot that the fat began to sizzle almost at once. The aroma of frying meat came on strong, helping to camouflage the sweetish smell of bad flesh.

While the meat was cooking, he helped John mix flour and water into a thick ball and pat out small round cakes that he laid around the edges of the skillet.

He unwrapped his wet pants and laid them near the fire. All these preparations were awkward because he had to keep the gun in one hand, ready, but he didn't hurry himself or get upset over minor irritations. He watched John and noted how he moved the gun along with him wherever he went.

There was a pleasure really in the preparations, in the smell of the frying bacon, in the hiss the water made as it boiled and ran over the coffeepot. John removed the pot from the fire and put it a little distance away to set. Then he went over to the packs and started rummaging around again. "Jest like them to steal our liquor on us," he said. "Drink it all up like hogs the first night." He was angry about the whiskey, unwilling like Mason Raymond to accept the fact it was gone. He said he had this idea that hot coffee mixed with good, strong whiskey would make a good drink for them. The coffee and whiskey would lift their fatigue long enough to get them about the arduous business that had to be done. But John, like Mason Raymond, couldn't find the whiskey, and that was an annoyance which kept grating on him. He was swearing now as he pawed over objects, talking about goddam sons of bitches who were nuthin' better than hogs. "But them hogs is all dead," he said with satisfaction. "They ain't gonna drink no more."

We could wait until morning, Mason Raymond thought, sleep off by the falls, and then do the moving in the morning, we'd be fresher then; but he discarded that notion because he knew they should get going early, as soon as the sun came up. Back there, without food and fire, Tom and the girl were waiting. He had obligations to them over his own agitations.

There was no whiskey, they'd drunk it, the buggers, John said, again, enraged. He hated the dead men for drinking the liquor, *his* liquor, and for making all this trouble. No need to take all of it, he kept saying, no need at all save they was greedy. We weren't goin' to take nuthin' off them. Why'd they want ours for? Because it come easy, because they didn't care nuthin' about nobody except theirselves, John said. They deserve jest what they got.

Mason Raymond wasn't sure about the equivalency of anything in this world. But he understood John was angry and edgy again; the camaraderie of an hour or so before was gone. John had slipped back into his old sullen state. He'll start blaming me for what goes wrong, Mason Raymond thought; even if he doesn't say the trouble is my fault, he'll think it.

He got a couple of cups, a spatula, took them to the spring, rinsed them, poured coffee into the mugs, turned the meat and flour cakes with the spatula, laid the spatula aside on a rock, squatted, blowing on his mug of coffee, looking at the bodies. They could maybe drag them out into the open and let the coyotes work on them. But they'd have to put them where Tom and the girl couldn't see them. Off the trail—way off, to the side, away from the regular tracks they'd be following. Still, there was the problem of moving them. They'd be heavy and inert. Use the horses, he thought. There are plenty of horses. They had our horse—the piebald, he said to himself, a picture forming in his mind of the girl swimming the hell out of that little horse. And some of their own. Plenty of horses. Git the horses and let them drag the bodies. The horses would give them trouble though, because they'd be spooked by the death smell. The horses would be more trouble than they were worth.

They could use the mule. Caboose would handle all right.

Mules didn't get so nervous about things like the smell of death.

He squatted, blowing on his coffee, trying to think of how to move the bodies, thinking he didn't know the names of these men so even if he and John gave them a decent burial, put them in a proper grave, they still couldn't put up any kind of sign to say who they were.

John came and squatted beside him, watching the meat sizzle in the skillet. "I'm hungry as hell," he said, "and mad as a wet hen, their guzzlin' all our booze like that."

"You got any idea how we're going to get *rid* of them?"

John looked at him. "No," he said, "I jest hadn't thought of it—you know, like right now."

Mason Raymond nodded. He understood.

After a time, John lifted the skillet off the fire and let it cool a few minutes; then he passed Mason Raymond some bread and bacon, his gun in one hand and the food in the other, squatting, eating, thinking, Mason Raymond saw, turning the problem over in his mind. But John didn't look worried. The West was a man's world, and John already counted himself a man. Though his methods were questionable, his motives weren't: He wasn't going to be the one to lose.

But here, among the dead, the nonsurvivors, Mason Raymond thought he had an objectivity John lacked. To be a winner meant others had to lose. He wanted a world, as he had told Bartholomew, where there were no winners or losers, just people who were left alone to lead their own lives.

"No," Bartholomew had said, angry at Mason Raymond's density. "In a world where there are men and women there is no way you are going to avoid conflict."

"I'm not talking about *that* kind of conflict. Let's say the men and women fight—all right, I can see you have a point there—but why can't the men just leave one another alone?"

"Because they have to test themselves," Bartholomew said. "And the easiest way to do that is to take on another man; there you're going to have a winner and a loser, no way it's going to break even. Every green young kid, he wants to prove how strong he is. His rawness and inexperience will make a lot of difficulties for him, but he's going to prove he's

a man or die trying. And that means force. That means violence. That means winners and losers." There's no way under
the sun (or stars, as the case was now) to deny it, admire it,
pay some kind of homage to it, Mason Raymond thought,
even if you don't agree with it. He should have had sense
enough to see from the start there was only one term appropriate for that kind of view of the world: a man's, he thought. The
girl doesn't think like that.

IV

The goddam horses and the mule were nowhere in sight. In the moonlight John cruised
the general area around the spring and there was no trace of
any of them, no trampled ground or gnawed bark, no nibbled
buffalo grass, nothing at all that indicated any foraging animal
was in the vicinity. He supposed he must have presented a
fairly strange sight, calling "Caboose—hey, you Caboose.
Where'd you go and get to?" Where the hell was the damned
mule, those horses? They ought to have been pegged out
within a reasonable distance from camp so that an eye could
be kept on them, and certainly he ought to have been able to
hear them—he ought, he thought suddenly, to have heard
them the whole time he was hiding behind Reed's rock, but
there had been no sounds at all from any animals except the
small grove creatures.

They couldn't have run off. They'd have been hobbled or
tied, more likely hobbled so that they could move about some
to graze. Made no sense at all. Still, a day had gone by: Maybe
they'd been able to move further than he'd reckoned. How far
could a horse incapacitated by leg fetters go in twenty-four
hours? Nothing to do but circle until he came on them, wan-

dering around in the moonlight calling, "Caboose," and tired right into the marrow of the bone, his feet pulsing with a life all their own. He could have dropped right there and slept, past caring about anything, if there wasn't Mason Raymond to drive him on, carping about the bodies and where to bury them and worrying about the nigger and the girl—why didn't he jest think about himself for once? What made him always have to take on the rest of the world?

John kept moving in a wider arc, squinting, trying to sight some shadow on the horizon that would identify large animals. A filter of clouds had begun to haze over the heavens, blotting out the stars now and again, some kind of front moving in that he was uneasy about. He understood weather changes back East, had grown up with them and absorbed their warnings without even realizing he was becoming a kind of automatic barometer of fluctuations for the climate and weather, would know a storm was coming on hours before it hit just by the feel of the air. But out here everything was a mystery. Look at how that murderous rainstorm had hit without warning. How was he to know what a haze on the horizon signified? Might be nothing at all, might be a sign of something really bad.

The weather wasn't all there was to bother about. He was beginning to feel the weight of Mason Raymond's concern over the dead bodies. He can't think of what to do with them himself, John thought, so he's dumped that problem on me. Those kind of men back at the camp weren't the types worth worrying about, but Mason Raymond would chafe himself raw if John didn't come up with some kind of fitting solution.

He tried to concentrate on his objective, finding the horses and the mule, tried to ignore the increasing perplexity that was making him dig around in his mind for an easy way to bury five bodies; he was half out of his mind with agitation, angry and irritated all over at Mason Raymond, who always had to worry something like a dog with a bone—he needs a good punch in the nose, John thought, somethin' to wake him up and see what life is all about.

He was exhausted and it was all just too much, and then Mason Raymond had started that business about not being clean, dropping his gun, stripping, sprinting, naked again save for his socks and boots, across the darkening plain toward the grove. John had followed after hollering what the hell was he doing, he'd just washed, Christ, not more than a couple of hours before, while Mason Raymond was frantically trying to get his boots unlaced, fumbling with his socks.

Mason Raymond plunged into the pool at the bottom of the falls, going rigid with cold but not seeming to care. John watched as he splashed and scrubbed, using a fist-sized rock to scour himself, beating at his body with the water and stone; after a time he began to calm, he said he felt clean. God, what a trial, John thought, he's been.

John had watched him leap from the water; the sky was darkening, a thickening layer of clouds descending. My god, what if it started to rain again? Dragging dead bodies in the midst of a downpour—we gotta do somethin' with them. He's just got himself clean, and now he's goin' to have to start touching those bodies. How's he goin' to take that? Drive him pure *loco.* I'll have a real crazy on my hands. A shiver went over John. *Cut that out,* he told himself. It's not like any of you knowed those men. They don't mean nuthin' to you. You never even really seen their faces. You never knowed their names. They ain't real like people. They jest bodies got to be moved same as you moved a dead sow or hog back home. You dealt with lots of dead animals, never even gave it a thought. What's so different about them?

You gotta do somethin' about them right now. You can't keep runnin' around this goddam empty plain lookin' for a lot of disappeared animals or watchin' that crazy cousin of yours jump in and out of the water.

He went back to the campsite and picked up a dead man's shirt, the dead man's socks, stood looking at them, considering. He commenced throwing all of the things that belonged to the dead men to one side and took all that the dead men had stolen from them and threw that in an opposite pile. The fire had gone way down. He can't keep *nuthin'* goin'. Got to build it up and git it goin' good, git these bodies dragged off. Take our stuff with us and go through theirs when we git back. Where the hell are those horses and that mule?

The pile of wood was nearly gone. His teeth were chattering, and his feet stung. He sat down by the fire and tried to think. It was hard to concentrate with Mason Raymond watching him that way, standing there half naked, dressing, watching his every move. Git wood, dry wood, git *them* moved.

I'm so goddam tired, it's all jest too goddam much. "We gotta build this fire up," he said. "Come on, we'll go look for wood."

They started foraging for wood. He didn't know whether it was his imagination or not, but the smell around the campsite seemed stronger. He kept going, trembling with fatigue and cold, pushing himself, wood so scarce it was like the ground was picked clean. Why not? Thousands of wood gatherers before him—they weren't going to leave something for anybody else. In this world you take what you need and to hell with who comes after. Nobody leaves you nuthin', he thought. It's like you got to start from scratch every time.

Goddam horses run off, no knowin' where that ornery mule's lit out to. So damned tired I can't do nuthin' but come apart at the seams, but if he catches on there'll be hell to pay. So long as he thinks I'm all right he'll try to hold on hisself, but if he sees how done in I am, he's goin' to break like there won't be a million pieces to put back together. These men gotta be moved.

He was in a rage with the emigrants who'd whistled up all the wood in the grove, with the dead men who had to be hauled off, with the mule and the horses, with the nigger and the girl back there counting on him, but most of all with his crazy cousin following him around with that hangdog look on his face.

He went high up past the spring and found a dead sapling; he broke some limbs free—nothing much to speak of, but a start—and he took these back and fed them to the fire, encouraging it. Mason Raymond was still out looking. He'll never find anythin', John thought, but let him look. It keeps him out of my hair.

He stood by the expanding flames and warmed himself a moment, closing his eyes and sinking into the marrow of fatigue. A wind was driving wood songs through the trees. He let the sound move, soothing, through his head; but his body was nagging at him, all pain and cold, and, oh, his fatigue was terrible, but worse was the deep residue of doubt about his ability to do what had to be done; you can't jest stand still, he told himself, you have to keep moving: There is too much got to be done.

He commenced the search for wood again, fruitless, exhausting. His feet were really bad, bleeding again from rubbing against the grainy leather of his boots and the grinding motion, too free, of the laceless ties. It came to him he was so tired that he was just wandering around hopelessly, past planning, past caring. But he kept moving automatically around the grove as if the motion signified he was still trying.

A small patch of some tree John couldn't identify, some western species with which he was unfamiliar, lay past Reed's rock; he was standing off a distance, scanning the area up past the boulder, resisting the idea that he ought to move in that direction, a new one, to look for wood because he had already pretty well exhausted the possibilities in the rest of the grove. He was hesitating because up by the rock he could look down on the mud flat where the last man had sunk; sinking in mud, maybe not even dead from the gunshot wound as he went down: No one ought to die like that. Nor like the others, shot while you're asleep, you don't even get the chance to fight back. *We never had no choice,* he told himself.

He traversed the gentle incline slowly; just before he reached the rock, he had a moment when his whole body was seized by a spasm and he had to stop, he was shaking so badly. Without any warning at all, his eyes began to water, and suddenly, convulsively, he was a shudder of spasms, his whole body given over to them. He closed his swollen bug-bitten hands over the sides of his head as if they might help him keep control of the pressure. He was gasping. It seemed to him he had never felt so tired in his life, never never in his whole life been so small and insignificant and powerless to control what was happening to him. And all those people, they depended on him.

] *280* [

But not long after the attack started it ceased as abruptly as it had begun. He was spent, but he felt somehow better; he got up and stood where Reed had chipped away at immortality; he looked at the carving, the date, and wondered what had happened to Reed, if he had made it to Oregon—probably no way of knowing whether he'd made it or not, so many hadn't, but he would thumb through the guides if he ever got the chance and see if maybe there was some mention of him somewhere. Hundreds of thousands had passed, but only Reed had carved his name. Maybe someone had taken the trouble to see what had happened to a man who had carved his name where others hadn't.

The wind was worse, the sky black, but there were dead trees up ahead; that much he could make out—fallen trees, easy to discern even in the blackness. Need an axe—must be one back at camp—and, oh god, he'd left his gun down by the falls. How could he be so dumb? If Mason Raymond had done that, he'd have raised holy hell.

He debated a minute whether to go on and see what he could forage ahead. Go ahead, he told himself, and stumbled forward. Loose limbs lay broken by past winds and storms; he picked up as many as he could and carried them back to the fire.

A few sticks of wood were simmering and sputtering as he laid his load on the hot ashes. Mason Raymond had found some scraps of wood somewhere. John added his, and there was a momentary lull before the dead wood caught, then a bright explosive blaze. You either git too much fire out here or not enough, he thought. No water or a flood. Too much sun or not enough. No excitement or too much. No in-betweens, a country of absolute extremes, crazy for anyone to come to. Yet once one man ventured out, a flow followed, people always hopeful for what was ahead. Seemed like what you had was never enough, even when it was good; you always wanted something more. That push was built into people. Not everyone—lots didn't mind stayin' put. They'd grumble, but they'd never push out. The ones who went on maybe wanted to see how far they could be pushed before they cried, "Enough," had to test themselves. It ain't enough to know what you are maybe; maybe you gotta keep tryin' to find out what you could be.

I never meant to be no murderer. But neither did Mason Raymond. Neither did Pa. Some killin' is there to be done and some men git where they have to do it. It comes from the probin' to see how far you have to push yourself.

I come a long way since I left home, John Buttes thought, and I kin go a lot further. I can lug those bodies away and bury them if that's what needs to be done. With or without him—looking at Mason Raymond stacking some odds and ends of dead wood. But first, I got to git me an axe and then I got to cut me some real wood and then I got to rest a little and then I got to take these bodies and drag them out where they got to go. Then I got to come back and fix up somethin' to carry water in and find the horses and that there *this* mule—I'll find them somehow—I jest got to keep circlin' till I find Caboose and them other horses and then I got to go back and git the nigger and the girl and haul them up here. It ain't all that hard, once you got in mind what you got to do. It's settin' the sequences in order makes it difficult.

"We're goin' to move 'em the easiest way I know," he said to Mason Raymond, "but first we got to get some rest. You can't move dead men if you is half dead yourself." Before Mason Raymond could fight with him, he lay down, dragged a dead man's blanket over himself, and fell down into sleep, too tired to care there wasn't one of them awake and on guard. The last thing he remembered thinking was, That's pretty much how *they* got shot. But when John woke up, there was Mason Raymond, sitting with a mug in one hand, Tom's gun in the other, turning his head this way and that: Well, I'll be damned, John thought, who'd ever have counted on that? He's stood guard the whole time.

He stripped two of the dead men of their blankets and commenced rigging up a sling with which to carry them. He got Mason Raymond to hold the blankets down while he dragged one of the men onto the blankets, but two blankets turned out not to be enough. A third did the trick. With a line of rope attached to the blankets as a sling for their shoulders, with the blankets knotted together, he rigged up a layout that would hold a body so that they could drag it with the weight centered and the strain minimized. He had slept some and felt better; the fire was banked so that it would last a good spell —altogether they were in pretty fair shape. He drank some of the old coffee, warmed over, and fried up some more bacon, stuffed his pockets with a portion of jerky he'd uncovered looking through the dead men's things. He gave some of the jerky to Mason Raymond; it wasn't much, but maybe it would have to do until he could get the nigger and the girl up here. "Eat," he said. "You ate it once before." Mason Raymond stared. "Back where that old man was—the nigger, he portioned out what that old man give us, don't you recollect? You et it then. Eat it now. It's *meat*," John said in exasperation. "Jerky."

"I ate meat?"

"You et it then. Eat some now. You need the strength."

Mason Raymond put it in his pocket. To hell with him. Let him starve.

"What we're goin' to do," John explained, "is drag them out—use these here slings to pull them out a ways—off, you know, from camp—and we're goin' to leave 'em out," he said fiercely, as if daring Mason Raymond to defy him, "and what happens to them out there is none of our business."

He had expected objections and arguments from Mason Raymond, but Mason Raymond only nodded abstractedly, as if he'd gone off into his private world again and really did not fully comprehend what was going on; a mistaken fancy, John realized a moment later when they harnessed themselves into the sling and began pulling, because Mason Raymond was alert and involved. He's jest detached hisself from thinkin' about what it is we're doin', John decided, so he don't have to face it. Well, I don't care how he wants to handle it so long as he don't make no fuss.

They strained and began pulling the first dead man over the rough terrain. "We got a distance to take 'em," John warned. "So—you know—there's no smell."

Mason Raymond said something that sounded like an agree-

ment, the actual words lost in the sibilant sounds of his straining. The ground was very uneven. The body kept catching.
John was exasperated by the delay and by the fact he had
devised the sling to appease Mason Raymond's sensibilities.
The commonest, best way would have been just to drag them.
But John was pretty sure dragging five dead men by the feet,
pulling and lugging and having to look back at them to see
when they got caught up on something, would have been too
much of a strain on his cousin. He would give out under such
circumstances and John would be left with the work all on his
own. Suddenly he stopped. All this sling stuff was absurd. Why
should he appease Mason Raymond, make all this work, just
because of him? He turned, fists clenched, and growled, furious, "What makes you so goddam special? How come everyone has to kowtow to you? Why can't you jest go and be like
everyone else? Why is it we always have to think about *your*
special feelin's, *your* special way of doin' thin's? Why the fuck
can't you jest be like everyone else *and stop causin' me so goddam
much trouble?*"

Mason Raymond, halted, sweating, with the sling half
slipped from his shoulders, didn't even have time to answer
before John ripped the blanket off and shouted, "We're draggin' these goddam stiffs—you understand? We're goin' to
drag 'em by the feet because that's the easiest way and I'm
tired, I'm shot right through, and I'm sick to death of your
goddam sensitivities and if you don't like it that's jest too
bad." His breathing came with difficulty because he was trying
to restrain himself from reaching out and grabbing Mason
Raymond and dragging him into one of his fists. Nothing,
John thought, would give him so much satisfaction as to beat
the blood right through the bones of his crazy cousin.

Mason Raymond stood under the patched moonlight calm
and serene. "Why didn't you say you just wanted to drag
them? It was you who rigged up the sling."

The logic of this was the last straw for John. He flung
himself on Mason Raymond and brought both his fists down
on Mason Raymond's back. He felt Mason Raymond stagger
under the blow and with a feeling of giddy release, John
brought his right arm back and cocked it for a smashing blow

to Mason Raymond's face when he saw, too late, Mason Raymond's knee coming up. He got it full in the testicles. Explosions went out of his privates into the whole of his thighs, bowels, groin, and all the way up into his abdomen. "You *cunt*," John raged, and fell forward, trying to claw his cousin. But Mason Raymond—whose face, partially viewed in the strips of moonlight that cut between the trees, was one John hardly recognized, fierce and determined as it came close— grabbed hold of John around the neck and squeezed with both hands, blocking off John's breath.

For a moment John thought he was going to lose consciousness, but he held on long enough to get a knee up into Mason Raymond's stomach, first once, then twice, aiming lower the second time but hitting the upper groin. Mason Raymond grunted and let go. John smashed up against him with his whole body, using his arms and legs to ram and kick and hit. Mason Raymond started to sag and John reached out and held him up while he brought his knee high enough to hit Mason Raymond's chin. Mason Raymond folded under John and went down, but on the ground he grabbed hold of John around the ankles and sank his teeth in John's ankle and hung on.

The ignominy of it was beyond John's comprehension. All he could think was, He bit me. . . . He *bit* me . . . while he bellowed and jumped, kicking, to throw Mason Raymond off. Mason Raymond reached up and grabbed his privates and pulled—John let out a scream—and Mason Raymond yanked harder. John came down on top of him clawing and scratching and biting and thrashing with his legs.

They tumbled over, flailing at one another, rolling first one way and then the other, getting whatever wounds they could in whatever way possible. There was no coherence or pattern to the battle. First one would be on top, then the other. "I'm goin' to kill you," John said at one point, and if he could have got his hands on a gun or a knife he would surely have made good the threat, but his fists were insufficient; both of them were pummeling and tearing and thrashing at each other, both panting and heaving, but they were too tired and spent, John saw, by the ordeal of the past days and by the intensity of those first blows to be making any real fight. As they tumbled about and finally came upon the corpse, he let go, trying to stop what to him now seemed childishly silly and a waste of time and strength. But Mason Raymond would not give up. He clung to John as if he were his fate, biting, scratching, feebly trying to beat John with his fists, but so exhausted that when John gave him a shove, he rolled over and lay, gasping, unable to go on.

John was propped up next to the corpse. His ankle hurt worst of all; Mason Raymond had sunk his teeth in and hung on. There was blood in his mouth and his privates ached with a dull, continuing throb, but oddly enough it was the ankle that troubled him most. He couldn't understand that, any more than he really knew what they had been fighting about or why he had grabbed Mason Raymond in the first place. He was shaking his head, trying to clear it, when Mason Raymond flopped over and smacked him on the mouth. In his surprise he didn't even try to defend himself; the next thing he knew he was lying halfway across the corpse and Mason Raymond was on top of him, trying to strangle him. "Give in," he kept gasping, "Give in."

"Oh, for crissake," John said. "I give in. What difference does it make?"

John took a canvas fold-up bucket and filled it three quarters full. Any more would slop over. He intended that they go as fast as they could back to where they'd left the girl and nigger almost two days before. They had dragged the men, struggling harder with each one, off some distance to the east, working together even if they weren't talking to one another. The thing that they both seemed to agree on, even though that agreement was unspoken, was that they had to get at least some food back to the two waiting for them by the riverbank. The water John carried was for them; to go back over that desert in full sun without water would be impossible in their present condition; but even carrying that small amount was going to be a hardship because he was so tired out; nevertheless, he had filled the bucket without a word, taking it on himself to do what had to be done, just as Mason Raymond was shouldering some of their belongings, the major portion, to bring along so that they would be safe. John got the leavings, which were not all that heavy, he discovered. He's gone and took the heavy stuff, he thought—and in the condition he's in. For though John had "given in," he was by no means as battered as his cousin; they both limped, but Mason Raymond lurched as well.

If he wants to have the heavy stuff, let him, John thought, but there was a grudging respect rising in him because Mason Raymond had fought right on, refusing to give up—a respect that began with the fact that his cousin had fought at all, let alone to the bitter end. Somethin' sharp as steel in there, John's grandfather would have said, and he would have been absolutely accurate. He's changed, John thought. Since we come across the river, he ain't the same. So crossing the river had made a difference after all. Alterations, he decided, are not always easy to see.

As he came out of the stand of trees, dust hit him like hail. The wind was hard out there where there were no trees to filter it. Regular storm of dust, as if the whole top of the earth were pulling itself free. He needed a cover for his face, some protection against the deluge. His eyes were already smarting, and he found it difficult to breathe, dust in his swollen nostrils, coating his cracked lips, even collecting, for godsake, in his ears. One goddam thing after another. Ain't none of this never goin' to stop? Water'd git all gritted up, too, if it didn't get covered. The hog is dead, dead, dead.

No choice but to go back. No choice but to use somethin' left over from those dead men's thin's as coverin' for our faces, he thought. It's bad enough as it is without no dust gittin' in the sores; water won't mind and if it don't mind, I guess I can put up with it. Maybe you got used to thin's as you went along. The idea of wearing one of those dead men's handkerchiefs didn't nerve him up at all. All he could think of was what a nuisance it was to have to waste the time on another trip back into Alcove Spring.

V

They had to fetch fresh water and John spent time fiddling around looking for a covering for the bucket—a kerchief for his face he found right off, watering it down and tying it over his nose and mouth. Mason Raymond couldn't bring himself to use a neckerchief off one of those men; it seemed so personal. He finally tore a sleeve from one of the shirts and put it around his face. His face was battered and bug bitten, sunburnt and dirt covered; the bruise from the gun blow still bothered him, and he had burns on the neck and ears and around his forehead; the blows from the fight had puffed his cheeks and lips up, but he felt a kind of elation the soreness couldn't suppress. He'd whipped John. John had had to give in.

Going to be hard going, he thought, all that dust between them and us, but there you were: Out here you came to see things were going to get worse before they got better, and what had to be done had to be done. Theory went the way of bad bread.

He handed an extra shirt from one of the packs to John to top the water, and he remembered Tom's gun. The remembering was automatic, so he guessed he was learning. Well, there had been a lot of lessons in the past few days.

They emerged out into the open and Mason Raymond was hit by flying dirt as if he were moving into the bombardment of a battle. Ground was so goddam hard he wondered how it was possible for the wind to tear it loose, but that wind had ideas of its own. He'd been through what people called "bad storms" at the Landing, wind that whipped the lake to a froth, wind so bad that a long time ago it had raised the lake so high it had carried off all the makings of the first Buttes homestead, a story people still told of how Guthrie Buttes, stubborn, like all the Butteses, the Butteses is all stubborn, people said, Guthrie was the first and they've jest gotten worse, Guthrie was so stubborn he wouldn't listen not to build down on the lake; we warned him, we did, lake would take his wood, but he wouldn't listen, too pigheaded, went and laid all that wood up on the rim of the lake, crazy place to put a house, and the lake come up jest like we warned him it would and carried the whole kit and caboodle off, left him clean wiped out, them lake waves was big enough to carry the whole of that pile of lumber off. All we could do when the lake died down was say, "I told you so."

So there were bad storms at the Landing, especially in spring and summer, great crashing thundershowers that uprooted trees and blew roofs off houses and sent floods into the bottomlands, but Mason Raymond had never seen anything like this. This wasn't a normal storm, one with thunder and lightning and rain; there was nothing in the wind but dust, acres and acres of loosened earth beating across the plains.

It was impossible to see, impossible almost to breathe. Even moving required a fierce concentration—and we haven't got all that much energy left, Mason Raymond thought. Nothing, though, he thought, would surprise him now about this place.

He was covered with fine white powdery alkali earth, a thick-coating white dust. The dust itself would have been bad enough, but the alkali it contained ate at every inch of exposed skin, made the raw parts from the fire a fresh fire of pain. Washed twice and scrubbed myself to the bone and now I'm back where I started, feel like I'll never get clean again. Maybe I won't. You don't wash some things away so easily; they hang on.

He began to cough, the wind so intense that it was driving

the dust right through the sleeve covering his mouth. He bent down, removed the sleeve, and groping in the dust for John, finally laid hold of him and pulled him to a stop. John looked ghostlike all covered in grayish-white dust. Even the kerchief had melted into his face, the dust was so thick. Mason Raymond, edging a corner of the covering from the water, dampened his sleeve and got it back to his face. Relief lasted for what seemed like only a second; then the cloth was clogged again, this time wet with suffocating dust. He could taste the alkali in the cracks of his lips and his whole stomach roiled. The broken part of his face was ooze and dust. His wrists were so white that he couldn't even see the broken blisters from the fire. His neck throbbed and hollered it couldn't stand any more. But it wasn't his neck hollering; that sound came from between the swollen rims of his lips.

But worst of all was his sense of disorientation; he could not really see, and the world, a whirling inferno of white dust, had no markers visible to guide him. He had lost John and had no idea in which direction he had gone. Mason Raymond simply blundered on, assuming if he went straight ahead he would find the river. Once at the water he could follow the shoreline —in both directions if necessary, first one way and then the other—until he stumbled on Tom and the girl. But with his distorted sense of direction, he was going to get himself lost sure. He always did. Before he went any farther and got himself totally dislocated, he should turn back—right now.

He had hoped that with his back to the storm, things would be better; but the wind was wild, running this way and that like a crazy woman, so that even though he was out of the main onslaught of the storm, he was still plagued beyond endurance by the blinding, stinging dust. He swung the gun over his shoulder, coming at a run the last few yards into the outskirts of the spring, dust-choked, winded, spent, past rallying. He got into the woods a ways and threw the gun to the ground; then he lay down, his arms covering his head. It came to him that in the past few days he had asked too much of his body; right at the moment he couldn't ask any more of it. It had done all it could for the time being.

He lay motionless, so empty in spirit and strength that he

was convinced he would never rise again—an illusion that lasted perhaps five minutes. Summarily and without preparation, his mind exploded into a melange of figures, three people without any protection at all in the middle of the onslaught of that storm. They would die out there unless he got to them. They would die if he didn't get up and get them help.

He couldn't believe he could get up, but he had not only risen, but he was also running, circling the camp grabbing up whatever lay open from the packs that might offer protection —shirts, underwear, tarpaulins, he didn't care what it was so long as it might be some sort of use.

If God wouldn't show him the way in the storm, he'd find it himself; he was in that kind of blind determination. He set off jogging and kept right on going, choking and spitting but absolutely resolved not to stop no matter how his lungs were exploding: He felt as if he might burst them in the effort of the run. One thing only remained in his mind: that running straight and true in the direction in which he had left the river was his only chance of finding Tom and the girl. He couldn't pause or look or question or even stop to breathe. He must just run.

How far was it—two miles, three miles, four?

I'll never make it, he thought.

I gotta make it. I've got to get to them and drag them back if I have to carry them myself. John can look after himself.

He'll make out, Mason Raymond thought grimly.

The land was level, which certainly was an advantage, but there was no vision at all, which most certainly was not; he kept going, his pace faltering, his heart knocking wildly against the strain, but pushing himself, lashing himself on with the image of Tom and the girl lying down on the ruin of the earth, the dust blowing them dry, covering them over, the two of them days now with nothing to eat and only bad water to drink, waiting out there for him and John because they'd said they'd come back.

Once he lost the picture; it was blotted out by a vision of the dead men still unburied back east of the spring, and he thought, Damn them, and kept running, putting back in his head the picture of the black man and the girl all defenseless, in the middle of the blow, waiting for him to come back and give them help.

The gun was a heavy weight pulling against his aching shoulder—the shoulder felt as if it would come right out of its socket—and his insides felt all turned around, as if they had slipped sideways, and he thought of the girl saying *this* meaning *shit*; and he wanted to burst out laughing, roar right into the heart of the storm, you *this* shit, you, and at that moment he ran into something and fell, a great bang from the loaded gun exploding into the white sky; it was a goddam wonder he hadn't gone and shot himself like so many of those ignorant pioneers, that would just have been his kind of luck; then he heard a whinny far off—so far off maybe he hadn't heard it at all; maybe his imagination was only working overtime. But no, he couldn't have imagined that sound; he got up from the tangle of brush that had tripped him and fired the gun again, calling, "Hey, horse, is that you? Where are you?" and realized for the first time the goddam horse didn't even have a name yet; but the whinnying came again, that little piebald knew his voice, and he ran toward the sound, screaming, "I'm coming, I'm coming, girl, hold on, I'm coming," running for all he was worth with a triumphant joy he wouldn't have believed was left in him after all he'd been through, flushed with jubilation, a regular running maniac of exultation; pausing once to shoot off the gun again and hear, nearer, the little horse cry back; sprinting like an absolute madman right up to where, dingy in the dust and only a big misshapen glob out on the desert, the piebald pony stood, waiting, running up screeching, "How are you, old girl? How in the hell are you?" and then pausing, rapt with disbelief, before he asked her, "Where'd you get them? Where'd your friends come from, for godsake?" Staring in wonderment and disbelief at the humped-up forms of four horses that had somehow hobbled all this way smelling and sensing company way out here on the vast and empty edge of space, bobbing and weaving their way foot by foot, and there in the back, bringing up the rear as usual, Caboose.

The horses were all over him; it was a regular goddam stampede, and for a moment he thought he was going to be trampled, but he was so wild with success, so giddy with lack of sleep and the force of fatigue, so elated with his fight and finding the horses and mule that nothing could dampen his enthusiasm. He was a lunatic of energy, jumping around freeing fetters, letting horses loose—let 'em run back for water if they wanted, but he was willing to bet they wouldn't go with the mare here because, it came to him, she must be in season, they were rushing her, not him, trying to mount her now that their legs were free; and he was so happy that he started shouting, because that meant they'd follow her anywhere, and she was a runner; oh god, she could run, she could outrun any of them, that little mare, he'd bet his life on that; she could run all those goddam horses right back to the girl and good old Tom; and the mule could do what it wanted, they could always round it up later, after the storm.

You're going to find them in this? that incessant inner voice demanded, and he had had enough of it, You're goddam right I'm going to find them, he said all in the same breath it took to untangle the rope tied to the halter on the little mare. He had to beat back the eager, rutting horses, but he took Tom's gun and hit out at them with good hard whacks, laying right into them, enjoying every blow; he was enjoying everything. The tide had turned. As John would have said, the hog lived, lived, lived.

He got the rope twisted around, stopped and gave the panting, snorting studs a couple of more good strong cracks, then tightened his hold on the piebald, beat off the stallions with the gun again, and swung onto the pony's back—he was wobbly, but he would hold; he gave the little piebald a smack across the rump; suddenly they were flying through dust and debris, spinning over the earth using it up so fast that it didn't even seem to exist; it was as if he and the pony were skyborne in the midst of all that twilight world of white through which, somewhere unperceived because of the dust, a sun was rising, a little light lifted through the blackened sky that made the storm like a gray robe thrown over the earth, one which parted its thick gray nap to let them fly through, then closed down its fluff as they passed, covering the world in white wool dust again, while in back of the piebald Mason Raymond heard the sound of the stallions' hooves and the loud high frustration of their cries.

Oh it was a beautiful, beautiful feeling he had, borne high over the earth with the mantle of dust making way as they went against its grain, whirling through a world of white in which it seemed only they existed, he and the little mare, and would go on existing suspended forever in this instant of both freedom and flight, a frieze that would hold through all eternity in one moment in which, for the flickering of an instant, beyond the oppressive permanence of evil, he would pass and fly into the face of heaven.

You've gone and got yourself lost again. You've gone and fucked the hog again. For a few seconds he felt he had held life in his hands; now it was swept up in the dust and blown god knew where; he was once again the ignorant fool who wasn't content just to endanger himself but had to pull along a lot of innocent animals as well. Who but a half-wit like himself would run around in such a storm?

He was blind and the horses were probably worse, maybe permanently ruined. And Tom and the girl god knew where. I've *got* to find them, Mason Raymond thought. Well, find them at a walk, the inner voice of reason said. Give a horse —or a boy—his head and there's always a run on foolishness.

Mason Raymond could no longer hear the other animals, lost somewhere in a swirl of dust, probably running around in circles winding themselves futilely. He lifted the gun and fired. If the pony had heard it and answered, maybe Tom could hear and holler.

There was an orange cast to the sky, as if above in the heavens a fire raged right over his head. Sun trying to break through, he thought. Dust seemed to be dying down, too— probably only his imagination. It is dying down, he thought. I can even see a little ahead: a lump of rock or broken brush which he could quite clearly make out ten yards or so ahead. He hadn't been able to see anything at the height of the storm, nothing at all past the pony's head and, while they were running, sometimes not even her head, just the grayish dust curve of neck and the blinding billions of particles of dirt whirling around the place where the head ought to have been.

He let the rope loose. He sure as hell didn't know what he was doing; maybe she had an idea or two. Animals survived on instincts that led them to watering holes and shade and small, hidden patches of grass. But the piebald's instincts apparently were as retarded as his own. She simply stopped, bringing her head around to gaze at him in bewilderment. They were stopped in the middle of nowhere, lost, dust-encased, incompetents on the range.

He sat in the midst of the blown alkali earth and waited. The horse waited with him. Somewhere the girl and Tom were waiting, too. God alone knew where John was—probably back at Alcove Spring where he himself should have stayed. A world of waiters, the dust eating him up with itching. Worse than the bugs had been back at the boulder. Just lies here, this land does, he thought, waiting for some simpleton to come along so that it can take him apart and leave the pieces lying around for the coyotes to come catch, paste a sign on you that says *Inferior*. No, he thought, the sign would say: *Here lies Mason Raymond, a nonsurvivor, like so many others who took to this trail.*

Here they come, he thought with a sinking heart, hearing the snorts and hooves, high stallion screams of the other horses somewhere in back of him. I can't sit. These animals'll be all over us. "Come on, girl, let's move."

The dust seemed to be tiring itself out in all that wind though, he thought, scanning the small distance ahead where it was now possible to make out shapes. More like snow than dust, a world of white, shrouded, empty as some people's souls, like some terrible pestilence and destruction the materials of war swept over this place taking everything with it and only the bones of the inner earth left. Bartholomew would love the scene.

He could not persuade himself Tom and the girl could have survived such devastation, not without shelter or food, testing in his mind the improbables of such a situation. But, he argued against the laws of probability, they're people who had gone without before and will go without again. That was the encouragement with which he tried to sustain himself, that and the senseless determination that everything depended on him.

The confused sky went first blue, then white, then a molten running of red where the sun poured through. He had reached the state, it seemed to him, where the mysterious laws that guided the universe must unbend for only a moment to make or break him; he could not go on being toyed with any longer. This landscape was a graveyard of how many dreams? Yet it seemed to him he heard something—not with his ears, no, not with his ears—but as if some secret string inside his skull had been plucked by a sound the ear could not hear but which was nevertheless there. Something called inside his head. He was hearing what could not be heard, but he believed in it nevertheless, just as he had believed Bartholomew when he said there was a special hole in the center of the earth from which the winds were let out and that at the drop between day and dusk hidden voices could be heard from the underworld.

He had, a second later, the confused idea someone was stumbling toward him, a body that looked as if it had been burned away from its bones and was flaking and drifting under the molten sun. It is dust, Mason Raymond told himself, just dust. The dead do not rise in revenge.

The figure fell, groped in the dust, half rose. Weak, Mason Raymond thought. I don't have to be afraid of something with so little strength.

The figure held up a hand and Mason Raymond inched a little more forward, recognized the small black eyes in the dust-caked face, the gold tooth that glittered through cracked dust-encased lips. He comes up with a poem, I'll kill him, Mason Raymond thought.

But the black man was too done in to versify; he fell against the mare with a kind of sobbing, hanging on to the horse and making queer raspy noises of recognition.

He did not know how he did it, but Mason Raymond got Tom up on the horse, beating at him as if he were a rug brought out of the Albany house in the spring to get a good cleaning: Dust rose in clouds, choking Mason Raymond, making the mare skittish. It wasn't just the dust; it was also the cries of those buck horses on the scent again. While Mason Ray-

mond was smacking away, they come ghosting out of the
storm and began circling the mare, trying to get to her, panting and wheezing and making blowing noises, throwing steam
and dust from out of their noses, creating a fearful clatter, one
of them banging against the mare and knocking Tom sideways
so that, for the first time since he'd held his face up for Mason
Raymond to try to recognize, he raised his head and stared at
the row going on around him. He even managed to croak out
a question: "Where the hell they come from?"

"You just stick on here with me," Mason Raymond said,
"and I'll try and keep these damn things away. But we got to
run or they'll pester us the whole time. This one—the piebald
—she's in season."

Tom didn't look as if he could hang on at a walk, much less
gallop, but they were going to have to make a run for it or one
of those stallions would pin the mare sure. Mason Raymond
got down, trying to beat off the stallions and to determine how
else he might help Tom, when the black man gave the little
pony a word and she started trotting out. The other horses
were right after her. The goddam nigger hadn't given him
enough time to latch on to a horse before he'd taken off. Why
the hell couldn't he have waited one minute? It's not his fault,
the voice of reason counseled; and Mason Raymond, all emotion, shouted at it, Oh, shut up. He was running his head off
trying to catch up, but the mare had taken off, she was really
running, what a runner she was, and he found himself, a
minute later, deserted amidst dust and desert.

He was filled with such a rage that he didn't recognize
himself. He who had always urged nonviolence and gentleness for the weak, sympathy for the lame and the halt, was in
the kind of tantrum he identified with his cousin John, stamping up and down, grinding his teeth, and beating his arms
against his thighs to try to relieve his frustration, but all he
could think was, That goddam nigger's run off and left me
after all I been through.

For a few seconds all reason left him; he was pounding
about as wildly as those rutting horses tearing after the mare.
He was spouting obscenities and shouting his anger up at the
sun, but the words were incoherent. He was plain crazy with

frustration, fatigue, and a fate that could leave him stranded all alone in the midst of this Great American Desert with nothing but dust and fire and death.

There were slow concentric circles of flakes whirling here and there; in another half hour or so the whole thing would probably be over. That didn't mean something else wouldn't start. Sit down and quiet yourself. *Quiet* myself? How can I quiet myself?

Something exploded to the left of him and out of the detonation the mare flew by, the nigger hanging on to her neck. The black man didn't even try to stop the horse—that was apparently beyond his strength—but he was trying feebly to circle her. Mason Raymond was nearly overrun by stallions. He tried to catch a halter, jumping up frantically and reaching out blindly as the horses stamped over him, dodging this way and that, grabbing hopelessly for something to catch hold of while the nigger got the mare steered in toward him again. As she came by him a second time, Mason Raymond lunged at her and grabbed a handful of leather. The halter caught around his hand dragging him, but the mare ground to a stop. "That's it, girl, hold up. That's a good girl, girl, hold still."

The black man looked down at him. "Mason Raymond?" he asked in disbelief. "Where the hell is John? I thought you was John."

Four

The Journey

I

*B*enjie *was enveloped* in powdery ash. She
had been lying that way she didn't know how
long with the sun stored in her even though it was blotted out
by the dust, giving her strength even though she could not see
it; but then the dust crawled over with such insistence that the
sun dissolved inside, and thousands of gray eyes looked down
on her instead. She felt she was being devoured by the dead
spirits of these plains, who had risen up to hover over her and
ask her the same eternal question which had haunted her ever
since she could remember: *Why must this be?*

Some people seemed gifted with a grace that moved with
them through the end of their days (she thought of the beautiful women in the big white mansions where the grass ran blue
on all sides and trees shaded the wide verandas and deep lanes
leading to them), while others (and she pictured the Klomp
shack amidst its profusion of weeds) seemed to walk over
ashes and clutch their gray miserable rags against dreams they
knew were spawned only for those more favored than themselves. All she knew, and that was a surety which bridged no
exceptions, was that this seemed the final abandonment; now
the desert would finally claim her, as it had tried to years

before; and all those years, all she had endured, she might just as well not have gone through them.

She thought of the safety offered by Bone Hand's tipi—she could see the calendar pictures that counted the winters, the most important events that had occurred during each year represented by a picture, what they called the Winter Count, from the picture of two sets of horses' marks, arrowed toward one another, signifying the winter when horse thieves had sneaked into camp and made off in the snow with one set of horses to that time, a few weeks later, when a band from Two Moon's camp had gone out and stolen another set back. The last marks she remembered were those which showed the white men coming to the *Paha Sapa,* but she supposed now Dark Hair Woman would have painted the story of the raid of the camp on new skins. For a moment she had forgotten the destruction of that tipi she remembered so vividly and which had promised safety, forgotten that it had been burned by the soldiers; a pile of ashes did not offer safety.

Ashes . . . dust . . . In the end it seemed to her it was all the same, everything ended in destruction, in ashes.

Pte-san win: White Buffalo Woman; Benjie Klomp—she didn't know who Benjie Klomp was; there was no translation for that, and maybe it didn't matter anymore—maybe it had *never* mattered; you were what you were forced to be; events around you did not stay still. You could be born into one series of expectations and end up in a totally different set so that your whole sense of the world was turned around. I held out my hand to be white and was turned back, she thought, and then I thought I could be Indian. Benjie Klomp, who had thought that fifteen years of her life were unreal, remembering each year of those fifteen marked by a painting on that tipi, the skins of which had pictures of years dating back to way before Benjie was born, those pictures like a vision, a fantasy I have where I'm neither awake nor asleep but somewhere in between, directing my dreams, and I see down into the crack of the earth and extract what I want to make my own poses. But those are only poses. They cannot *be,* no matter how real, at the moment, they seem. What is at the heart of the earth is not the same as what is on its outer rim.

I am thinking like an Indian, she thought, surprised. No white thinks like that. No white sees layers of the world the way an Indian does; for an Indian the vision is always what is true, not the externals, not the here and now; the outside of the earth belongs to the whites, with their iron-locked logic, blocked off from that inner world inside the earth, which belongs to the Indians. An Indian can slip in and out of different worlds. He can ride hard after the buffalo or the enemy or in the fracas of races and be in and of this world, right on the lip of its edge; and then, at the same instant, he can fall through the rim and be inside his own vision, out of this world as Crazy Horse was out of it and into the heart of the spirit of himself where he took himself away and went in search of his visions.

Names were not important to the Indians, she must try to remember that. Crazy Horse had first been Curly or Light-Haired One until he was a young man; then he became Crazy Horse and after that Strange Man. Sitting Bull had once been Jumping Badger, and Bone Hand, before he grew into his enormously strong hands, had been Bird That Goes Wild. The Indians were like seals that slipped in and out of their selves as if they were skimming skillfully through shining waters— they dipped and turned and disappeared and reemerged, still the same and yet someone else; that momentary submergence had changed them—or changed the eyes of those watching them so that an Indian was never himself, he was always at the slippery edge of emerging into someone else, for which a new name was needed; and yet it was true, too, that at the same time there was a hard core of himself that stayed centered, a balance to the constantly shifting nature of all things, that she, Benjie Klomp, who clutched desperately to hold on to herself, lacked. You cannot keep changing names, she would think. What if the water was not called water tomorrow, or we kept referring to the buffalo every time by a new name: How would we ever hold on to the world around us? We need names to know.

My world, the world I wanted, I thought, was in my white name. I will not be White Buffalo Woman, I would say to myself, I am who I began to be, Benjie Klomp, no matter who tries to change me by calling me something else. I did not know that for people names are not important, only for things. People die and rot away; they cease to be; but the world of things stays put, and to share it with others we need the names to be constant, for the sake of telling one another what we want to say. But people—people can become as many people as they want. They are constantly whirling and flying about, like this dust, searching for some place to land.

Now, as she lay with a million images shattering her mind, she no longer knew what was, what anyone might be named. *This* was a world she had never seen, did not know, could not identify by name, as if the real world had ceased to be and what followed after was some twilight space which had slipped out of the earth, as the Indians believed, from that same hold from which the *wasna,* the buffalo, had emerged.

To die alone buried in dust, without even the honor of an Indian scaffold, the platform on four stilts that held the body off the earth—it rotted and fell apart, but still there was *some* kind of marker. Everyone wanted to be remembered in some way. That's why Benjie Klomp had not understood the Indians' changing their names; she had felt that was like losing who you were; but, again, the Indians didn't look on things the way the whites did; theirs was a different kind of self—she thought she could understand that now. To be one name for part of your life and then another the rest of it was like having two separate selves (which was what had happened to her), and that was the way you linked those two together, by changing names.

She threw her hands over her head to try to keep out the dust. No one would ever remember any of the Klomps. We didn't do nuthin' to be remembered for, she thought. We just tried. And even that didn't work out too well. This is one time I ain't goin' to be able to say, Well, I got through *that* day, one time when one door doesn't close so another can open.

I kept wanting, she thought, and this came to her as a revelation, not as logical knowledge she had weighed and balanced and thought through, but as an intuitive flash brought on perhaps by thirst and hunger and fatigue, the ultimate terror of being buried alive, a slow suffocating horror

that surpassed anything she had ever known. But the knowledge was also outside of these and clear, in spite of her dust-
heavy brain inside, because the knowledge had nothing to do
with her mind; it was centered purely and solely within her
heart, the seat by which all such irrational knowing came, and
the insight she had said with absolute certainty, I kept wanting
to be white. *But I am not white. I am not Indian either.* Just as
there are two worlds, red and white, just as there are two kinds
of knowledge, interior and exterior, just as one can live in this
world or escape from the outer rim of the earth and slip down
inside, so can I swing between two worlds, and what I have
got to do is learn how to balance each so that the weight does
not fall too far one way or the other and plunge me down to
depths from which I can never climb back. I have got to learn
to live with more than one name.

There was a Sioux story that said Crazy Horse had fasted
and purified himself during one of the worst times the Lakotas
had suffered, when many were poisoned by the white man's
whiskey (what Bone Hand always called "the burning
drink"), when children were starving because there were no
skins to trade for food and the hunts were poor; and among
the Oglalas, Crazy Horse's own people, there was quarreling
and killing, and Crazy Horse's father, who was then called
Crazy Horse himself, had helped his son, who was called Curly
at that time, to construct a sweathouse where he could purify
himself and meditate and seek his vision. And Crazy Horse,
the father, who was Crazy Horse then, went himself to a sweat
lodge and asked for a vision.

In the Paha Sapa *long before, the older Crazy Horse, the father
of Crazy Horse, had also had a vision. A bear came to him and gave
him great powers. "He gave me powers to conquer the things of this
earth," the older Crazy Horse had said, "and that also includes the
whites who come into our land. I am old and grow infirm and so I
give my powers to my son, who is young and strong so that he may
become a great leader of the Lakotas. And he will fight many whites
and bring great death and destruction on them and on one who leads
them against our sacred lands; he will bring not only him down but
also all his men. It will be the greatest of Indian victories, a sign from*

*my son of the power of the bear." The spot where the vision had come
to the older Crazy Horse was known as Bear Butte for the bear who
had visited the old man.*

Thus Crazy's Horse's father saw that his son would be a
great man and that he himself could no longer claim the name
Crazy Horse, which had first belonged to his father before
him, and his father before him; so Crazy Horse's father came
back and said:

*I give him the name of his father, and of many fathers before him—
I give him an illustrious name, I give him my name, Crazy Horse.*

So Curly became Crazy Horse and Crazy Horse's father
took the name of Worm. Then Crazy Horse went again to seek
his vision; he fasted and let the evils in his body out and waited
and prayed, and yet nothing had come to give him a sign.
Then, just as he was about to give up, the Great Spirit had sent
him the vision that told him what would happen to his life.
Crazy Horse would move forward and look into the fire and
talk slowly, in a soft voice, of that vision. It was as if he himself
had become the vision in his telling, and he would tell them
what he saw.

*He ran toward his horse who had been hobbled below. He felt weak
and dizzy, afraid really, but he could not identify his fear; it had
simply seized him and held him fast in the center of its palm, and he
could not force it out of him, so that he felt the final despair of
weakness, for courage was an Indian's principal armament.*

*He saw his horse grazing peacefully, and he stopped to catch his
breath, to push back the fear, and the horse lifted his head. And then,
he said, I must have fallen through the crack in this earth to the next.
For there was a rider on my horse, and the horse was no longer my
horse but first bay and then white with sun-colored spots, and the man
who rode the yellow-spotted horse was not painted or dressed for war.
He had only one feather in his loosely hanging hair—and this was
oddest, behind one ear was fastened a small stone, blue I think it was.*

*I could understand him, though he did not speak—he gave me his
thoughts. He sent his thoughts out of his head into mine. He was a*

great warrior, I knew this, even though he wore simple clothes and had no paint or war bonnet. I could see shapes of enemies gathering round and I was afraid for him, this man who began to ride my horse and then had turned it into a sun-spotted horse from the gods. Many warriors came; they wanted to count coup against the man with the feather and the blue stone; they were dressed and painted for war, and as they rode the paint streaked and melted and ran down their bodies and covered their clothes and they shot guns and let arrows fly from their bows, and though there were many of them, they could not touch the man who was unpainted and who wore plain clothes and only a feather and a small blue stone as an adornment.

Many times the lone figure was pulled back by his own people, but always he broke lose and rode out again against his enemies.

It began to storm. Lights fell from the sky. Great roars of thunder lifted up the earth. Hail cascaded down and made spots upon his skin and there was a stripe of lightning that cut across his face.

When the storm was gone, a hawk came and it had red upon its back; the red hawk came and cried out to the lone warrior and his people. And then I saw no more; that was the end of what I saw.

But the Indians understood the vision very well. It meant that Crazy Horse would be a great warrior who could not be brought down by an enemy's bows and arrows or bullets; when Crazy Horse went into battle, he could fill his mind with his vision and come away unharmed. He must ride as the man in his vision had ridden—unpainted and in plain dress, with a single feather in his loose hair and a small blue stone hanging from his ear. And a hawk would hover over him.

Crazy Horse the son, unlike other Indians, never painted or dressed for his coups; he dressed only in the white buckskin shirt and dark-blue leggings of the man in his vision; he gave away horses he took on his expeditions, keeping only one or two for war; he did not sing or dance the way the others did, did not make the Sun Dance; he did not take scalps or count coup, as if the taking of scalps and counting of coup were of no importance to him; all he seemed to care about was the little red-backed hawk pinned to his head, and the little stone that hung behind his ear; he kept, for a fact, very little for himself; even among the Indians, who prided themselves on what they could give away, he was known as a generous man. He had really never wanted anything for himself. No, that was not really true either. He had not wanted material things, but he had most certainly wanted Black Buffalo Woman. For Black Buffalo Woman, Crazy Horse had broken sacred rules, and because of this there had been a time when he was unholy —because he had ridden into camp and taken No Water's woman; Crazy Horse and Black Buffalo Woman had brazenly ridden out of No Water's village together, Black Buffalo Woman's cheeks crimsoned with big red circles, the sign of one who is greatly loved and admired.

No Water had tracked the party, and their second night out burst into their tipi and aimed a gun at Crazy Horse. Crazy Horse had a knife, but Little Big Man grabbed his arm, and the fire from the gun caught Crazy Horse in the face. He should have died. His jaw was shattered, the bullet wedged in his head so that his speech was gone, and his eyes burned red.

Bone Hand was sent for—Benjie remembered the messenger riding in on the lathered pony crying out to them that Crazy Horse was dying, probably dead, and Bone Hand rising —his face had looked all caved in for a moment, he had looked like someone Benjie had never seen; then his face went back to being itself.

Bone Hand had known that in one of the visions about Crazy Horse a very important thing had been told: Only with one hand held behind him by one of his own people could Crazy Horse be killed. "He won't die," Bone Hand said, but no one would believe him. "Strange Man is dying," they all cried, and there was great weeping and grief in the camp.

For the rest of his life Crazy Horse carried a black scar across his white face. Black Buffalo Woman had been sent back to her own camp so that the trouble between peoples of the same tribe would be avoided, and Crazy Horse grew more silent and distant and withdrawn, so that more and more people were calling him Strange Man, and even though a new woman was brought to his tent he did not ever again seem like a young man.

"Each time there is a loss of love," Bone Hand said, "there

is a kind of death. A man grows old quickly who loses his friends and his woman fast. His is an old heart," he said sadly. That last year Benjie had been with the Indians Bone Hand spent more time than ever with Crazy Horse, as if to say, I am the last left, I will not desert you. Benjie remembered how Bone Hand and Two Moon had come in from the destruction of their camp and Crazy Horse had come out to meet them. "Even the little we have they have taken," Bone Hand said to his friend, and Crazy Horse had said, "Yes, that is the way it goes now. Even the little we have is taken from us."

Crazy Horse would never let the white man's black box take his picture; he wanted nothing that could hold him still in one place, he said. He spent time alone, or with his good friend Bone Hand, who sat and shared visions with him and had ridden with him along with Lone Bear, who had been killed in the fight with men who were cutting wood under Fetterman, and Hump, a great teacher; they had all ridden together, but now only Bone Hand and Crazy Horse were left because two winters back Hump had been killed in a Shoshone raid. When Hump went, Crazy Horse had been so reckless that he had tried to get himself killed, riding in the direct path of the Shoshone warriors for over an hour, but neither their arrows nor their bullets could bring him down. The Lakotas said that no arrow or bullet could ever kill him.

And Bone Hand believed this implicitly. He had been with Crazy Horse during the bloody year on the Plains when Red Cloud had been a great leader among the Indians, a warrior unlike any other; now Red Cloud was like a white man's woman, sitting waiting for handouts; Bone Hand had been with Crazy Horse against Fetterman and at the battle of the Wagon Box when Hump and Crazy Horse rode against Powell's men, using four hundred braves against Fetterman's woodcutters. Crazy Horse and Bone Hand remembered this battle perhaps the best of all because it was the first time, Bone Hand repeated again and again, the bad new medicine was used against them, the black fast-loading guns that shot so fast the Indians could not believe it, the new Springfield breech-loading rifles that the white Captain had been very proud of. He had shown it to Benjie as if it were some kind of sacred instrument with which the gods gave men power. Perhaps he was right. The Indians had strong medicine but the white men were always inventing stronger ways to get what they wanted. "Custer's goin' to teach them a lesson this time," the Captain said. "He's goin' into the Hills and get them buggers."

Benjie wondered if he had gone. In the *Paha Sapa* there were many Lakotas and Cheyenne gathered north of the Little Bighorn and Bighorn and some, a few, now had the black fast-firing gun, but all were, like Crazy Horse, determined not to give up the great lands where the pines grew so thick and dark and black; when Long Hair had first come to the *Paha Sapa* two years before, Crazy Horse had not been able to believe the whites were coming into the Hills. "To the *Paha Sapa?*" Crazy Horse had asked disbelievingly, shaking his head that no, it couldn't be so because the treaty Red Cloud had signed said so long as grass shall grow and water flow the land belonged to the Sioux. But it was true. Long Hair— Custer, she thought bitterly, an *Army* man—had come into the Hills; he had gone right past Bear Butte where Crazy Horse's father had had his vision, and he had found out about the yellow metal; then the yellow-metal diggers had come and there had been trouble at the fort, over a flagpole, which Sitting Bull and Young Man Afraid of His Horses had stopped; but Crazy Horse would not go to the fort; he stayed in the sacred hills, and those last two winters had been bad ones, with deep snow and, in the Moon of Frost in the Lodge, snow blindness, she had suffered from it herself, the Hungry Times, Bone Hand called these winters. The Indians at the agencies who had come in had no adequate food either— stinking meat and moldy flour, and one blanket for every three Indians, conditions so bad even the agents sent complaints back to the place the President was, and when nothing happened the word had come to the Indians who had stayed away not to come in, their people at the agency were starving. Bone Hand and Two Moon's people had taken the little they had and separated it into two piles, one for themselves, and one to send down to their people at the fort; but even this did not help the agency Indians—they were starving and freezing and finally, in desperation, they took their ponies before the fort so the Captain could see, and slit their throats, built fires, and roasted and ate the horseflesh so that the whites could see how bad things were. The bones stayed in front of the fort, a daily reminder of their needs that the soldiers would pay no attention to.

But of course the soldiers didn't care, Benjie thought. They never care a one of them about anything but theirselves. Men who would come out into the Indians' country and take it away and let them starve and freeze, what do they care?

In the *Paha Sapa* the fighting went on between the Army and the Indians, the miners and the Indians. She remembered now, buried in dust, how cold and hungry she had been chewing on *wasna* bladder in order to still the cramps in her stomach. Yet no one complained, for what lay ahead was inside all their minds; they *saw,* Benjie thought, even as I couldn't, how it would go. Nothing could get better or ever be resolved until all Indians were hanged or caged or in chains. This Bone Hand and Crazy Horse and Sitting Bull and Worm and Young Man Afraid all saw, but I only felt the hunger and cold and only cared what happened to me. I only wanted to get back to the whites. I didn't care if they were hanged or in chains or driven out, and all the time Bone Hand and the others were desperately trying to survive, it was their terrible hardships I took for my own hope; I lived then on the sufferings in the camp, the hope we would give up and go down to the fort and I would go back to the whites. Even after the second boy came I never took in my children or my husband or Dark Hair Woman or any of the others as having *connections* to me; they were all just impediments to my getting back where I thought I belonged.

Red Cloud and Spotted Tail and many Lakota chiefs went far away to the Great Father, and he asked them to sell the Hills, and they could not believe the words and said they could not do such a thing without asking the people, and so the great black train went back on the iron tracks and called the great chiefs together, and Bone Hand went down and when he came back he was so bitter that he said he would never race his horses again until the Hills were his and his brothers', and all the white men were dead or driven out.

His tent had never been one known for its laughter or careless ways; now it became a place of bitterness, Bone Hand's determination so intense that it entered the very air inside the tipi; and sometimes Benjie could even imagine that anger taking shape: She saw it, not in the way she looked at ordinary things in the normal world around her, but as if Bone Hand's rage were so strong that it took dark shapes and made the air dense with black pulsating weights.

In the Moon of Frost in the Lodge word had come in that all the Indians must come down to the fort, but the snow was too deep even if they had wanted to get in, and many of the braves were far away seeking meat for the starving bands and could not know they had been called in; and when all the Indians did not come in and when the whites saw there were many, with power in the councils of both the white and red, who said they would never sell the Hills, word was sent from Three Stars that guns and fire and cannons would come to clear the Indians out.

"So we shall all be warriors again," Bone Hand, old and tired and bent under the pressure of his anger, said. And then, after the raid: "We shall send the light one back. Black Buffalo Woman had to be sent back; now White Buffalo Woman must go, too. These women were not meant for us," he said to Crazy Horse. "Perhaps giving her back will placate Three Stars. At least perhaps the Bluecoats will leave us alone for a little while."

Bone Hand and Crazy Horse will come and kill them, Benjie thought, and it was as if after the dust and thirst and hunger and fatigue she, too, were leaving her own body and rushing like the wind through that small crack in the earth where one passed from the normal life into the center of what was and what was to become. And this was the dream Benjie had:

In the Moon of Making Fat, the moon that usually came in the month the whites called June, the tribes would gather for the sacred Sun Dance. Benjie saw the Indians coming in from many miles away, the ponies dragging the travois with their tipis wrapped around all possessions; the great tests of endurance would be held near the rocks the Indians called Deer Medicine, and in her dream she saw all the well-known figures

—Bone Hand and Two Moon, Sitting Bull and Young Man Afraid; but in her dream she did not see Crazy Horse. It was Sitting Bull on whom her vision focussed: He was lifting an awl over his arm and slowly cutting away scraps of flesh, first all up and down one arm, then shifting the awl and starting on the other, fifty on one, fifty little cuts of flesh on the other, a hundred pieces of flesh she saw carefully laid out as an offering to the great god. Sitting Bull turned his head to the sun, his eyes never moving, and began to dance. . . . He danced, sun-blinded, the blood covering his arms, until he could no longer see nor hear nor stand but lay on the ground as one dead. And Benjie saw inside her head the vision Sitting Bull had: of many soldiers falling dead.

All this came to her as if she were there herself, and yet she knew quite well she was lying on the desert floor enveloped in dust, but the dream was so real that she felt the dust fade and the desert dissolve; it was as if she were hovering in the background of the great ceremony, which she had always despised, considering it bloody and barbaric, and the Indians who took part in it uncivilized, but now there was a kind of hypnotic trance to the sun-dazzled man with blood running from his arms, dancing on and on, his head turned up to the sun, eyes open and dazed, feet moving rhythmically, arms outstretched, the red of the sun and the red of the blood mixing in Benjie's mind, and the soldiers falling, red and bloody, on the plains—she was back again within herself, huddled up under the heavy dust, her throat parched, her body faint, a dizzy lightness lifting her head until for a moment, quite clearly, she saw the dust-whirling ground around her, and she thought, *I'm not gonna get through this.* Then it was as if her mind refused to accept that understanding, and she released her hold on the state of seeing that included the world around her and she retreated back inside, back to the Indian world inside, where she was safe—and immediately, as if by the sheer force of her will, she held that faraway world together and set it in motion as an entity outside herself. She *saw* it. It existed for her with far more force than the dust-enclosed prairie which ran with its millions of grams of dancing dust all around her.

It was not Sitting Bull she saw this time but Crazy Horse. He had on his usual dark-blue breeches and his plain buckskin shirt; she saw the black-powdered scar on his face, the hawk pinned in his hair, the single feather, the little blue stone behind his ear; he was leading many painted and feathered braves, many Lakotas and Cheyenne; first she saw Crazy Horse on his yellow-spotted pony charging again and again until the little horse was so done in it could not be whipped to a run anymore; the blue-coated soldiers had panicked and fled from the boulders and brush beside the river that could have protected them, driving their horses across the stream and up the high bank, many clubbed or killed as they crossed, the others scattered up a hill, and yet just at the moment when the whites seemed caught, more soldiers came up; and Crazy Horse took his bay and went back into battle again. The blue soldiers crowded together and their guns smoked. They were pushed back, leaving a rim of dead around them; they went on firing, more frantic now, as the Indians pushed in, Crazy Horse rushing back and forth on his little bay, urging them on. The soldiers were firing and dropping and falling back; the Indians were riding wildly and firing with what guns they had, shooting their bows, the arrows whishing through the air; the Indians came with clubs and knives and dropped down from their ponies and beat and hacked and mutilated the dead. Dust flew up so strong she could see nothing, and Benjie thought, Ah, this is where the vision comes from, out of the dust. Now I see. And what she saw was more dust with figures emerging and firing or bending their bows, then disappearing back into the dust; a cloud of sand and grit and smoke was left, and she saw the Bluecoats—there were fewer of them firing and some had been forced back to back, they were being pressed so hard.

There was chanting. She heard it clearly, first from the Indians raising their voices in praise and thanksgiving for this great fight against the whites, and then, softer, from the soldiers: They were praying, some of them, or calling to someone to save them, the ones who had fallen and were still alive and could see the clubs and knives coming at them. The Bluecoats who were still firing made cursing chants, their faces contorted with rage and helplessness and disbelief, as if it had suddenly come home to them they were all going to be killed and cut up and left lying for carrion out on this wild bluff, and they could not believe the long-yellow-haired man had led them into a fight they could not win and yet all around them they saw the dead being butchered, they heard the Indians singing their great war chants, they saw the light-filled faces of those sure of victory; all the signs were unmistakable and yet the soldiers could not believe; they huddled up against one another and fired and fired until their guns were so hot that they could hardly hold them, their hands were blistered from the heat, and someone cried the ammunition was running low and someone else cursed; there were the wails, hollering, screaming, one voice crazed with anger and excitement, but no one could understand what he was trying to say as the Indians drove their ponies in again and the dust whirled up again, the soldiers firing their smoking, sizzling guns; and Benjie saw above the dust and noise and hubbub the clear figure of Crazy Horse whipping his horse to drive the Lakotas on to a final charge, his Winchester like a flag held high above his head, while he cried out to them the Indian chant, "This is a good day to die." Crazy Horse rode out, exposed, so that they could see his courage and partake of it. All this Benjie saw, as well as the warriors thundering after him, plunging over dead horses and men through the whirling bullets of the whites, and they were close enough to see now what Crazy Horse could see, that the whites were afraid, there were only a few of them still standing, and their faces were frightened; even Long Hair had stopped his craziness and seemed to see, finally, what was happening. He stood in the midst of the small circle of blue-coated men watching the Indians come with their war clubs, scrambling from their ponies for an instant to scoop up a carbine or take a knife to a man who had fallen, either dead or half alive, and with a slice of the blade and a flash of hand, hold the testicles or scalp in the air; and then, at that moment, there came a piercing, frantic cry from a bugle, a young soldier trying to rally the men left, and the soldiers huddled closer together and fired again, and Benjie saw many Indians fall and the wave turned back.

But there were more Indians at the river by the Little Bighorn, and as they saw the fight lag they beat their horses toward the front and came, like a wave, down on the Bluecoats in a great roar—and, when the smoke cleared, Benjie saw there were no more Bluecoats to kill. All lay still, a silent hump of bodies on the little hill, their horses rounded up by the river and kept in check by young boys.

Crazy Horse sat on the ridge—she could see his light-skinned scarred face quite clearly; it was impassive, as if no flicker of emotion, not one inkling of the triumph of this great battle, would be allowed to pierce through the rigidly held skin—he watched as the Bluecoats were stripped and left naked under the great bolt of sun burning down from overhead. One Indian had the bugle she had heard earlier and another hoisted aloft a flag; many of the Indians had put on soldiers' clothes and many carried white guns or were collecting ammunition, and there was dust and noise and confusion and then a voice calling Crazy Horse to come up on the hill and look. He rode high up and saw many more soldiers on a ridge a few miles away and at the same time he saw more of his own warriors splashing across the river toward the hill where the other Bluecoats had fallen back.

But these Bluecoats had a good place and the Indians could not seem to get through to them. Crazy Horse whirled his horse and galloped down the bluff and tried to rout these Bluecoats, but the sun was failing and the Indian dead had to be put on scaffolds, the proper mournings must be made; he rode back to the encampment to rest and plan.

Benjie saw him lying in his tent scheming ways to destroy the Bluecoats on the hill the way he had wiped out those on the Little Bighorn. But in her dream she saw more and more soldiers coming; for every one killed more and more came. She saw Lakotas and Cheyenne taking down their tipis in the wash of a new day and moving on and on, with the Bluecoats like millions of small ants swarming over the plains after them, the Indians riding harder and faster, farther and farther, trying to escape; but there were too many Bluecoats and no more places to hide, and the dust rose as the men and women and children fled on, a long line of people desperately struggling into the mountains and trying to find refuge in the cracks and crevices of the *Paha Sapa.* The Bluecoats came on and on; this Benjie saw, as if the advance were unending, as if the Bluecoats represented the idea of the never-ending, and she thought, It's as if they have no home—first that they exist to fight and destroy and one Bluecoat is like another and even such as Bone Hand and Crazy Horse and Sitting Bull and Gall and Worm and Young Man Afraid cannot stop the flow, no matter how brave or hard they fight. They will all die, she thought, and the white man will crush their bones into the Hills and take the gold.

In her dream she saw death looking over their shoulders, tiny shadows waiting to envelop them; when Crazy Horse turned his head, he caught the flicker at the edge of his eye; he knew. Then Benjie saw John. He was doing something that looked like hoeing, but he wasn't farming. He was in the mountains. She recognized the crags, the needlelike rocks, the swift-flowing streams, the thick pines. He is taking out gold, she thought. They are all dead and he is taking out the yellow metal the whites want. The whites have won.

II

*W*here the hell is John?"

It seemed impossible to Tom that Mason Raymond could have survived and the Buttes boy be dead; yet life was full of just such dumbfounding reversibles. Time and time again he had been witness to the subversion of justice, the triumph of the weak, the wrong, the worthless. Why should this instance be any different from all the others? But Buttes was so—Tom had no one word to describe John Buttes; what he thought instead was, Jest his anger alone oughta a kept him goin'.

> *Men who hates puffs up and swells,*
> *Men who got the power knows the spells . . .*

"The spells" were, to Tom, a way of describing how hate could carry a man farther than love. I thought he'd anger hisself right into the Hills, Tom thought. I even seen him diggin' gold right out of them ornery peaks with his own bare hands, he was so set on bein' somebody. Jest goes to show you you can't trust what ain't there to see but you think you knows. That there boy was so full of poison it shone off him like it was

] *318* [

light. I figured he had enough orneriness in him to keep him goin' a long, long time, almost up to forever. I been wrong before, I'll be wrong agin. But I'll miss his piss 'nd vinegar. The other one (thinking of Mason Raymond) was easier, but we don't always take to what's smooth on us. Human nature being what it is, we enjoy a challenge. He watched as Mason Raymond came galloping at him on the piebald. Tom was too spent to try to stop the little mare. He just had to hope Mason Raymond could maybe get the mare pulled in and come round. He jest gits her quieted enough to turn, the others'll follow, and if he comes by agin I can mabbe grab hold of her, Tom thought. It don't never end. But every man ought to have the right to go to hell in his own way.

How we gonna git them ruttin' animals to stay still long enough to git me and the girl up on one of them? Most of 'em ain't got one single solitary holdin' thin' on them, a couple got raggedy halter is all, look like they'll come apart in your hands, and there sure as hell ain't anythin' here. Yet a thought came to him: Maybe he or Mason Raymond had a belt that could be used around one of the horses' necks; that would make an anchoring piece. How you gonna hold the girl on, you so low the dogs would bark back at you if they could.

The little piebald circled Tom, Mason Raymond hanging on and looking grimly determined. He's learnt to sit, Tom marveled. He almost looks jest like he been born to the range. I wouldn'ta believed it iffen I hadn't seen it with my own eyes. Look at the boy hang on to leather.

Mason Raymond was getting the pony harvested in. She came right up to him as if she were grain and he was the barn. "He's back there, somewhere in the storm," Mason Raymond hollered hoarsely. He looked so wild-eyed and mean and made that breezy noise with every breath he took that Tom had trouble recognizing him. I never thought I'd see him able to horse up proper, Tom thought. "What's that?" he asked. "What's that you say?"

Mason Raymond stared at him out of two holes of dust; his eyes glittered and winked. "I said he's out there in that dust. We got separated. *John's out in the dust*," Mason Raymond said as if he were talking to a held-back child.

Tom's mind gave him the pleasure of a sigh of relief. I got attached to that boy without even knowin' it, he thought. He's so damned ornery he's outstandin'.

"Are you all right?" Mason Raymond asked anxiously. "You look kind of—you're all covered with dust and you look —you look terrible," he said with his usual tact.

"I ain't gonna die. I'm gonna shoot like a star," Tom said, half grinning. "My stomach's sort of vacant and my throat's parched dry, but there's still fire inside. The girl's took bad though. We gotta do some hustlin' to pull her around."

Mason Raymond grabbed him so hard that Tom's teeth rammed up into his head; Mason Raymond pulled him down to the ground and, as he hauled him through the air, he plastered Tom to the side of the piebald. Before Tom had a chance to speak, the herd of horses was running over them. How'd he hear them and me not? he asked himself. He developin' powers, Tom thought. Ain't that somethin' now?

"We have to get her—" Mason Raymond began, flailing out at the stallions. "Get," he shouted, "Get away. Oh my god," he said, "they're just driving me crazy. Why can't they let up a minute? We have to get the girl and we have to go back and get him—get John—he's lost out there in all that dust. Get away, get away," he hollered, trying to beat the horses away. "Get back up on this horse," he shouted into Tom's face.

"I ain't got strength enough no more to hang on, son, not with them devils flyin' at us."

"You have to," Mason Raymond said. He sounded desperate.

"I ain't got it in me. I know my limitations."

"Oh, god," Mason Raymond said and it sounded more like a prayer than an exclamation. He grabbed Tom and looped him over the horse. Tom just couldn't believe that tall long drink of water had that much in him; and yet he was sacked out across the little mare like a canvas of potatoes. Horses were flying at him from every direction; one behind him had almost mounted the piebald when Tom saw Mason Raymond give him an enormous blow across the muzzle. "Damn it, git," Mason Raymond said, Learnin' to ride and swear at the same time, Tom thought. The wonder of it.

Mason Raymond hoisted himself up behind Tom awkwardly and gave the piebald a kick. "Where's she at? Where's that girl at?"

"Back yonder." Tom was bouncing up and down so violently his insides were being thrown this way and that. I'll never git them straightened out, he thought.

"Where's that?"

"Jest keep"—he was so jiggled that he couldn't get the words out right —"goin'," he said finally. He wasn't really sure exactly where she was, but he was grateful the storm had almost ground to a halt because it was easier to see and safer to look. In the thick of that dust they could have gone right by or over her without even knowing it. But she was closer than Tom had figured. "There," he said. "She there—*that* lump, there. Next that other lump—the big one, that horse of yourn."

Mason Raymond got down and tried to put his arms around the girl. She lay stone still. He bent down, disengaging her gently from a mound of dust. Tom slid down and held the pony and tried to shoo the other horses off. They were mauling Mabel now. He was afraid they were going to stamp on her. God, they were a wild bunch. Just like their former owners. People were right when they said animals took on the characteristics of the people who owned them. These outlaw horses were like their outlaw owners, and Mabel was like Mason Raymond—turning the other cheek as they tried to stampede her. That horse had had a hard time, worse even than them—beat down by the stream, the plains, and finally done in by the dust. And that girl was really in a bad way, just like her family had been. There was an inch, an inch and a half of dust all over her, and she didn't even flop in Mason Raymond's arms as he raised her. She was dead rigid like she was gone. Maybe there was a little somethin' still left in her they could fan up, but she wasn't what you could call likely to leap on no horse on her own and grab mane and run it cross desert to Alcove Spring and git saved.

Still, there was a slight rising and falling of the chest that denied the obvious. The girl had always been what you might call a heavy breather (probably come from all the talkin' she done, Tom thought, kind of a gassin' up swolled her lungs), but the motion now was so feeble that Tom wasn't encouraged. She looked as if she were sloughing out her last.

Mason Raymond jackknifed the girl back and forth so that her lungs could get a cleaning out. In cases of emergency, Tom supposed, you didn't have the right to waste valuable time on being gentle and considerate. She was bad, and there was no tellin' what condition John was in. He better than this one, Tom thought. Bet my bottom dollar on that. She bad.

The girl coughed, choked, heaved, and began to give way to gusts of abrasive sound that seemed to come from the friction going on inside. She was all clogged up. Mason Raymond shook her, pounded on her back, bent her double, and wobbled her back and forth, trying to knead the dust out of her any way he could. She was a symphony of noises, but sound, any sound, was encouraging. Look at how quiet she had been.

Oh god, those horses had give up on Mason Raymond's horse and were making another run on him.

Mason Raymond let go of the girl, who tumbled in a heap and lay still. He jumped up and grabbed the halter of the piebald and hung on; Tom sank like a stone onto the ground. I'm plumb tuckered out, he thought. It's jest too much, jest too damned much; all these damn ravin' horses, *enslaved in their lust,* he thought, a phrase so ludicrous he could not possibly imagine where it came from and then, an instant later, remembering the shack down South when he was a small boy, sitting up on his pallet and his mother was holding out one of those cheap books she traded for on the sly, spending the few free hours she had collecting nuts and herbs to pass along for what she could, never hard cash, but discarded clothing she could still mend and patch, extra flour or salt, a bone of meat, and once in a while a torn pamphlet with pictures and writing. Niggers were not supposed to read and write. But she had it in her heart he was going to get away, go North and get free. "Your granddaddy was set on that," she would say, and somehow or other she would lay her hands on a book and smuggle him out a night a week to get learning. She was completely without any training herself and therefore could not know the precious book she had found for him was trash, a romance with heavy passages where passion and virtue locked in battle and made a deadly fight to the end, carrying the moral that those in whom lust rose were enslaved. Naturally the words had stayed with him.

Mason Raymond held on to the mare while the stallions came thundering in. He ran with the pony. He didn't want them stomped. No horse but an outlaw would deliberately trample a human being, but in all the confusion accidents could always happen, and any way you looked at it these horses weren't normal. If something can go wrong it will, and not jest one thin' at a time: a law his white friend Jonathan, who had given him his watch, had been fond of quoting. Something will go wrong if it can, and not just one thing at a time. That summed up Jonathan's whole philosophy: They don't just rob us, he had said, getting up out of the dust and brushing himself off. They hurt us—kick, stomp, punch, no need for that, but they done it. "Here," he had said, dangling the watch, "you take it. I ain't trustworthy enough to own nuthin' decent." Jonathan was always givin' me somethin', Tom thought. A giver, he thought, and I never seen jest how givin' he was till now.

Mason Raymond held on tight to the mare, twice flailing at the other animals. He can't go on doin' that forever, Tom thought. I gotta move. He gotta have some help. He can't hang on to the mare and drive off the horses and help git us organized to git back to the Spring all by hisself. Nobody can be called on to do what's beyond him, especially that boy. But he changed. Oh, he changed.

Mason Raymond smacked a horse across the nose and turned and kicked out at another trying to mount the pony from the opposite side. He was beginning to work himself into a fury, the rage of despair, Tom could see. He might even beat those horses to a pulp if he got worked up enough, and he was sure on his way, for he had begun to scream—incoherent, violent curses, flailing this way and that—as if he were burning with a blind passion to punish. He's lost all control, Tom thought. It seemed impossible for one so committed to gentleness and grace, but there was the living example of repudiation right before his eyes. "I can't take any more, I tell you,"

Mason Raymond was shrieking, "I just can't take any more."

The mare was bobbing this way and that; the stallions crowded in, determined to make contact. She shrieked in a high horse way. The girl lay still. And inside Tom's head Jonathan dangled the watch.

Tom stood up. I'm with that boy, he thought. It all jest *is* too much. How many times this trip had he come to the same conclusion and what good had it done him?

Mason Raymond let go of the mare. Apparently he had decided that if she wanted to run off and get bred, that was her business. If those horses wanted to drive themselves to dust running after her, that was their business; he was through.

"Don't let her go!" It was the girl, croaking and struggling to rise, her hands raised in a supplicating gesture while Mason Raymond and Tom stared blankly. Rose from the dead, rose right out of the plains, spindly as a yucca, dust-drenched beyond recognition—all covered with white that way and lurching toward them like a symbol of vengeance risen from the grave to set the score straight. Take what you want. Take it, but pay.

"Grab hold," she croaked. There were holes in her voice as if passing out through her throat it was torn apart by sharp obstacles. "Hold."

The mare reared around and nearly ran over Tom; she had caught him off guard. The studs were crowding in. He had a confused impression of haunches and withers, flying legs, dilated nostrils, plumes of steam, flying flakes of white lather, he and Mason Raymond and the girl groping to bring some kind of order to all this chaos. The girl was so weak she kept stumbling, throwing herself against Mason Raymond to brace herself, but still managing to hang on to the mare. "Drive them *this* animals off," she said in that eery, ragged voice.

Drive them off? Drive five horses off? Of course she was crazy. They were all crazy—and that includes me, Tom thought.

She went down on her knees, still hanging on to the pony's halter. Tom just wished she'd found someone else to survive with. He grabbed hold of her and hauled her up. There was nothing to her at all, just a few skimpy bones and a little weightless flesh.

She hung to the mare obstinately. "Git them back. Drive them off." Mason Raymond ran out and began waving his arms and shouting at two of the closest horses. The two others on the off side were crowding the pony, raving and steaming. The girl lurched under the pony's head and beat feebly at them.

Three ain't no better than two of us, Tom thought.

But it wasn't three now. A fourth figure was stumbling around. John Buttes was wobbling from side to side, futilely trying to drive the raging animals back. He's done got here, Tom thought.

Mason Raymond ran around and grabbed John. "Get on the mare," he shouted. "And haul the girl up and get over to the grove. Just run the mare straight ahead back toward the spring. I'll git Mabel and bring him in—"

Mason Raymond dragged the girl, not listening to John's response, some protest no one had any interest in.

Mason Raymond shoved the girl next to the mare and boosted her aboard. He had to give the girl a crack across the arm before she would let go of him. She was babbling, furious about something. Greatest bunch of arguers Tom had ever come across.

"Get up," Mason Raymond said peremptorily, and he shoved her along. Tom remembered her weightlessness and wondered why she hadn't just blown away in that wind. "Listen, don't fight," he said to her. "You're jest wastin' time."

She was a torrent of meaningless sounds, but Mason Raymond had got her up. "I gotta tell you," Mason Raymond began in a worried voice, but the mare was already under way, John running alongside. "Go on," Mason Raymond was hollering. "You go on. We'll catch up." Whatever it is, we'll find out soon enough, Tom thought. Bad news don't really wait long to spring itself on you. And dead men tell tales of a sort.

He should have stayed put down there on the Abilene Trail. Old man his age had no business startin' to roam around again, go places he got no business. There comes a time you got to bow to the will of your joints and stay put.

He must look dead gone, eyes especially, deep dark potholes outlined by dust.

He needed fire and water and a boiling of beef broth to make any kind of earnest attempt at resurrection. Maybe they'd jest leave me, he thought, a characteristic punishment along the trail, to cast out the offending members of a band to fend for themselves, often without even a gun. (He had no idea what had happened to his own gun and, in his present indifferent, fatalistic mood, didn't really much care.)

I can't git to the Spring on my own, he thought. It ain't that far, but I'm too done in, even to hang on to a horse. He could make it, Tom thought looking at Mason Raymond. I'm the one holdin' him up. I ain't goin' to come this far and done what I done jest to end up as pickin's for the coyotes. On horseback I got strength enough to make it partway on my own, but I ain't sure I got power enough to get there all the way.

You gotta try. *You gonna jest give up?*

"That horse can't carry anyone," Mason Raymond said, as if reading his mind.

"We ken walk ourselves," Tom said.

Mason Raymond looked doubtful. "I don't know," he said. "It seems like an awful long way back."

I ain't gonna use energy arguin' with him, Tom thought.

He started cross-desert to where there was food and water and horses to get him to the Hills. He should never have tried to play God to a bunch of kids. Served him right to be called to account like this. You get big idears, nigger, you gotta pay for your high-and-mightiness. You ought to know that by this time.

He trudged through a desert of desolation under a scorch of sun, trying to sort out the possibilities of what lay ahead. You have to be prepared in order to survive. He knew that. Behind him Mason Raymond stumbled along, pulling his horse behind him.

He's weak. No, he ain't. He's jest tired. He ain't weak the way he was. I never seen sech a transformation. What those two boys do at that there Spring? That there *this* Spring, he thought, grinning, thinking of the girl. Come into the camp I'll find out.

Been through so much, don't even care; jest drink and

maybe chew something to eat and lie down and try to git some rest. Like as not, load up the gear, pull out—why should any of us care what happened to those men? They kill them? Like as not. Scared them off more like it. Mason Raymond, he ain't gonna kill nobody.

He stopped and wiped grit from his face. His face struck back at him with pain. Git washed up, git some food, lie down and rest. Wouldn't take no time to git to the Hills on my own. It's always others hold you back. I try to play it big and done nuthin' but brought trouble down on all of us.

His eyes were acting up. The horizon rose and fell, undulating in front of him. When he trudged toward the distant grove and tried to take a sighting on it, the world tilted and spun and turned upside down, trying to fight him out into space.

Mason Raymond grabbed hold of him. "You all right?" He sounded real worried. Tom shook his head. He really didn't know. Everything was topsy-turvy. Even Mason Raymond's face looked upside down. "Too old," he began, but the effort of explaining was too burdensome. "Better off—your own," he finally got out.

Mason Raymond's face was all screwed up in the concentration of trying to understand. He obviously didn't. "On your own—better off," Tom said again. He had the strange sensation he was looking at Mason Raymond and, behind him, the wobbling image of the horse through a kind of double vision; the landscape pulsed and throbbed; he couldn't sort it out and get it straight. He wasn't even sure they were going in the right direction.

He shut his eyes and tried to concentrate; when he opened them again, the whole earth heaved up at him and he stumbled, trying to hold his balance while the world seemed to sway and bend and break; he shut his eyes again and tried to grab hold, but he couldn't stop the feeling that the ground under him was falling away and that he was about to hurtle through the endless emptiness of space.

All he could see was a world of whirling white, a world whirling so fast that its dizzying speed made him nauseous, a world dividing and multiplying its white dots so fast that in no time at all he would see nothing but one solid mass of white. I'm done in, he thought, really done in when I start thinkin' white. The sun or the dust, maybe the two of them, somethin' permanent's unhinged.

He could be angry and rage; he could succumb to a flood of self-pity; he could rant and rave against the injustice of existence: All of these were feelings he could deal with because he had experienced them in the past, but the fear he felt was so persuasive and uncontrollable that he simply didn't know how to handle it. It swept over him and he felt weak and trembling and desperate. You go against what's laid out, swell yourself up with the pride of being powerful, you're committing some basic sin that has got to be punished. So he was going to be punished, he was goin' to die, the perfect punishment for someone who wanted to do more than other men, white or black.

My god, he thought, I ain't *never* hurt so.

He couldn't even close his jaws without the whole nerve center inside his head setting off an alarm. It's where that Mason Raymond grabbed me so quick and rung my teeth agin my head, when he went and git me to save me from them ruttin' horses, he thought. His skin vibrated, split; he felt lost out in the middle of nowhere—a fitting end to a prideful man set out to make himself as good as white, thought he knew so much he could *lead* others. They was only children really, he told himself. You set yourself up ahead of them though, didn't you? It give you a good feelin' to think of you, the nigger, bein' the leader and them, the whites, followin' after.

He felt Mason Raymond patting his leg, as if in reassurance. You growed fast, boy, he thought. A week ago you couldn't have done what you been doin'. It ain't easy to learn you have to do thin's you don't want. All the time, every day, that's the one thin' a man can count on—he's gonna have to make hisself do thin's he don't want to do. You don't have no choice, boy, if that's any comfort to you. You ain't got no way you ken back away from a demand that comes so final. You understand? That was what he wanted to ask Mason Raymond.

"You stay still and rest," was what Mason Raymond was saying to him. He the leader now, Tom thought, that crazy boy no one would give spit for is growed up and haulin' us all around. "It's too much sun and dust," Mason Raymond said. "You wait and I'll go back and see if I can't get some help. Maybe that horse is up to another trip—don't trust those others somehow. They're all stirred up."

Goin' to be helpless, like a little baby, weak and helpless, an old man, dependent on other people. That was the one thing he abhorred, the notion of having to depend on other people. It's what everyone always expects of us niggers, that we ain't capable of gittin' on on our own. Got to fall back on someone else, always need some kind of help, ain't never really growed up, we's always some kind of children.

Jonathan, he never figured like that. Never treated me nuthin' but white and I got angered up because he said jest that and I left him 'cause I had too much pride. Down deep that always been my sin. Too much pride.

Stranded out here in the middle of nowhere, dependent on a couple of kids and a squaw girl—squaw's a name like nigger ought never have been invented. He remembered a story he had been told by a Mex on the trail, that squaw was a word like greaser that no one should ever use because it came from an episode whites ought to regard with shame, but that for people who had color in their skins whites had no sense of shame. "I will tell you," the Mexican had said in his formal, polite, slightly condescending way, "what squaw means because I, too, once used the word and I, too, did not know what it stood for. Then once, in the ways of the trail, a man explained to me. He said he was an Indian, not of the tribes here, but from a far place back where the whites first began, a place where the word came from. He said some white men who had been away trapping for many winter months came out of the forest in the spring and they had their furs and their things with them and they were wanting badly women. The first village they came to was an Indian village and these white men could not make the Indians understand what they wanted so at last they pulled down their leggings and exposed themselves and pointed, making gestures. The word for a man's parts is *numsquaw* in that Indian tribe, and the trappers, not understanding what the Indians had said, thought they had got the trappers' meaning and they started hollering, 'Squaw! Squaw!' thinking the kind of women they wanted would come. But, my friend, the truth is the word has nothing to do with women, and no women came, but the trappers took that word away with them anyway."

Mason Raymond gripped his leg. "We got to do something right away. You can't go anywhere the way you are now. And I can't leave you lie here. If you can get up, maybe I can help you though," and he confessed this reluctantly, "I'm kind of banged up myself—the burns and the bites. The two of us though, we ought to be able to move on some and then they'll be coming back with the horses; we might meet them half-way."

Tom didn't answer. What Mason Raymond was asking was beyond him, but he didn't want to discourage the boy. A boy likes to have plans.

"Get you set first, then—" Mason Raymond stopped talking and Tom heard a horse; he assumed it was one of their horses because of the flat-footed fast-running sound it made and because he just couldn't believe their luck was so bad that someone else was on them.

The girl came up in a clatter of questions—no denying that voice, insistent, angry, demanding. "How come you look so funny like that, starin' like that? What's the matter with the nigger, that's what I axe you? How's come he's down like that? What you gone and done to him? What you gone and done to that old man?"

"I haven't done anything," Mason Raymond protested. "He's just resting a little—"

"I don't believe you. You was gittin' ready to run off and leave him 'cause he was old and trouble. You was goin' to go off and leave that old man—"

"My god," Mason Raymond said, "haven't we got troubles enough without inventing new ones? I'm not going to run out on anyone. Maybe you don't know that, but I'm not."

The girl was squeezing Tom's other leg, as if she were trying to squeeze information out of him. She'd ask a question and then squeeze, ask another question and squeeze; his leg felt as if it were undergoing an inquisition.

"Let's get him up on the horse," Mason Raymond said, and the girl started struggling without stopping her chattering. "What's the matter with him he's so done in? We was all took with the dust, but you get a little rest it leaves up on you. He looks half dead. What's wrong with him? How come he went down? He ain't never looked frail before. You seen how strong he been—why should he give in now?"

Mason Raymond, straining to lift him, didn't answer right away. Only when Tom was aboard the horse—a strange horse, one of the outlaws', he supposed, they were probably giving the piebald a well-deserved rest—did Mason Raymond, huffing, say, "He just came to his breaking point, I guess. You both went through an awful lot—"

"We all been through a lot," she said sharply, and there was something funny in her voice that said to Tom, She seen plenty at that spring. He pulled himself up and opened his eyes, but nothing happened. He shut his eyes and opened them again, and nothing had changed. The world was a whirl of white. Desert got me in the eyes, he thought.

"You all right?" the girl asked, belligerent, as if if he weren't she'd have Mason Raymond's hide.

Mabbe it'll go away. These thin's come and go, best not to worry them. "Fine," he said. "Mite tuckered but—"

"You stay on the horse," the girl ordered. "Won't hurt us to walk, ain't that far."

Tom just wished he could open his eyes and see what shape that girl was in. She had been near gone no more than an hour before. Young come back easier, quicker. You gonna be *fifty*.

Half a hundred.

The horse was hard for them to hold, he could tell; it was a dancer, bolting this way and that; he could feel it get out from under their control every once in a while and drag them along. He hung on and tried not to think because the thoughts inside his head were bad and he didn't want a lot of bad notions filling up his mind.

They came close to the falls—he could hear the steady splashing—the horse halted, and the girl and Raymond boy helped him down. Helpless as a babe—he was going to have to tell them the truth.

He struggled to stand upright and walk straight, but there were problems. "A little trouble with my eyes," he said. "I ain't seein' so well as I might."

He heard the girl catch her breath. "You makin' yourself worse doin' that," she said, as if she understood for the first time the troubles he was having. She took his arm and guided him through white spacelessness. She was using one hand on his shoulder in a gentle downward push to indicate he should lower his body and sit. He went down slowly, gingerly, until he came in contact with rough material, probably a blanket they'd found in one of the packs. He sat, waiting, dependent on them. I'll be helpless like this the rest of my life, he thought. There was a bad smell that lingered over the place, too. Killin' been done here, he knew that right enough. Don't ask, he told himself. Iffen you ask, they'll haff to tell and iffen you don't you can all pretend nuthin' really bad happened.

Someone took his hand and put a tin cup in it. It must be full because it was heavy. He drank water and when the cup was empty held it out. Someone took it away. He would have to concentrate and try to differentiate their hands. The boys' hands would be rougher, though the girl had had a hard, fighting life. I'll know a woman's hand, he thought, no matter how toughened up it is.

That's her hand, she give me the cup.

He was beginning to separate out sounds, too—fire crackling, the hiss of something cooking, the two sounds of water —first plashing over rocks and then the sound of smooth-flowing free water, a small stream. The first would be the falls. The image of water formed in his mind, and with that image a name. It was The Sweetwater they'd been going to, that name must have been special to those two boys because they had insisted that's where they were going, even if it was somewhat out of the way. The name called him now. Funny how names could come to mean so much. Like the name Jonathan. Now he might never see the stream. Might never see anything again—except white. The irony of that was not lost on him probably because he'd always set such a store by the difference between what was expected as opposed to what was.

Now he tried to work with his voice, tried to get it out of

storage. He thought of how it, too, seemed dust-shrouded; things that had been put aside gathered a coat of dust, had to be cleaned before they could be put to use again. He felt as if his voice were all grainy and out of commission.

The girl's hand pressed something into his. Hot bread with something greasy inside, bacon maybe. He could hear bustling around the campsite, too. Once in a while one of them talked, but he concentrated on eating, not paying much attention to anything but trying to get the food up to his mouth.

"Eat, you ain't eatin!" she said. "You got to eat to git your strength up."

He could hear her doing something, but the sound didn't make any sense, not until she forced a bit of bread and meat between his lips. What she had been doing to make those strange sounds was breaking bread and shredding meat. She wasn't going to let him give up. She knew, then, how bad his eyes were. Mabbe it's like the punishment is I can't never see no more and I ain't supposed to speak neither. Mabbe it's like I gotta go through this world not seein' and not speakin'.

She left him to go do something. She told him she was going, explained in great detail all she was setting out to do, how she was going to help fasten a sling on a couple of the horses and get things ready to move so that they could get on; he wasn't to worry, they'd be back before dark; it got dark, those men—she never said *dead,* but he knew—would attract coyotes and they had to get going; being very meticulous as she went over plans in detail with him, Tom not answering, his voice wouldn't work on him, all dusted up the way it was, just nodding, listening to her set out while he stared sightlessly into his world of white, identifying the sounds of the three of them going, sounds at first harsh and quite clear, then rapidly growing fainter and less distinguishable as the caravan got farther and farther from camp. The word he thought of was *forsaken,* an old-fashioned word. He had heard his mother say disapprovingly about some man who'd run out on his wife and children, *He forsook her.*

You
don't
do
that, her voice said.

It was a strong voice, far stronger at this moment than ever before. That's a part of my punishment, he thought, to hear voices but not to be able to see. I been left in this world of white with nothing to see, so I can't never git away from the voices inside, they goin' to keep at me and keep at me all the days of my life.

Won't be nobody but me and the voices saying over and over, You shouldn't oughta have done it. You shouldn't never have run off and left home. You went and left us and never sent no real word back nor money neither, and you knowed we was old and poor and hadn't got no money and wanted to know what had happened to you. I'm gonna carry what I don't want to see or think or hear around with me wherever I go. No way to make anything right, it's too late, he thought. Gambled away what I shoulda sent back. Give in to impulses. Never had no discipline, jest done what I wanted— No, didn't even never do that, jest carried on the wind, a creature carried on the wind, blown this way and that. That ain't no kind of freedom, jest to be blown about by whim.

He was exhausted, but his mind wouldn't let him rest. It was all tightened up into a spring that kept turning and turning, twisting up his thoughts. What am I goin' to do? he asked himself, a black man gone blind out here in the middle of nowhere, and there was no answer, no answer at all.

Horses were whinnying, the mule braying in that funny singsong cry jackasses made, stomping about, restless at its mooring because of something. Horses git lonely by theirselves; they miss not being together. They . . . they *what*? he asked himself. They know enough to see it's easier when you ain't all alone.

Sometimes, he thought, people never consider what's goin' to happen, they jest barge ahead askin' for the immediate need to be met, don't think nuthin' about no future. Man was so full of gullibility; he believed he moved himself about in a careful, rational, planned program. But everything was unknown: You see one day and are completely blind the next.

He felt the roar in his heart of that word *fifty*.

He hunched inside, his sense of loss overwhelming. They

take an infant and they educate him from one painful minute to the next until he finally begins to understand and that knowledge really only starts to come at the end, when it's time to die. How nice, he supposed, to believe death was only a switching of states; he couldn't.

It's all nearly up with me, he thought, but the lungs of life still breathe on. Yet life was also possibility, anything *might* happen—probably wouldn't, but might. To the end it seemed some, like himself, held on to illusions, clouds like floating pools in a brilliant blue sky. Any other way would be for him to be sealed in defeat.

The whinnying became more frantic. Maybe those kids was having problems. The sling might not hold with too much weight. Left them with all the dirty work, he thought. That was the last thing he remembered until he awoke the next morning and saw the world was still a whirl of white. He smelled coffee and heard rustling sounds around and last night's final thought came back to him—had to do my dirty work. He wanted to ask what had happened to the outlaws, then remembered it was best not to know. Couldn't git his voice up anyway. He sat up, white flakes whirled, rose and fell, like one of those magic paperweights he remembered seeing once when he was a small boy, some treasure of the white world he had gazed on in awe, a winter scene inside glass of a man and woman, a little boy and a dog, all bundled up making their way through mounds of snow and when you picked the paperweight up and shook it a blizzard obliterated the people and the dog for a moment, then the snow dwindled and diminished until only a few flakes were falling.

Git washed up, he'd feel better. But when he went to stand, he was so rocky that he swayed. Must be all scooped out inside, ain't nuthin' more to draw on.

He stood weaving back and forth for a moment, then abruptly folded up, collapsing back onto the blanket the girl had laid him on the night before. What was really the matter was that he didn't want to get up; he never wanted to wake up again and face a new day; sleep—hiding out being black was better than being in this world of white. You're so god-dam smart, what you gonna do now? he asked himself.

He sat facing all over again the shock of his sightlessness. I ain't never goin' to see agin, never.

Her hands were handing him a mug and he took it and put his face over the brim letting the strong fumes work their way into his head. Only way I'll ever git anythin' is somebody give it to me. He shook his head, an involuntary reaction, one he couldn't help because he was trying to deny what was, saying automatically *No, I won't,* but the simple fact was there was no choice.

"You drink up," she said in that bossy tone he knew so well. She got all the cards on her side now, he thought. Well, good luck to you, you be my guest in the game.

"God, but you be a sight. Git you all washed up and dust-free, you'll feel more like yourself. How's your face this mornin'?" He noticed she said face instead of eyes. "What's the matter, cat got your tongue?" He shook his head, just wishing she'd go away. But of course she wouldn't. "Drink," she said, and just to shut her up he did.

The scalding bitter brew could hardly have been called coffee, but whatever it was it awakened his stomach. He was hungry, hollow with hunger, weak with it; maybe that's why he had had trouble staying on his feet. She was handing him something hard and oily—jerky, he took it to be—and he chewed. He had a terrible longing for something sweet. Sugar, he thought, remembering the sugar beet back home, sweet and cool to the tongue when he sucked the root, or boiled up into syrup, hot and sticky, sometimes burning the roof of his mouth; he was so greedy to get a lick in that the skin would come right away from the top of his mouth and for a day or two after his tongue would touch it wonderingly. There would be a flash of raw pain and he would try to see how something as good as the hot syrup could produce the aftermath of this rawness in his mouth.

He could plant over the blank white frame of his mind with the trees and fields around the big plantation; he could picture the big house with its wide porch running all around three sides where the rockers and swing were set out summers; he saw the master and missus gently swaying back and forth. That white woman always had something in her hand—sewing or crocheting or tatting. The master sometimes sat on the steps and other men perched on the porch rail. Some liked to lean against the house. They would drift out there one at a time hot evenings to look at the last dying light on the wide yard in front of the big house, the wafer moon as it was raised like a signal in the sky. No place prettier nor more peaceful. For the whites. Out back it was different.

She see me now, Tom thought of his mother, what she think (but never say) was that I'da been all right if I'da jest settled down somewhere; all that running off to strange places that had no rhyme nor reason for going was what brought me down. Courtin' trouble. You court trouble, trouble gonna take you to trial, she always said. And who knew, maybe she was right. If I had stayed put I never would have killed no one nor run off and left my best friend, wouldn't never have got myself in none of this. I'd be gettin' up in the dark gropin' around for my pants and boots, start downhill to the bottom hollow jest as the light comes up, streaks of red stab right across the sky and the land the color of caramel boilin' up. He heard the twack of the milk-heavy cows as they pushed against the fence, wanting to be let out to go up to the barn; the milk hurt their udders when they got too full, and they liked eating while he and the other hands released the pressure with the milking; he heard the stream of milk as it hit the pail and smelled the heavy scent of urine and manure as the cows let go their wastes inside. A good farm, he thought, a woman, children—it wouldn't been impossible, but I always held on to a pair of itchy feet, I always had to see what was around the next bend or over the next hill.

He shook his head, trying to brush away the peaceful pictures he had inside, and the girl's voice, a stranger's voice it took him a minute to identify, started its nagging again. "Keep chewin'," she said, and he let her have her way. He chewed while inside his mind he took a long udder in his hands and began to to massage, gently but firmly, the milk from out of the long pendulous white tube into the waiting pail. He could smell the sweetness and taste the hot freshness of that milk and hear the cats mewing to get their taste, and over to the right a horse stamping impatiently in his stall, waiting for its morning corn and ration of hay. In the rafters overhead the pigeons cooed and a songbird rose with morning and gave its call.

He knew some things about women most men didn't, he thought, because he had been mostly woman-raised if not woman-tied all his life. The young years were the teaching ones. Old dogs only infrequently indulged in new tricks. So it didn't seem to him of the highest importance he'd never married—all right, so in that area he was a casualty of the kind of wandering life he'd chosen—but he'd always *liked* women; he wasn't one of those men—he thought of John—who saw women as inferior, as vessels for a man's seeds and servants to his pleasure, but then, considering, maybe he was just putting on airs to himself because there were plenty of women he'd taken advantage of, no way to deny that. Vessels, indeed— where else had he poured his seed? Stop seein' yourself as highfalutin, old man.

No, no, poor suffering souls, who once were young and pure,
Man makes you all to suffer, that's for sure.

Now, in the girl's ministrations as she bent over him and wrung out rags she used to soak his eyes, he recaptured in her sighs echoes of his childhood; as she leaned forward and pressed the cool cloth against his face he smelled from her hands some of the same acrid herbs that his grandmother dried in the kitchen, some of those roots and tubers passed on from ages past as home remedies for the ills of the poor. White people had universities where they studied skeletons and blood systems and scientific mixtures of medicines; blacks and Indians had other kinds of healing. He leaned his sightless head closer to her and said, "You got faith in this here remedy, don't you?"

"It's all we got, but even if you was laid up at some Army post where they got the walls lined with all them bottles and jars I'd still sneak some of this in—if I could git in. I seen what happen to you happen to lots of others. The Indians have a whole time they call the Moon of Snow Blindness when the eyes is affected. You ain't snow blinded, but the way I see it it comes around to about the same thin'. The dust and sun done what the snow does."

He lay back and rested. He felt tired. Yet there was something he wanted to ask her; it was about this feeling he had that there was a new tension in the air that centered on the two boys and her, the kind of strain that, though unspoken, existed precisely from what was *not* said. Maybe there wasn't really a name that could be assigned to the invisible push and pull that extended from one to the other of those three and which made him so uneasy. It was bad enough he was blinded, but to feel currents building up to the point where they would burst out and cause trouble—real trouble—and to know he couldn't handle the situation forced him to ask himself how it was that he who had been convinced just a few days before that the three others could not survive without him could now be as dependent on them as a small child.

World goes topsy-turvy, turns upside down afore you know it. Don't do for a man to count on what little advantages he's got, they ken be grabbed away from him that fast. "You and that boy," he said, "you two gonna team up?"

"*What* boy?" she asked sharply.

Just her asking which clarified in Tom's mind why he felt so uneasy: If both boys assumed they was winners the hogs was in the corn. "You don't know which one?" Always poking, always prying, nosy old buzzard.

"I don't know nuthin' about nuthin'," she said and her voice sounded both exasperated and evasive.

"You don't, who does?"

"I'm goin' back where I belong," she said, and Tom recognized the stubborn, retreating tone of her voice as one that said to him, This ain't none of your *this* business. But the whole point was that it was. He persisted. "You fancy one of them over the other though? You got yourself set on one of them, that's what I guess I'm askin'."

He heard her suck in her breath. Finally she said, "I learnt not to set my heart on nuthin'. It don't pay to do that."

"But if you was to have your way?"

She did a strange thing. She reached over and patted his hand, just as if he were a child and needed comforting. He allowed his hand to close over hers for a brief second. "You had a hard time, girl. You deserve somethin' good come into your life. And I'll tell you somethin' else. I hope you git it."

"I go back," she said slowly, "I find my boys, I'm jest let be, that's all I axe."

"Still," Tom said, "it's like thin's ain't the way they were. It's like there's a change in the air here. That's what I'm talkin' about."

"Ain't nuthin' changed, 'cept you done got ahold of this piece of bad luck. Maybe you imaginin' a change 'cause you got time on your hands to do too much thinkin'."

"I ain't imaginin'. I feel it plain as day." And he laughed at the incongruity of that image. "But mabbe *you* so busy you don't see it like it is."

She put a fresh rag against his eyes. "You don't feel no change at all?" she asked. "Inside your head, not *out.* I'm worried about what goes on *inside.* You worry about what you want."

"It's still the same. Ain't that a pretty predicament though —I can't see nuthin' but all this white. After all these years thinkin' about nuthin' but black I've gone and got myself enveloped in white."

"It's gonna change. You wait and see. Gradually it's gonna lift and you gonna go down into darkness and then gradually that gonna lift and you gonna start to see a little, bit by bit." She sounded absolutely convinced. But Tom could also hear in her voice the concern he had heard so often expressed by his mother for those in distress: My heart just goes out to you. What the girl said instead was, "My ma, she used to say, 'One door don't close but another opens.' She didn't have much goin' for her, my ma. But she never give up. The more I think about back then, the more I see that. Ain't like she was one of them danced with silver buckles on their shoes," she said. "But she was always tryin' to go on ahead, no matter how hard the times was. It's like some people they jest born to push the wheel and others, they jest born to enjoy what the wheel grinds."

"How'd you keep all them white words with you all that time? You always comin' up with all these words hit so close to the mark, and I gotta axe myself, 'How she able to say somethin' like that when she been away so long and I been right around all the time and I cain't put it so good?' "

"I never done nuthin' all that time but think white—for all the good it done me," she added bitterly. "That's all over now though," and now it was her turn to give a short, ironical laugh. "One door closes, you got to open another. You got to unlatch the lock yourself, it don't open for you. Otherwise you left hangin' 'round the hall."

The dull weight of fatigue was pressing down on him. The blind sickness took something out of him, but not so much maybe as just his years. Fifty. It was such a final mark.

The worst part of growing old was that all your mistakes were more than held against you: They added up to the meagerness of what you had made of your life. All I got to show for my life is a gold watch don't run. But that wasn't right either. The fact the watch itself didn't work wasn't really important. What mattered was that Jonathan had given it to him. Only left my pocket once, he thought, and that was when I give it to the Buttes boy, and that was like necessary, it meant stakes to go where we had to—for all of us. Jonathan woulda wanted me to do that. Where he at now? Dead mabbe. Bad not never to know. Well, I ain't and it's my own fault. Stubborn old nigger, you gonna reap what you sowed. Your mama always told you to be careful how you laid up your youth 'cause you was gonna be called to account in old age.

I ken carry all I got in a roll on the back of a saddle—or on my back if it came down to it. Always been that way—all my life nuthin' to show but a bedroll of nuthin's. But there had been more than that, he knew. That Captain . . . Jonathan . . . good men on the trail . . . these boys . . . this girl . . . and mabbe even himself. I got myself, like I ken hold myself in hand, and I ain't sorry for what's been, I jest hungry for more ahead, and the end's closin' in. Ain't gonna be much more ahead, he was too far into his life.

I don't want death, Tom thought. That's the sum total of it.

Old and tired and probably permanent blind now, don't mind layin' up, but they's young and impatient, they want to head out, I'm holdin' them up. Only decent thin' is to have them go on.

You gotta let them go on, he said to himself. It's no use your actin' the wounded sparrow at your age. No one takes an old wounded sparrow serious. This here land is for the young, you know that, even though mabbe the pains of loss hit the old the hardest. Do what has to be done.

"You all right?" the girl was asking. Her breath smelled of poisonous roots and herbs, was hot as fire; she scorched him leaning over him breathing on him all her worry. "Don't you worry now. You gonna be all right. It's gonna break free. Hold on—you hear, jest hold on, you gonna be all right."

You hold on, he wanted to say back at her, but he was too tired for arguing. Groaning, he went down with a sudden falling, just like the girl had said, into darkness. Goddam girl. Nuthin' but trouble and self-righteousness. Jest like a woman always bein' right.

III

---

*M*idmorning they set about scrubbing the nigger. They stripped him clean and got him into the water and then lathered him up with something that smelled so strong that it hurt John's nostrils and was so power-ful it stung his skin, but they had to get him cleaned up and the girl said this was the way to do it. She'd mixed the concoc-tion herself, some Indian recipe, he supposed, and he was just as glad he didn't know what had gone into it. It was bad enough to smell it.

Tom stood patiently letting them flay him, water pouring off him; finally they hauled him up on the bank and toweled him dry with a rough blanket. They got him into new duds—dead men's things—and laid him up on some strippings the girl had bundled into a bed. John had quit talking to him; he saw that his voice was useless—or he didn't want to talk, one or the other—and he could see no sense in pressing a man to talk who didn't want to talk; but the girl spent a lot of time telling about how she was going hunting for some special plant things the Indians used and how she was going to make another potion and put that on Tom's eyes, that would work wonders, she said. Her face looked like something patchwork with that clay still plastered over her nose; it had dried and seemed an integral part of her features. She said when he was all well and better (she didn't say *see*), they could get on. They had a powerful distance to go and anyway, as far as she was concerned, she'd had enough of this place. The sooner they could lift harness, the better she'd like it. And she knew he felt the same way. She didn't even look for an answer out of him, just chattered on, trying to sound cheerful.

When they had Tom done up to her satisfaction, she took to pouring some kind of salty hot concoction down him; it would fire up his system, she insisted, and get his blood going again. "He's jest plain peaked," she said at least a dozen times.

Yet she spoke over and around him all the time she was talking to him, as if he were some kind of foreigner who couldn't understand English.

The thing that troubled John was the puzzle of what to do with him. Tom couldn't go to the Hills and mine; that was obvious. They couldn't leave him. We left him food and water, he'd be all right until the next people come along and give him somethin' to tide him over, John thought. We can't take him with us, can we? What's a blind man goin' to do on the trail? He'll be all right here. People'll give him a hand. It's not like jest leavin' him.

The girl was yammering about her Indian plants and Mason Raymond wasn't paying attention, too busy telling how he was going to take one of those rambunctious horses and go back and do what had to be done. "It bothers me we don't have any markers there," he kept saying. "You know—to tell where they're laid up."

"You could maybe like take one of them rocks and carve somethin' on it," the girl said. Neither she nor Tom had questioned the cousins. They had not been told details and they had not asked.

"You think I could get it all down?" Mason Raymond asked uncertainly. And she said, "Up there, with the Indians, they make pictures."

"Well, we could maybe leastwise have a rock where they lay," Mason Raymond said. "Maybe put a little something on it indicates what happened. It doesn't need to be carved. We could just write on it." One of Tom's poems, John thought.

Under the yucca set in the land of the plains,
We have laid these men, outlaws of stage and trains;
Some called them wild; some said they was guileless as a child,
But think of it, pards—now they is straight as rods
Where we covered them with the great desert sod.

God took them from us,
He knew what was best.
They'd outlawed long enough
That's why He let us put them to rest.

The girl was being officious by the fire, concocting Indian stuff. John gave a snort. She was a marvel of madness, singing a little song over the fire, brewing up some crazy potion a lot of savages used; there was no use arguin' with her, she even believed that spirit nonsense about the dead tellin' the livin' what to do.

Lately she had begun to bother him more than usual. At first he thought she was just getting on his nerves a little more than average with all those small annoying habits which are at first almost unnoticeable and then begin to take on monumental proportions. One of his brothers used to bite his fingernails and the short snapping sounds of his teeth grinding down on the nails could at times drive John to fits of almost uncontrollable fury. This girl had bad habits, too. She was a neck rubber, for instance—forever raising her left hand and massaging the base of her skull; she also had a nervous way of scratching her elbow in moments of distress; she was a shrieker and a hollerer and her voice, even when it wasn't raised in one form of desperation or another, had funny lapses, Indian inflections, he supposed, that grated on his nerves. The freckles bothered him, too. Why should she have so many freckles when most girls didn't have any? So he blamed her for them the way he blamed her for her name. Benjie Klomp. That was no name for a girl. She was obstinate (as her name somehow implied) and willful and she'd gone and broke that horse on him which rightly she shouldn't have been able to do because that showed she was superior to him in some ways. She looked crazy with her nose done up in clay that way; she didn't show him the proper respect—it was as if she considered him nothing more than a mere boy, as if he had no real importance in the outcome of their survival, and that was the worst insult, especially coming from a girl that was nobody, who'd been picked up by Indians and was nothing better than an ignorant squaw, not that John thought of girls on the whole as much (his mother excepted, course; mothers were in no way the same as "girls") but he was used to dealing with them to show them how things stood, who was boss—he had nothing but contempt for the kind of men who let women put claims on them, who let women giggle and grab them in public as if declaring, "You see, he's mine, you keep your hands off him, you hear"; and so John had learned that if you stayed aloof and showed you weren't going to be taken in, women didn't really trouble you too much. They took you on your own terms. John's were very stringent: He didn't want to get involved. So he avoided the "nice" girls and got what he wanted with the ones that were "easy." The Landing girls were divided into those two categories: ones who expected a ring and ones who were willing to—well, some were more willing than others. These were usually the ones who got "in trouble," or, as his mother described it, "in the family way."

But this girl, with all her annoying and exasperating ways, didn't seem to follow any of the old rules and patterns he understood. For a fact, she didn't pay any attention to him at all, as if he didn't matter—that was the worst of it. She didn't take him seriously. So when this girl began to bother him, he laid his edginess to all her faults and deficiencies and decided that the more he stayed away from her the better off he'd be. The trouble with this was that in practice it only increased his irritability—the less he came in contact with her, the more she obsessed his thoughts. It came to him now that she was *all* he was thinking of; he pictured her rubbing the back of her neck and a little flash ran over him, except that it wasn't a flash of annoyance, there was a kind of pleasure in it; he started thinking about all her freckles and he found he didn't think maybe they were so ugly after all as maybe interesting; he remembered her hollering and screeching and he almost got to laughing, thinking how funny she looked when she was all excited, jumping up and down; even the alien lisp came to have a peculiar kind of charm; it marked her off, she was different from any other girl he'd ever known; and now when she started scratching at her elbow in her impatience, he was positively tickled, he thought it was one of the most endearing, comical movements anyone had ever made. He took a deep breath and swallowed, hard, and said to himself, Oh, no, not *her,* and then he shook his head, reassuring himself, No, not *her,* and he felt better. He was just trailblazed, a common symptom for the bad time he'd just come through. Everything got distorted; fatigue could shake up your whole perspective. She was a girl and any girl, even an odd one like this, was bound to have her points if you were way out in the middle of nowhere and there was no possible way to make appropriate comparisons. Any girl would look better under the circumstances. No need to take her seriously.

"Oh, lord, lord . . . lord," he heard her cry and something went crash and a hiss of something spilled into the fire. "Oh, god," she cried again, and he saw her running, a frantic, hysterical galloping as if ghosts had taken after her.

He jumped up and started running, too. "You hurt?— Benjie, you hurt?" It was the first time he remembered using her name. "You've gone and burned your hand."

She was sucking at the seared flesh.

"Here, let me take a look at it." He bent forward and put his hand on her shoulder and a terrible current ran through him; he almost jumped back, but she didn't seem to notice, standing there sucking at her hand. "It boiled up, that pot boiled up," she whimpered, "and I went to pull it back and it boiled over on me."

What good is breathin' and bein' alive, he asked himself, if you don't feel? But I don't want to feel this, he answered himself. You can't decide which feelin's you want and which you don't, he was answered from inside.

The girl went back to the fire and put a poultice over her hand, the wet rag full of fat first pressed against the earth, then against her hand. She's goin' to git dirt in that hand, John thought. "Don't do that—you'll git infected, you do that. Ain't you got no better sense than to git dirt in a wound? What kind of curin' is that, puttin' dirt in somethin's all raw? Ain't you got no sense atall?"

He could feel her hostility go right through her and out toward him, an anger so intense that he even imagined a shudder passed over her. Can't stand me, he thought. To her I'm worse than that there dirt. That there *this* dirt, he thought.

The rag stank. God knows what she'd put in that pot she'd dunked it in. Some ratty array of bitter roots and weeds that made his nostrils flare. But she went on holding the cloth in place, stirring the pot with her good hand; her faith in her Indian herbs was like someone praying when his lungs was knocked out with the consumption; the praying might make him feel better but it sure as hell wasn't going to repair his lungs. Still he couldn't keep his mind off the idea she was hurt. He wanted to do something to help her, and he couldn't think what. He had never felt quite so helpless—and restless. He got up and began to pace, watching her stir the pot and tend to her bad hand. Funny how she'd changed ever since they'd picked her up. He could see it very clearly now. When he looked at her now it was like seeing a whole new person, not the girl he had known before the dust did them all in. A few decent meals had filled her out, and even though the freckles were still there and she was spattered with mud on the face like that and looked baked brown enough to be a real Indian, her eyes, gazing back at him, had the defiance of feeling in them. When the tides of change come, they do not necessarily announce themselves with calls of trumpets and flows of red roses. They might just as easily move in on mud and slime and chaos.

In the late afternoon the girl took the pot off the fire and let it cool. She tore one of the dead men's flannel shirts up and put strips in the pot to soak and then she used them to bandage Tom's eyes. John went over and tried to help, but she gave him such a look that he finally just stood and watched. She was very deft. She reminded him of his mother when she had to do up one of their hurts back home. It was the gentleness with which both of them worked, the sureness, the concentration and steadiness. The girl had taken her own bandage off and John saw that her hand looked like it always had; there was no trace of a burn. He couldn't believe it; he had seen the burn himself and it had been bad, and now there was nothing there on the skin except a smooth expanse of untouched flesh.

Mason Raymond had come over to watch. He squatted down and followed intently the movement of the bandages from the pan to Tom's eyes, back to the pan for resoaking, back to Tom's eyes again. His passivity annoyed John; he was getting in the way again the way he always did. Always in the way, always getting lost, always underfoot when you didn't want him, always getting turned around or tangled up. Why the hell couldn't he sense he wasn't wanted?

Because Mason Raymond never had any sense about anything.

He could not imagine anyone less like himself anyplace in the world, not even niggers or Chinks or even those cracked Mormons with all their wives. He looked at his cousin: a complete misfit. Then he thought of that moment Mason Raymond had fired, how they had run together and embraced, tumbled about laughing and pounding one another on the back. He remembered their fight. He thought about Mason Raymond back in Albany and Mason Raymond now at this moment.

These were two different people. He had changed and John knew it, but he was still trying to think of him as the same person who ate one meal a day and no meat at all, who had been back in that austere room in Albany with the almond-eyed saints, the incense, and the small square pallet he used as a bed.

Well, he still carries that same goddam book, John tried to argue with himself.

But he ain't the same.

Never will be no more. You want him to be like you and he ain't, that's what's the trouble with you. He ain't never goin' to be like you, he couldn't be.

Well, John thought, you can waste your life tryin' to think

] *349* [

you can remake everyone over the way you want or you can accept what is and try to make some kind of peace with it. Which you want? The first will kill you, he thought, and the second ain't no better.

Accept what is, whether you like it or not.

I can't, he thought, that's jest askin' too much. Why couldn't the world be the way he wanted it? Everything was so divided and confused that he couldn't deal with it; he felt powerless because he recognized that he stood at the gates of himself and refused to let others in. Maybe that was what made him rage so inside—because he couldn't make the world the way he wanted it; and because he couldn't he was filled with a sense of impotence and he didn't want to be weak, he wanted to be strong, so he raged against his sense of weakness.

To hell with him. To hell with the girl. To hell with all of them. It was all so complicated. He looked at Mason Raymond and thought, Well, he's changed, I guess I can. Some, leastwise. He looked from Mason Raymond back to the fire and the girl. The nigger sat quietly, letting the girl work with him. Every once in a while he'd grunt and she'd say, "That too hot?" and the nigger would shake his head. Not to see was terrible. But seeing was terrible, too.

We oughta leave him, John thought. But it ain't right. We can't.

The girl was putting new bandages on Tom and John looked at Mason Raymond and he could see that Mason Raymond's reaction would not even be one of questioning. He'd never leave him, John thought, even if it meant he had to die waiting around for him. I don't know, I don't know. How's come he would feel like that? Why couldn't he feel the way most people would, that it would be *sensible* to leave him provisions and move on? You had to think about the majority. There were the three of them as opposed to the one. But the girl wouldn't leave him either. She'd been left herself. So they'd let me go off on my own, he thought, and wouldn't probably hold it against me neither. They'd just think, Well, that's the way he is. He wants to go on, let him go. But they wouldn't go. I don't know, I'm just all turned around trying to know what I do think.

It's funny how I know what they think but I don't really know how I feel. I want to go and I don't. It's right, it's sensible to go, but it ain't exactly what I want to do neither. Maybe because I had this picture of Tom and me goin' to the Hills together, don't seem right I should jest take off on my own.

The girl finished wrapping the bandage and went back to the fire and started working with some new plants and leaves. John went over to her and bent down. "Is it permanent, his not seein?" he asked.

"I don't know, not for sure." A pause. "Maybe yes, at least probably unless somethin' unexpected happens."

Maybe could be a very big word, enclosing a whole world of possibilities. John did not know how the universe set its laws right; perhaps there weren't even any laws at all. Who was to know? But killing all those men— "You gotta pay some way for what you do," his grandfather was convinced. Him and Mason Raymond, though, they had been the ones to do the killing, not Tom.

I been using his name, didn't even know it, John thought. It's like my bein' mad at him ain't important now. The blindness blotted out every other consideration.

He got up and went and found some tobacco and searched around to see if there were any papers left. He couldn't find any, but he came across a pipe in one of the packs and filled that. When he put it in Tom's hand, his whole face lit up with pleasure. John bent by the fire and got a long twig going. "I got a light here," he said. "You suck on the pipe and I'll hold it up." He held the ember to the bowl and Tom inhaled; little pieces of tobacco began to pop and sputter. "Wasn't your fault these men got what they deserved. It was me and Mason Raymond's. You shouldn't git punished for what we done."

"You mean killin'? You done some of that, too, ain't you? Well, you ain't alone. I killed one of 'em, too. You disremember about that half-breed? And I done some shootin' before, on the trail. You don't go back and forth from Abilene as many times as I done without makin' no marks on your six-shooter. Tryin' to live right all the time is like tryin' to catch the wind. . . ."

] *351* [

He bent closer; his breath was hot on John's face, the smell of tobacco overpowering. "You was mad, wasn't you—mad as a hornet I didn't go with you, wasn't you?"

"I couldn't understand why the hell you'd let *him* go out with me when—you know how he is. Any fool knows you don't send a greenhorn out to deal with men been fightin' and shootin' most of their lives, and you ain't no fool. You ain't no fool and I ain't no fool," John said. "And that's twice you done me in—I mean, you coulda got me kilt. He's a loser," John said angrily. "You know it. I know it. It ain't right to saddle other people with him—especially when thin's git hot. But . . . I guess I seen a point to it, too, like you was tryin' to help him out."

"You lay your hand right on the key. You and me, we seen he had gaps. But you and me, we also knowed we got to help fill in them gaps. He ain't goin' to go off on his own with no prospects iffen we didn't git them gaps filled in. So you might say your expedition was in the nature of pluggin' up some of them gaps."

"You coulda got me kilt," John said again, but he wasn't really as angry as he had expected, as he once would have been. It was funny, but it was almost as if the black man were teasing him.

"You ain't gonna git kilt, you too ornery."

"That's easy enough to say, but nobody but a fool would believe it, and you ain't no—"

"I been fool enough in my days, I gonna be agin. Lissen," Pepper Tom said, "you look at that boy now and he ain't the same boy went out. You ken see that even if I cain't, but I ken *feel* it. He ken ride, he talks different, he acts different— because he thinks different. He knows he ken count on hisself to come through when the chips is down. Why," Tom said, reaching for a little levity, "who knows—mabbe we'll even teach him how to handle the cards one of these days. Don't you want him to come into his own and go off and leave you so it don't sweat your conscience none?"

"I only said I'd take him to Independence. I didn't sign up for the Pass nor any redoing of his character. He was supposed to be strictly on his own after Independence and he would have been, too, if you hadn't gone and opened your mouth—and without even askin' me neither."

"You ain't got all that wealthy on the cards you ken git by yourself all we needs for the—"

"All *we* needs? How's come you don't win your own stake? How's come you all of a sudden so dependent on me? How's come I got to put out for *both* of us?"

"You don't. You can git your money offen him anytime the fancy takes you. And you ken take what you won. Won't nobody hold it agin you no way. You ken mosey along all on your lone self any time the notion takes you. Ain't nobody gonna hold you back.

" 'Nother thin' I wants clear and out in the open air. You wasn't payin' my way," Tom said. "You was tradin' what you had, which was some gear, for what I knowed, which, the way I see it—or at least the way I seen it when my eyes was good—was a lot more valuable than some thin's you ken pack up. It was what was stored up in here," and he tapped his head.

"You want to go on your own, you be my guest. I ken git where I'm goin' all on my own even if I ain't got my eyes back, so don't you worry none, you go on you want to."

"I ain't sayin' you wasn't offerin' nuthin' in return," John said sullenly.

"But you was implyin' it."

"All I'm sayin'," John said stubbornly, "is that you had no right to send him out. You shoulda gone yourself."

"He done what was needed."

"Yeah, but—oh, the hell with it, ain't nobody can talk to you—or him—or her. I ain't goin' nowhere and you know it. We're gonna hole up here till we see how thin's is—"

"Mabbe take some time."

"I guess we can wait."

"Every day there's men goin' up there into them Hills, layin' out stakes. You don't want to set around lettin' others git what could be yours."

"I reckon I can wait."

"I don't want you to jest because you thinks you should. You don't owe me nuthin'. I don't want to be in your debt. I don't want to owe you nuthin'. Before, when my eyes was good, I had somethin' to trade. Now I got nuthin' and I ain't never been beholden to no man in my life, and I ain't plannin' on startin' now. I don't want you to wait. I ken go with them."

"Go with them? Go where with them?"

"Up to them Indians. Lots of black go with the Indians. They call us Buffalo Men up there on account of our black hair. Our hair's like the buffalo's hide, they say. Ain't you never heard that?"

"You're thinkin' about goin' up with the girl and Mason Raymond to the Injuns?" John couldn't believe his ears.

"Course I could. Comes down to it we're all flesh and bones, ain't we? I could do it," Tom said with that absolute basic assurance that made John admire him. "What's so crazy about that?" He held his hand up to the bandage. "This thin' smells—smells strong enough to do some good. You can say that for it."

You couldn't argue with a man like that. He was always one ahead of you. "What makes you so smart, what makes you so goddam smart, that's what I want to know?"

"Jest tryin' to keep up with you, boy." And that damn nigger had the gall to smile.

What his father and grandfather had preached was a code more individual and yet more universal than John had imagined. What their beliefs involved was continuity and courage as the foundation of all else. To John, looking at the girl with the middle of her face encased in clay, and at Mason Raymond with his burned neck and wrists and hands and still bruised at the temple, and at Tom with his sightless eyes, there came an understanding—at least partial—of how that continuity and courage worked; he had been watching it all his life but he had perhaps taken the wrong things from what he had seen. He had only accepted the outward manifestations, for instance, of what it meant to be strong and to stand up for what one believed—violence had been so much a part of what he had witnessed that he had not seen that that came only to good men after all else had been explored; in someone like Mason Raymond, for instance, it was even possible to get him to kill if there was absolutely no other choice open. To Tom the sense of continuity came from a strange set of propositions that he lived by and would not violate—for instance, the notion that he had things in his head that were more valuable than money—and since he knew this, the fact that he was poor did not make him humble. The girl had her own special and crazy kind of courage and continuity as well: She would live and adapt, and try, as best she could, not to look back too hard and long when looking back would cancel out any hope for the future. These lessons were hard for him to understand; they were even harder for him to put into practice, but that perhaps had been what his father was trying to show him that last morning when he'd taken down the Civil War saddle whose workmanship Tom had admired so much that first day John had run into him. John thought of how his father reached up and took the saddle off the wooden mount where it was always kept on the wall. It was always oiled and kept polished, and under the layers of saddle oil that had been lovingly applied it shone, a handsome piece of work, something to admire. His father had come down from the back field, where he's been spreading manure to pep up a field he said was loggy. He'd caught John at his last milking in the down barn. It was the day before he was scheduled to leave. His brother Lyman had spent the last few weeks apprenticing, getting to know which cows were temperamental and had to be watched for sudden bad behavior, which were stubborn milkers, which were apt to prank about in the barn; at sunrise the next day Lyman would be in complete charge, but he had anticipated already his coronation and was swanking about the barn as if daring anyone to dispute the divine right of kings.

If Lyman was dumb enough to think herding cows was the crowning credential of power, he would also draw water from a sieve, but John certainly wasn't going to be the one to tell him that he was puffing himself up over milkweed; he watched his brother strut from one cow stall to the next flapping his mouth at the cows as if they could understand all his crowing while John systematically milked, hunched over the old, scarred stool, using his hands rhythmically and mechanically, drawing a steady stream of steaming fluid into the waiting half-full pail. But in his silence he was exulting. Never again to have to rise in the yeasty morning to fumble about in the semidarkness dressing, never again to have to lurch downhill to the barn through mud or snow or rain or early morning fog, never never again to have to massage one cow's udders after another, empty pails, clean up manure, fetch grain and lay up hay, never again to have to nurse a colicky cow throughout a night or assist in a messy early-morning birth. In less than twenty-four hours he would be free.

He had not been expecting his father. When the barn door creaked open, groaning the last few inches where it hit the upslant of the hill, he looked up in surprise. Lyman was delivering to the manger what seemed to be some kind of address of state, but John's father was not paying attention; his concentration was focussed on John. Finally, sighing, he turned to his second son and said, "You mind, Lyman? There's somethin' I want to talk to your brother about—private?"

Lyman was all excitement. "You bet," he kept repeating. "You betcha. You go right on, Pa. I don't mind one bit."

I hope he ain't goin' to git into a lot of sentiment, John thought, rising, wiping his hands on his pants, considering how lucky he'd felt up to now because talk about his going had been kept to a minimum; now he was filled with dread because he feared his father had held back his sorrow and disappointment as long as he could and now it was all going to spill out.

His father was heading off toward the side room where the animal tack was stored; they had partitioned off a whole long narrow room on one entire side of the barn where harnesses and saddles, bridles and halters, driving devices for the training of young horses, and buggy equipment were hanging from big thick hooks driven into the wall. The room smelled of leather and oil and animal hair, a strong pungent smell that always flushed John with pleasure. Standing here, he experienced the feeling all was in place and right with the world. Everything was orderly, labeled, oiled, and in place; you knew right where to put your hands on anything you wanted. Outside all was confusion and chaos, but here he felt utterly in control. It was the only place he could think of where he had that feeling.

His father was looking down the long lane of dangling

harnesses and straps, measuring the wooden horses on which the saddles were propped with a calculating eye. "You startin' early, I take it?"

"Don't do no good to waste light when you got a long way to go."

"I won't argue that." He had stopped beside the holder where his own saddle was stored. That saddle was a work of art, the tooling intricate and involved; a man his father had known in the Civil War had sold it to him during the panic of '73 when he'd been wiped out by the Depression.

"I didn't want to take it offen him," John's father had said. "But like he said, it was gonna be me or some other bugger because there was no way he couldn't have sold it and he'd rather see me git it, he said, than see it go to some stranger he didn't even know."

Now John's father ran one hand absentmindedly along the tooling; he fingered the pommel, almost as if he were kneading it. "You won't be back for quite a spell, I reckon," he said.

"Don't seem that way."

"No way neither of tellin' what ken happen here or out there." He paused, picking and choosing his words with consideration. "I don't claim no powers to look into the future; all I know is everyone's got to pay the price of life."

He's talkin' about dyin', John thought. That's what he means—the price of life is death.

Another pause, then the dry, laconic voice talking slow and almost amused. "Ain't never felt right about takin' this offen Eben, maybe 'cause I was conscious how I coveted it. Nobody will ever know how much I wanted this here saddle. Right from the first time I laid eyes on it, I wanted it. Weren't no piece of horse gear I ever seen could hold a candle to it, and then when I got it, there wasn't the pleasure in it I'da counted on. Thin's is mabbe never as good when you git them as you think they is goin' to be when you want them.

"More than likely I felt guilty about gittin' this because gittin' it meant old Eben goin' under. I want you to take it, John—" He had started to say "son," and then changed his mind. An "s" lay on the air like the fluttering of a bird's wing. He lifted the heavy saddle and looked at it appraisingly. "You gotta put the right saddle on the right horse, or you ain't gonna go nowhere in this world. You remember that," he said, and this time he added the "son."

Now John looked at the saddle and then at the girl. She had that same dead-determined look she got when nothing was going to move her, not even barbed wire in her mouth. Rather be cut to pieces than give in. His father was like that, too. Guts, John's grandfather would have said. They all of them got guts, John thought, looking around—most of all *him* (looking at Tom and thinking, There's more than one way to think the word nigger). He put out a hand and touched the black man. He wanted to talk.

He wanted to give Tom a sign of appreciation, and he searched his mind for the right gesture, something that would signify he conceded Tom all his past accomplishments, some token of appreciation that announced, *All right, I see you was a big man, still are.*

"Bastards drunk up all the whiskey," John said, "or we'd have a drink on what we gonna find in the Hills, me and you." He paused. "A little thin' like weak eyes ain't gonna make much of a dent in the plans we got after everythin' else we been through."

"How many of them was there?"

"Six."

"Six?"

"Six," John said.

"Leave him rest up a bit," the girl pleaded.

But John had a couple of other things he wanted to finish first. "That there Reed," he began, "the one put his name on the rock over there—he carved his name on a rock by the Falls, I seen it, waitin' out a last man got away, and the whole time I was layin' up waitin' him out, all I could think was whatever happened to that Reed who did the carving. You suppose I could take that book, that guide, and look and see if it says?"

"You want *to look up* ole Jim Reed?" Tom asked indignantly, just the way John had hoped he would be insulted because Tom knew most of what had happened on the Trail even if he hadn't seen it himself. "I ken tell you what hap-

] *358* [

pened to Reed, you don't need lookin' up nuthin'. You want to know who Jim Reed was, I'm gonna tell you who Jim Reed was. Reed, he set out with his family—had hisself a wife and a girl, couple of boys, a little girl, and Jim's wife had a mother and she come along. They called her Grandma Keyes. She was on her way out, Grandma Keyes was, to join up with one of her other sons who'd gone on ahead.

"They was in the Donner party. Reed, he had some misfortune and wasn't with them when they all got laid up there in that pass and the food run out and they had to eat their dead. What happened to Reed was that he got hisself in a scrape on the Trail, killed a man, they say, in a fight; and he was took out of the party and told to go on by himself, so he wasn't with the others when the real hard time come on. His gittin' put out like that mabbe saved his life. But his family had stayed with the Donners and they went on into the mountains. It took them Donner people three months after they left Reed to git to the Sierra, and they was so late gittin' there that the snows come and they got locked in them mountains.

"Some of them people couldn't hold theirselves together. Their minds give. A few saw they wasn't goin' to make it and set out on snowshoes to git relief. There was eighty-some-odd started out and thirty come out.

"Some folks say they drew straws on who was to die, but that ain't accurate. The fact is they et those had gone. They et Jacob Donner's brains, and that's a fact. Reed come in with the rescue party to try to find his family and seen Jacob's head cut off from his body and the skull opened up, and that's how the story finally come out that the survivors had done et human flesh. Reed saw that when he brung in the rescue party.

"They say it was right here in this grove Grandma Keyes give up the ghost, and if you was to search it out mabbe you'd come across her grave somewhere in the vicinity. Reed, he was said to make a stone and that he carved her name on a tree at the head of the grave. Reed buried her hisself. They give the little girl a lock of her hair. And that little girl, she had that hair in her hand when Reed come in with the rescue party and got the survivors out. I told you-all that part 'fore we got in all this trouble, remember?"

There are always survivors, John thought, and he's one, too, John conceded, looking at Tom, even for someone so long in the tooth. A nigger was important in my life once, he would have to say one day. He made me see things no white man ever had, even my father. Reed . . . the Donners . . . Hugh Glass . . . the Sublettes . . . the stories of this land. Tom was one unto himself as well. The history of the land, like maybe the history of the country when you came down to it, was here, in the men and the land and how they had come to work on one another. White Buffalo Woman. Benjie Klomp. The Klomps. Pepper Tom. The Sweetwater. The West. They say so much, he thought. That's what power is, to know what sweet water is, to name it right, to come to the spring and drink down to its heart, John thought. It was odd. All along he had assumed his anger raged mostly against Mason Raymond when in reality it had been running against himself. And this land, that used to drive me to despair. I thought it was the land I was out against, to fight the land, but it wasn't. It wasn't gold or the desert or any of the other thin's I had to lick that pushed me out here; it was the empty places inside myself, those gaps Tom was talking about in Mason Raymond, but he meant me, too; I just didn't see it at the time. I had gaps inside myself I had to fill up. And I couldn't find the way when I was back home.

Why was that? Because I wanted to go West. It wasn't just the gold it was, as much just wanting to get away and be free and push on, like there was this awful need that raged inside that said, Go out and *see*.

I jest wanted to see for the sake of seeing. And I couldn't explain that because back home they weren't like that. They wanted to stay with the land because the land was what filled up their gaps, but I needed somethin' more to fill up mine, and I was mad because I couldn't explain it to them and they couldn't see it for theirselfs; it all got so complicated and the complications was what made part of the anger. I couldn't explain to them—maybe I can't ever really explain to anyone —that there's so much you can do you can't stay put long, you got to keep movin' so that you can get in as much as you can before the end comes. I got to run and run, he thought, there's so much up ahead.

IV

He awoke to darkness and a great jolt of joy raised him up; he gazed overhead wanting to see the stars, remembering how once he'd said, I ain't gonna die, I'm gonna shoot like a star.

There were no holes in the sky, no moon; overhead was as dark as the outside had seemed when he first opened his eyes. I give up white to go back down to black, he thought, and laid his head against his knees, taking refuge in the comfort of his own arms.

I got the world's heavyweight voice inside, he thought. And that voice told him now not to hold out too much hope. Let the girl cite all the Indian stories she wanted, he'd seen enough cases of sun and dust blindness himself all those years roaming around to know that a man who was bad-took never came back to himself all in one piece. Wasn't just the eyes involved neither; there was a kind of craziness hit the mind, worse mabbe even than blindness.

He tried to pull himself up and think straight. Voices were burning to be heard inside his head—his grandfather . . . his mother . . . the Captain . . . Jonathan; Jonathan the worst, shouting to get his attention; and then, suddenly, Tom had a vivid picture of Jonathan, tall and elegant and angry, waving his arms and demanding to know why Tom had been such a damn fool as to get mad and go off like that.

"I don't know," Tom mumbled. "I jest didn't have good sense, I guess."

"You should have knowed better," Jonathan said back.

"I know, I know. *Now* I know but what good is that?"

He had betrayed Jonathan's friendship and there was no way now of ever finding Jonathan and making it right. No way to—his mind cast about for the word—no way to *atone*; and then he understood where that word had come from because a voice opened up the present part of his mind from the part spun out in the past; that voice was from here and now and had given Tom the word because he associated the word with that particular voice. Where am I? he thought. And whose voice is that? It's that Raymond boy. He trying to talk to me. Tom raised his head from the cradle of his arms and tried to concentrate. ". . . get you on . . . doctor in one of those towns . . . help, you need help . . . a doctor . . ."

Tom shook his head. No, he didn't need help. He ought to be left behind. He began to try to explain but Mason Raymond shut off the speech. "I'm not moving unless you do," he said. "What you're doing is just giving up before there's time even to try, but even to think 'I'll try' is to say you're not going to, you've already given up. What you should be saying is, 'I'm going to do it.' I know. I been 'trying' all my life instead of 'doing.' This friend of mine, lived in a cave, a man I cared about and I think cared about me—Bartholomew cared about *everything*," Mason Raymond said passionately, as if the cry of that man was still there inside his heart and who could say that maybe Bartholomew hadn't even heard him? Maybe Jonathan—his grandfather, his mother, the Captain—could hear when they were called out to. Tom wanted to believe so. "Bartholomew, he was so close with the world he could talk to all of it, even his stuffed animals, even the plants and shrubs he walked through, whispering these strange messages in the middle of the wilderness. 'Don't eat meat, and only the parts of plants they can spare,' Bartholomew used to say. He was so close to me he made me feel— We're not going to leave you, I don't care what you say. We couldn't leave you because—because we need you, you know that."

Tom felt touched in unknown parts of himself. The ordinary places of the world had never in the past few years existed with so much importance as they did at this moment; he felt now he had burst through the outward surface of things and his heart beat with the undescribed; he felt flooded with a feeling of expectation, as if after all it was not impossible to be fifty if there were still things to do in the world. For it seemed to him, even in blindess, a great world of possibility and choice might open up before him.

Damn fool nigger, he told himself. Where you *at*?

Don't mabbe nobody know that ever.

That boy, he got a structure like steel, Tom thought, don't do none to sell him short. He could hear Mason Raymond shouting to the others. "Listen," he was hollering. "Listen, come here and talk to him. He's being pigheaded again."

They care, Tom thought. They care way past what I worth. Ain't that somethin' for a nigger near fifty go and find out? Put that in your pipe and smoke it.

"We put you on Mabel," Mason Raymond said, "you won't have any trouble at all. She's *reliable.*" He said that with great pride, helping Tom to his feet and leading him across an area full of tricks to trip him. Tom was trying to concentrate on keeping his balance; it was a great relief when he smelled the familiar dusty horse odor, acrid and pungent, that trail smell he'd come to love. He put his hands against the side of the horse just to be reassured by its touch. Touch and smell, those were left to him even if sight wasn't. "You reckon you ken get us to the Big Blue?" he asked.

Mason Raymond laughed, but it was not self-conscious or ashamed; he sounded amused. "I'm not leading anyone *any-where*. That's one job nobody ever wants to hand me. John, he'll give the directions. Here, let me hoist you up."

"I ken still git up myself." He sounded crosser than he meant, but he was jealous of the few areas of independence left him. "No offense," he added, hoping to take the sting out of the words.

"No offense," Mason Raymond answered and it seemed to

Tom he was laughing again. What puts him in such good humor all of a sudden? he asked himself and a little voice said, raising its pesky head, The girl?

"But you look smart seein' we don't run into no trouble, you hear? We had one bad experience, we don't need no more. You got to look real sharp all the time." He had begun to worry himself John wasn't up to the responsibility, he was so young and inexperienced. What did I have to go and git blind for? he asked himself for perhaps the hundredth time. There's goin' to be all kinds of problems they can't handle and I ain't gonna be no help to them, ain't gonna be nuthin' but a hindrance. They ought to leave me behind, old man who ain't— He began to bicker.

"You hush up that talk," the girl said. "We got troubles enough you ain't peskyin' us every other minute to leave you behind. We ain't gonna leave you, and that's that. You gonna be able to ride that there *this* horse?" she asked one of them anxiously. Which one? It was Mason Raymond who answered. "My knees is swoll up some, but they're better than they were."

"You done washed all the poison out. I never seen a man so set on water. Can't no more than turn around and you're washin' away. What you washin' anyway?"

"I don't know. It's just like I feel dirt all over me," Mason Raymond said defensively. "Maybe it's the alkali."

And mabbe it's a feelin' of bein' guilty, Tom wanted to say. But that'll wear away. You don't wash it off, but time ken take it away. Ain't that right, Jonathan?

Sightless, riding the horse, he started out with them. He might not be able to see, but he could feel the land begin to pitch and heave; he could imagine it stretching and yawning, under a red haze of sky.

They crossed the Big Blue near Marysville at the Independence-Mormon crossing, what some had called the California Trail, the last real settlement past the Missouri. Here thousands of covered wagons with settlers bound for Oregon, Mormons for Utah, gold seekers for California, had crossed the river—five hundred thousand according to John's guide, which he read to them pretentiously, informing them that

Frank Marshall's wife Mary had given her name to the town, a fact Tom could have lived without, but those guides were always full of that kind of useless information when what you really wanted to know was whether or not this was the kind of town filled with doctors who could cure your eyes and horse buffs liked to lay a little money out on a race. We git a little race rigged up, Tom thought. His spirits rose. Nuthin', he thought, like the prospect of a pack of cards and a nice little horse wager to pep a man up.

In 1860 Marysville had been the first home station of the Pony Express, John read on. The little sod building was still standing, according to the guide, a reminder of those seventeen months of agent stations from Julesburg to South Pass, ten, fifteen miles apart where riders changed ponies and carried the mail in one long gallop across the Plains. Probly ponies like the piebald, Tom thought. Nuthin' like good Indian stock; ain't a white man's horse can match it.

He thought of the pony riders galloping the two thousand miles from St. Jo to Sacramento. Took eight days and letters cost five dollars a half ounce and people had written on tissue paper to save cost. A wonder really when you thought of it. Somethin' I'd liked to have tried myself, he thought. Would have been real excitin'.

> *Spare your horse? —Yes and no;*
> *Treat him square, boy, of course;*
> *But the mail's got to go through,*
>   *And it's up to the horse*
>   *To carry it through.*
> *Though his heart thumps his side,*
> *Get the best he can give;*
> *If he drops on the trail,*
>   *Just grab up the mail,*
> *Get another and ride,*
>   *Just ride like the wind.*

"Want to look around for a little action," Tom said. "Mabbe find ourselfs a sawbones can give us some hard facts on these here blinkers of mine—'' He wanted to sound as if he didn't have a worry in the world, that of course there was just some medicine waiting for him in Marysville that was going to fix him up fit as a fiddle, but he was afraid his words came out edged in anxiety and he was annoyed at himself for letting his feelings show. He rushed on, trying to cover up. "Fix ourselfs up a little stake race, run up a few nice solid bets, no trouble gittin' a stake together atall.''

When he said *stake* the excitement reared; he could almost actually envision the race, could hear the jingle of coins in his pockets from his share of the winnings; he could taste success and smell the rich pine woods up north where the touch of earth was wet and dank as he panned, separating the gold from the gravel. This sudden longing for the Hills was sharp and intense. Hard as life was up there, there were many rewards —or the expectation of them—to make up for all the drudgery. A man took his hands out of the muddy water and often saw the "colors," flakes of gold that stuck under his fingernails. He thought of that crazy Chink who could play cards like God had given him a set all marked with nothing but aces and eights. He remembered, too, the patient Chinamen who inched their way over the abandoned mines, reworking what the whites no longer wanted, looking for the small scraps that had been left.

He had had mixed feelings about these Orientals. Being black, for the first time he'd had the luxury of looking down on someone else; yet the contempt which those hardworking, long-suffering men, so far from home, experienced had raised in him feelings of affinity as well. A puffed-up nigger from down South could find common cause with a spit-upon Chink —much as he might not want to.

Tom thought all this as they rode into Marysville, and he asked himself what kind of impression *they* made: two young kids got greenhorn written all over them, a girl rode like an Indian and had clay over half her face, and a trail-beaten blind old nigger on a broken-down horse from some nowhere place back East.

He would remember that doctor working on him all the rest of his life—and always shudder, trying to block off the incisive memories of the cutting and probing, the pushing and realigning, some salve that was stuck on his eyes and seemed to dissolve them in acid; things got so bad that after a while he went under, but just before he did he heard his grandfather shouting, "Don't you dare holler out and disgrace us. We ain't none of us complainers nor whiners, you hear?"

Tom's jaws jarred him back to consciousness, the nerves throughout his head aflame. He'd been grinding his teeth under the pressure of the pain; he really couldn't see, but he wasn't immersed either in white or black anymore; at first everything seemed indistinct, but then gradually began to blend into large unidentifiable objects.

The doctor was one of those noisy obstreperous talkers who tried to make up in enthusiasm what he lacked in talent, banging around the room talking about all the great cures he had effected and it was criminal with the insights he had to be stuck in a little hick town like Marysville. Tom didn't ask him why he didn't move on if he was so dissatisfied; he didn't have to. He had smelled the liquor on his breath and every once in a while he would hear the gurgle from the bottle as the man paused in his diatribe and refreshed himself and then, re-fueled, ran on about "the lack of opportunities." Tom's contingent suffered in silence mostly; occasionally Buttes would chime in about how he knew something about small-town thinking himself, he'd lived in a little hamlet back East; but the doctor paid no attention to this attempt at amenity, rattling on, running over anyone else's ideas, utterly absorbed in his own dissertation.

Tom's head ached and he was apprehensive waiting to see if this hack's efforts were going to work any real results. A drunken sawbones was hardly the type to inspire confidence, but in the midst of the Great American Desert you didn't expect diplomas out of a real doctor school; still, it gave a man pause letting someone so out of control mess around with your eyes. "You only got one pair of eyes and they cain't be re-placed, boy," his grandmother would fret. "Read closer to that fire."

Dull throbs in his head threatened to rob him of reason; he surged up and down on waves of pain; an hour passed and then slowly, so slowly he wasn't really sure it was happening, he began to distinguish, he thought, some change, a gradual lifting of the veil, the darkness dissolving very slowly from black to gray. He wasn't sure at first; then the vague outlines of figures began to emerge. He could detect large movements, particularly the medical man crashing from cabinet to cabinet lamenting his liquidation in the wilderness.

A wild whoop of Tom's heart gave forth to joy. He wanted to jump up and down and shout and holler his head off, but he was reserved and cautious by nature (maybe, he thought, one reason he'd never been able to extend himself to the point of making any lasting commitment to a woman) and he waited for further proof the curtain was in fact being lifted and there would be fine scenes to view.

The three people around him he found strange to sight now after getting to know them of late through touch and smell. The girl was banging and bustling around in a doctor-busy manner, making syrupy sounds in her throat to indicate how seriously she took her responsibility. It was difficult for Tom to discern what the two boys were doing, but it looked as if they were leaning against the wall just maybe waiting—or watching. Certainly the doctor must have made some kind of spectacle. "Nice bunch of animal flesh you people brung in," he was saying. "Understand you're not averse to a little wagerin' on that Indian pinto pony you got." Tom's heart gave a happy leap and he tried to focus; he could recognize greediness when he heard it. "We got some horseflesh around ourselves, a couple of first-rate bays. You think you might be interested in a little race—that is, if you got some stakes?" A born sucker, Tom's brain registered. It took one to know one. "You been boastin' that little pint pony can outrun anythin' we want to put up—" Tom wondered when they'd been doing that. When I was under, he thought. He was proud of them; they were learning. "Them piebalds never last, don't have no stayin' power, but if you was to want to put up your good hard-earned cash to prove a point, who am I to turn you down?"

Who, indeed? He should no doubt be babbling out heartfelt gratitude of thanks for the gift back of his eyes, but all he could feel was a fierce, congealed contempt. I hope he loses every cent he's got, Tom thought, he's such a superior son of a bitch. Drunk and boastin' and bettin' all at the same time. How come he didn't put me under before he started all that pokin' and proddin'? They got thin's nowadays they ken give you, but like as not I wasn't good enough, I wasn't white, he wasn't goin' to waste good stuff on me.

Banging around, the doctor asked John if that little runty mare could really run. "Some," John muttered, and Tom blessed the tone of his voice, which sounded unsure. Jest leadin' him on like a pro, Tom exulted. Lead him on, lead him on, don't let him git away.

Ain't you got no gratitude in you atall?

Let him put his money where his mouth is, he's sech a big talker. If his own greed's gonna sucker him in, that ain't *my* responsibility.

You owe him somethin'.

When the time comes, I'll like mabbe give him a little warnin'.

Excuses, excuses, excuses.

What do you want from me? Why this everlastin' mutterin' and naggin'?

Lissen, let me tell you somethin' you done disremembered. Sick people ain't jest sick, they's bad luck. Bad luck rubs off. You ain't mabbe gonna be all that welcome around no major bettin'. I ain't missin' this for *nuthin'*, he grumbled to himself, I don't care how superstitions run. Yet he was uneasy, wondering how his little group was going to react to him. He'd been such a nuisance to them already.

The drunk hauled him up and splashed something in his eyes and the first thing he saw was that the girl had the plaster off her nose. She was standing right beside him peering at him with great concern. "You done taken the clay away," he said and a big happy smile split her face. She bent over and held out to him a handsome new hat with which he could crown his recovered head. He was so taken aback that he didn't know what to say. The last people he could remember giving him anything were the Captain and Jonathan *years* ago. He fished around frantically for words of gratitude. Then he smiled himself:

*"Dakota comes! What varied wealth of mount and plains she
brings!"*

he sang out,

*"How vast a golden light athwart the coming years she flings!
Her mines exhaustless, soil the richest, healthy balmy air,
She holds to give and gives to bless—her bounties all share."*

Athwart? Well, why not? How often did the blind not only
see but also get a new hat to crown the miracle? Shy for the
first time since Tom had known him, John presented his gift,
a little homeopathic number (28) for "nervous debility, vital
weakness or depression, a weak exhausted feeling, no energy
or courage, the result of mental overwork, indiscretion, or
excess." Indiscretion or excess, that was a hot one. Athwart
that one. What lay in store for him from Raymond? A book,
of course. *The Golden Moments of Verse: A Garden of Inspirational
Songs.* "Very fittin'," Tom said, "very fittin', indeed. I'm not
only gonna look the rake and feel the rake"—holding up his
medicine—"but there ain't gonna be nobody stop me from
actin' one neither with this here ammunition," and he glanced
down, with eyes that had halfway begun to see, at the volume
of verse which lay now in his lap. But, oh gawd, he was
touched. Imagine their spending all that money on *him*. There
was nothing for it but a little celebration.

He lay groaning at the edge of what looked like, through
his foggy eyes, a trough. He had a vague memory of leaning
over water, trying to clear his head, but of being unsure
whether it was the bad eyes or the liquor he had been trying
to get rid of.

"Oh, lord, you all come quick," he heard the girl crying.
"He's gone and give out most of our money. He's gone and
got hisself all liquored up and now he's laid up like one of the
fallen, ain't no way to git him on his feet and— You ain't never
seen the like of the amount of liquor that there *this* nigger put
away."

Liquor always had been an awful temptation to him, liquor

and cards. I don't resist sin too well, he thought. It's like it's ingrained in the bone. "But they's not bad vices to speak of," he pleaded, "compared to some I knowed."

"To speak of?" she said, furious. "I hate whiskey," she said passionately. "I seen what it done to—" She shook her head. "The Indians would be lyin' like logs all over the plains, so dead drunk they didn't even seem to breathe. They'd fight and knife and go at their women—men so gentle you couldn't believe they could git as wild as wolves like that." She took a breath, collecting herself. "It ain't meant for out here. This here is Indian land. It ain't got no place out here.

"Indians and niggers," she said, "they ain't made up for puttin' that down in their insides. And they always pick the worst times. You ain't gonna be in no mood to ride when you comes out of this. He ain't gonna ride," she announced. "He ain't maybe even goin' to be able to stand." She looked at John and Mason Raymond. "And the two of you, you ain't in much better shape, him all burned in the knees and you wore out with all you been through. You can't neither of you git up and ride smooth, the conditions you in. You'd come apart as sure as can be under the strain, and he can't ride, he's so liquored up. What got into you?" she demanded. "We was countin' on you—"

"How could you count on me? My eyes—"

"Your eyes was goin' to be fine iffen you took care of them the way you should. But, no, you got to go out and git yourself all liquored up. Oh," she cried in exasperation, "what made you do it? We got so much involved, what made you go and do a thin' like that?"

Weak in the flesh, Tom wanted to say, but his head was pounding too fiercely for prolonged recriminations and debate. He lay stretched out feeling the miserable sinner he was.

Oh god, take this old reprobate
And cast him out the pearly gates.

"He ain't ridin," she said. "You two can't. So that only leaves *me.*" She said the *me* with a menacing sound of satisfaction.

"You can't ride. You can't ride out there in front of all them men. Girls don't ride in races," John Buttes said.

"Lose your money then! It's you who's so keen to git it all piled high, you who's greedin' to git to them Hills you got no business bein' in and takin' out gold ain't yours. I don't need none where I'm goin'. I ain't ridin' for me. It's for you"—indicating the dead-drunk man on the ground and looking from John to Mason Raymond—"for you, for all of you. It ain't for me. What I need that kind of money for?"

"Listen," John said. "I ain't tryin' to insult you. All I'm sayin' is it ain't seemly for no girl—"

"Seemly?" She started laughing, great whooping gusts of mirth flying out of her. "You're jest too much sometimes, you really is. Seemly," she said, shaking her head in wonderment. "If that ain't the livin' end."

"They'll hoot us off the field they see you come ridin' in."

"We'll see," she said. "We'll jest see."

The race was set for seven, before the bad heat of the day set in. But it was one of those plains hot dawns, streaked gold and silver and cut across with fire, a red-hot sun bursting up off the desert floor. Tom's eyes, even only half functioning, felt scorched out by the intensity of the light. His head ached; his stomach was jostling up and down.

All night Indians had been riding in; they were camped all over the plain. They had come riding down from the hills, hundreds of them dressed up in fancy feathers and buckskins and beads, painted, too, a whole host of savages, made his flesh run cold just to get a glimpse of them. But they weren't the real hostiles, the girl explained; those were up north with Crazy Horse and Bone Hand and Two Moon and Young Man Afraid; probably Sitting Bull would be there, too, getting his warriors together, she said. Though these Indians looked fierce they were what was called "friendlies," and she said that word sarcastically, showing she had no use for them, Indians who had put down their arms and come to live around the white men's forts, take what the white man cared to dole out to them, miserable as it was, and have to act grateful to get that, "white-men Indians," she called them. The girl shaded her eyes with one hand and made a quick survey of the scene.

] *372* [

"Word's out," she said cryptically. "They love a good race. No need for you to keep lookin' like that. That ain't war paint —the ones you want to watch out for ain't gonna come near no fort. They're like as not up on the Powder or in the Hills around the Big Horn waitin'. That's where they're goin' to be, watchin' and waitin' to catch them Army men come in their Hills, not here bettin' on no horse race."

He took her at her word. John had told him she'd been moseying around talking with this Indian and that ever since they'd ridden in. He supposed she had all the dope straight from the medicine man's mouth; while the white doctor was working his special brand of magic, out in the hills her kind of medicine men were casting their own spells and making their own magic. She made him uneasy though, talking so certain of where the Indians were laying up and what they were planning to do, just like she knew the whole plan. He turned away abruptly, a signal to lay off giving out information he didn't want to have.

She got the signal and silenced up, but there was a dark hooded look to her eyes that he would remember in July when the news came into Nigger Hill that Custer had been overrun. He was up with the rest of the niggers in the dry gulch when the news came in—living with John, the two of them keeping to themselves because after being with the girl and Mason Raymond they couldn't seem to accustom themselves to other people's ways, especially the white ways. Tom had been worse, he felt, than John, but that was probably natural, his being black. He just couldn't get used to how arrogant and superior these whites seemed after Mason Raymond and the girl. But then he never thought of the girl really as white; she seemed more Indian to him. Crossbred was the way he thought of it. So finally he'd said to John he couldn't take no more, he was going over with the other blacks on that water-less spot known as Black or Nigger Hill, and John had stayed put with the whites maybe a week before he'd packed up his tools and come over and asked if he could stake out with Tom. "I don't belong there neither," was all he ever said. "They's fools."

He'd gone up and asked the niggers if he could lay up with

them, he didn't want to barge in. They'd given him queer looks and cold shoulders at first, but gradually they'd taken him in and he'd been given fair divvies; maybe even the niggers hadn't had any hope for that dry run they'd been given as a joke and which, in the end, had bubbled up the last golden laugh and made them all rich, richer than most of the white men around, except of course for John. He got rich with them on niggers' findings on that claim nobody white had ever thought worth a damn; that was the kind of joke Tom liked. They were all rolling in gold, golden golden black men and one white, but that was later. It was July when he stood listening to the news about Custer and thought of the girl and all she'd seemed to know back in May in Marysville. Tom stood reading the special edition of the *Black Hills Pioneer* and Captain Jack's sorrowful poem:

> *Did I hear the news from Custer?*
>   *Well, I reckon I did, old pard.*
> *It came like a streak of lightning,*
>   *And you can bet it hit me hard.*
> *I ain't no hand to blubber,*
>   *And the briny ain't run for years,*
> *But chalk me down for a lubber,*
>   *If I didn't shed regular tears.*

How'd she know way back then? he would wonder. And he thought, Injuns got ways of knowing, like she said, white men don't even have an inklin' of. I ain't never gonna argue that no more. She knew back there jest as if it had already happened.

He wondered if she and Mason Raymond had got to the Oglala camp in time for the big attack; and then, later, when the mine came in, he stood thinking part of what he was going to get belonged to them because it was those two who'd helped him get his eyes back and get the stake together and he'd never know where to go and find them; it was like Jonathan and the Captain, disappeared into another time and place. And he said to himself, White Buffalo Woman, Mason Raymond, where are you? Safe somewhere, I hope, because it

ain't gonna go good with you. Injuns don't kill a Custer and
run free to brag about it. "The only good Injun is a dead
Injun." "The only good nigger is a dead nigger." "The only
good Chink is a dead Chink." Brigham Young? "The only
good Mormon is a dead Mormon."

Today she stood in the wind and in the blood-red sun and
announced she was going to ride bareback and John kept
arguing how there'd be a protest about that, too. It was bad
enough he was going to have to fight about a woman riding,
he didn't want to have to argue about her riding bareback as
well. "Weren't nuthin' said about saddles," she argued. Then,
after a pause, she said, "Jest like when you and him had that
bet, weren't nuthin' said *he*," nodding at Mason Raymond,
"had to bring his coon in dead." So he done told her all about
that, Tom thought. What else they been talkin' about, them
two? He looked quickly from one to the other trying to discern some special, secret relationship they had established, but
he couldn't find anything except the ordinary. Still he was easy
to deceive on a thing like that.

He perked up for a moment, thinking, It wouldn't be a bad
thin' though she got one of them to protect her. Still *he,*
looking at John, he ain't really likely to stick. He ain't the
stickin' kind. Better she set herself on someone who'll be
dependable.

"You don't use no saddle, you lessen the weight. The lesser
weight you got, the lighter the load. The lighter the load, the
faster the horse can run," she pointed out.

"That pony can run fast enough with a saddle to win. A
saddle ain't all that heavy if it fits snug and there won't be no
disputes like there'll be iffen you come out there with nuthin'
next to the horse but you. It ain't ladylike."

"Oh my gawd," she said.

"Well, it ain't," John insisted. "That's what they'll say."

"I don't care what they say. Ain't nuthin' to me what they
say. Ain't nuthin' set out in the rules says I got to sit a saddle
and I ain't, 'ladylike' or no. I'm ridin' the way to win and that
don't include no saddle."

She was set in her way, Tom could see, and he watched her
come out with the pony to a great hoot from the men who'd

gathered and wild nose noises from the Indians. They were hollering a girl couldn't ride, this was a man's race, they hadn't put their money up to see no girl ride. But that wasn't from the few who'd bet on the piebald. The rest were just letting their derision make itself known. For a moment everything was noise and confusion and Tom envied himself his hangover; he was too done in to have to take charge of anything. He hung over a barrel and moaned the truth, which was that he was give out inside, he'd never touch another drop as long as he lived if only God would give him another head. John and Mason Raymond were mad at him; they kept ignoring his misery, but he wasn't going to be bypassed on good advice. "You tell her to let that pony out all the way. Tell her not to hang back none. That pony got more wind than she needs to make that run."

"I heared all about your reform before," John said. "You tole me you was never goin' to touch another drop as long as you lived the last time you got yourself in a state like this. Your word is mighty weak when it comes to liquor. That's all I got to say."

"Give me a gun and let me git it over with."

"You got your own gun. Mason Raymond give it back."

"Jest tell her to let 'er go," Tom said again. It was important. This was not the kind of race to hang back. I ought to be in there riding, he thought, and just the thought made his stomach sick.

"She knows more about it than any of us," John said. "I ain't about to give her no advice."

Mason Raymond and John helped the girl with the final rubdown of the pony and then, as the girl got up bareback, there was that terrible explosion of squealing and howling. This goin' to be somethin', Tom thought, but the girl was cool as anythin'—there might not even have been a single soul in sight, not them thousand or so singsongy Indians, not all those yelping men, just her and that little piebald pony out for a morning run. The piebald looked scruffy as ever, careful as they had been not to slick her up too much and make any of the bettors edgy. The girl was hardly what you would call a vision of loveliness, decked out as she was in old trail gear, her hair tucked up in a round braid like a ball atop her head, and her feet bare—it was the last part that got Tom the most, the bare feet. She had on greasy pants and an old shirt, the sleeves rolled back (probably one of them dead men's shirts) and all her freckles showing, and not even a kerchief round her throat for a little color, the drabbest thing you'd ever laid eyes on, and those dangling bare feet. The hoots were at yell level as Sculley, the Marysville man who had been elected to ride, came out, immaculate as if he were going to be reviewed by General Grant on his way out of office in disgrace but all dressed up anyway and full of the importance of saying good-bye to the troops. Sculley had on an old Civil War uniform and his boots were so highly polished that you could see faces from the crowd reflected in them.

Some of the men were bent over laughing their guts out. Others were scowling and shouting, saying that racing a girl didn't show no respect. The Indians were just chanting; Tom had no idea whether their noises were in favor or not; but the girl went cool as the day's first dew, swinging her way through the little lane that opened up to the starting line, a line with red flags where they would set off, a mile to the barrels, race around them, and come a mile back, a little over two miles in all.

She had nerves of iron, sitting there barefooted, paying no heed at all to the fancy-dressed Sculley haranguing her about what was right, what wasn't. Finally she turned and in a brief pause, while he was catching his breath, she said, "You ride like you want and I'll ride the way I want. Don't make no matter to me iffen you stoke your saddle."

"It ain't right," Sculley kept protesting. "It ain't proper."

Tom, supported by Mason Raymond and John, ceased paying attention to the debate. He had more important matters on his mind. Something was the matter with that pony. It kept turning its head right and left, shuffling nervously back and forth as if it were searching for something. Tom had never seen the piebald like that, all nerved up and uncertain. He ransacked his mind for a clue. The bugle was sounding the five-minute warning. Sculley was carrying on fit to be tied. The girl swung her bare feet. The little mare was pawing the ground angrily.

My god, what if she don't run? Tom thought. That's the way

she's acting, like she's done took it in her mind not to run at all. That jest our luck. We a hard-luck crew. Have been from the start. One damn thin' after another, like the good God above set on doin' us in.

John let him drop back on Mason Raymond and sprinted up to the girl and the pony and began talking frantically. "What is it? What's the matter? All these people botherin' you, that it? Don't pay them no mind, girl, you jest run. We got everythin' we own in this world staked out on you—you run, you hear, you run your heart out."

The piebald's ears were twitching. And for a fact, she seemed quieter, but she still looked as if she were hatching plans of her own that bode well for none of them. She's as bad as me, Tom thought in despair, jest plain undependable. You can't never count on what either of us is goin' to do.

The little mare turned her head and looked round; her eyes were filled with all the wickedness in the world. You gotta come through, Tom thought in desperation.

The bugle sounded the one-minute warning. "Git back," the girl hissed. "*Git out of the way.* You're gonna mess up the start." John stumbled free of the cord. That would be cut when the final blast of the bugle came. The girl was hunched up light against the pony; they appeared one and the same, the girl like some growth sprung from out of the horse's back.

There came the sharp harsh blast of the bugle; the rope flew free; John screamed at the top of his lungs, "Run, goddam it, run for all you're worth." Tom felt as if he were going to be sick. He was losing air and couldn't breathe. He saw that was because, in his excitement, Mason Raymond was clutching him and squeezing him in and out in time to his screams, shouting, "Oh, lord, let her win," squeezing Tom so that his breath was shut off, then letting him go so that he gasped for air, squeezing him again and hollering, "Lord, let her go, let her run like the wind."

Dust flew from the horses' hooves. Mason Raymond was shrieking and grinding Tom in the deadlock of his excitement; John's frantic blows were now raining down on Tom's back. Then Mason Raymond started kneading and squeezing again. Ain't gonna be nuthin' straight left in the structure of me, Tom thought.

He fought his way free of both boys and rose to his toes trying to get a clearer view. He felt he was looking at the wind bundled up in the tunnel of a tornado. "Who's ahead? Which one's in front?" he cried. "Ken either of you see?"

"It looks like the dark one, the bay," John screamed. "It looks like the bay."

Both animals rounded the barrels and were thundering for home. Tom could see quite clearly now with the dust in back of them, and he wished he couldn't because the Sculley horse was way ahead, two whole lengths at least, just tearing up the prairie with his flat-footed run. My god, what a horse that was. Tom had never seen anything to equal it. Even in his horror at losing the race he couldn't stop his admiration. A beautiful, beautiful piece of motion, a magnificent animal, absolutely flawless, and then, just for a faltering instant, the bay seemed to hang suspended before it took its next stride and Tom thought, I jest imagined that—then he saw the faltering again, longer this time—you might even imagine you could clock it —and the girl, flattened down on the little mustang, pulling away. My god, Tom thought, she's been holdin' back. John told her not to hold back. She been holdin' back—she likely to give me heart failure. What got into her, holdin' back?

The piebald leaped right out from under the girl now that she had given it the go-free sign; that pony struck the hard ground with such violence that Tom thought he saw sparks fly from her hooves. The little piebald mustang roared past the tiring bay, who was dropping back, spent, its energy used up in the first mile; it was a sprinter, not a stayer; the little mare outdistancing it first one, then two, finally four lengths as she came pounding across the finish line, the Indians wailing their feather-happy heads off and half of the men of Marysville throwing their caps in the dust in disgust while the other half were screaming foul, foul, unfair, they were going to lodge a complaint, she ain't rode right. The judges stood, glacial, in the midst of the horse dust and heat, gaping at the bedraggled little Indian mare that had beat the *this* out of their best horse. They just couldn't seem to take in what had happened. It was as if for the first time the notion had occurred to them that looks ain't everything.

The girl sat, hardly a breath out of place, just panting a little;

she bent over when she got to John and Mason Raymond and said, "You take in the money. I'm goin' back and look after the horse."

She ain't got no sense at all and never will, Tom thought. She held that horse back. We'll be lucky to be rid of her. But he didn't feel lucky. For the first time he thought about South Pass and Mason Raymond and the girl going one way and him and John another. He couldn't take the idea in. They had all been on the trail so long that it was like they were welded together, nothing would ever separate them. We come a long way since Independence, he thought, a long, long way.

V

All their journey before Marysville had been through prairies; now they were entering the plains, a vast sweep of blue sky, low green undulating hills, stretching and turning as far as the eye could see. The trail followed the general course of the Big Blue, ran through the big valley which in days past had been the favorite range of the Pawnee. The ancient road led straight to the Platte, the great river road that wound into Fort Kearney, the turning point for many: Beyond, the Great Desert stretched, and many of the faint-hearted turned back. Lots of people said the plains didn't really start until after Kearney, but them what knew counted it plains from the Big Blue on. "Damn sheep men," Tom said. "It's them ruined the country. Them and barbed wire. The two of them has ruint the plains."

They rode on, Tom gazing back at the sad scramble of Marysville shacks and houses that had tried to call itself a town. "I'm a bushwhacker. I been back and forth across the Chisholm Trail more times than you got fingers and toes," he said proudly. "And I'd still be goin' back and forth free if all them interlopers hadn't come pilin' in stringin' up their wire and fencin' off everythin' in sight, drivin' all the good men out," he said to no one in particular, but in fact it seemed to Benjie that he was giving a final farewell to the runty little town they had left behind where they had cleaned out half the grown men in the place.

She was riding the piebald and the two boys were on big burly animals that kept prancing and playing, young frisky uncut studs, Tom had commented depreciatingly, but it was a marvel to Benjie how handy to the saddle Mason Raymond had got. She expected John and that old *this* trail whacker to sit astern, but Mason Raymond was a real revelation. They had all insisted Tom ride a thick ugly Roman-nosed black with enough years on it to have forgotten its colt tricks; it plodded along, making as little effort as possible, a blessing considering how spent Tom looked. Yet the minute he sat in the saddle his spirits seemed to lift; he was so happy, he claimed, just to be able to distinguish the bluffs and valleys, to jog along and feel the prairie air on his face, that he would never complain again. Benjie didn't doubt he'd be back to himself before the day was out, but for the time being his gratitude was a pleasure to have around. It made them all feel glad, that and the heavy sack of money they'd took out of Marysville. We done all right, she thought proudly. *I* done all right, too. I didn't let nobody down. I knowed how to run this horse and I run it right.

Four, she thought, looking at Mason Raymond and John and the black man. Four was a magic number to the Sioux— the four seasons of the year, the four points of direction, the four basic elements, the four divisions of nature, the four ages of development, and now, Benjie thought, the four of us.

If there is something you cannot change, accept it, the Sioux said. If there is something that you want that you cannot have, do not set your heart on it. If there is something that is making you confused and torn, flee from it. Ask yourself what it is you want and direct your eyes toward that. But do not ask for the impossible.

Crazy Horse's great love had been Black Buffalo Woman. Bone Hand named me White Buffalo Woman in Sioux—why in Sioux? There was a connection here she saw for the first time as important. Bone Hand's great Sioux friend Crazy Horse had had Black Buffalo Woman. It wasn't just the similarity of names between those men who were so close but also, she thought, the name probably had to do, for Bone Hand, with one of the central stories by which the Sioux lived as well, the legend of the great White Buffalo Spirit, that mysterious albino buffalo that had come up out of the fog to two Sioux hunters and as they came close to it, it had turned into a blinding flash of light and white, they had shielded their eyes against that brilliance, and a woman had emerged and stood tall and beautiful, all in white. One of the warriors had reached out to touch the apparition and had been consumed by flames.

Maybe they won't take me back, she thought, maybe they'll only see me as bringing bad spirits back into camp.

I got noplace else to go, she thought.

Strong emotions were working in her; she tried to suppress them and think of the strong points in her favor. They were making good time, having got an early start, and if they rode the way they were now they might even get past Kearney without having to stop. She didn't want to lay over there but she wouldn't say anything. She never wanted to stay in an Army town again, but of course everything would depend on how much time they made, mostly how Tom held up. He rode up ahead trying, she supposed, to show that he wouldn't hold them back. They were passing through one of the endless prairie-dog villages that dotted the Plains and Benjie turned in her seat to watch the little animals sit up on their hind legs and yelp and chatter as the four riders and the mule and pack horse went through. The little animals were sending out alarms, and from little mounded holes all over the desert the little squirrellike animals poked out their heads to see who the intruders were. The thin coughy bark was like a dog's and the fear that sent the hundreds of tiny animals scurrying this way and that reminded her of the same frantic feeling she had had the night she had tried to escape and the soldier had come and put his hand over her mouth.

There were no young around. They were born in May but did not come up above ground until a month later; then you could see great circles of eagles overhead waiting to dive and pounce. "Sentries" were constantly on duty to alert the colony to the danger of the great birds and to the menace of badgers and ferrets, the natural predators on the young. Violence was everywhere you looked; it seemed to Benjie the one sure law that ruled the world.

She had dropped behind and she noticed that John was pulling back, slowing down, to come abreast of her. There was something about being too close to him that made her uncomfortable, something she couldn't put into words. She started to urge the little piebald on, wanting to run and catch up with Mason Raymond, perhaps a quarter of a mile up ahead, Tom behind him. She had not realized how far she had fallen behind.

"Crazy little buggers, ain't they?" John said as she tried to trot by him.

She thought of the alternatives: to go on and seem impolite or to rein in and chat and seem natural. "Guess so," she said and kept going. He had let his horse out to keep up. They were going a little faster with each stride, Benjie squeezing the sides of the piebald to keep her going strong. "Goin' to make Kearney in no time at all," he said sociably. "I reckon so," Benjie answered and kept the little mare trotting out. "Can't wait till Laramie though. Nice place, Laramie, I heared, lots of bettin' there," and he was smiling. She wondered if he had another race in mind. I ain't ridin' in front of no soldiers, she thought.

"Nobody there now at Kearney," Tom, who had heard them, called. "It's closed up," he said. "Ain't nuthin' left but squatters and rattlers," he went on. "Indians burnt it out after the Red Cloud treaty."

"You sure is in a hurry," John said to her.

"I jest don't like to fall too far back." She bit her lip. "I mean he ain't all cleared up in the eyes yet and—"

"I don't hear no complainin'."

"No, but it don't do to be too overconfident."

"That ain't a fault of yourn, is it?"

She glanced across at him hastily, but he seemed like himself. Still there was something in the remark that made her uneasy. It was saying one thing on the surface and meaning another underneath. "I mean," he went on, "you don't trust nobody, do you?"

"Some," she said shortly. I don't trust you, she thought, but

I trust *them.* But why shouldn't she trust him? He hadn't ever done anything to her. It's like he'd use me and forget it, she thought. Like he wouldn't see it as serious. But she wasn't even sure herself what she meant by serious. She kicked the horse and let it run for all it was worth until she caught up with the other two; then she felt all right. She felt safe.

She had still expected soldiers at Kearney for some reason, no matter what Tom had said. Maybe it was because she had never paid much attention one way or the other to the differences of the forts. The Indians didn't call them by the names the whites used anyway and she had just naturally assumed Kearney would be a real fort with real soldiers. But she was wrong and Tom was right. It was nothing but a deserted dilapidated cluster of mounds lying in a low flat bottom of the Platte about forty miles from Grand Island, a spot treeless except for the cottonwoods on the little islands that dotted the river. Tom's guidebooks said there once had been a substantial garrison here, from 1848 on one of the principal posts of the West, but the completion of the railroad had rendered Kearney obsolete and it had been abandoned except for a few squatters. No direct attack had ever endangered the fort, it had just been let go. They rode through the ruins of former greatness, looking at the gutted and tumbling walls of once-solid barracks. The Platte Valley stretched ahead, turning and twisting, snaking its way through nothing but waste save for an occasional clump of trees, nothing moving in the fort except a few lizards. "Look at it," Tom said, nodding his head toward the river. "A mile wide and an inch deep. And totally useless. Ain't no way to use it 'cause it's too shallow for boats to float and it's full of quicksand and treacherous to cross and you go down to git water and you likely to git swallowed up in that sand." He sat in his saddle regarding the long ribbon of river that stretched out ahead. "And that's the great road the emigrants followed all the way they could 'cause though it weren't good for nuthin' else it was the greatest natural route the country ever had."

They came into Cottonwood Springs and made their way toward Ash Hollow where they wanted to put up. The area

] 385 [

had been the scene of endless skirmishes between the Pawnee and the Sioux and the beginning of an ascent up a steep hill so perilous that in the old days no emigrants were said to have spoken for the two miles that they had to pit themselves against the hill, wagon wheels locked and chained, horses riderless, men braced against wagons, straining against the laws of gravity, the mules and oxen thrashing about in terror as the wagons threatened to give way. The ravines were filled with wrecks and animals' skeletons and smashed wagons. Benjie leaned over her saddle and peered down. She was used to the long line of junk rusting out on the prairie—clocks, chairs, sofas, tools, pots and pans, a line from which the Indians often scavenged—but the broken remains of wagons and animals below was an awesome sight.

Tom was explaining how ropes had been attached to the wagons in order to act as windlasses and how the emigrants had used their bodies as levers and brakes. Because the wagon wheels were still swollen from the crossing at the South Platte, the wagons often bogged down in the steep incline up the hill, the last half mile having been called "hell" or "the hill's hell," but as they came up toward the top of the steep hill there was a magnificent panoramic view of the valleys and the chasm, bluffs of limestone spread out before them. Such a view must have made the terrible climb almost seem worthwhile to the pioneers, Benjie thought. She wondered what her parents would have thought of such an incredible sweep of space. Back in Kentucky there were views but nothing that ran so far as this. This was a land of far views.

She smelled wild cherry and wild roses. High up like this she looked out on a pink prairie where the roses ran as far as the eye could see. Hundreds of birds had found the spot as well, and in the shade and safety of the ash and cedar their songs promised to blot out old memories of burnt-out or bloody lands.

"Look at all them graves," Tom called out. Dyin' everywhere, Benjie thought, even here where it looks so safe and pretty. Can't turn around without stumblin' on sickness or weapons or death.

She got down off the horse and took it over to hobble it up. A land of far views and a land of flat graves. She secured the piebald and began to unpack and reorganize—there was always unpacking and repacking and reorganizing to be done (that was the whole story of their trip, of every trip, white or Indian, as far as she was concerned), and she was uncomfortable because it seemed to her John kept watching her. She was all nerved up and jumpy, him watching her every move that way. Once when she looked up and leveled her eyes at him and looked at him, really looked at him, it was almost, she thought, as if she were trying to plead, "Please leave me be. I don't mean you no harm so please jest let me be," and the look he gave her back was so cool and level that she knew the answer was no.

He crossed the camp and stood in front of her, looking down at the bedroll she was laying out. "You mind?" He pointed at his own blanket. She bit her lip to hold back an obvious refusal. He had the right to lay up where he wanted. "It ain't *that* bad, is it?" he asked, trying to make some kind of joke, but she knew he saw right away there was no joke as far as she was concerned.

"You set up where you want," she said. "I'm goin' to git some water for fixin' up."

There was a thin trickle of water with long green reeds standing like pipe stems out of the shallow bottom an inch or two down. Benjie had begun with two pails. She'd started off alone with both, but John had stopped her and made such a fuss about how she needed help that she had finally surrendered one to him, sighing, All right, all right, if you insist, but I've carried this and heavier before. Indian heavy, she had said.

Now she knelt by the water, letting it run into the pails, a slow business because of the shallowness of the stream, but grateful for even this thin inch of clear water running over the earth and sprouting green whiskers. Most of the only water they had seen had been the slime green alky puddles of the desert.

There was a small fish about two inches long gliding through the narrow ribbon of water and, as she watched, a snake slithered out of the bearded stubble of grass and unhinged its jaws and began to swallow the small fish. It moved slowly forward, its mouth gradually closing over the fish until the jaws had completely covered the little fish; then the snake gently moved through the empty water swallowing the large lump that first lay in its neck and then began to make its way gradually down its long slithering body. The snake slithered back into the weeds; the grasses looked as if they had been combed apart, and the snake went down to the narrow channel where the water ran. One instant the fish had been there and the next it had been swallowed up, and yet the swallowing had been beautiful to see, the slow, sure, and graceful opening of the snake unlocking its hinged jaws, the snake gliding closer and closer toward the unsuspecting fish, the snake slipping its head farther and farther along the fish's body until the whole fish had disappeared, a large elongated lump in the snake's neck; she could see it making its way down the whole length of the snake's body, the muscles and juices inside rippling as they broke the fish up and digested it.

I'm like that fish for him, she thought. He's come down here to swallow me up. She couldn't move, squatting by the edge of the water letting the stream trickle into her pail. He put out his hand and let it close over her shoulder and a shudder went through her just as the snake had shuddered as it broke apart the fish. "Don't—please," she said and her voice sounded funny.

He had dropped his own pail. It lay on its side in the water. He's done lost the water he did git, she thought as he put his other hand on her and turned her around and her own pail upset and she let out a little cry; then his mouth was on hers and she tried to struggle and couldn't; she felt completely weak and useless, as if any struggle she might make would be worthless, it always had been, hadn't it? And he was pressing her so close that she could feel the hot male urgency rising out of him. He seemed feverish all over. He can't wait to git hisself off in me, she thought, same as all the others, and she felt such a sense of anger and rebellion and push—that was the only word for it, a gigantic push of revulsion—that it lifted her up and made her heave against him so that he fell back, surprised, his eyes flying open and looking at her in astonishment. She thought probably the freckles were popping out all over her face, like red flags. "I wouldn't have you if you was to walk from here to Independence for me. You ain't never goin' to know, never in this wide world, what it's like bein'—" She couldn't express her outrage and her sense of helplessness, and tears were coursing down her cheeks, and that made her angrier because she sure in this *this* world wasn't going to cry over the likes of him. "You and your big high thinkin' about yourself," she panted in anger. "The way you always jest assume that of course naturally because you're so—"

"I didn't assume nuthin'—"

"Yes, you did, too," she interrupted. "You think you're better than us, than everyone else. It shines out all over you, that feelin' of yourn you is so superior. But I got somethin' to tell you. There's what some people git from bein' born rich or high and mighty and there's a natural kind of superior that some men jest has inside. You too love-struck on yourself to see either of *them* is worth ten of you—maybe it don't make no nevermind to you," she raged on, "because maybe for you my livin' with Injuns don't make me as good as you, so maybe what you think is that you can do what you want, what difference does it make to me, someone got won in a card game and had soldiers doin' all kinds of bad thin's to her. What's one more or less? But let me tell you one thin'. I ken recognize a man when I see one." Her contempt and anger were so complete that there was nothing to do but try to get them out or they would eat her up. She didn't want to hold back; she wanted to throw her rage out at him. "You think 'cause you come from back East you're somethin' special," and when John started to protest, she just went right on, running over him with words. "But the truth is—the truth is you don't know nuthin' about nuthin'. What you need," she said with that absolute total finality she hoped there was nothing he could do but accept, "is git out of yourself and learn a little, listen and learn in this *this* world which ain't, no matter what *you* think, been hoved out jest for you to play around in. You listen to me. I wouldn't have you if you was give to me. Oh, I know what you're thinkin' in that superior shut-in head of yours. You think, She's nuthin' but a squaw woman, how come she's takin' on so. That's the way all you people"—she said *all you people* with utter revulsion—"think. You don't none of you know what's real and what's jest made-up false in your head. The trouble is they is so many of you people and so few of us."

Her voice slid suddenly to a stop, as if the unexpected vision she had now led her to confront in her ranting that, right as she might be, she was also wrong because there *were* more of the false-see-ers, as she had pointed out, than the ones that she thought saw true. So maybe in the long run he had won. He had come and swallowed the same way the snake had moved silently and unknown to the fish and locked its jaws over it and crushed it before it had even had a chance to know it was being devoured.

From Ash Hollow on the first great monuments of the plains began. The first was Court House Rock which rose, shimmering, like a great white tower in the distance, so that Benjie imagined an ancient castle rising suddenly out of the sand, as if it had been built in an instant, and yet as she came closer she saw the structure was of soft sandstone, ready to crumble at the touch; the "castle" was in point of fact jagged and eroded, gnawed and disfigured by the teeth of time.

Tom said that the early settlers thought the big rock looked like the Court House in St. Louis and the smaller one the jail, and that's how it had come to have its names. The initials and names of the emigrants had been etched in the soft stone, but the chalklike rock was not the kind that could stand up to the ravages of wind and storms. Tom warned them not to get too close either, because a spot like that was a terrible temptation for rattlers.

From Court House Rock there was a turnoff to Sidney and Deadwood, the trail to the Black Hills which crossed the North Platte over the Camp Clarke bridge, but they were not going that way because there would be too many soldiers in the area asking questions and because from the start the plan had been to get to The Sweetwater and then go north.

There was a small stream that ran at the base of the rock— Pumpkin Creek, because a fur trader had given the Indians pumpkin seeds to encourage them to leave off wandering around having good times on the plains and frolicking with the buffalo (as he saw it) and settle down to the boredom of growing things (as the Indians saw it). These Indians hadn't wanted to settle down to farming—any more than the ones Daniel Boone had tried to teach wanted to sit still and parcel out one piece of land and live on it; they liked going around free with the buffalo—and so they had thrown the pumpkin seeds in the creek and that was how it had got its name. She would have liked to stop and wash, but she held her peace. During the long trail ride she had learned that though Indians bathed every day whites weren't so concerned.

They rode slow around the rock, admiring it, and she could see names, some carved, some painted, a lot scratched in with pencil. There had been apparently a great competition to see who could carve his name the highest. Men had hacked steps out of the base in order to raise themselves up over other men and carve their names higher and higher. It seemed to Benjie a lesson in the futility and vanity of the world: to carve your name in sandstone.

They had fifty miles to go between Court House Rock and Scotts Bluff, the really last big familiar sandstone structure on the trail. Most of the valley was dotted with bluffs and in the distance mountains that rose strange and dreamlike, as if they were unreal. But they were real enough, as the Donners could have told you.

The mule was beginning to act up again—though the pack horse had long since settled down—and John was whacking it with a stick, trying to get it to move. It stood single-mindedly determined not to, and even Mason Raymond began hollering at it to get the hell on the move. It was a comical scene to her; she sat watching and smiling when the black man came up and reined in beside her. "You ain't smiled like that since we left Independence back there," he said. "You done laughed once in a while but you ain't never smiled straight up out of you."

She looked at him, serious again. "Don't take too much to unlearn you the habit," she said.

"I hope you done relearned it back," Tom said. "It looks good on you, that little smile."

Benjie was embarrassed. She didn't know how to tell him that when some things have happened to you you feel as if you will never laugh or smile again and that it's easier to get up a laugh—even if it's forced—than to let a simple smile out. Smile's a thing you don't think too much about, but laughing is most of the time kind of rehearsed.

She was happy because they were leaving her alone, all of them now, John having stopped badgering her after the little episode at the stream, and she was free to float up the Platte River road through the sand castles and cathedrals that were strung out over the desert, to muse under the enormous bluffs and gaze out at the great endless avenue of prairie that shimmered in the sunlight and glazed into a mirage in the distance. They came almost immediately to the greatest of the sights on the long road, Chimney Rock. Some of the emigrants, Tom said, had even called it the eighth wonder of the world, seeing it stuck up needlelike in the midst of the long low desert. They made the approach over badlands and past soda flats and over alkali beds. It looked like a lighthouse from a picture in her childhood, Benjie thought, not a chimney. She couldn't understand why it had been called a chimney until Tom explained that to early travelers, mostly English, it had reminded them of a great tall chimney on one of the factories back home and that was how it had got its name. "Rattlesnakes here, too," Tom warned, and though John was eager to make a break and carve his name, Tom told him to hold off and do it at Independence Rock. That was where it *counted* to carve your name, he said; but Benjie wanted to tell them it didn't matter where you carved here in this sandstone, your name wasn't going to last. Nevertheless, they paused and gazed at the great tall column in wonder. It was strange and unsettling, unlike anything else they had encountered, as if some hand had deliberately molded a beacon to set on the plain, one that would say, Yes, this is the way. She thought of those signs, so simple, that said This Way North and This Way West, and she thought maybe all of the big things often were said that simply. He jest give me a name, she thought, and it had all the significance in the world and I never even knowed it till now. When he give me the name White Buffalo Woman, he was saying something special to all the others and I never even had the sense to see that until now. I shoulda seed and appreciated it but I was too blind.

The campsite was five miles away from the base of the Chimney, and they pulled up there, seeing the column fade into darkness; even so, under the stars, she could keep an eye on it off and on through the night, for she slept restlessly, thinking about how Bone Hand had been so taken with her that he had bestowed on her a privileged name and she had only repaid him in resentment and scorn. Now she was going back and if he would only take her back she thought she could make it up to him. He's an old man, she thought, and he's been through terrible things, I'll do what I can. It ain't much, Benjie thought, but all the strength I got I'll put into making it up to him. Don't jest let him be dead by the time I git back, she supplicated, I got so much to make up to him. When dawn came, she had a desolate feeling, something to do with the early light and the mournful quality of a new day on the desert and something to do with the utter sense of desolation inside her own heart. How had she lived so long among the people of the plains and understood so little?

From Chimney Rock to Scotts Bluff they passed curious mounds and buttes, high sand hills, before they saw a great towering fortress of clay and sandstone, a kind of Gibraltar, Tom said of it, standing in the midst of the desert, an old favorite rendezvous, Tom explained, for fur caravans. "Gone," the black man said, "gone like all the good thin's from the old days—put up barbed wire fencin' everyone out," he grumbled, "and rig up windmills and settle in and *farm*," he said contemptuously, with the same anger—it occurred to Benjie—the Indians felt about a settled way of life. People wasn't maybe so much different by way of skin as by way of thinking.

They took Mitchell Pass with Dome Rock at the left a mile away, the old ruts from the emigrants' wagons as much as eight feet deep in the sandstone where the pass was so narrow that no more than one wagon at a time had been able to pass. The great Laramie Plain stretched ahead of them, a vast desert uninhabited save for a few buffalo and some Indians, an occasional trading post. They saw some old Sioux encampments and burial scaffolds, an Indian, a young one, buried in a blanket and skin in the top of a tree. They stopped to look, silent, the bundle so small that it looked like a small package they could easily pick up and carry with them. If you had any need for bones, Benjie thought, moving her pony on. The scaffold had reenforced the memories of the many dead in Two Moon's camp and reawakened the trembling apprehension that by the time she rejoined Two Moon's people Bone Hand might himself be dead. Grief could kill as easily as a weapon and what, after all, did he have to live for?

When they got to Fort Laramie, that would mark the end of the plains and the gateway to the Rockies; the great Laramie Peak beyond told them that they were not now that far away. Its snow-covered crown seemed to say, This way, this way.

The old emigrants had liked Fort Laramie because they thought of it as midway through their trip, even though they had only traveled a third of the two thousand miles from St. Jo or Independence to Sacramento. Still, it was the end of the blistering dust plains and the entrance into the mountains, and the sight of the snow on Laramie Peak, looming in the distance forty miles away, gave promise of coolness and the end of cholera. Once they reached a sufficient elevation, about a hundred miles past the fort, the danger of cholera, which had haunted them all along the trail, was over.

The fort did not have a good reputation among the travelers, who spread inflated stories about exorbitant prices, marked cards, murderous Indians, fleecing women, but after miserable weeks of dust and sun and storms it was still a welcome sight in spite of those tales.

In single file they crossed the steel bridge that had been built across the North Platte the year before over the same spot where Marcus Whitman had crossed in '36 on his way to Presbytyrannize the Cayuse Indians; his wife, Narcissa, had been the first white woman in the Far West. Their little girl, Clarissa, had been conceived in the great fort where white women had never before been seen. Narcissa had kept a record of her scant two years on the Walla Walla with a steady stream of letters back East, where they had been widely published after her death in '47. Benjie's father and mother had read and discussed those letters. Perhaps the tragedy of Narcissa and her family had been what had delayed them so long from starting out.

Narcissa Whitman had written she'd packed sugar and flour, salt and beans and bacon and rice, coffee and tea and vinegar for the long trek; talked about the milk cows they had taken along and the cattle, and the two Indians boys who had to manage the livestock. In her new homeland in Washington she still used the old recipe of the trail, mixing flour and soda and salt with water to make flat cakes she baked in a Dutch oven buried in the coals of a fire.

At the Whitman place of adobe and bricks in Washington, later travelers could eat these cakes and pick up provisions that Marcus and his bride had lacked on their own pioneering expedition—beef at six and seven cents the pound, potatoes at fifty cents a bushel, flour five dollars for the hundredweight, even melons which the Cayuse Indians, who never had any interest in the mission, stole. The Whitmans had tried so hard and had never really managed to turn up evidence of one real convert. It struck Benjie strange how all these white people kept pouring in to change the Indians and how little success they had, but that failure hadn't seemed to make any impression on the others that followed.

Like the Whitmans, all the missionaries believed so passionately in the right of their missions that they had never thought through how little the missions had done for those they were trying to change. But it was interesting how the missionaries themselves seemed to prosper. She thought of what John was saying in between thumps on the backside of Caboose, how he'd read about the Whitmans and how terrible it was that after all they had done for those Indians the Indians had gone and massacred them. By '44, he said, Marcus Whitman had even managed to have a sawmill going—that showed how hard *he* had worked—and he had taken in seven children whose parents had died on the trail. John didn't say what this showed, but the tone of his voice certainly indicated pride. Injuns take in children, too, she wanted to say, but she rode on, letting him expound the superiority of the Whitmans to the Indians.

Narcissa and her husband, and Clarissa, the little girl, and ten other men and two children had been hacked to pieces by the Cayuse. The Indians had burned the mission, chopped down every tree in the orchard, destroyed the gardens, and set the house afire. It was not an ending to a story of Westward migration that was likely to encourage the timid, and Benjie supposed her mother and father might be counted in that category. No wonder they had talked and wavered for so long before her father had finally made up his mind. By then it had seemed the Indian threat was over. Now, she thought, they would have lived, if they *had* lived, to see it again. Up there on the Powder and in the *Paha Sapa* they ain't goin' to jest let white men come into their Hills no matter how strong them white men think they is.

Soldiers, she thought unappreciatively, as they came into Laramie. She rode straight and tall in the saddle, not looking to right or left. She knew the kind of impression she would make, and she wasn't even going to bother looking to make sure she was right. The men would all be licking their lips and the women would all be wanting to pray over her. "Underpaid and underappreciated," Tom said, and then as he looked at her, he added, "and undermannered." He looked back at John. "You keep a good eye on that there saddle of yours. This the kind of place they got a lot of light fingers. And they ain't probly seen the like of a saddle like that since they passed over the Missouri. It's a temptation."

In spite of herself, Benjie felt fear rising. She saw the heads turning as she rode in, and it was little wonder—an old bent-up black bushwhacker, a white woman looked like she'd seen more than one Indian or white war, and two trail-weary boys, both of whom might have lost the look of back East off them but who still hadn't acquired completely the restless hard look of Westerners. "Jesus," John said, "what a place."

Benjie was looking the Indians over carefully, searching for a face that might look familiar. She looked from Indian to Indian, paying the whites no mind at all, particularly those women who stopped and stared at her because even in this ragtaggle you had to say one thing, she thought with a kind of grim humor: She stood out. The soldiers, lollying and lounging, reminded her of the scars in her mouth and she threw her head contemptuously as they hissed and whistled as she went by.

She wanted to scrub up, but they had to go about the necessary business of getting the horses and the mule to a barn where they could keep them safe while they went out and got fresh supplies. Have to keep an eye on Tom, too, she thought. He git away from us, he won't be up to no good, damage hisself with all that liquour, git hisself hung up on the cards, find women ain't goin' to improve his health none. This is one place I ain't in no way goin' to enjoy.

But she was wrong. They didn't even lay up at all there. At first she couldn't understand it because Tom was so keen on getting into a place where, as he said, there were a few "accommodations." But they'd no sooner pulled in and a crowd of the curious had begun to back up around them than he took to cussing and shoving and swearing and finally, in total exasperation, shouting. "We ain't some kind of show," he hollered. "Git back. You want to gawk, you ken gawk for a price. Take her on out," he said to the two boys. "You heared me. Git goin'. I ken stock up on the little we really needs and catch up." But no one had wanted to leave him, though not one of them had had the courage to say why. But he knew. He was a smart one, he was; he saw all right. He was so disgusted he threw his new hat in the dust. "You go and buy the stuff then," he said to John. "But I'm takin' your horse and your saddle 'cause I don't trust this riffraff. You in the store they uncinchin' your saddle before you ken git a little salt and git out. You take this here nag, ain't nobody in his right mind goin' to make off with him. I'll see they"—looking at Mason Raymond and the girl—"git out. You ken meet us on the outskirts. Git back, you miserable cussed curiosities yourselfs," he hollered at the men and women piling up all around them. "Ain't you never seen a nigger before?"

Said that about hisself, Benjie thought, so I wouldn't think they was lookin' at *me*.

They struck out from Laramie toward Register Cliff. It was hard riding, enormous sandstone ruts cut deep through the hills. No wonder it was called Deep Rut Hill where they cut through.

At the Red Buttes they turned north, making their way

through a hostile landscape of angry stones upthrust out of the earth, the foothill country where the going was really rough, a sterile, barren place where the pronghorns ran and all the water tasted of some strange mineral Benjie didn't know.

The air was a little cooler, but the land was so barren and alien that it cowed all of them. Even the ponderosa pines looked stunted. Tom had let off his everlasting travelizing and poeticizing to warn them again to keep a sharp lookout for rattlers. This was bad rattlesnake country, he said, bad country all around, not even fit for Injuns. Then he bit his tongue.

Day after day they rode on, outcasts in sand and sage and scruffy little brush that made the desert a study of brown and gray and pale milky green. They were waiting for the first sight of Independence Rock, the Fourth of July stopping-off point for most of the early emigrants which had given the enormous protruberance its name. They would be a month early because they had been able to move so much faster than the slow caravan of wagons. Independence Rock rose like a gigantic turtle squatting in the sand, the remains of campgrounds all around. Once the entire plain had been covered with whitetop wagons and on the rock thousands of home-seekers, chisels in hand, had carved their names in "the register of the Desert," as the famous Father DeSmet had called it.

They were a day riding up to it, the whole time Tom encouraging the boys by reminding them that this was where they were going to carve their own passage over the Great American Desert, but what Benjie kept thinking was, The Sweetwater runs on its south side, the Sweetwater runs on its south side. . . . I come all the way and now it's nearly here, and it don't seem possible—not that jest a name could git you thousands of miles over the lonesomeness of this land.

"How's come you didn't come up there with us and carve your name?" Mason Raymond dropped down beside her, feeding sticks to the fire. "It was pretty up there."

"I don't remember much about writin' and though I guess I could work out my name all right I ain't especially keen to," she said after a moment, looking off into the dark plain. "I wouldn't know what to carve anyway. Ain't nuthin' I got to say." She felt she had offended him. "Looked like a big turtle, didn't it, comin' up on it that way acrost the desert. There's a big turtle lyin' out there, I said to myself. It wasn't what I imagined it would look like atall."

He shook his head. "There were so many names up there," he said. "We had to climb and climb to find a spot that wasn't full up, but John he always was a climber and he was determined. From the time he was real little John used to go way up in the top of trees and swing. The rest of us would hang around on the ground watching while he went way up and then swung out. It was something to see. He's always been like that," Mason Raymond said, "someone who climbs way up and does what others are afraid to do."

"*You* ain't all that afraid the way I look at it."

"I'm no climber the way he is," Mason Raymond said. "When we got way up there it made me dizzy, I didn't want to look out. But John, he was determined I should. He said it was quite a sight, and he was right. It was beautiful up there. You could look out forever and it didn't seem possible we had come over all that." He was shredding a sliver of wood apart, looking down with clouded dark eyes. "It's like—like it's endless, and it was crazy thinking anyone would ever come up there and see where we carved our names, but we stayed and put them in just the same. I guess you do it because it's the thing to do," he said at last.

"I don't understand you at all," Benjie said, "wanting to go up with Injuns when you could be back home, comfortable and all."

"We just own houses," Mason Raymond said. "They've never been what you might call homes." She looked at him, puzzled. "A big house in Albany—mostly my father 'lived' in it; my mother and I just sometimes stayed over. But I always hated that place, and at the Lake, where he comes from," nodding toward John who was polishing his saddle, "there was a big place, it had a nice view, too, but it was always my grandfather's house to me. It's like I've been wandering around looking for a home, my own home, all my life."

"And you think you're goin' to find a *home* up there with the Injuns?"

He shook his head. "That's not what I'm looking for any-more." He picked up the short stick he'd been fussing with —the only wood they had been able to find was scarce, was scraps—and began chewing on it. "I don't fit in. It's hard to find a place to belong when you're not like everybody else. I had this man I knew—when I was up there in the wilderness —Bartholomew was his name and he was a kind of hermit; you know, he didn't want much to do with other people so he went off all by himself and whenever he'd feel like he was so differ-ent from everyone else that he didn't belong anywhere, he'd tell me there was going to come a time when this world would be sliced open and if some people would try they would be able to see through the darkness and look at this world turn into another. He was full of ideas like that—about all these other worlds existed that we couldn't see because we didn't know how.

"Bartholomew thought that if you got off by yourself and sat and did nothing but concentrate on one spot—but it had to be the right kind of spot—and you looked and looked, you really concentrated, you might see one world overlapping into another. Sometimes it seemed like he was right. There are a lot of ways of looking at the same thing." He had a grave, concerned look on his face, as if his full concentration were absorbed by her and only her and by the thoughts he was trying to express to her, and the experience of anyone wanting only to concentrate on her because he wanted to share secret ideas and concerns with her was so novel that she was not quite sure how to deal with it; she felt uncomfortable, but flattered.

Mason Raymond was gazing into the fire with a look of profound steadiness on his face. When he raised his face and looked at her his eyes said, You and me, we're alike; and Benjie wanted to throw her arms around him and bury her head in his shoulder and weep her heart apart; she wanted to start all over again, as if the past had never happened.

She sat, rapt, trying to get the words together to tell him how she felt, and when that failed she looked at him with all her feelings in her eyes. He reached up and fumbled with the pocket of his jacket and extracted that everlasting *this* book he was always burying himself in. He put it on his lap, and his hands ran over it once, twice, a third time, as if he were smoothing it out. But how could you smooth out a book? She couldn't help thinking that no matter how you thought a person might understand, there always came the moment when the awful separateness of people filled in that belief with the knowledge nobody can ever really understand, and you knew you were always going to be alone, always, forever and ever, going to remain apart from everyone else on this earth. Benjie remembered that all the time the wagon jogged along and her father tossed and turned, fever-hit, and cried out how he loved her, that she was his favorite, she never once had taken the hand that squeezed hers so frantically for affirmation, had never once lifted that pleading hand to her lips and held it there, had never once said to him, even in the barest of whispers (after all, there was no need for her sick mother to hear), "I love you best, too, Pa. You know that."

Now she wanted to take hold of Mason Raymond and turn him around so that he would look at her and concentrate on her and solely her instead of being distracted by that everlasting book, and she wanted to say to him, "Tell me, do you know what love is? Ken you tell me what it is—explain it so I *know* it?"

"I had this teacher," Mason Raymond said, removed from her forever, it seemed to Benjie, "he was really a very great man and I think he knew he had it in him to be great but he was caught and he couldn't get free of what had caught him so that he could go out and find his greatness, and that was just destroying him, that being caught and not being able to be what he could.

"I would look at him and I would think, He knows things the rest of us don't, and I wanted to know what those things were. I'd go to his room and talk to him and he'd talk to me, and I'd listen and wait to hear about this thing that was in him, this thing that was there but was all bottled up and he couldn't get out, but he never let it out once, he could never get it out to go free. Once or twice I thought maybe it was almost out, but then it would jump back and hide, and I'd think I just imagined I'd seen it, he hadn't really been about to let it go at all.

] *401* [

"He set a lot of store by this book," Mason Raymond said, "and so I figured that some of what he knew might be in it, and I started carrying it around and reading and studying it and trying to find out."

"And did you? Did you find out?" She really needed to know. Maybe there was a lesson in it for her, too.

"Some," Mason Raymond said. "It's about a very great man who must fight and knows he's going to lose because there's no way in the world he can win. But Hector, he fights with all his strength, even though he knows he's going to lose; and he's a good person, much better than those who are going to win—"

Crazy Horse, she thought, and Bone Hand, Young Man Afraid and Gall. Worm and—once—Red Cloud.

"And in the end when Hector goes down to this terrible death—he's dragged around the wall and the dogs come and lick his blood—his death has meaning," Mason Raymond said. "It has meaning because there's nobody else to care about, just him, because he was so different; so maybe it's right to be different, maybe being different is the sign that you've got the possibility to go beyond what most people see. Like Bartholomew said. Maybe that's what I'm trying to do when I go with the Indians, see things that I couldn't see any place else."

"It's not like you think," she said, "up there with the Sioux and Cheyenne."

"Ain't we *ever* gonna eat?" John Buttes called from across the fire where he was putting his saddle aside. She got up abruptly, started toward the pot boiling on the fire, then suddenly stopped. "You said it was nice up there where you carved your name, that it was beautiful. How was it nice up there if you was scared?"

"It was like you could look on forever," Mason Raymond said. "If you knew how."

There was a great rift in the granite rocks on the other side of Independence Rock, a tremendous chasm and to the west a magnificent valley. The Sweetwater flowed in between Devil's Gate; they got off their horses and bent down, putting their faces to the water. It was true; after the Platte the water was so sweet. Benjie looked at the reflection of her face in the clear, pure, rapidly running water, a bed of sweet water sliding through Devil's Gate and running clear and cold and pure out of the granite rock up toward the hills. The face looked distorted but it was her own and it had a lift to it that said to her, I'm all right, I'm all right as long as I think that way. It's only when the others make me feel bad that I feel bad about myself. I got to go where nobody makes me feel bad. That's the way I'm going to be all right.

The trail ascended, with The Sweetwater at its head—far away, higher even than South Pass, it entered Green Valley, and if you followed its bed it would take you up toward the Snake and Soda Springs, and the parting of the ways where the homeseekers had to make up their minds between California and Oregon. For John and Tom there would be another kind of decision, a different sort of parting, there at South Pass.

They rested their horses and the mule and drank again themselves, filled their canteens, and then began the long slow pull up the hills to South Pass. South Pass wasn't like any pass anyone would ever imagine, neither narrow nor steep nor like a gorge between mountains, but rather a broad, gently sloping incline twenty miles wide, The Sweetwater on one side and the Rattlesnake Hills on the other.

The black-backed hills held them all day; each mile they rose higher and higher; the air grew cold, and the wind was a mountain wind, never tiring, pulling at them with the chill of snow from the far passes, and calling out in a soft moaning voice as if carrying some message they must stop and listen to. But they could not stop; they were behind already, and now that the end was in sight they pushed themselves, wanting to get the parting over with.

Near the top Tom was so winded he had to call a halt. Benjie's pony was restive, wanting to move on. John and Mason Raymond had hauled their horses up and were waiting, quiet in the saddle, gazing back from the summit of the pass down one long vast plain that they had slowly—so slowly they had scarcely realized they had been climbing—traveled upward all day, their eyes dazzled with the great panorama stretching on all sides of them. They looked as if some deep well within them had suddenly been infiltrated with a mysterious substance that went into the blood and altered their basic chemistry; they were looking out on a montage of images they could not seem to accept as real, as if their eyes were tricking them, as if all were a mirage or a part of a hallucination; shaking their heads as if to clear them and looking, wondering, right and left at the Great River Valley they had left behind.

She came up to them at a walk, the piebald dancing about in impatience. Tom was grumbling he didn't know what he was going to do; all his life he couldn't see no good in jest digging and making do, the way it looked he'd been doing again, but what choice did you have—you could either dig or not dig and there was at least a likelihood of luck in digging.

Benjie suspected his complaints were a way of masking his emotions. An old man didn't need much encouragement to break down, and Tom had been through a hard time. He was too proud, too, to show how he really felt.

The four horses nuzzled side by side in the wind. The fresh, brisk mountain air ruffled the spiderwort, crowned with its blue coronet, tossed the skeleton weed and bunches of black-eyed Susans. A rare day—and such a view. Benjie burned inside with the pain of it. She could never have believed until this moment how much she cared.

She thought *black man,* two distinct and separate words and images, *black* separate, *man* separate. Tom was both, black and a man, and a friend, and now he was turning, he and John, whose anger she saw at last was part of his restlessness, part of a pushing energy he could not help, the kind of demand inside that drove people on—even her timid mother and father—sent them West where violence was a way of life, even with the weather and the land and the people who survived. If you were timid and had no strength to kill or be killed, you could not last out here. He would last—and do well.

She thought of the hailstorm, the tornado of dust, the fire, the long, lonely stretches of plains, a savage country that was an expression of the excessive kind of energy that burned in some people, people like John. He would indeed survive, indeed prosper.

She turned and gazed at Mason Raymond, and he was gazing back at her. He did not have John's burning violence creating chaos inside him; his was a different kind of energy, a different way of looking at the world, which, if you thought about it carefully, called out voices from the past. Perhaps he would not last, but something, she thought, that he expressed —something close to what she had seen with Crazy Horse and Bone Hand and the rest—might, she hoped, endure. When they are gone, she thought, who will carry on what they have, that way of seeing the world between twilight and dark, between dawn and day?

White Buffalo Woman, she thought, that's who I am, the *woman* part embedded in her mind next to the word *man*. They were going together, she and Mason Raymond; they would be all right some way she did not yet understand.

They were joined animal to animal, looking out, absorbing for the last time the great plain over which so many thousands had toiled and over which they had come through so many turmoils. Then, almost imperceptibly, the black man made a slight movement with his rein hand. Benjie turned her head to him. But he was staring past her at Mason Raymond. "You take care, you hear?"

"You, too."

"Yeah," John said. "You both—you and her, you both take care."

"You ready?" Mason Raymond asked her. He started to turn his horse and John called out, choked, some bubble of words Benjie couldn't identify. The high wind was in those words, hollowing them out with the pain of loss, the end of a friendship whose depths John hadn't recognized until these final moments.

John got down and began to unstrap his father's saddle. The saddle seemed terribly heavy as he took it off the horse, heavier than it had ever been, heavy maybe as the feeling he had inside at this moment. He held it for a moment, looking at it. "You take it—with you," he said to Mason Raymond.

Mason Raymond shook his head.

"You take it," John said angrily.

Mason Raymond got down and unbuckled the cinch around

his own mount. Silently they exchanged equipment, each working carefully with the new saddle as he put it on his own horse. They did not look at one another. "And you take this," Tom said, not looking at any of them, grubbing about in his pocket until he finished fishing around in the thousand places that seemed affixed to his coat and shirt. Something glittered —the watch, Jonathan's watch. He held it out to her. She couldn't take his watch. "No, go on, take it."

In the silence pierced by the small singing spasms of wind they stood; then the black man looked at John. "You ready?" he asked and John nodded, looking down. She tried to say something, but there were some things that could never be said. Those were the kinds of words that were kept locked inside.

Mason Raymond was working with his jacket. He got it unbuttoned and took out his book. He handed it up to Tom. "It's got a different kind of verse in it than you're used to," he said, smiling. "But somehow I think you'll kind of take to it. There's a lot of good quotes in there a man like you could use."

Then Mason Raymond locked his hands around the pommel of John's saddle and heaved himself up on his horse. "Long live the hog," he said to John.

"Don't do nuthin' with your mouth your hands and feet can't back up," John said back to him.

Tom turned one last time in his saddle. He was looking straight at her. "If you ever need us, you know you can send word. Deadwood," he said. "Jest axe for Nigger Tom. That's how they call me up there in Deadwood, Nigger Tom. Won't take us no time at all to come, you ever send word you need us. I guess it's time we was goin' on now," he said to John. John kept his horse upwind as they turned and went slowly, in single file, northbound toward the mines. She and Mason Raymond turned and started toward the Hills, toward the land of the Sioux and the Cheyenne. As they came to the top of the hill, they both turned back for a last look. Tom rose in his saddle and waved his new hat after them. But John never moved at all. He kept going, straight, not looking back.

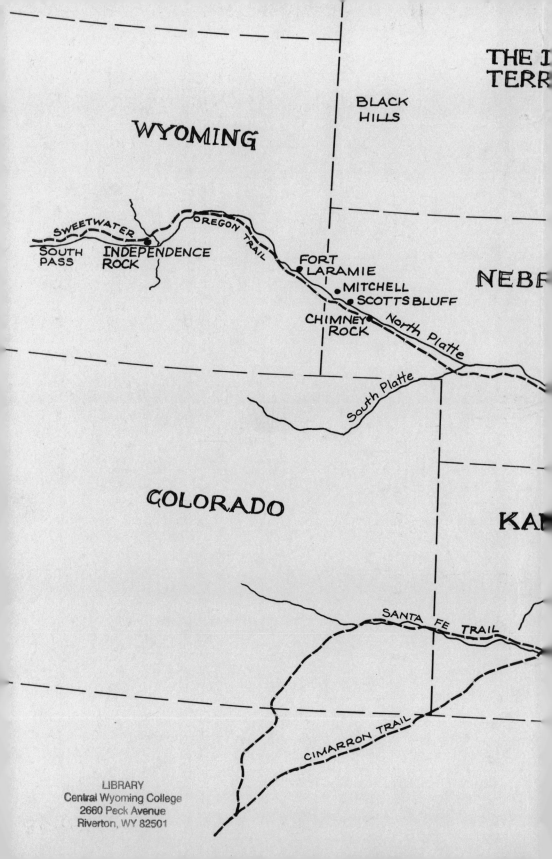

THE I
TERR

BLACK
HILLS

WYOMING

NEBF

SWEETWATER
OREGON TRAIL
SOUTH
PASS
INDEPENDENCE
ROCK
FORT
LARAMIE
MITCHELL
SCOTTS BLUFF
CHIMNEY
ROCK
North Platte

South Platte

COLORADO

KAN

SANTA FE TRAIL

CIMARRON TRAIL